Ghirlandaio's Daughter

Also by John Spencer Hill

The Last Castrato
John Milton: Poet, Priest and Prophet
Imagination in Coleridge

GHIRLANDAIO'S DAUGHTER

John Spencer Hill

St. Martin's Press ⋙ New York

Library of Congress Cataloging-in-Publication Data

Hill, John Spencer.
  Ghirlandaio's daughter / John Spencer Hill.
     p.   cm.
  ISBN 0-312-15133-0
  I. Title.
  PR9199.3.H4787G48   1997
  813'.54—dc21   96-48765
                                                    CIP

First published in Great Britain by
Constable & Company Ltd

First U.S. Edition: March 1997

10   9   8   7   6   5   4   3   2   1

For my daughter

KATHERINE

who waited a long time

for her turn

With special thanks to

my old and dear friend David Ormerod, for permission to use his poem *'Musée des Beaux Arts, 1994'* (© David Anthony Ormerod), whose 'onlie begetter' is Michèle O'Sullivan – the poem appears on p. 171–2; Laurielle Ilacqua, for help with matters Italian; Frances Hanna, a tremendous agent, critic, and friend; my dear wife Jan, sole partner and companion in crime for thirty years.

PART ONE

A Cast of Exiles

1

'Great Scott!' Nigel Harmsworth exclaimed, sucking in his breath with a sharp rasp. The violence of the event, its suddenness and the remarkable thoroughness of its devastation, had stunned him into temporary immobility. He stood as if rooted to the spot, his eyes round with wonder. After a moment, gathering his nerve, he leaned cautiously forward and peered over the edge of the shattered patio table at the figure on the far side. It lay on its back, arms flung wide, eyes dilated and mouth agape, its torso pinned to the turf, like an insect on a display board, with the bronze spear of a Mycenaean warrior planted squarely in the middle of its chest.

The man was most certainly dead. Nigel could see that at a glance, although he was no doctor. The vacant eyes of the corpse stared up at the vacant sky. There was no hint of motion in the body, no indication of life or struggle, no sign of breath. The corpse lay splayed on the manicured lawn, the spear protruding stiffly from its sternum and the bronze figure of a Greek myrmidon suspended over him where it had toppled forward from its concrete pedestal. The pair of them looked, Nigel thought, like dance partners who had fouled in their footwork and tumbled ignominiously to the floor in a tangle of limbs. He stared down at the scene as one transfixed, his eyes wide in disbelief. Yet, in spite of the bizarre and grisly circumstances, his artist's eye couldn't help noticing how the blotch of dark gore flowering in the middle of the dead man's chest seemed to blend, in a satisfying and aesthetic way, with the pattern of delicate earth-tones on his expensive print silk shirt.

'Jesu, Maria, and all the saints,' Nigel muttered, unable to tear his eyes away. He ran the fingers of one hand through his mane of silver hair and tried to gather his thoughts. It had all happened so fast that he didn't know what to make of it. His mind was in a muddle. And the worst of it was that he hadn't the slightest idea who the man with the spear in his chest was. Their conversation hadn't progressed that far.

The man was an American, of course. That much Nigel knew. From one of the northern states, he thought. although his knowledge of their various accents was limited and all American speech struck his refined Home Counties ear as harsh and vaguely plebeian. His feeling on the matter was, he knew, the product of a cultural bias tinged with envy, but it was a nationalistic partiality that he nurtured with grace and dignity as well as tenacity, and one that he had absolutely no intention of altering. Albion was everything to him. There was no acceptable alternative anywhere in the world to England's green and pleasant hills. (Oh, how he missed them!) At the age of seventy-two, Nigel Harmsworth was too old to change, too set in his ways to entertain cosmopolitan sympathies. He was neither desirous nor able to be other than what he was: an anachronism, a dinosaur, a bred-in-the-bone subject of the British crown.

Which made it odd, of course, that he should find himself in the heart of Italy looking down at the body of an unknown American locked in the death embrace of a Greek warrior. But there was a long story behind that.

The San Felice estate in northern Tuscany, where he now stood, dominated the shoulder of a hill that formed a spur of the Apuane Alps which ran, in a series of bony fingers, out into the flat, fertile valley of the river Serchio. The villa, erected by the Guinigi family at the end of the eighteenth century, was an elegant yet rather modest structure by the usual standards of that flamboyant dynasty. The ground floor, with its recessed portico, was surmounted by a continuous balustrade decorated with vases and marble busts. From the middle of this balustraded terrace rose the two-storey central block, a simple white rectangle, broken by symmetrical rows of tall shuttered french doors on the first floor and large shuttered windows on the second floor. Above the central doors on the first level was embossed in bas-relief the Guinigi escutcheon: gules a cross argent charged of eighteen spearheads azure.

The villa faced west, looking out on the ranks of ascending peaks, white in winter, that rose to obliterate the horizon. The grounds were spacious, and the view from the garden behind the villa, where a water chain tumbled down the slope, was, if anything, more spectacular than that seen from the front of the building. Beyond a spreading lawn, girdled with clipped yew and set off with a fountain of sporting nymphs, the ground fell abruptly away to reveal a panorama of spacious plain, dominated in the centre by the walled medieval city of Lucca, her red-brick ramparts rising from the valley floor and planted around the circumference with a leafy coronal of chestnut and plane trees. Off to the right, one could even pick out, on a clear day and with the aid of binoculars, the humped back of the 'Devil's Bridge' spanning the Serchio on the winding road that led to the sulphate spa at Bagni di Lucca.

It was to this terraced garden at the rear of the villa that Nigel Harmsworth had brought his unexpected visitor. When the door chime had sounded just before eleven, Nigel had been in the kitchen, his feet up, a pot of steaming tea at his elbow, reading the letters to the editor in *The Times*. Every morning at eight, as regular as clockwork, he drove the old grey Bentley down into Lucca to retrieve the copies of *The Times* and the *Guardian* waiting for him at the Doroni Franca bookshop in Via della Rosa. They were his only link now to the land which he had left in self-imposed exile more than a decade ago, his only way of keeping pace with events and personalities in the country he still, despite a long absence, regarded as *home*. He relished the daily arrival of his papers and resented bitterly any interruption of his reading time. The staff at Villa San Felice had long ago learned to steer clear between the hours of nine and noon and were discreetly studious in their efforts to give Signor Harmsworth a wide berth during those interdicted hours.

But today, being Wednesday, he was alone in the house. The maid and the gardener both took Wednesday as their day off, and the cook, Signora Capponi, was in town replenishing the contents of the villa's depleted larder. She would not return until mid-afternoon and, in any case, she would never, for anything short of the Apocalypse itself, have been able to muster the temerity required to ring the bell in the front portico. There was a service entrance at the side for her and the other staff.

When the silvery chime rippled over the inlaid marble of the foyer and sought him out in his private retreat, Nigel had lowered the paper fractionally, squinted at the clock on the mantel, pursed his lips and given a quizzical grimace. It was odd, decidedly odd. He was expecting no one. The fact that he was alone in the villa meant, of course, that he had to attend to the matter himself. With a sigh of resigned irritation, he folded the paper and laid it on the table next to his half-drunk and cooling cup of Earl Grey, then rose to his feet. He passed through a series of ante-rooms into the dining-room, pausing briefly at a gilt-framed mirror to adjust the paisley cravat at his throat. He always wore a cravat, preferring its ambience of relaxed elegance to the more formal constriction of a necktie – and he had always, for as long as he could remember, been partial to paisley. Today, the September air being cool, he had donned a lemon angora pullover over his open-necked white shirt. He looked, he noted with approval, every inch a man of means and cultivated leisure.

The door chime sounded again, insistently, three times in quick succession. Nigel cast a scowl in its direction before returning his attention to the mirror to flatten an obstinate tuft of straying hair, and then turned finally away, without haste, to answer the imperious summons. It was, he recalled thinking later, precisely that aggressive pounding on the bell that had first led him to suspect that his visitor was an American.

Passing through the main salon, he reached the entrance foyer and swung open the oak door. The figure who awaited him in the portico was tall and well built, about thirty-five, with tousled, thinning hair into which had been shoved, at a rakish angle, a pair of tinted aviator glasses. Behind him, on the paving stones of the drive, sat a red Maserati sports coupé, its convertible top turned down. The man wore a breezy smile on a face cratered with the scars of adolescent acne, and his tanned features, insolent mien, and casual but expensive dress gave the appearance of a motion-picture producer on holiday. Nigel half expected to see, waiting over his shoulder in the Maserati, a platinum blonde with enormous bosoms spilling from the front of a flimsy dress. But the man was alone. He was also a stranger. Nigel had no idea who he was or what had brought him to San Felice. Perhaps he'd lost his way and come in to ask for directions.

The man cut the Gordian knot of his curiosity with a single stroke.

'I'm looking for a guy named Nigel Harmsworth,' he announced in a grating nasal accent before Nigel could formulate a question of his own. 'Are you him?'

'I am he,' Nigel said, tacitly correcting the solecism.

'I thought you might be,' the man said, stepping in past Nigel and closing the door. 'You're certainly the right age.'

The speed of the manœuvre took Nigel completely by surprise. Flustered and struggling for composure in the face of this astonishing invasion, he drew himself up and said stuffily, in his most daunting Oxbridge accent, 'May I enquire, sir, as to the nature of – '

'Let's cut the hoity-toity,' the intruder interrupted with a curt wave of the hand. Then, his boyish grin returning, he threw an arm around Nigel's shoulder and drew him close. 'Now, what d'you say we find a comfy spot somewhere and get acquainted?' He gave Nigel a penetrating look and said sadly, like a schoolmaster addressing a truant charge, 'You see, we've got quite a lot to talk about, Nigel. Yes, indeed we do. A hell of a lot to talk about, in fact.' Somewhat relaxing the iron grip on his victim's shoulder, he threw an admiring look around the shell-shaped foyer with its inset niches of classical sculpture, its filigreed reception table, its crystal chandelier, its veined marble stairs ascending to the upper floors, and said appreciatively: 'You know, this is really one hell of a pad you've got here, Nigel. Much swankier than I expected. A real palace, I'd say.' He added in a quiet, darkly mocking tone, 'And I'll bet my Yankee ass, old buddy, that you'd really hate like hell to lose it all, now wouldn't you?'

Alarmed and utterly baffled by the alternation of threats and caresses, Nigel struggled free of the encircling arm and salvaged what he could of his dignity by straightening his sweater. Ever the English gentleman, he suggested they retire to the terrace and offered his guest a drink. Americans, he knew, liked to drink. It put them at their ease.

'Yes, indeed. A drink is just what the doctor ordered,' the man agreed, his smile returning like the sun through cloud. 'Make mine a long scotch, if you don't mind. Single malt, if you've got it.'

Nigel led the way to the bar in the smoking-room and poured a stiff Cardhu for the visitor and a very small dry sherry for himself. He couldn't abide the thought of alcohol before lunch. It always played the devil with his stomach – but then, of course, one had to be polite too. Handing the American a glass, he led the way across the patio and down a flight of travertine steps to the garden below. In a protected nook, surrounded by replicas of Greek statuary on concrete bases, was a white wrought-iron table and set of matching chairs.

'Well now,' Nigel said, turning, 'perhaps you'll be good enough to tell me what this is all about.'

The man dropped into a chair and crossed his legs with insolent bravado. 'Certainly,' he said, raising his glass to Nigel in a kind of toast. 'Certainly, I'll do just that.'

13

And so he did.

Nigel stood across from him, unable to sit, and listened with mounting horror to what the man had to say. His astonished senses could hardly take it in. His mind grew fuzzy and his knees felt as if they might buckle under him at any moment. He fought a green nausea that rose in his throat like a silent trout through weeds. The man spoke on. Swirling his drink and flipping the toe of one hand-tooled burgundy wingtip in a rhythmic way, his mouth moved implacably and the terrible words rolled out between his parted lips like the announcement of Armageddon. At last, Nigel could stand no more. He was overcome by the grotesque enormity of it all. The forgotten sherry glass fell from his hand and he tottered helplessly, like a man in his cups, against the statue of a Mycenaean warrior holding his spear aloft. The concrete base supporting the statue, cracked and eroded by a hundred winters, gave on one corner with a snap and the statue toppled forward, overturning the table and falling directly on top of the wide-eyed victim who tried valiantly, but alas too late, to launch himself backwards out of the destructive path of its descent . . .

A sudden flash of colour to his left caught Nigel's attention, returning him to the present and the corpse over which he had stood, for how long he didn't know, replaying in his mind the improbable events that had led to its becoming a corpse in the first place. The colour flashed again. It was a large butterfly, electric blue tipped with black, with a wingspan of perhaps five inches. He turned to watch as it fumbled briefly at an oleander bloom, then started across the lawn toward him. An amateur lepidopterist, Nigel followed its weaving, bobbing flight with fascinated interest. At first, he couldn't be sure, but, as it came closer, no room for doubt remained. It was a Blue Morpho, *Morpho menelaus*, first described by Linnaeus, from the family Nymphalidae. What was odd – indeed, quite remarkably strange – was that a specimen should turn up in Tuscany. Its native habitat was limited to the steamy South American rain forests of Venezuela and Brazil, and he had neither read nor heard of a single sighting in Europe. With rapt attention, he watched its progress toward him only inches above the well-trimmed grass. A protracted sirocco might perhaps have explained the arrival of a wayward traveller from tropical Africa, but there was no precedent, and no rational explanation, for the appearance of a species from as far

14

away as South America. The advent of a Blue Morpho in Lucca was a mystery – an utterly inexplicable event.

Unerringly, as if directed by a secret intent, the splendid imago made its way across the lawn. When it reached the fallen American, it hovered briefly over the lifeless face, flapping exploratively, then landed on the forehead and spread the glory of its wings wide in the September light. It was, Nigel saw then, a mature male of the species, with sable-tipped forewings and characteristic elongated hindwings trimmed in velvet black. For a moment the insect sat motionless, as if entranced, then rose suddenly into the air in a flash of iridescence and disappeared over the hedge, its desire (whatever it was) apparently accomplished. Like Psyche, Nigel thought, coming in to carry off the soul of the departed.

'Extraordinary business,' he said aloud, when it had gone. 'Perfectly extraordinary.'

He waited for several minutes to see if the butterfly might return. When it did not, he turned reluctantly, leaving the scene of carnage untouched, and made his way up the balustraded steps into the villa. It was cool and dark inside and his eyes took a moment to adjust to the gloom. He picked up the telephone and pressed the number on the automatic dialler for the police. The line was opened on the second ring.

'*Questura di Lucca*,' a voice announced. '*Pronto*.'

Nigel cleared his throat. 'Ah, yes,' he said thickly, hardly recognizing his own voice. 'This is Nigel Harmsworth, at Villa San Felice. There has been, I'm afraid, the most ghastly accident . . .'

2

Detective Inspector Carlo Arbati closed the suitcase that lay packed and ready on the bed and glanced around the room. No, he hadn't forgotten anything. He snapped the hasps on the case and checked his watch. There was still plenty of time. His train didn't leave for over an hour and Giorgio would no doubt be along any moment to pick him up. Although he was licensed to drive and occasionally, under duress, did get behind the wheel himself, Arbati avoided doing so whenever possible. The reason was simple. He disliked and, if he was perfectly honest with himself, actually *feared* that subspecies of *Homo Sapiens* which an otherwise charitable God had, for inscrutable reasons, permitted to survive and even to thrive on the planet in the form of The Italian Driver. The mere thought of them made Arbati shudder. There was, he was convinced, some bizarre quirk in the Italian spirit, some impulse built into the gene pool of the race itself that, once behind the wheel of a car, transformed normally placid men and women into rancorous savages inflamed with a wild bravado who refused to yield even an inch of pavement to those around them. The sirens one heard so often in Italian cities were always – or so it seemed – ambulances rushing to the aid of another stricken pedestrian or hapless Vespa rider. Arbati had no intention of casting his lot among them. His idea of hell, in fact, was to be trapped for eternity in the clogged arteries of the old city – going round and round and round – while drivers pressed in on all sides honking, cursing, and shooting obscene fingers at him. Whenever possible, therefore, he let his partner, Giorgio Bruni, do the driving. It was easier that way.

He carried the suitcase into the living-room and set it by the door. He never took more than a single medium-sized bag when travelling because he believed – and two decades of experience had, in his view, irrefragably proved the truth of his conviction – that half a cubic metre was ample space in which to compress the essentials of existence required for a two-week vacation. If he'd been married, of course, things would have been different. Wives had a tendency to pack everything but the furniture and the heavy appliances for even a weekend jaunt. But Carlo Arbati wasn't married – and half a cubic metre of packing-space had become his inflexible rule.

He was looking forward to this trip to Lucca, his first real vacation in several years. Lucca was a quiet retreat, a place where time had eased imperceptibly to a stop several centuries ago and where serious villainy hardly existed. Arbati smiled to himself. If he could be certain of anything, it was that there'd be no call for his professional services during the next two weeks. He could lay the policeman in him aside and relax for a change. He'd already planned it all out. There'd be lingering dinners at his favourite restaurant, the Antica Locanda dell' Angelo in Via Pescheria, followed by evening rambles along the tree-lined ramparts; there'd be – not far away – the green sea and the trendy art nouveau cafés on the beach at Viareggio on the Tuscan Riviera, and perhaps, if he was feeling particularly energetic one day, a little mountain climbing in the Garfagnana. But he was also looking forward to the visit for another reason. It would give him the chance to renew his old and, in recent years, sadly neglected friendship with Giancarlo Bonelli, his best friend during their days together as cadets at the Carabinieri academy. They'd been close in those days, very close – in fact, they'd been inseparable: two peas in a pod, twins born of separate mothers. They'd studied in each other's rooms and eaten every meal side by side at the long wooden tables in the college refectory. They'd shared their hopes and dreams, their fears and frustrations, encouraging each other when the going was rough. But then, after graduation, Arbati had stayed on in Florence and Giancarlo had returned to his native Lucca. Since then, they'd met only sporadically, on those few occasions when their paths crossed in the line of duty – but never for long enough to recapture the special bond of youth and all they had been through together. But *that*, Arbati vowed, was about to change. The halcyon fraternity of youth was something too precious to sacrifice to devouring time without a fight, and certainly too important to be lost through inertia and simple neglect.

The fact that the Società delle Arti di Lucca had voted to award him their gold medal for his most recent volume of poems, although it was the ostensible *raison d'être* for the trip, was, in Arbati's view, no more than an added bonus. Three months ago, the secretary of the society had written to inform him of the honour and express the hope that he would be able to spare the time, despite a no doubt hectic schedule, to attend the September meeting of the society and accept the award in person. Arbati had jumped at the chance. Lucca was one of those cities – quaint, romantic, and mercifully off the beaten path of packaged tourist itineraries – that it was always a pleasure to revisit. And Giancarlo, of course, would be there to meet him at the station.

There was a tap at the door and a moment later Giorgio Bruni, a tousled knot of sandy hair perched on his head like a bird's nest and his bad eye drifting furtively off to the left as if on a private assignment, stuck his head around the corner.

'Well,' he enquired, 'is our peerless poet packed?' He added with a grin, 'Note the alliteration. I worked it up on the way over in the car.'

A diminutive body, clad in a creased suit, the tie knotted loosely at the neck and twisted askew, followed the head into the room.

In appearance, Giorgio never failed to remind Arbati of Peter Falk, the American television detective: short, unkempt, always looking as if he'd just rolled out of bed. They made a strange team: Arbati and Bruni, the odd couple of the Questura. Arbati was tall, good-looking, fastidious in clothes and manner; Bruni, in contrast, was small, slightly grotesque and invariably rumpled. At least today however, Arbati noticed, his partner had managed to locate a pair of matching socks. It was one of his good days.

'Yes, all set,' Arbati said, ignoring the attempt at alliteration. He was at the sideboard pouring himself a scotch from a glass decanter. 'Like a drink before we go? There's plenty of time.'

'Officially, I'm on duty, you know,' Bruni reminded him.

'That doesn't answer my question.'

Bruni grinned. 'Okay then, a short one,' he said. 'To be polite.'

Arbati handed him a glass and they sat on either side of a coffee table on which a neat pile of magazines, an engraved cigarette box, and a large ceramic ashtray were set out. The silver box was something Giorgio recognized with a pang. It had been, he remembered, a gift from Cordelia Sinclair, an American girl Arbati had dated for several months. They had been, in many ways, an ideal couple and everyone expected the match to end with confetti and wedding bells. And yet in retrospect, Giorgio saw, it had been a relationship doomed, perhaps from the very beginning, to fail. Arbati and Cordelia were star-crossed lovers, fated, in a modern variation of the old Shakespearean theme, to founder on the rocky demands of separate careers. In spite of all they had in common, in spite of the fact that they actually loved one another, their love hadn't been strong enough to survive the competitive pressures of that great twentieth-century disease – the drive to fulfil oneself, to carve a career and a reputation out of the flinty rockface of self-imposed expectation. Cordelia, on the rebound from a bad marriage, had needed the security of knowing she could make her way in the world without a man to fend and fight for her. Carlo, wedded to his job at the Questura and to the Muse who inspired his poetry, was unwilling – or perhaps just unable – to make room in his life for yet another mistress. Whatever the cause, they had drifted apart, love cooling into friendship, and at last Cordelia, her thesis written, had packed her bags and gone back to the United States. It was truly sad, Giorgio thought, that love should wither and die in such a way, that two lonely people should choose to embrace celibacy in the forlorn hope of somehow finding and preserving their fragile identities. Giorgio saw the world in a different light. Marriage, in his view, was the only door that led to real happiness – and he was damned glad he had his Tessie there at home waiting for him, to keep him warm at night and to pick up the pieces when he got frazzled and life was just too much to bear.

Arbati leaned forward, took a cigarette from the silver case and lit it, dropping the spent match absently into the ashtray. He was thinking ahead to the succulent *osso bucco* and fine Brunello to accompany it that he intended to consume when he reached Lucca.

'Do you still hear from her?' Bruni asked.

'Who?' Arbati asked, knotting his brows. Then his expression relaxed. 'Oh, Cordelia. Yes – yes, we write occasionally. Why do you ask?'

Bruni shrugged. 'Just curious. I wondered how she was getting on, that's all.'

'And why things didn't work out between us, I suppose?'

'That too,' Bruni admitted.

'It's water under the bridge,' Arbati said. 'It was never meant to be.'

That's not how Bruni saw it, but there was no point in arguing the point. Carlo was a bachelor – and no doubt would always remain so – because he could never give himself fully to another human being. At the heart of his complex character lay a centre of cold reserve, of stingy privacy that refused to share its joys and pleasures, or even its sorrows, with anyone else.

Bruni ignored the implied rebuke. 'So, how's she getting on?' he asked.

Arbati launched a plume of smoke at the ceiling. 'Oh, fine,' he said. 'She's found herself a position – a tenure-track assistant professorship, she called it – at a liberal arts college somewhere in Indiana. She sounds happy enough. I suppose she'll be a full professor and running the place in a year or two. It's what she's always wanted.' He added, 'Maybe then she'll feel like settling down.'

'Maybe then,' Bruni nodded. He finished his drink and looked at his watch. 'We should be on our way,' he said. 'The FS waits for no man, my friend. Not even you.'

A black Carabinieri Fiat was parked outside the apartment. Arbati put his suitcase in the back and then, with Giorgio at the wheel, they set off at high speed along the quiet cobbled street.

19

'How many pedestrians did you kill on the way over?' Arbati enquired, clutching the handrest.

Bruni shot him a grin. 'Three,' he said. He shrugged theatrically: 'It's not my fault if the fools aren't quick enough to get out of the way. It's very Darwinian out here, you know. Survival of the fittest.' He geared down and rounded the corner on two wheels, cutting up an alley toward Via Maggio. 'You'd know that, my friend,' he added, shifting up again, 'if you ever bothered to get behind the wheel yourself.'

'It's precisely what prevents me from trying,' Arbati said between clenched teeth.

An old man approaching on a bicycle, wobbling precariously, driven to the wall, shook his fist at them as they roared past. Arbati closed his eyes.

Giorgio Bruni had the reputation of being the worst driver in Florence – worse even than the legendary taxi drivers of Rome. If he hadn't been an officer of justice, he'd almost certainly be wasting away in prison for a long and incorrigible history of moving violations.

They crossed Ponte Santa Trinità, weaving and dodging, and turned up Via Tornabuoni. Tourists swarmed the pavement, peering in at the windows of Gucci, Valentino, and Ferragamo. Woe to the careless soul, his mind on bargains, who ventured into Giorgio Bruni's path! Arbati bowed his head as if in silent prayer. It would be quieter in Lucca, he reminded himself – and considerably less stressful.

Bruni braked suddenly and swerved sharply left. Arbati's head came up in time to catch sight of a stout matron springing like an Olympic hurdler for the safety of the pavement. Without batting an eye, Bruni accelerated and carried on as if nothing had happened. In his mind, nothing had. It was all part of driving in Florence.

'Santa Maria dei miracoli!' Arbati breathed to no one in particular.

It was a close call. Still, he reflected, his heart falling from his throat back into his chest where it belonged, Bruni had a flair for it – a definite flair. Like a grand prix driver, he had an instinctive feel for speed and distance, coupled with an iron nerve and lightning reflexes. He was good. Yes, he was very good – you had to give him that.

At Via Panzani, they shot the amber light and made a sharp left in front of an ATAF bus. Traffic was moving at a crawl and Bruni drummed his fingers on the wheel impatiently, debating whether to switch on his roof lights and pull up on to the pavement.

'Don't even think about trying it,' Arbati growled, 'or I'll turn you in myself.'

'I wasn't,' Bruni lied. 'Well, not seriously anyway.'

As they crept past the Feltrinelli bookshop, Arbati noticed in the window a prominent display of *Tommaso incredulo*, his new volume of poems. It always came as something of an embarrassing surprise to see himself in print, to stumble over his books in a library or a bookseller's display, to be suddenly confronted by the secret thoughts of his soul, over which he'd laboured for months in private, laid out for public inspection in brightly coloured dustjackets. It was, somehow, he thought, like being photographed as you stepped from the shower.

Bruni followed his gaze. 'It must make you very proud,' he said. 'I know that's how I'd feel if they were my books stacked up in there.'

'Proud?' Arbati mused. 'Oh, I don't know. In a way, it feels more like being a rape victim, I'd say.'

Bruni rolled his eyes. What a strange man Arbati was. Even though they worked together every day, how little he understood what made his partner tick. 'Then why publish them?' he asked with surprise. 'Why bother to make them public at all?'

Arbati was silent for a moment, considering the question. 'Vanity,' he said finally, still gazing at the display in the bookshop window. 'Simple narcissism, I suppose. Vanity, vanity, all is vanity, saith the preacher.'

It was another of his quotations, Bruni knew, though he didn't have the faintest idea where it was from. Arbati had a quotation for every occasion. He must, Bruni thought, sit up at night with old, forgotten folios hunting out phrases and committing them to memory.

Traffic crept forward, easing finally when they passed the bottleneck at Piazza dell' Unità. At the first sign of an opening, Bruni tramped down the accelerator and they bolted forward, shooting at right angles across the traffic circle in front of Santa Maria Novella station. Several uniformed Carabinieri were on duty in the piazza, leaning on their motor cycles, and they grinned when they recognized the driver. Giorgio's reputation preceded him wherever he went.

He drove up the ramp reserved for buses and stopped outside the station entrance.

21

'Hardly a record,' he said, 'but you're here in plenty of time. You want me to come in?'

Arbati shook his head. 'No, I'll find a compartment on the train and read,' he said. 'You get out there and staunch the tide of crime. That's what the government is paying you to do while I'm away after all.'

'And you, my friend – ' Bruni cautioned, '*you stay away from crime* for the next two weeks. I don't want Giancarlo picking your brains to solve his cases for him. This is a holiday and you remember that. I want you back here fit and rested when it's over.'

'I promise,' Arbati said, retrieving his case from the back seat. It would be one of the easiest promises to keep he'd ever made. After all, what ever happened in sleepy Lucca . . . ?

'Well, I'll be off then,' Bruni said, extending a hand through the open window. 'You have yourself a fine time and knock 'em dead at the awards dinner.' As an afterthought, he added, 'Oh – and by the way, Carlo, *we're* all very proud of your poetry back at the Questura. Even if you aren't.'

Was it imagination, he wondered, or was Arbati blushing as he turned away?

Bruni smiled to himself with satisfaction. It wasn't often in their five-year partnership that he'd managed to get in the last word. It was a red-letter day.

He watched Arbati disappear through the glass doors of the station. It would have been a more gratifying sight, he reflected, if Cordelia Sinclair had been on his arm – but that eventuality, he knew, was about as probable as the everlasting fires of hell burning out. Although they had once been deeply in love, Cordelia would never come back to Florence looking for Carlo, and Carlo would never go off to the States to seek her out. Careers and egos, Bruni thought with a grimace, could be such terrible burdens.

He put the car into gear and pulled away from the kerb. Too quickly, as usual.

3

The convoy of two Carabinieri Fiats and a red-and-white ambulance of the Croce Rossa Italiana turned at the fork and started up the narrow, winding track that led to the San Felice estate. There had been more traffic on the usually quiet road in the past two hours than there had been in the past month. First, perhaps an hour ago, a powerful red sports car had slowed to a stop, then reversed and shot up the path to San Felice scattering stones and trailing a cloud of dust – and now, inexplicably, there was this sober municipal cavalcade. Something had happened at the villa. Something, clearly, was amiss.

From the garden of her cottage at the junction, Cecilia Hathaway watched the vehicles pass her gate at the beginning of their ascent to the villa five kilometres further up the road. Dressed in a twill jacket and a broad-brimmed hat to ward off the effects of solar radiation, she paused in her pruning and stood, hands on her hips, with a look of alarm etched on her hawklike features. Bunter, her brindled bull terrier who had been sleeping on the grass nearby, scrambled to his feet and stood four-square at the edge of the garden-plot, his ears erect and his head cocked to one side, watching his mistress through speculative, triangular eyes. Bunter missed nothing. He was in some mysterious way an extension of his mistress's soul, attuned to every variation in her mood, every feeling and intimate sensation. It was as if, in a previous life, they had been siblings or perhaps even twins born of a single mother.

'Well, Bunter,' she said, compressing her lips thoughtfully as the vehicles went past, 'this is extremely odd.'

'Aaarrgh,' Bunter concurred with a throaty rumble.

The events of the morning really were quite unaccountable – and, even before the cavalcade had disappeared from sight, Cecilia had made up her mind about what she was going to do. Decisiveness ran in her family; determination and resolution were qualities transmitted to her in her genes. Her father, in 1941, had led a spontaneously heroic – if ill-fated – charge on a Nazi machine-gun emplacement, for which he had been awarded a posthumous medal by his grateful country; and his daughter, no less impetuous, was wont to leap impulsively in wherever danger threatened. Certainly, she was not one to stand by and twiddle her thumbs when the safety of loved ones hung in the balance. And only one consideration motivated her now: *Nigel needed her.*

Doffing her gloves and laying aside her secateurs, she strode into the house and exchanged her gardening boots for a pair of stout walking shoes. Of all days, she thought testily, for the telephone to be out of order! If it had been working, she'd have rung first to let them know up at the villa that she was on her way.

In the mirror on the bureau she paused briefly to consider the image of her spare, wiry form. Yes, she judged with a curt nod, she was remarkably well preserved for a woman of sixty-five: trim, pink-cheeked, clear-eyed, feisty. She plucked a stray rose-cutting from the bodice of her jacket and fastened the cord of her hat under her chin. She was ready. From the umbrella stand in the front hall she snatched up a stout ashplant, gnarled and venerable with age, and sallied forth like a latter-day Dorothy Wordsworth on her mission of mercy.

When she emerged from the cottage, Bunter was waiting at the garden gate, anticipating a ramble over the hills that would bring a thousand new and exciting smells.

'Not this time,' Cecilia said, reaching down to scratch between his ears. 'It's Nigel, I'm afraid.'

A look of visible aversion passed over Bunter's pointed face and his ears fell. For reasons that Cecilia had never fathomed, Bunter and Nigel had disliked each other intensely from the start – a case of loathing at first sight. At the bottom of it lay something visceral and atavistic – an instinctive antipathy, something born in the blood. In any case, it wouldn't do, she knew, to turn up at San Felice with Bunter along. No, it wouldn't do at all.

'I'll be back as soon as I can,' she said, standing and turning the latch on the gate. 'You look after things here while I'm gone.' She addressed him as if he were a fellow human being.

'Aaarrgh,' Bunter rumbled, promising.

As she closed the gate behind her, another car rumbled past – a battered green Opel – and Cecilia turned in time to see at the wheel the taut, unsmiling face of Dottore Bindi-Santi. Yes indeed, serious business was afoot at the villa. There wasn't a moment to be lost. Without further delay, she set off at a brisk, lung-taxing pace, the metal tip of her ashplant and thick soles of her Oxford hikers crunching in purposeful syncopation up the steep gravel track.

Five kilometres away, Nigel Harmsworth swung open the oak door in the portico of Villa San Felice to admit the waiting constabulary. They had drawn their vehicles up in a line behind the red Maserati and now stood – a dark-suited detective flanked by three uniformed constables – in a sombre wedge of unsmiling officialdom. The black Carabinieri uniforms, with their ominous, high-peaked caps, sent an involuntary shudder down Nigel's spine. They made him think, in spite of the triumph of parliamentary democracy around the world, of bygone Fascist days and the German *Schutzstaffel*. Behind the wedge of policemen, two ambulance attendants, shrouded in anonymous white coats, waited with a collapsible wheeled trolley.

'You are Signor Harmsworth?' the detective enquired, removing his hat.

'I am,' Nigel replied. 'Please follow me.'

He led them through hushed salons out on to the rear terrace, then down the balustraded steps to the garden below. The dead man lay as he had left him, arms cast wide and body pinned like an insect to the turf, the impassive Mycenaean warrior mounting, as he had done since toppling from his concrete pedestal, a vigilant guard over the cyanosing corpse. A startled woodland bird, tugging at a grub in the lawn nearby, squawked angrily and flapped away to the solitude of the surrounding forest. There was however, Nigel noted, no sign of that other and more mysterious wayfarer – the Blue Morpho butterfly.

The detective, a spare man in his middle thirties, short and already balding, with a dapper little moustache, surveyed the scene with a practised eye. He noted the position of the body, the expensive clothes worn by the deceased, the forgotten sherry glass that had tumbled unregarded from Nigel's hand, the crumbled lip of the statue's pedestal where the cracked masonry had given way. He knelt beside the body and, quite unnecessarily as it seemed to Nigel, felt for a pulse in the carotid artery on the victim's neck. Satisfied that there was none, he prised the tumbler from the dead man's hand, raising it first to his nose and then running a finger around the inside rim and touching it to his tongue.

'Scotch,' he announced to no one in particular. 'Single malt.'

'Cardhu,' Nigel supplied helpfully.

The detective rose to his feet and turned toward Nigel.

'You have touched nothing, Signor Harmsworth?' he enquired, wiping his fingers on a linen handkerchief. He had the disconcerting habit of delivering his questions as assertions that became interrogatory only at the final instant.

'Nothing at all,' Nigel replied. 'I telephoned you directly the accident occurred.'

The little detective nodded. 'So you told the duty sergeant,' he

25

agreed, with what probably passed with him for a genial smile. 'And the red Maserati in the drive belongs, I assume, to the deceased man?'

Nigel nodded in the affirmative.

'Very well,' the detective said, turning back to the body, 'if you'll be kind enough, Signor Harmsworth, to give me a few minutes to complete my investigation here, I'll rejoin you in the house shortly. I'll need a formal statement from you, of course.' He turned to one of the uniformed officers and said, 'Go up with him, Paulo, and take a look over that Maserati. Oh yes – and send the coroner down when he arrives. He won't be far behind us.'

The road was narrow and snaked its way up the mountain in a series of switchbacks. On the right, the ground fell sharply away to a fern-floored valley where an unseen stream rushed by in the undergrowth, gurgling cheerfully over its rocky bed. On the left the land rose, equally abruptly, up a steep hillside plumed with large conifers. Overhead, the midday sun spilled down without relief, like molten metal poured from a copper sky.

Cecilia Hathaway paused to rest on one of the posts supporting the guard rail. She was hot and parched; she was breathing hard and her calves ached from exertion; there were beads of perspiration on her brow. She'd acted, she realized now, precipitously. If she'd had her wits properly about her at the start, she'd have worn lighter clothing and brought along a thermos of chilled rosemary tea.

In the old days, she thought with a grimace, I'd have managed better. She remembered the time, one spring when the gorse was in glorious bloom, that she'd climbed to the top of Porlock Hill and retraced the steps of Wordsworth and Coleridge along the Channel coast, past Lynton and Heddon's Mouth, all the way to Ilfracombe and then back through the gloomy confines of Exmoor. She'd scarcely broken a sweat the whole journey. Later, in a long vacation when she was an undergraduate, she'd walked through France and Switzerland to see the Jungfrau, reciting passages from Byron's *Manfred* aloud to pass the time. But those far-off days, alas, were now no more, and all their aching pleasures.

She pulled off her hat and fanned her burning cheeks. Age was an encroachment on liberty and a debilitation of physical strength that she refused to suffer gladly. She hated growing old: it clipped the wings of her desire and curbed her freedom to function as she once had. It imposed restraints on her craving for action, driving a wedge between aspiration and ability. It was also, in a most unsettling way, a premonition of the icy silence of death, when all motion and feeling would cease forever. A chill stole over her in the glare of noon and she felt a strange sensation along her spine, as of a distant tramp of footsteps on her grave.

She shook the dismal mood off with a decisive shrug. She could pity herself later. Just at the moment there were more important things that required her attention.

Something was wrong up at San Felice. Nigel was in trouble.

What on earth, she wondered for the hundredth time, could have happened at the villa that called for *two* police cars and an ambulance as well? Had the place been burgled? Had there been a struggle? Was poor Nigel lying wounded? – oh God! perhaps even *dead*! Were the police, even now, drawing an outline in chalk around the corpse to mark its exact position . . .?

Vividly, mercilessly, her imagination sketched the image of a splayed figure, face down on the cold marble, dark blood pooling like a grotesque aureole around its battered head.

Stop it! her mind commanded. *Stop it at once!*

A flash of blue in the undergrowth caught her attention. It was a butterfly – large, iridescent, beautiful. She didn't know what kind it was, only that she had never seen one like it. And as so often in her experience, a phenomenon in nature turned her thoughts, not to biology, but to her reading of Greek mythology. Psyche, she thought instinctively: the emblem of the departing soul.

Subtle images of death were all around her.

She watched in fascination, mesmerized, as the fragile creature, bobbing and weaving, its jerky flight controlled as if by an unseen wire, frolicked in the dell below her. And then, quite suddenly, it disappeared behind a clump of fern and was gone. She waited for its return.

The passing seconds lengthened into minutes. Still she waited.

Nothing.

She had been wearing a blue dress, she remembered, the day she'd first met him. That was the summer of 1985 – eight . . . no, nine years ago. Was it so long, really? Oh dear, how time flew, the subtle thief of youth! Her mind, drifting, traced back link by link along the iron chain of memory. Yes, it was certainly 1985: the year she and Bunter (then a pup) had left England, taking early retirement from her position as headmistress of Holford House, a private girls' academy on the edge of the Quantock Hills in rural Somerset. She hadn't missed the job at all. She had always, right from the beginning, hated the administrative part of it – the struggle in so isolated a setting to attract and retain a committed staff, the endless paperwork, the acrimonious and unproductive meetings with a penny-pinching board of governors. During her last years at the school, even the teaching of English poetry, once so great a pleasure to her, had become an onerous chore: a futile attempt to impart to callow girls, whose giddy minds and hearts were elsewhere, an understanding and a love of the music of their native tongue. Thus, when word had come, quite without warning, that a long-forgotten uncle had died, bequeathing to her his cottage in Italy, she had submitted her resignation, taken a reduced pension, and packed her bags without regret.

Yes – yes, she had been wearing, she remembered, that royal blue evening gown from Harrods and a Hermès scarf the first time she'd seen Nigel Harmsworth all those years ago. It all came back to her now in a flood of memory. It was at a soirée after a performance – of *Tosca*, was it? – at Teatro del Giglio, and she had fallen in love with him at first sight. He was warm and witty and intelligent – and he was a bachelor. He was, in fact, the man she had hoped all her life to find. They had talked about music and painting; he was a painter himself, she'd discovered, and had retired to Italy only a year or two earlier after a long career as a refurbisher of old oils for an internationally respected auction house. She had listened to the story of his life with adoring fascination. He had smiled and laughed and charmed – *oh, he had sparkled that night!* He had bewitched her and stolen her heart. But Nigel Harmsworth was not, alas, the marrying kind. In the months and years that followed he had cultivated her friendship but never courted her love; he had opened his house to her but never his heart. Yet Cecilia Hathaway had never abandoned hope. What was it Alexander Pope had said so long ago? *Hope springs eternal in the human breast; Man never is, but always to be blessed.* The same patient wisdom, she was certain, applied with equal force to Woman. All good things came eventually to those who waited for them with a believing heart.

Oh – ! but what if now he lay, as her worst imaginings feared, in a lifeless pool of blood? Poetry would provide no balm for *that* bitter reality . . .

She stood abruptly and snatched up her walking-stick.

No, he was alive – injured perhaps, but alive – and she would be there for him. Suddenly, she was strong again and infused with an iron sense of purpose. He could always, yes always, count on her.

His investigation of the accident scene completed, Inspector Bonelli appeared in the doorway of the smoking-room where Nigel, fortified with a brandy and soda despite the early hour, awaited him. Bars of yellow light, filtered through slatted shutters, lay in horizontal strips on floor and furniture, and motes of dust, like miniature snowflakes, floated languorously through the shafts of laddered light. The only sound was the distant ticking of a clock. The atmosphere of strained apprehension in the room was like that in the lounge of a private clinic where relatives have assembled to await the news of a loved one's condition. When Bonelli appeared, the police officer at the door stepped silently aside and the inscrutable detective entered the room, smoothing down the sparse remains of his hair with a fastidious hand.

'Ah, inspector . . .' Nigel said, rising with a pained smile and twisting the brandy glass awkwardly in his fingers.

Having never before encountered the minions of justice at such close quarters, he found himself agitated beyond his expectation by the prospect of the impending interview – although of course, he consoled himself, there was nothing whatsoever for him to be concerned about. How could there be? Accidents, even fatal ones, were beyond anyone's control. What had happened that morning in the garden must be obvious at a glance to the disinterested observer, and Inspector Bonelli, it was abundantly clear, was a keen-eyed professional of considerable acumen and experience. Yet still, unaccountably, Nigel found that the glass he held was trembling in his hand. There was something – he didn't know what – in the inspector's wary taciturnity that alarmed and frightened him, that put his nerves on end. He felt somehow that he was presumed guilty in advance of some heinous crime from which he was presently to be given an opportunity, if he performed well, to clear his besmirched name.

Inspector Bonelli took the seat opposite and crossed his legs. He removed a notebook from an inside pocket and opened it on his knee. When he looked up finally at Nigel, his face was an expressionless mask. He said:

'There are a number of questions, Signor Harmsworth, that I must ask you about this unpleasant business. Do you feel up to answering them now?'

'Of course,' Nigel said, sensing the hemp tighten around his neck. 'As you please, inspector. Now is fine.' He planted his feet and squared his shoulders manfully. 'Yes, yes – fire away then.'

'Perhaps you'd be more comfortable sitting down,' Bonelli suggested.

'Yes, quite. Perfectly so,' Nigel agreed, sitting.

Bonelli touched the pencil to the end of his tongue. His eyes flickered down to the notebook, then up again to Nigel's face. 'Let's begin,' he said, 'by reconstructing the events of this morning. Tell me what you remember. From the beginning.'

Nigel leaned back awkwardly, feigning relaxation, and said after a moment's reflection:

'There isn't, in fact, much to tell, inspector. It was just coming up to eleven when the door bell sounded. I was in the kitchen reading the letters to the editor in *The Times*. I was alone in the house, of course. The maid and gardener both take Wednesday as their day off, and the cook, who lives here with me, was shopping in town. She has still not returned.'

He paused, giving Bonelli a questioning look, as if to enquire whether the level of detail was sufficient. The inspector gave a curt nod.

'Well,' Nigel continued, 'I folded the newspaper and walked through the dining-room to answer the door. The man who was waiting there said he had something – he didn't say what, I'm afraid – that he wished to discuss with me. I offered him a drink, which he accepted. He asked specifically for a single-malt scotch, and I obliged, taking only a small sherry for myself, it being not yet noon. We took our drinks and walked through to the back garden, where I knew the sun would be warm and pleasant. He took a seat on one of the garden chairs and had just begun to tell me why he had come when I felt suddenly faint – the effect, perhaps, of sherry on a morning stomach – and tottered heavily into the Greek bronze beside which I was standing. The pedestal on which it stood had apparently cracked and weakened over the years. In any event, it broke away and the statue tumbled forward and – well, the rest, of course, you know.' He debated including an account of the strange business of the Blue Morpho butterfly, but the laconic inspector didn't strike him as one to be interested either in entomology or in the finer points of the Psyche myth,

30

and so he refrained. 'Directly I realized what had happened,' he ended, 'and had ascertained that the poor chap under the statue was quite beyond my help, I returned to the house and telephoned for the police.'

'I see,' the inspector said, taking his eyes off Nigel for the first time and making a jotting in his notebook. When he had finished writing, the grey eyes flickered up again. 'For how long, Signor Harmsworth, had you known the deceased?'

Nigel cleared his throat.

'He was, in fact,' he said, speaking as if through a drainage pipe, 'a complete stranger to me. I had never seen him before this morning, inspector, when he rang the bell.' He added: 'I must confess that I don't even know his name.'

Bonelli's brow wrinkled. 'I see,' he said. 'And yet you invited this man, a total stranger, into your house and gave him a glass of expensive Cardhu single-malt whisky. You are a remarkably hospitable man, it seems, Signor Harmsworth.'

'*Noblesse oblige*, inspector,' Nigel said stiffly. 'The man had business to discuss with me – or so he said. I was merely being polite. I did what any gentleman in my position would naturally have done in similar circumstances.'

'Quite so,' Bonelli agreed, making another jotting. 'But the nature of the business that he came all the way out to San Felice to discuss with you remains a mystery?'

Nigel nodded. 'A complete mystery, I'm afraid. We had barely begun our conversation when the unfortunate accident occurred.'

'And you have no idea – cannot even guess – what it was he came to talk about?'

'No, inspector, I cannot,' Nigel said evenly. 'He was, as I have said, a man previously unknown to me. I haven't the remotest idea what he wished to discuss.'

Outside the villa, the attendants loaded a shrouded trolley into the waiting ambulance, supervised in their endeavour by the coroner and watched impassively by two Carabinieri, smoking cigarettes, who were leaning against one of their black Fiats.

'Tell me, Signor Harmsworth,' Bonelli said suddenly. 'How much do you weigh?'

'Just over ten stone,' Nigel replied, surprised. 'Why? Is that relevant?'

'Ten stone,' Bonelli computed, 'is what? – about sixty-five kilos.' He made a notation in his book, then looked up again at Nigel. 'Is that information relevant, Signor Harmsworth? To tell you the truth, I really don't know. But that statue is extremely heavy. It took four of us to lift it free of the body. You must have *tottered*' – the word was in italics – 'into it very heavily, I think.'

'I suppose I must have done,' Nigel shrugged. 'All I know is that it broke free.'

'That fact,' the inspector agreed, 'is beyond dispute.'

Leaning back and running a thoughtful hand across his chin, Bonelli changed direction again. 'The dead man's name is Dearing,' he said, pausing fractionally to note Nigel's reaction. 'James Dearing, of New York City. He was born, according to the birth certificate in his wallet, in Boston in the State of Massachusetts on 27 June 1961. Does the name James Dearing mean anything to you, Signor Harmsworth?'

Nigel shook his head. 'No, nothing at all, I'm afraid.'

'The Maserati is a hire-car,' Bonelli went on. 'Oddly enough, however, the signature on the lease agreement we found in the glove box is not that of James Dearing, but of a certain Martin James Peterson. Perhaps it is an alias. Is that name, perhaps, familiar to you?'

Nigel furrowed his brow and then shook his head again.

'I know no one of that name,' he said.

Bonelli retrieved a package of cigarettes from an inside pocket, enquiring by a look if he might indulge.

'Go right ahead,' Nigel said, declining the proffered package himself. 'I gave it up years ago, but I'm not one of those killjoys who inflicts the moral superiority of their suffering on others.'

For the first time, Bonelli's lips cracked in a genuine smile. 'I've tried to give it up myself – frequently,' he confessed, striking a match and touching it to the tip.

Nigel nodded. 'The first two years are the easiest,' he commiserated.

Outside, the ambulance with its shrouded cargo, followed closely by the coroner's battered green Opel, eased around the red Maserati and started the descent down the steep, winding road to Lucca. The two Carabinieri left behind slouching against their car looked at their watches and lit fresh cigarettes. Inspector Bonelli was never one to hurry an investigation.

Back inside, the inspector tilted his head back and launched a plume of smoke at the ceiling. 'Tell me, Signor Harmsworth,' he said conversationally, 'how long have you been so fortunate as to live here at Villa San Felice? This is the first time I've actually seen the place.' He glanced with approval at the veined marble and polished wood around him. 'An elegant house,' he said. 'It was originally built, if I recall correctly, by the Guinigi family.'

'At the end of the eighteenth century.' Nigel nodded. 'As for myself, I've been here nearly ten years, ever since I retired.' He added quickly, 'I don't own the place myself, you understand. I merely look after it for my former employer, Sir Richard Danvers. He visits occasionally, usually when it's snowing in London, but most of the time his duties keep him busy elsewhere. He's a rather well-known figure in the international art world. Perhaps you've heard of him?'

The inspector nodded. 'Danvers' House Auctioneers, specializing in Italian art and antiques.'

'With rooms in London, New York, Paris, Rome, and Firenze,' Nigel supplied, feeling more at ease now with the tone and direction of the conversation.

'A prestigious firm,' Bonelli agreed. 'You worked for them, you say.'

An impish grin crinkled the corners of Nigel's mouth. 'Actually,' he said, 'Dickie – Sir Richard, that is – and I were at school together many years ago, at the Slade in London. We fancied ourselves the Raphaels of the coming age, but abstract impressionism and the distinctly avant-garde prejudices of our instructors drove us out into the cold world without diplomas. I chose to starve in a garret in Paris pursuing the dream of a classical revival. Richard, more wisely, turned his hand to commerce. By the time he found me in the Rue Gabrielle in Montmartre several years later, he was already a wealthy man and I was down to my last franc. I had sold, if memory serves me, only one painting – an imitation in modern dress of Fra Angelico's *Annunciation* at the Museo Diocesano in Cortona – and that for a mere pittance, a "song" as Americans say, to an eccentric Texas oilman. It didn't take much persuasion for Dickie to convince me that I'd do better coming to work for him cleaning and restoring old canvases in preparation for the gavel. That, inspector, was the beginning of a long and fruitful collaboration, and this,' he said, sweeping his hand around the room, 'is my reward. An annual living allowance and unrestricted use of an historic Tuscan villa.'

'Distinctly preferable to starving in a garret,' Bonelli agreed. 'And now, I suppose, you have sufficient leisure to pursue your original dream of painting?'

Nigel laughed. 'A sere and faded vision by now, I'm afraid, inspector. It is Dali and Mirò who have triumphed, not I. I have a studio in the back, of course, and I still do some painting. But I paint from habit now, not from the heart. I have nothing to say to the world, and the world, it must be said, ignored me when I did have something to offer it. No, the old fires burned themselves out long ago, inspector, leaving behind only the charred cinders of a forgotten desire.' He tossed off what remained of his brandy and added: 'Happily, however, I've learned to accommodate myself to anonymity and a life of slothful ease.'

This comfortable tête-à-tête was interrupted by the appearance of one of the two policemen from outside. He crossed the room and muttered something into the inspector's ear. Bonelli nodded and the officer disappeared as swiftly and silently as he had come.

'A Signorina Hathaway is at the door and insists on seeing you,' he announced, stubbing out the remains of his cigarette. 'Since our business is nearly finished, I told my man to show her in. I hope her visit is not an inconvenience.'

'It wouldn't matter if it were,' Nigel said with a grimace. 'Cecilia is a woman not easily turned aside from her purposes.' He added with a grin: 'It would, however, have been substantially more diverting, inspector, if you had chosen to try and keep her out.'

The measured tramp of stout shoes echoed in the hall, coalescing in the doorway seconds later with the bonneted apparition of a woman, flushed and breathing deeply after the exertion of her five-kilometre climb. In her right hand she bore, like a weapon of war, a gnarled walking-stick, smooth and shiny with use.

'Nigel,' she cried with evident relief, 'thank heavens, you're safe. I saw the police and an ambulance go by and came as quickly as I could.'

She paused, casting a glance at the seated figure of the police inspector.

Nigel rose. 'Cecilia Hathaway,' he said, performing the introductions, 'this is Inspector Bonelli of the local Carabinieri.' Turning to Bonelli, he added: 'Miss Hathaway is a neighbour. Her cottage is at the fork at the bottom of the hill. You would have passed it on the way up.'

'A pleasure, *signorina*,' Bonelli said, extending his hand.

She crossed the room and shook the offered palm, then turned again to Nigel.

'What on earth is going on?' she said. 'You've given me a terrible fright, Nigel. I was worried to distraction about you all the way here.'

Her face was red and her breathing still laboured.

'Before we get into that,' he proposed, 'perhaps I could fetch you a glass of water – '

'You can tell me, first,' she said shortly, 'what's going on.'

Nigel knew when he was beaten. Glancing at Bonelli, he said slowly, 'There's been a dreadful accident, I fear – '

Bonelli, recognizing his cue, interjected: 'A man has been killed, Signorina Hathaway. He was crushed by a statue in the garden.'

'Heavens!' Cecilia breathed, dropping on to the sofa as if the air had been let out of her. 'A man killed!' She recovered herself quickly and fixed Bonelli with a steely gaze. 'You don't, I hope, suspect Nigel of killing him. The notion is perfectly absurd. I've known him for years, inspector. He wouldn't harm a fly.'

'The evidence,' Bonelli said reassuringly, 'suggests the death was accidental.' He added: 'The circumstances, however, are unquestionably bizarre, and the coroner, I believe, intends to hold an inquest into the matter. But I'm confident the only verdict the facts will bear, unless other evidence comes to light in the meantime, is death by misadventure.'

'But the possibility of foul play does exist?'

'It's possible, yes, but not probable.'

'Dear Nigel, of course, has been completely exonerated?'

'I think, Signorina Hathaway,' Bonelli cautioned, 'that we're best to let the coroner pronounce on such matters in due course, when he's in possession of all the facts.'

Inspector Bonelli rose to depart. He turned to Nigel: 'We've covered the central facts, Signor Harmsworth, and I can always contact you if I need more information. I wonder, however, if we might have a word in private before I go? There are still one or two nagging details that I'd like to clear up.'

'Of course,' Nigel said. 'You'll excuse us for a moment, Cecilia, while I show the inspector out.'

Side by side, the two men made their way along the inlaid marble corridor toward the foyer where, only two hours previously, the enigmatic James Dearing had thrust himself so suddenly and unceremoniously into the placid centre of Nigel Harmsworth's life. As they walked, Bonelli asked:

'Does the name Ghirlandaio mean anything to you, Signor Harmsworth?'

Nigel raised an eyebrow. The inspector had the knack of blindsiding an interlocutor with his questions. 'Of course,' he said.

'He was a Florentine painter in the second half of the fifteenth century. Why do you ask?'

Bonelli gave a thin smile. 'It's odd, isn't it, that we should have found the name written on a scrap of paper in the dead man's pocket? Nothing else – just that single word: *Ghirlandaio*. I wondered, Signor Harmsworth, you being a painter yourself, whether the name held any special significance for you – anything that might help explain why Signor Dearing should have turned up here with that particular name in his pocket?'

Nigel furrowed his brow, then shrugged and shook his head. 'No – none that I can think of, at least at the moment,' he said. He added: 'Poor old Ghirlandaio, you know, was a rather dull and prosaic artist, inspector – an anachronism even in his own lifetime. His greatest claim to interest for posterity is the fact that he took Michelangelo on as an apprentice in his studio. Why Mr Dearing should have had the name in his pocket is, I must say, an enigma to me.'

Bonelli pursed his lips. 'Ah – a pity, alas,' he confessed. 'I'd hoped we might have a useful lead there. Still, you'll let me know if you do happen to think of something. I have a feeling the discovery is an important one.'

They continued in silence and entered the foyer with its crystal chandelier, its statue-filled recesses, its balustraded marble staircase.

'You hinted, inspector,' Nigel reminded him, 'that there were two points you wished to raise with me. Is there something else?'

Bonelli stopped and, turning slowly, fixed Nigel with a serious eye. 'There is, yes, as a matter of fact. Did you know, Signor Harmsworth,' he said with deliberation, 'that Signor Dearing was armed?'

The look of stunned horror on Nigel's face was the only answer that was required.

Bonelli went on:

'He was carrying a 9mm Beretta pistol concealed under his shirt in the small of his back. We also found a screw-on silencer in his trouser pocket. Signor Dearing was a man, it seems, who prepared himself in advance for trouble. What, I wonder, Signor Harmsworth, led him to suppose that he might need such preparation in visiting you?' He removed his notepad and, turning to a fresh page, wrote down a number. 'I have reason to suppose, Signor Harmsworth,' he said, tearing out the sheet and handing it over, 'that your life may be in some danger. This is my home telephone.

If you can't reach me at the Questura, you can call me there at any time, day or night.' He added: 'If you should recall anything – anything at all, no matter how apparently insignificant – you won't hesitate, I know, to contact me immediately.'

The door clicked softly and he was gone.

As if recovering from a physical blow, Nigel lowered himself gingerly on to the marble steps and dropped his head into his hands. The incident in the garden – which he'd considered a tragic aberration, now closed and best forgotten – was apparently a beginning rather than an ending. What, he wondered, was to follow? Would there be other surprises, other visitors – perhaps in the middle of the night? He shuddered. What should he do to prepare and protect himself?

He hadn't the slightest inkling of an idea.

He sat for several hour-long minutes, his mind turning mechanically but totally blank, then levered himself to his feet and, like a man condemned, retraced his steps along the corridor to face the enthusiastic charity of his well-meaning neighbour. In the circumstances, of course, there was nothing else he could do. *Noblesse oblige.*

4

Ilse Kleist geared down and took the hairpin bend like a Formula One driver negotiating a chicane. On the straightway, she shifted smartly up through the gears and jammed her foot down on the accelerator. Her leased Alfa Romeo convertible, sharing the fantasy, responded with every enthusiastic ounce of thrust that its 4-litre heart could generate. There was a smile on Ilse's face. Her pulse was elevated and her hands were slightly sticky on the wheel. Life was good. Catching the mood, the puckish wind snatched at the collar of her dress and twitched her blonde hair provocatively in its gamin currents. She pushed the speedometer up to 100 kilometres an hour. The Italian countryside flew by in a giddy blur on either side.

Ilse lived in the fast lane – or at least that's the image, in the secret places of her heart, that she cherished of herself. She saw herself as a thoroughly modern woman: emancipated, daring, living life to the lees. She was young, she was beautiful, she was married to a man – a man nearly twenty-five years her senior, it was true – but a man, nonetheless, whose position in the world guaranteed her a more than acceptable level of security, prosperity, and status in society.

The mountain road dipped and entered the Serchio valley, hugging the shallow, boulder-strewn course of the river whose jade-coloured waters were lined with sallows and thickets of oriental-looking bamboo. Overhead, in an opal sky, tropospheric currents tugged patches of ragged cloud across the sky. It was a gorgeous day – the kind that made one forget one's mortality and gave a comforting illusion that lingering autumn afternoons would never end.

The road she was travelling acquired a name – Via del Brennero – and plunged into the outskirts of Lucca. Through gaps in the rooftops rose the tree-lined ramparts of the town, high red-brick walls with a leafy plumage of chestnut and plane trees. Ilse eased up fractionally on the throttle and kept a weather eye open for traffic patrols. Willi, long-suffering husband though he was, would kill her if she got another speeding ticket. She'd managed to pick up three of them in quick succession in a bad patch over the summer, and there were definite limits, she knew, to Willi's patience.

Via del Brennero came to an end in a Y-junction at Borgo Giannotti. She slowed for the flashing light, then wheeled left, heading into town.

The nearness of her destination made her suddenly aware of the dampness between her thighs. There were some urges that couldn't be denied and Peter Morgan was one of them. They'd met four months ago – it was hard to believe it was really that long – at an otherwise dreadful party at Marchesa di Lena's palazzo and had carried on a steamy and tempestuous affair ever since. Peter Morgan was the forbidden fruit that Ilse had waited all her life to taste. And now that she'd found it, she wanted nothing more than to taste it again and again. She was a glutton for pleasure.

She geared down and shot irritably, abruptly, around a fat woman on a bicycle wobbling in the road ahead. *Mein Gott*, Ilse thought, if I looked like that old cow, I wouldn't be caught dead out in public. Ilse was fastidious about her appearance. She ate wholegrain breads and jogged to keep her body fit and firm.

At the traffic circle in Martyrs' Piazza, she bore left, following Viale Marconi around the base of the fortifications. On the grassy common below one of the spade-shaped bastions, a group of boys had struck up a scratch football match, using empty milk cartons to mark the goals. Their shouts reached her ears like sounds from a distant planet. She glanced at her watch and wondered what Peter was doing then, right at that very moment. She liked imagining where he was, what he was doing, what he was thinking. It made him seem that much closer.

Thought led to thought, and then –

I wonder, she asked herself suddenly, her lip curling into a testy pucker, why the miserable *Scheißkerl* didn't tell me he was coming into town today?

It had been a week since they'd last met and he knew she had nothing on that afternoon. A second thought struck her like a mallet blow: what if he was with another woman? Her face twisted into a vindictive pout and her grip tightened on the helpless wheel. He was an attractive man. He could have any woman he wanted. If he snapped his fingers, they'd queue up to have a go at him.

Her eyes narrowed dangerously. By God! she swore, if I catch them at it, I'll kill them on the spot. And her fertile imagination began to survey a range of weapons suitable for the task.

Ilse Kleist was one of those personalities who, born with nothing, had grown up expecting a great deal out of life. She was aggressive and self-centred – a restless spirit never satisfied with her lot but never able to identify what it was exactly that she was missing out on. Her early years had been spent in grinding poverty, without a father. His sudden disappearance when she was seven was a mystery for which her mother had never offered a solution, although from hints she'd dropped it seemed probable that he'd been killed in a bungled bank heist. But Ilse didn't care. Her past was something she had left behind her – a sorry episode that was buried and best forgotten. She lived for the present and the future.

At the age of twenty, working days as a file clerk in a shoe factory and going to night school, she had won an entrance scholarship to Kiel University. There, she'd taken up the study of biology, not out of a disinterested love of science but rather because the human body – the only aspect of the subject she deemed worthy of investigation – endlessly attracted and fascinated her. She was devoted to the sensuous contours of the human anatomy, the erotic curve of thigh and instep, the rippling grace of biceps and deltoids. But life never serves up quite what one expects. Ilse had spent her days as an undergraduate cataloguing stamen types, squinting through microscopes at sections of sheep intestine, and ploughing through textbooks on statistical analysis. Finally, however, in her final year, one of her professors, an entomologist recently widowed, had fallen in love and proposed marriage. After thinking it over for a weekend, Ilse had accepted. She'd been hoping for a younger man, of course, preferably a surgeon or a stockbroker; but a professor of insect morphology would, she decided, have to do in the circumstances. Social mobility exacted its sacrifices and involved, inevitably, certain inconveniences in the ascent.

Someone more ruthless and cynical, more sure of herself, might have considered these triumphs an adequate victory over destiny, but, for Ilse, they led only to increasing insecurity and a pushy determination to cling for dear life to the things she regarded as rightfully hers. And those things most emphatically included Peter Morgan, her lover from Philadelphia. The thought that he was cheating on her, that he was tumbling in scented sheets with some shameless hussy, some *Flittchen*, was agonizing for her. It made her skin crawl. It made her blood boil. It made her eyes fill with tears so that she could hardly see the road in front of her. How could he betray her love in such a callous and unfeeling way? And how *dare he* – !

She would do them in, she decided, with a butcher's knife. It would be easy enough to pick one up on her way through town.

But at that moment reason asserted itself and prompted her to reassess the situation. Peter might, of course, be screwing some-body else, but it wasn't all that probable that he was. Ilse kept him too satisfied. She wasn't good at many things – like cooking *saltimbocca*, for example, or discussing Etruscan bronzes – but she was a good lover. No, she corrected herself, *a great lover*. It was her special gift in life. She could be quite certain that Peter wasn't sleeping with another woman. Between what Ilse – and, presum-ably, Peter's wife as well – demanded of him, he wouldn't have the surplus energy needed to run his plough into strange furrows.

With that happy thought, Ilse's self-confidence returned and, with it, her smile. She didn't need to buy that butcher's knife after all.

But still, why hadn't he phoned her? Was it possible he'd wanted to get out of the house without having to see her, that he hadn't called because he was tiring of her? The thought sent a tremor down her spine. No, the idea was absurd. The chemistry when they were together was magnificent. Most probably, she reflected, he'd sneaked out for one of his hush-hush meetings with that supercilious twit in the designer shirts. She couldn't remember the man's name and she didn't care to know it. He was boorish, vain, and probably, she thought maliciously, a homosexual as well. Business dealings made for strange bedfellows. She wondered briefly what kind of business it was that had brought Peter Morgan together with an *Arschloch* like what's-his-name. It couldn't be anything good, she knew. She dismissed the thought. It didn't really matter. Whatever it was, it had nothing to do with her.

By the time she passed through Porta Elisa and entered the old city, she was feeling quite her old self again. The cloud of jealousy that had crossed the sunny face of her libido, dampening its heat, had been dispersed by the combined forces of special pleading and proleptic lust. Once again, she was aware of a flutter of expectation in her stomach and a pleasant oozing dampness in her crotch.

She found a place to park in Piazza Napoleone. She didn't need to guess where she would find him. She knew exactly where to look: the Hotel Universo. They had always, since that first fortuitous meeting, used the same venue for their trysts; and Peter Morgan, a creature of habit, would be there now. He lacked the imagination to search out a new location for his assignations, whether for business or pleasure. Ilse smiled to herself. She knew him better than he knew himself.

There was a seedy elegance about the lobby of the Hotel Universo. The reception rooms were small and sparsely furnished, as if the owners had fallen on hard times and been forced to sell off a portion of their patrimony. The mahogany tables and leather chairs had a look of decayed grandeur, a patina of anachronism and nostalgia. Even the spiky palm in its brass planter seemed reminiscent of another age. Everything spoke of a down-at-heel gentility basking in the memory of better times and bygone days.

The concierge looked up and smiled as Ilse approached the reception desk. They were old acquaintances, discreet conspirators.

'Is he in?' she asked.

'Room 213.'

'Alone?'

A knowing smile. 'But of course, *signora*. Until now.'

'Thank you, Franco.'

'*Prego, signora.*'

She took the stairs to the second floor. Room 213 was half-way along the corridor overlooking Piazza Napoleone. If Peter had been looking out of his window, he'd have seen her arrive and park the car. She tapped on the door and waited. There was no response. She tapped again, this time more loudly. Still no response.

She knew what it meant, of course. He was asleep – or indisposed.

She pushed the door. It swung open and the match-folder inserted to hold back the latch-tongue fell to the floor at her feet. (It was a trick he used when he was expecting someone.) She stepped inside. The room was empty. Ilse smiled. Good, she thought, her visit would be a surprise. She liked to surprise him. It kept him on his toes.

The bathroom door was half-way open and she could see steam and hear the sound of the shower running. From somewhere in the swirling mist, Peter's voice, gravelly and off-key, was wrestling an old Beatles tune to its knees. He had many gifts, but song wasn't one of them. Ilse looked around the room. The bed, she noticed immediately, was untouched – still made up with the drum-skin tautness achieved only by nurses or a professional housekeeping staff. She felt a pang of guilt. She'd been wrong to doubt him, wrong to flirt for even an instant with the absurd notion that he was sleeping around. She knew him better than that. He was as much in love with her as she was with him. All the same, however, it was a relief to discover that the empirical evidence supported her implicit faith.

She hung out the DO NOT DISTURB sign and closed the door, locking it behind her. She wanted no intruders for the next hour or so. If the obnoxious American in the designer shirts – old what's-his-name – turned up, he'd just have to leave a note and come back later. Whatever his business with Peter was, her needs were more pressing. She took a condom from her purse and, slipping it under the pillow, pulled the covers back into place. Then she turned a chair so that it faced the bathroom door and, throwing her legs seductively over the padded arm, sat down to wait.

'She Loves You – Yeh, Yeh, Yeh' gave way to Elvis's 'Blue Suede Shoes', equally execrably performed. Then there was a thump in the pipes as the water was shut off and, a minute or two

later, Peter Morgan, a towel secured around his waist, material-
ized in the doorway like a man stepping out of a London fog. He
was drying his hair with a second towel and, for a minute, didn't
realize that he had a visitor.

'Oh!' he said at last. 'I didn't hear you come in.'

Ilse grinned. 'You were sterilizing your equipment. I didn't like
to interrupt.'

He crossed the room to the frigobar in the bureau. 'Like a
drink?'

'A bit early for me, thanks. But don't let that stop you.'

'I won't,' he said, tossing some ice in a glass and cracking open
a mini-bottle of Dewar's scotch. Swirling the amber liquid, he
turned and said, 'How'd you know I'd be in town today, by the
way?' He didn't sound disappointed to see her.

'I telephoned your wife.'

'*You what?*' he spluttered, the glass frozen at his lip.

'Relax. I got the housekeeper. She told me you had business in
town and were expected back for dinner.' She added, 'If I'd got
your wife, I'd have hung up, naturally.'

'I should damned well hope so. And what's the housekeeper
supposed to think?'

'Let her think what she wants, as long as she keeps her thoughts
to herself.'

'Remind me to tell her that,' Peter said, tossing off his drink
with a convulsive swallow. 'And in the meantime, my sweet, do
me a favour and keep your itchy fingers off the dial.'

'I haven't seen you for a week,' she countered accusingly.

'I've had things on my mind,' he said. He walked to the window
and scanned the piazza below. He seemed edgy, Ilse thought.
Turning back into the room, he said, 'I'm expecting somebody.
I've been expecting him, actually, for the past two hours. If he
doesn't get here soon, I suppose I'll have to send the police out
after him.' The tone was forced, a transparent attempt at levity.

Ilse studied him leaning against the sill, his body glistening, his
hair wet and shiny from the shower, the muscles of his chest and
shoulders rippling like the sculpted form of a Greek athlete. She
didn't give a rat's ass about his meeting with what's-his-name.
She had other things on her mind.

'Come over here,' she said throatily. 'You look good enough to
eat.'

'Not now, Ilse. I told you, I'm expecting somebody,' he said
without moving.

43

She stood and walked over to him slowly, seductively, undoing the buttons at her throat. 'He'll have to come back later, I'm afraid,' she said. 'I've locked the door and put out the sign. Your meeting will have to wait. You have to deal with me first.'

Peter gave a grimace. He knew when an argument was lost.

She loosened the towel at his waist and it fell to the floor, then she reached down and cupped him in her hand, squeezing softly. Peter groaned and closed his eyes. Right from the beginning she'd known the right buttons to push. With gossamer fingers, slowly, gently, she circled the head of his organ, feeling it grow and stiffen in her hand. She wondered if his wife knew how to do it half as well. The low moaning that came from deep in his throat excited her, stirring her hormones like a stick in a hornets' nest. She could have been standing in the middle of the piazza outside and still have noticed nothing around her. Her genes were on autopilot, cleaving the air, thrusting her up through infinite space.

He took her mouth in his and the taste of his tongue was warm and salty – and then she felt his hands on her breasts, her buttons opening, her dress falling. She kicked it aside. She stood on tiptoe and nestled against him, thrusting her tongue between his lips. She wanted all of him. And then his hand was between her thighs, exploring the secret places that dripped with warm, light oil. And she felt herself rising like a bird, carried aloft on downy wings of rapture. The world was unfocused, lost in a sensuous void where time and space could never penetrate, where pleasure was a whelming tide that drowned all other sensation, all other thought, all sense of place and hour.

He carried her to the bed. She retrieved the condom from under the pillow and flicked the paper sleeve aside. He lay on his back and she bent above him, taking the furled sheath of the prophylactic in her mouth, as he'd taught her to, and unrolled it down the length of his penis with her lips. It wasn't something she particularly enjoyed, although from his quick intake of breath she knew what it did for him. Oh well, different strokes for different folks. She couldn't help thinking, somewhat irreverently, as she unrolled the latex down his hardened shaft, that the male anatomy was a particularly odd bit of biological engineering. There was something incongruous and vaguely comic about it – like pieces of fruit stuck on to the crotch of a suit of armour. But still, she thought, however silly it looks, it serves a delightfully useful purpose.

She straddled him and leaned forward, whispering sweetly into his ear. 'Fused and ready, capt'n. You can fire at will.'

Twenty minutes later, they lay spent and sated, stretched side by side like marble effigies carved on a sarcophagus. Ilse was in a ruminative daze. Oh yes indeed, she reflected dreamily, orgasm really is, as the French say, *une petite mort*, a little death. It had been only a week since they'd last made love and yet she felt as if she'd died into pleasure for the first time and was now, against all desire and inclination, in the process of being dragged painfully back toward the grey light of the mundane, workaday world. She wanted to prolong the mood of elation, the euphoria of love; she wanted to float forever, folded in the petals of the post-coital lotus. She resented the prospect of cold reality intruding on her idyll.

It was at that moment, unfortunately, that Peter farted.

'God,' she groaned, 'you really do know how to make a woman feel romantic.'

'Too much wine at lunch,' he grunted. 'Wine always gives me gas.'

Ilse rolled her eyes at the ceiling. 'Thanks for sharing that with me. I'll always treasure it as part of this special moment together.'

'Suit yourself,' he said, rolling off the bed and heading for the bathroom.

A moment later, there was the sound of a flushing toilet and then of water running in the sink. She knew what he was doing; he was fastidious about hygiene, a classic anal-retentive. It seemed suddenly a sad and reprehensible waste to her: the seed of future generations flushed to destruction in a rubber sack. All those little genetic tadpoles struggling manfully toward their goal, ambushed and sent swirling in a latex shroud into the dark tomb of an anonymous drain. It was like a kind of genocide. She remembered from her Lutheran background the Old Testament story of Onan, whom God killed because he cast his seed upon the ground. She wasn't a religious person – she'd never believed that superstitious claptrap, not really, or so she told herself – and yet the thought of all those potential lives so callously ended made her feel unaccountably melancholy and even, perhaps, a little apprehensive, as if a disapproving genie were scowling at her from somewhere in the shadows.

Peter emerged from the bathroom and dressed quickly, then went to the window and looked out again over the cars parked in Piazza Napoleone.

'You might as well get dressed,' he said, turning back into the room and noticing her. 'The party's over.'

Ilse shoved herself up on one elbow and fixed him with a stony stare. Christ, he could be a philistine sometimes. 'Wham, bang, thank you, ma'am – is that it?' she said. Why, she wondered, couldn't he be more sensitive ... more – *oh, more what?* She just couldn't find the right word, damn it all. Well, why couldn't he be less of a goddamn rutting boar? Her eyes were glacial, Medusa-like. Her mind was working but her face was a blank mask, showing nothing at all of what she felt. It was one of her rules never to betray any weakness, never to give him the satisfaction of seeing that he'd touched a nerve. Irony and satire were her substitutes for emotion. She said in a deadpan voice, mimicking his American accent:

'That's strike two, lover. One more and the International Orgasm Committee will revoke your Romantic-of-the-Year award.'

'That's not what I meant,' he said petulantly. 'You know I'm expecting somebody.'

Ilse threw her legs over the side of the bed. They were great legs, she noticed approvingly: long, silken, shapely. Legs worth killing for. She stood up and caught sight of her naked form in the mirror over the dresser. The rest of the body wasn't half bad either. He was damn lucky she was willing to put up with him.

'Somebody who's apparently not coming,' she observed coldly.

She retrieved her clothes and began dressing, watching him dispassionately. It struck her again that he looked agitated some-how. On edge. Perhaps even afraid of something. He was prowl-ing the room like a great shaggy bear, restless and preoccupied, his mind clearly elsewhere. She said on a whim,

'Is it anything I can help with? Maybe there's something I can do.'

'What?' he said. He hadn't been listening and she'd caught him off guard.

'This business deal of yours,' she repeated. 'Maybe I can help.'

'It's private,' he snapped.

Ilse shrugged. 'Okay, okay – sorry I asked,' she said. 'Just trying to be helpful.'

Peter seemed to recollect himself. His shoulders slumped and he looked penitent. He took her in his arms and kissed her forehead. 'Look, I'm sorry,' he said. 'It's an important deal. A make-or-break deal. I'm a bit uptight about it, that's all. Forgive me?'

With his arms around her and his musky smell in her nostrils, she would have forgiven him for the Treaty of Versailles. She snuggled close against his chest, luxuriating in the sinewy strength of his encircling arms, drinking in the manly scent of him, and said:

'Kiss my butt, mister. Do I look like a priest?'

'You know, that's what I like most about you,' he said, giving her a hug that made her eyes bug out. 'You never bear a grudge.'

She debated giving him a playful knee in the groin but thought better of it. That was the one part of his anatomy she wanted well toned and in peak working order. There was no point in running unnecessary risks with so delicate a mechanism. She contented herself with muttering seductively into his ear:

'Let's do this again, shall we? Soon – preferably very soon. A week's just too long, lover. I need my batteries charged more often than that.'

Peter nodded. 'In a day or two, okay? I'll give you a call.'

She pushed him away and wrinkled her nose in a peevish moue. 'When the deal's done, then I come first, is that what you mean?' She had a pathological loathing of being second. In her mind, being second was tantamount to being rejected. It meant that something she didn't care about – something from which she was excluded – was more beguiling to him than she was. Her vanity found the notion insufferable. The rotten pig, she thought. The least he could have done, if he really cared, was lie to me.

'It's an important deal,' he said in a conciliatory tone. 'A *very* important deal. Listen, I'll call you. I promise.'

Not 'I love you' – just 'I'll call you'. Bastard.

'You do that,' she said, snatching up her bag and starting for the door. 'It'll save me the trouble of phoning your wife to find out when you're free.'

'That sounds like blackmail,' he said.

'Call it what you want,' Ilse said, her hand on the knob. 'I need to see more of you – and I'm an easy girl to get along with when I get my own way. Try me.'

She smiled sweetly and closed the door without giving him a chance to reply. Having the last word in an argument was the same thing as actually winning it.

In the corridor, she paused and straightened her dress in front of the ornate mirror at the end of the hall. Her hair, she noticed, could use a trim and a body perm. It was starting to look stringy and lank – or, to be more precise, it was starting to look *as if shortly it might begin to look* stringy and lank. Which amounted, in Ilse's lexicon, to the same thing. She decided that she'd drop by

Leonardo's on the way out of town and set up an appointment. The tiff with Peter – which she'd won – behind her and forgotten, she felt happy and fulfilled. Ever since she was a little girl, the prospect of having her hair done had always made her feel cheerful. On the stairs she started humming to herself. The song was 'Waterloo', an old Abba tune. She was content, yes, and life was definitely good.

The hotel lobby was deserted. There was no one in sight except Franco, the concierge, who was arranging flowers in a vase in one of the reception rooms with his back to her. His must be a tedious job, she thought. Fussing constantly over this and that, always being organized and efficient, putting on a happy face for ten hours a day, even when you felt like hell, and then going home at night to warmed-up pasta and the mindless round of programmes on the television. *Der armer Hund*, she thought, the poor bugger. It wasn't the sort of life she could have tolerated for a week without running a razor blade over her wrists. She shrugged. But then, of course, she didn't have to.

Under the awning at the front of the hotel, she paused and fished in her bag for her sun-glasses. The day was bright and she found herself squinting in the glare. As usual, the cobbled piazza was full of tourists in casual slacks and culottes, interspersed with locals on bicycles. They were an easy-going people, the Lucchesi. Never in a hurry. Always warm and friendly, ready with a welcoming smile. And yet there was, too, a kind of ambiguous sadness about them, as if the proud race who had warded off the Medici princes of Florence for centuries had finally lost their city, without ever quite knowing how it happened, to a flood of outsiders with their pockets stuffed with Deutschmarks and pounds sterling. The formidable walls of their ancient city, converted into a tourist attraction, provided no defence against the onslaught and served, in fact, to attract rather than repel the invaders. But it was for precisely this reason that Ilse loved Lucca. It felt like the holiday atmosphere in Lindau on the Bodensee. It was as if she'd never left the security of home. A third of the people on the streets – or so it seemed – were German, another third English, and the rest were natives. Everyone, it seemed, spoke either German, or English, which she'd learned at school; and the smattering of Italian she'd picked up over the months was more than adequate to get her around and out of tight corners. As a result, Lucca hardly felt like foreign soil at all.

She made her way under a row of towering plane trees to the

parking area adjacent to the hotel. Approaching her Alfa Romeo from the rear she noticed something strange. There was a head of curly black hair in the passenger's seat. A head she recognized.

'*Teufel auch!*' she muttered to herself. 'Damn it all, what's *he* doing here?'

The head belonged to Willi Junior, her husband's oldest son by his first marriage. Willi Junior was twenty-five, four years younger than Ilse herself. He was a freeloader of considerable skill who, masquerading as a professional student, had managed for years to defer graduation and the attendant pains of moving out on his own, finding a job, and earning a living. In a vain search for his niche in life, he'd muddled his way through the early stages of degrees in chemistry, political science, art history, microbiology, and modern Slavic literature. And he was now enrolled, by correspondence, in something called Leisure Studies – a discipline which, from its title, seemed admirably suited to his particular aptitudes. *Schwein er hatte*: Lady Luck had smiled on him.

Early in their relationship, Ilse and Willi Junior had learned to despise each other from the core of their respective beings. Willi Junior resented Ilse because she was the replacement for a dead mother he still adored and because, paradoxically, he was jealous of his father's connubial rights with a woman whose body he secretly coveted for himself. Ilse detested Willi Junior because he refused to get a job and leave home and because, under the veneer of his snivelling self-interest, she sensed a dark lust aimed in her direction that, while it flattered her vanity, outraged her sense of decorum. Her private morality facilitated adultery with ease but recoiled in loathing and disgust at the mere hint of something as unnatural as incest. She saw Willi Junior as a prurient Peter Pan, a sorry little boy-man who refused to grow up and was alternately baffled and terrified by the enigmatic signals emanating from his pent-up gonads. He was also an ugly cub: short in stature and tending to corpulence, with soft, pouchy features and a nervous tic in one eye that made it seem as if he were perpetually winking at you. She wondered why a good Darwinian like Willi Senior hadn't tied the bugger in a sack and drowned him at birth.

She opened the door and, with an air of exasperation, dropped into the seat beside him.

'So,' she said, turning an icy smile in his direction, 'what brings you here, *Söhnchen*?'

He stared at his knees, not daring to face her, and fumbled his fingers awkwardly in his lap like an infant with a handful of thick pencils. Finally, gathering up what passed in him for courage, he said without looking up at her:

'You're having an affair, aren't you? You're cheating on Father.'

Ilse's eyebrows shot up – whatever she'd expected from him, it wasn't *this* – and then her eyes narrowed dangerously. What must have happened was suddenly transparently clear to her.

'You were listening on the phone,' she growled. 'And then you followed me here, didn't you, you miserable little turd?' She wished she *had* bought that damned butcher's knife she'd thought of using on Peter. If it had been in her hand right then, she'd have taken a considerable pleasure in slitting Willi Junior's gullet on the spot.

She turned away and looked out of the window. Her breathing was husky and shallow. *Verdammt!* He'd caught her off her guard and trapped her into virtually admitting her guilt.

Be calm, her mind cautioned. Get hold of yourself.

She decided the only course was to brazen it out. When your hand's in the till, you can always claim you were putting money *in*, not taking it out.

'So,' she said evenly, wondering exactly how much he did know, 'just because you heard me ask about a man on the telephone you've come to the conclusion that I must be having an affair with him, is that it? That's pretty feeble logic, *Söhnchen*, even for you. How many men, then, do you suppose that means I'm seeing? Fifty? seventy-five? – a hundred, maybe? Let's see: there's that hairy mechanic at the garage where we service the cars ... and there's Signor Lupo, the man I phone to make theatre reservations ... and Leonardo, my hairdresser, who's gay and wouldn't touch a woman with a barge-pole ... and Monsignor Pacciani, that handsome priest I talked to about the flowers, who just *has* to be a real stud when you get him out of his surplice ... and, oh yes! that sweet old man at the Caffè della Mura – you know the one I mean – the wine steward who lost his leg in Ethiopia during the war – '

She was counting them off on her fingers, mocking him, and he cut her off.

'You came out of the hotel,' he said in a surly voice. 'I saw you in the rear-view mirror.' Ilse feigned surprise. 'You saw me come out of the hotel *with a man*?'

'No, alone. But you came out of the hotel.'

Ilse shrugged. 'So what? Lots of people come out of hotels.'

'What were you doing there?'

'Minding my own business,' Ilse said coldly.

'You were in there with a man,' he said. 'I know you were.' He was beginning to sound like a record stuck in a groove.

Ilse had had about enough. 'You should spend more time doing your homework, *mein Junge,* and less time following people around like Sherlock Holmes. It inspires too many phantoms in your dirty little imagination. And besides, didn't anybody ever tell you it's bad manners?'

He ignored her. 'You're cheating on Father. I think maybe somebody should tell him.' He was a persistent bastard.

Ilse opened her bag and lit a cigarette, taking her time.

'Then that "somebody" better have some pretty solid evidence,' she said slowly, spitting the words out like bullets, 'or he'll find his sorry ass out in the cold without so much as a Pfennig for a pay-toilet.' A sudden thought struck her: why was he telling *her* all this? Why not just go straight to Willi Senior with his suspicions? She said:

'You want something, don't you? What is it? Money – ?'

He was staring at his knees again and fumbling maladroitly with his fingers. 'Yes,' he said, 'I need money. I got a speeding ticket following you in.'

Ilse threw back her head and laughed. That was rich. The irony was delicious. She'd like to see him try to explain *that* to Willi Senior! Anteing up for another speeding ticket in the family would please him no end.

'You drive too fast,' he mumbled. 'You're crazy when you get behind the wheel.'

Ilse fished two fifty-thousand lire notes out of her wallet and tossed them into his lap. If that's all it was going to take to shut him up, it was cheap at twice the price.

'Keep the change,' she said.

Willi Junior didn't budge. The money lay in his lap and he didn't move a muscle.

So, she thought sourly, it isn't going to be as easy as I thought. There's something more. She said:

'What else?'

His fingers started working as if he were trying to pull them out of their sockets.

'Spit it out,' she snapped. There was nothing more disgusting than a wimpy blackmailer.

'I want – I want you to be *nice* to me,' he stammered in a small, thin voice.

Ilse's tongue froze in her throat. The inflection on the word 'nice' implied a suggestion that wasn't nice at all. The thought of his pudgy hands on her body, his lips pressing her lips, his tongue on her nipples, made her want to throw up.

She gripped the steering wheel in front of her for control. 'Get out of here,' she hissed. 'Take the money and get the hell out of here!'

'I love you,' he said in a choked voice. He was crying.

'You're a smutty little toad,' she spat. 'I wouldn't let you touch me if you were the last man on earth.' She gave him a rude shove toward the door. 'Now, get out of here before I lose my temper and call a cop.'

When he had scuttled off, his tail between his legs, she sat for a long time staring blindly at the instrument panel. Shock, horror, and fear took turns passing over her face. She was in a tight corner and she knew it. It wasn't the thought that he'd go to Willi Senior that disturbed her. No, she could talk her way out of that easily enough: she was a more convincing and practised liar than he was. And besides, he was only guessing. He didn't know anything – nothing certain, that is – about Peter Morgan. She'd only used Peter's Christian name on the telephone. Moreover, Willi Junior hadn't seen her go into the hotel, had no idea what room she'd been in or how long she'd been there – no, when she'd arrived, he'd been somewhere behind her, taking receipt of a speeding ticket. Later, he'd made his way to Piazza Napoleone and found her car by luck, though it didn't take much luck to find a red convertible in a place as small as Lucca.

What frightened Ilse was not that he'd run off and tell tales behind her back to his father, but that, precisely because he was *unable* to go to Willi Senior, his next move was totally unpredictable. And in a secretive and vindictive personality like Willi Junior unpredictability was a dangerous trait indeed. He was capable of anything.

She fitted the key into the ignition and started the car. As she turned her head to reverse out of the parking space, her eye fell briefly on the place where he'd been sitting. The money was gone. In spite of everything – his lust, his degradation, his tears – he'd remembered to take the money. It was precisely that element of calculating self-possession in his character, even in the face of a soul-withering shame, that most alarmed and frightened her about him.

As she eased the car out of the parking space, she was aware that her forehead was bathed in a cold sweat.

5

The FS train eased into the station and stopped with an expiring shudder. Carlo Arbati stood and stretched like a man coming out of a deep sleep, then hefted his case down from the overhead rack. It had been a good journey – just over an hour – and he'd been lucky. The train wasn't crowded and he'd had a compartment to himself the whole way. A couple of bearded students carrying backpacks had parked themselves in the corridor outside and spent the journey leaning out of the window, drinking bottled water and soaking up the passing scenery. Arbati had seen it all before, so he'd closed the compartment door, stretched his feet out under the seat across from him, and managed to plough his way through the first fifty pages of the most recent Umberto Eco novel. It was, as usual, dense and tangled fare – a lexical labyrinth. There was something, it was clear, in the post-modern spirit that recoiled in horror from old-fashioned values like clarity and simplicity.

Bag and book in hand, he descended from the carriage and got his bearings. There were only three or four other disembarking passengers on the platform. Lucca was a quiet stop, unlike Milan or Florence. The steps leading down to the *sottopassaggio*, the pedestrian underpass, echoed with the sound of his footsteps alone. When he emerged into the light at the other end, coming up beside the terminal building, Giancarlo Bonelli was there waiting for him, smiling like a Cheshire cat.

'Welcome, my friend,' he said. 'It's been a long time.'

'A long time,' Arbati agreed. 'Too long.' He stepped back and looked his old friend up and down, noting with pleasure how little the years had changed him. The only significant alteration was the depilation of what had once been a head of bushy hair. But the quivering smile, the sensitive lips, the ferret-like eyes that missed nothing were still the same. He remembered the day they'd met, almost twenty years ago – two raw, frightened recruits with shaved heads standing rigidly at attention in the courtyard of the Carabinieri barracks listening to the commandant's speech of threatening welcome. What was it Giancarlo had said afterwards, mimicking him? 'Well, boys, you'll have your crack at the criminals eventually, if you can just manage to get by me first.' That remark had pretty well summed up the gruelling mixture of physical and mental abuse they'd endured as police cadets over the next two years. The memory made Arbati smile. But then, it was easy to smile two decades after the reality of what had followed that comment.

'Come on then,' Bonelli said, taking the case from Arbati's hand. 'The car's just outside. We'll get you checked into your hotel and then we can spend the evening raking through the entrails of our lost youths. It'll be fun.'

'For an old man like you, I suppose,' Arbati grinned, clapping a hand on his friend's shoulder. Bonelli was the older of the two by three months. 'We youngsters, you know, can only remember back so far.'

Bonelli gave a grimace. 'I see – yes,' he said, pursing his lips as if he were making a diagnosis. 'A selective memory about memories. It's a well-documented condition in frustrated middle-aged males. As it happens, I know a doctor who can treat it.'

'You can give me his name.'

'I would if I could remember it,' Bonelli said.

The car was in the car-park outside the station. They turned right into Viale Giusti, the tree-lined ramparts of the old walled city rising on their left. Arbati leaned back and allowed himself to be seduced by the atmosphere. Lucca was so peaceful, so rustic and relaxing after the hustle and bustle of Florence. He'd almost forgotten, he realized suddenly, what real serenity was like. For the first time in a long time, he actually *felt* what it was like to be free. He was a man on vacation: a man with no deadlines to meet, no calls to return, no suspects to interview, no leads to follow up. Oh, yes – and it felt very, very good.

'What about dinner tonight?' he asked as they turned into Via Elisa. 'I hope you're still free. I've been looking forward to it.'

'Everything's taken care of,' Bonelli said, 'and of course I'm free. Crime has been cancelled in honour of your visit, didn't you know?' They passed between the imposing twin keeps and under the medieval arch of Porta San Gervasio, and he went on: 'I took the liberty of booking ahead, actually. Nine o'clock. At the Antica Locanda – your favourite restaurant, as I recall. There's time for a shower and nap beforehand if the fancy takes you.'

'Sounds wonderful,' Arbati said. He put his head back and closed his eyes. Yes, he was going to get used to this life of leisure very quickly. Like a duck taking to water.

'And since it's a special occasion – a reunion of sorts,' Bonelli went on, 'I asked the wine steward to lay aside a special vintage for us. I think you'll like it.'

'Intriguing,' Arbati said, opening his eyes. 'Do I get a hint?'

Bonelli shook his head. 'No hints. Just turn up with a trembling palate. I can promise you won't be disappointed.'

'Okay, you've got my attention,' Arbati said.

Bonelli smiled. 'I thought I might,' he said with satisfaction.

They turned off Via Santa Croce into Via Cenami, winding through narrow lanes until Bonelli pulled up finally outside the awning-fronted entrance of the Hotel Universo.

'Nine o'clock,' he warned, retrieving Arbati's case from the back seat, 'and don't be late.' He added: 'And, Carlo, it's damn good to see you again. We've let it go too long '

Today was something special. She'd been looking forward to it for a week and her excitement, as the moment approached, was almost palpable. Penny Morgan *loved* Italy: she loved its people, its food, its scenery – but most of all she loved its architecture and its art. She had grown up surrounded by fine things. The family home, set in a boxwood park where stately carriages had once, in palmier days, rolled up a long drive to the pillared portico, was an ante-bellum mansion handed down through nine generations. Located in rolling hills outside Charlottesville, where her father – a distant relation of Thomas Jefferson – taught political science at the University of Virginia, the Palladian house, though fallen in recent days on leaner times and much of the land sold off to please the IRS, was filled with heirlooms. From childhood, Penny had been surrounded by the aura, if not the material reality, of landed gentility and a sense of history. But nothing in her New World background had quite prepared her for the overwhelming antiquity of Italy. This, her first visit, had been a cultural awakening for her. Wherever she looked, she felt an intimation of immortality, a sense of something almost as old, it seemed, as man himself. And she wanted more than anything else to share these joys and marvels with her children. Her husband she would never share them with, she knew, for Peter Morgan, raised in a middle-class family in an outer suburb of Baltimore, considered art a frivolous waste of time unless it was an investment promising a high return. There was no sense of culture in his commercial soul, none of that gentle breeding and refined love of elegance that Penny had imbibed with her mother's milk and that still made her quiver with delight when she stood before a well-executed painting or felt her soul melting to the strains of Chopin or Schubert. There were cultural values, she believed, that it was her duty to transmit to those nearest and dearest to her – and if it was too late for Peter, it was all the more imperative that she should pass them on to her children.

Today was special because it was reserved for the cathedral, the Duomo di San Martino.

They stood before it now – she and the two children, Chad and Brooke – looking up from the sun-drenched piazza at the fourteenth-century façade by Guidetto: three arcades surmounted by a trio of airy loggias in green and white marble. It was stunning, unlike anything in her previous experience, and it left her speechless. Seven hundred years of history unveiled themselves before her eyes. A patina of antiquity clung about the stones, infusing them – or so it almost seemed – with life, and she fancied for a moment that she could hear the voices, the shouts and laughter, the ringing hammers of the old stonemasons at their work as she stared in wonder at the symmetry of arches and pillars rising like a canticle of stone into the azure sky.

'Well, let's get it over with,' Chad grunted.

Chad was sixteen, a handsome lad, tall and well-muscled like his father, with long blond hair, meticulously tended. Italy was a drag, man – a real bummer. There was no baseball, no hockey, no *real* football. Only soccer, a wimpy sport where nobody ever got anything broken. He looked at the façade again. It was exactly like the other churches their mother had dragged them to since they'd arrived, and they weren't even Catholics. What was the point? Was she planning to convert or something? Well, he thought, steeling himself for the task ahead, at least maybe there'd be a good-looking girl inside, something to take his mind off all the dumb paintings and statues – although, judging by his past experience of such places, there wasn't much cause for optimism on that score. Pretty girls and old churches just didn't seem to go together.

Brooke, his sister, aged fifteen, was bumping and gyrating in a private world of her own to the rhythms of the CD in her Sony

Discman. Music was her life, and she used it to block out all new experiences that might broaden her horizons. At the moment she was listening to something called 'Venice is Sinking'. The song's allusive lyrics – 'beauty is religion,' 'christened me with wonder,' 'the old come here to kiss their dead' – meant nothing to her. In Brooke's narrow world, words weren't important. It was the beat, the *music*, that counted for everything in a song, and she kept the volume wound high in order to savour it fully.

Her mother tapped her on the shoulder, fracturing the mood.

'Come along, dear,' Penny said, 'and take those things out of your ears.'

Brooke made a face. 'Do I have to?'

'Yes, dear. This is an interesting church and I want you to learn something. You'll thank me for it some day.'

'*Oh, mom . . .!*' Brooke whined, the words drawled into a peevish parody of her mother's refined Southern accent. But she obeyed eventually, sliding the headphones down around her neck and turning off her machine. 'You should make Daddy come with us,' she grumbled in a parting attempt at turning defeat into a sort of victory. 'Then we could all suffer together.'

'That will be quite enough of that, missy,' Penny snapped. 'No one is suffering and your father has other things on his mind.'

That Peter Morgan was preoccupied was abundantly apparent to the other members of his family. Although their visit to Italy had been planned as a family vacation, Penny and the children had seen little of Peter since their arrival. He was always, it seemed, locked up in the room he'd converted into a study in their rented villa or else off on business – or so he said – in Florence or Lucca; and even when he did manage to find a little time for them, he was restless and irritable and would fly off the handle at the slightest provocation. Something was wrong, Penny knew, and her intuition told her what it was: there was another woman in Peter's life. A pain like a dagger stabbed in her chest. She forced the thought of his infidelity from her mind; she couldn't bear the pain of her own suspicions. The fear that he was betraying her made her feel lost and panicky, as though the world were coming apart at the seams. She put on a brave face and said:

'Now, are we ready?'

'Yes, Mother,' Chad and Brooke chorused in unison.

In breathless adoration and bored surrender, they advanced

together – a trio of pilgrims – on the medieval façade of San Martino di Lucca.

Peter Morgan waited for an hour after Ilse left before finally giving up.

He consulted his ruby-studded Rolex for the hundredth time and cast another jaundiced look over the car-park below his window in the Hotel Universo. *Where the fucking hell was he?* Jimmy wasn't the most trustworthy sort, of course. He'd known that much about him from the very beginning, from their first meeting in that trendy bar on West 57th Street in New York City where they'd met and planned the whole thing. Jimmy had been late then too – not *this* late, but late nonetheless – tossing off some lame excuse about being tied up with a 'prior engagement' that had gone on longer than he expected. What a load of crap. Jimmy didn't have *engagements*, prior or otherwise. He was a small-time hood with no money, no prospects, and an inflated sense of his own importance. Peter gave a sour grimace, remembering that first meeting. He'd probably, if the truth were known, been in bed with a hooker in some sleazy dive in the East Village and lost track of time. That would have been just like him.

Irritably, Peter wondered why he'd ever trusted the man, why he'd brought him in on the scheme in the first place. Well, there was an easy answer to that. It was a marriage of convenience. In the normal course of things, Peter Morgan didn't associate with characters like Jimmy Dearing because corporate lawyers didn't spend their time consorting with grifters and petty extortionists. But Jimmy possessed certain skills and had certain contacts in the criminal world that Peter needed – like the engraver who'd forged a flawless false passport and phony driver's licence for him. And besides, Jimmy had come to him highly recommended.

It was Peter's gambling debts that had made it all necessary. Penny, thank God, knew nothing about them. As far as she was concerned, the decision to rent a villa and spend a few months in Italy was simply a long overdue vacation, a belated recognition on Peter's part that he needed a break from the high-pressure world of corporate litigation and that he really *should* spend a little time, for a change, with his family. As far as she knew, they had more money than they knew what to do with. Peter was a senior partner now, at the age of only forty-seven, in a prestigious law firm with walnut-panelled offices in Rittenhouse Square, the most fashionable address in Philadelphia. They lived in a Georgian mansion in Society Hill, owned a Jaguar and a Mercedes, kept a 40-foot yacht at an exclusive marina on Chesapeake Bay, and were season-ticket holders at both the Academy of Music and Veterans Stadium. But it was almost all of it a sham. What Penny didn't know about were the immense gambling debts, the threatening telephone calls from some very unsavoury people, and the fact that Peter had several times seriously contemplated suicide. He'd kept all that from her – and, of course, from the kids as well. For almost a year, he'd lain awake at nights bathed in a cold sweat, wondering how he could get himself out of the mess he'd somehow – he still didn't quite know how – managed to get himself into.

And then one day, quite by accident, he'd stumbled over the Ghirlandaio business. At first, it hadn't seemed like much – a notarized letter, short and cryptic, that turned up unexpectedly in a stack of affidavits related to a corporate take-over he was working on. Someone had apparently misfiled it. The letter was from a museum curator in Amsterdam concerning a Renaissance painting of a girl, and the document caught his eye because it was so incongruously out of place in the pile of torts and court briefs he was wading through. It was an intriguing letter. The painting – by somebody named Ghirlandaio of whom Peter had never heard – had been sent, by an American who had recently inherited it, to the Rijksmuseum in Amsterdam for cleaning and evaluation with a view, apparently, to offering it for public sale. But the painting was a fake – or at least that was the blunt opinion of Dr Frans van den Eshof, the Dutch curator who examined it. On a hunch, but mainly out of curiosity, Peter had started digging around, seeing what other interesting titbits he could turn up – and what he'd unearthed had both stunned and delighted him. That little letter, it turned out, was the innocent entrance into a labyrinthine conspiracy touching a half-dozen countries and some of the richest men in the world. And suddenly Peter Morgan had seen a way out of his problems. With the right kind of pressure, that letter could be worth millions of dollars – yes, *millions!* What he owed for his gambling indiscretions was peanuts in comparison.

The next step was easy. Peter met with his creditors, convinced them – revealing no more than he absolutely had to – that he had a viable scheme to get back their money with accumulated interest, and then asked for their help. And that was how he'd ended up with Jimmy Dearing: his passport into the underworld – and also, of course, his creditors' insurance policy that they were backing a sound horse.

But now, Jimmy was missing.

Something had gone wrong. But what – ? Jimmy had been raised in the south Bronx and knew how to look after himself. What threat could Nigel Harmsworth – a man in his seventies, for God's sake – possibly pose to a street-smart operator like Jimmy Dearing? It made no sense. Jimmy would have eaten the old codger for breakfast if he'd tried anything cute. No, there was nothing to worry about there. An accident then – ? Peter pressed his lips into a thin white line. That was certainly possible given the crazy way Jimmy drove the Maserati they'd rented for him in Florence. (He'd insisted on having a flashy car, and Peter, although he resented the exorbitant rental charges, had eventually given in.) Was it possible then, he wondered, that Jimmy had never even made it to the damned appointment? that he was lying now in some hospital bed swaddled in bandages – or maybe crumpled and broken at the bottom of a mountain ravine? God only knew. *Damn it all, though!* Peter thought bitterly – damn it all, Jimmy *knew* how much was riding on this roll of the dice, how important the meeting with old Harmsworth was. How the hell could he screw it all up by driving himself off a goddamn cliff? *Shit.*

He paced the room, muttering to himself, and tried to sort out his next move. He couldn't go to the police, of course. That was out of the question. What then? And suddenly it hit him. He'd do what Jimmy would no doubt have done if the tables were reversed. He'd fudge up a story about a missing friend and check the hospital for recent admissions; then, if that failed, he'd make discreet enquiries at the Misericordia about ambulance calls that morning. He could explain that he was expecting his cousin and, when he hadn't shown up, he'd started to worry. That would do. The truth about lies was that one was as good as any other. Peter smiled to himself. He was beginning to get the hang of it. Yes, by God, he'd make a respectable criminal out of himself yet.

He gathered up his things and left the room, closing the door and locking it behind him. There was no point hanging about the hotel. He'd only start stewing if he didn't keep busy. *Damn!* – he paused with the key in the latch, remembering suddenly that Penny and the kids were supposed to be coming into town on one of their historical excursions. 'They can't miss so much school-time at home,' Penny insisted, 'and not learn something while they're away' – and so she forced them out on regular pilgrimages to sites of historical interest. Oh well, he thought, better them than me; they're young and resilient. He tried to remember what was on the agenda for today. The duomo, was it? Bugger. That was just around the corner. What happened if he ran into them in the street? Well, he'd say his meeting in Florence ended early and he'd just that moment arrived back. One lie was as good as the next. He started off down the hall, pleased with himself, his bases covered. Oh! – and another thing, he remembered: he'd promised them dinner in town. Christ, that meant making a reservation some place. Well, it would have to wait until after he'd checked with the hospital and the Misericordia about Jimmy.

The thought of so many picky chores ahead nettled him, made him feel suddenly peevish and out of sorts. Patience, of course, as Penny was always quick to remind him, wasn't his strong suit. Still, he resented mundane detail and the constraint it imposed. He was born to be a chief, not just one of the Indians; and it was Jimmy, after all, who was supposed to be doing the dog-work. Peter's job was to co-ordinate and command, to ensure from a distance the smooth execution of the plan he had masterminded. He hated staining his fingers with the day-to-day minutiae; but there wasn't much choice in the matter now. Damn Jimmy anyway! he thought. Why did the bastard have to go and screw everything up?

By the time he reached the bottom of the stairs and entered the lobby, he was in a thoroughly testy frame of mind. There was a man talking to Franco at the reception desk. Peter started forward, then froze in his tracks. He knew that look: the man was a policeman, a detective of some sort. It was written all over him – in the way he dressed, the way he stood, the subtle way his presence exuded an aura of power and menace. What was going on? Who was he after? Had Jimmy broken under interrogation and spilled his guts? Peter felt a coldness creep over his skin as if he'd been quaffing hemlock. His pulse rate was elevated and he was starting to sweat. He hadn't always reacted this way to the presence of the law; but they affected him this way now, ever since the start of the Ghirlandaio business – for the police had become the enemy.

He deposited his room key at the far end of the counter and caught the concierge's eye.

'Just put it on my tab, will you, Franco?' he said, turning quickly away.

Once outside, he heaved a sigh of relief as if he'd escaped from a clever trap by the skin of his teeth. It was silly, of course. The man inside appeared to be checking into the hotel, not conducting an investigation; and besides, whether he was a policeman or not, he was no threat to Peter Morgan. It was foolish to suppose he was. After all, Peter reflected, I haven't done anything against the law – yet. It was just that, knowing what he was *going to do*, meant that anything even remotely connected with the criminal justice system made him jittery.

He started toward the car-park, then changed his mind. No, before he started looking into Jimmy's disappearance, he needed a drink – a damned stiff drink. If something untoward *had* in fact happened, then Operation Ghirlandaio would be in his hands entirely – and that bleak thought made a couple of double whiskies, straight up, seem an absolute necessity.

Nigel Harmsworth poured himself another sherry and contemplated in its amber glow the vision of a future which, since noon, had darkened with each passing hour. Inspector Bonelli's parting words tolled in his brain like an interminable dirge: *I have reason to suppose, Signor Harmsworth, that your life may be in danger.* Dearing, he had said, was armed – a 9mm pistol under his shirt, a silencer in his pocket. God in heaven! Nigel shuddered, what have I landed myself in the middle of? In the hours since the police had left, as his imagination had worked to fill the gaps deserted by reason, the danger that confronted him had grown more ominous and more palpable, looming inevitably and menacingly closer. It was out there – yes, he could feel it – circling like a shark, biding its time, waiting to surface and snatch him suddenly in its jaws. Of course, *what exactly* that danger was he had no idea, for he had managed with a quite remarkable ineptitude to kill the only person who might, had he been given a chance to finish his story, have revealed that information. Pacing the Persian carpet before the grate, Nigel sipped at his drink, staring disconsolately, as if in the hope of a saving revelation, into the crackling fire that he had built to keep himself company.

It was the coming on of night that he feared most. Darkness gave him the willies: darkness with its moving shadows and strange noises, its creakings and groanings as of restless, anguished spirits. But it wasn't ghosts that Nigel feared; it was the flesh-and-blood accomplices – for surely there *were* accomplices – of Mr James Dearing. Who were they? he wondered helplessly. What were they planning for him? Dearing had carried a pistol. There was no reason to suppose that these shadowy friends, out to avenge his death, would be any less determined or intimidating in their methods.

An arctic chill rippled down Nigel's spine.

He had taken, of course, all the precautionary measures he could think to take in order to secure himself. He'd locked and bolted the many doors and windows of the villa. He'd secured the garage doors and stuck pieces of Sellotape in unobtrusive places high on the frame – a trick he'd learned from a detective show on the telly – so that he'd know in the morning if they had been tampered with. He'd rummaged through every cupboard, closet and cranny in the house until he'd turned up a box of ammunition and an old bolt-action hunting rifle, which he now bore with him in his travels from room to room like a besieged sahib at a remote army outpost in Kashmir. And yet in spite of his preparations, he still felt exposed and depressingly vulnerable. A sitting target.

He knocked back the sherry remaining in his glass and reached again for the decanter, then changed his mind. No, he'd had enough. He needed a clear, quick mind and unimpaired faculties for what was coming – whatever it was.

He paced the carpet, fighting to remain calm, searching for a solution to his dilemma.

He couldn't remain passive, that much was certain. He couldn't sit there quivering and quaking, like a hare in a hole, waiting for them to come and get him. He had to *do* something. What was that trendy word they used nowadays? Proactive: yes, that was it. He had to become proactive. He had to *anticipate* trouble and do what was required to render it ineffectual in advance.

But how?

Dear, dear, he thought sadly – *that* was precisely the problem. How could he be proactive if he didn't know anything? Who the opposition were, for instance, or what they intended to do with him. All he knew was why they had sent Dearing in the first place and why, therefore, it was certain they would return. Not only was their business with him unfinished, but he'd made the whole sticky mess infinitely more perilous for himself by killing off their messenger. Who could predict how they might respond to *that*? Yes, he was in a right pickle all right.

Dearing hadn't told him much before the Mycenaean's spear

had silenced him, but he'd said enough – more than enough – to strike terror through every inch of Nigel's ageing frame. For a start, Dearing had known about the Ghirlandaio – *all about it*. He'd known where the painting was and how it had come to be there in the first place. Nigel dabbed nervously at his forehead with a linen handkerchief, recalling their interview. *God, what an unmitigated fiasco!* As Dearing had ranted on, it had become apparent that he'd known a great deal – far too much, in fact, about too many things – and that he'd had the time, before the spear transfixed him, to divulge only a tiny fraction of that information. Only the tip, indeed, of an insidious iceberg of knowledge that reached down far out of sight into the glacial depths of his callous soul. Mr James Dearing, it was clear, was a dangerous man with impeccable sources; and their brief encounter had convinced Nigel of a further, even more terrible, truth: Dearing's associates, whoever they were, were more menacing still, for they possessed both wealth and power. It was perfectly inconceivable, of course, that a bounder like Dearing himself, merely a *petit fonctionnaire* on the fringes of serious villainy, should have commanded the resources and the network of international contacts required to expose a conspiracy so carefully executed and so painstakingly concealed over so many years. No, but *someone* had had such contacts – and that someone was about to use them to destroy Nigel Harmsworth's comfortable world. A terrible thought struck him. Was the Mafia involved? Nigel shuddered. Oh, dear God, he thought. Dear God in heaven . . .!

He snatched up his empty glass and splashed three fingers of scotch into it with a trembling hand. Cardhu single malt.

Great Scott! he remembered, *the very drink he'd given that poor devil, Dearing!*

But it was too late for superstitious fears. The deed was done, the Hanged Man already drawn from the tarot pack of fate. Right, he thought, then bugger it – and he raised the glass in a cavalier, devil-may-care salute to fortune, then put it to his lips and drained it in a toss, feeling the fiery liquid scorch down the length of his oesophagus. Within seconds, the flame modulated to a velvety glow and he felt calmer – once more in command.

So, right. He needed a plan; he needed somehow, he reminded himself, to be proactive.

And then it hit him. Yes – yes, of course. Why hadn't he thought of it sooner?

He refreshed his drink, then walked through to the library

where a powerful computer, squat and imposing, sat draped in a plastic dust-cover on an antique escritoire. He approached it with caution, half expecting the thing to growl suddenly and lunge. Technology was not Nigel's forte. He detested complex machinery and routinely spurned it, preferring to do things the old-fashioned way. He'd made concessions in the cases of the telly remote and the microwave oven because modern life was impossible without them; but a computer was another matter altogether. It was an intimidating apparatus – byzantine in its complexity, eleusinian in its demands. Normally, he ignored it, left it safely shrouded under its protective wrap. Normally. But not now. Now he needed it.

It wasn't *his* machine, of course. It belonged, like everything else at San Felice, to Sir Richard Danvers, his employer, a man who prided himself on having his various properties plugged in to all the latest gadgetry; and Nigel, despite his indifference, had been subjected to a lengthy tutorial on the rudiments of operating the system by the technician who had driven out one day, on Sir Richard's instructions, to install it. Since then, he had used it to compose a letter or two, treating it as a glorified typewriter, and he was not, therefore, entirely ignorant of how to work it.

The only approach, he decided, was to take the bull firmly by the horns. He sat down before the monitor and lifted the cover, then, throwing caution to the winds, flicked on the power switch. The machine beeped and burbled like a genie disturbed from a thousand-year sleep, and a moment later a cursor began blinking in the upper left-hand corner, awaiting his command. He took a deep breath, then flexed his fingers in an experimental flourish over the keyboard. What would Tolstoy, he wondered, have made of such an invention? The old Russian, he decided, would have embraced it with a cry of delight. It would have delivered him forever from capricious quills and ink-blobs, from strike-outs and aching fingers – and *War and Peace*, in consequence, would doubtless have mushroomed to thirty volumes. It was a caring God, Nigel reflected, who had kept so dangerous a weapon out of the hands of such a man. His own intentions, of course, were considerably more modest – a single page at most – but still a daunting prospect: for he was about to step boldly into uncharted territory, to commit himself for the first time to the perils of the Infobahn.

The manuals were in a drawer of the escritoire. He selected a photocopied pamphlet entitled *Accessing the Internet* prepared by the technician who had configured the system and, opening it, began to read. Yes ... yes: it *looked* easy enough. He paused for a sip of Cardhu, then continued. A tiny grin curled at the corners of his mouth. Yes, he concluded with a nod, eminently feasible – not nearly as difficult as I'd feared.

He logged on, then opened the e-mail program, selected NEW MESSAGE, and began to type:

Dickie –
I had a visit today from an unpleasant cove by the name of James Dearing, an American. (Does the name, by the by, which meant nothing to me, ring any bells with you?) He was frightfully well informed about things that are none of his business: the Ghirlandaio in Chicago, for instance. Lamentably, he is now dead. A Greek bronze in the garden – the same one, in fact, that fell once before: you'll recall the one I mean – toppled from its pedestal and crushed him.

The motive for Mr Dearing's visit was blackmail. He is well connected, and there is every reason to think we must expect the most serious consequences as the result of his untimely demise. I suggest, Dickie – indeed, I most earnestly implore you – to take steps to protect yourself and to consider how we shall deal with this unfortunate business. We've not heard the last of Mr Dearing and his friends.

In the interim, I have, of course, secured San Felice against intruders and await your instructions. The local police were around to investigate the death, but I told them nothing.
Nigel

He leaned back and read what he had written with satisfaction. Sir Richard Danvers wasn't the sort to be shaken easily, but this, Nigel gauged, would do the trick admirably. His fortune – not to mention his reputation, his liberty, perhaps even his life – were all at stake. Yes, he reflected, there would be a prompt response this time from London. That thought offered a certain consolation. He wasn't in the thing alone any more – nor, indeed, should he be. The scheme, after all, had been Dickie's in the first place: it was *his* greed and love of danger, of living on the edge, that had made it happen. Now, let him share the terror as well.

Oh, how easy it had all seemed at the beginning! He remembered with a pang of regret the bright spring day – what was it? forty-five, no nearly fifty years ago now, just after the war – that

Dickie had turned up in Paris out of the blue. They hadn't seen one another for years. Dickie had somehow found his way to the seedy garret in the Rue Gabrielle in Montmartre where Nigel, ever the idealist, ever the traditionalist intent on turning back the hands of time, was struggling to keep body and soul together executing neo-classical canvases in a post-impressionist world. Nigel smiled at the memory of his youth. He had painted with fire and conviction, but no one would buy his work. Still, he hadn't given up – no, he'd persisted out of stubborn pride, subsisting on crusts and hard cheese, a man of vision, of principle: *un artiste maudit par ses convictions*. And then, Dickie Danvers, his old friend from the Slade, had turned up in a Savile Row suit and treated him to a fashionably late lunch at the bistro Benoît. Over the house *foie gras* and a vintage Bordeaux, they had reminisced about the old days, about the deplorable state of modern art, about what the future held for the serious artist – and then, just as the waiter arrived with their *cassoulet*, Dickie had leaned forward conspiratorially and, curling the wispy tip of his Vandyke beard around an index finger in that funny way he had when he was particularly thoughtful, had said, 'I have a proposition to put to you, my friend.'

Nigel remembered it all as if it had happened only yesterday. Through the *cassoulet*, through the coffee and Armagnac that had followed, Dickie Danvers, his face animated, his eyes suffused with a lambent radiance, had held forth, unfolding a scheme, diabolical in its simplicity, that had taken the citadel of Nigel's imagination by storm. It was risky, yes. It was daring. But it would work too. He had seen that immediately. And best of all, it would provide him with a prosperous living doing the only thing in life that he really wanted to do: to paint like the old masters. To paint like Giotto and Giorgione, like Pollaiuolo and Leonardo and Raphael. To paint inspired visions mediated to sense through the sensuous veil of flesh, bringing the divine into the world through human form and figure and at the same time, through the transforming alchemy of art, transfiguring perishable images of blood and bone into metonymies of eternity. Dickie suggested he take a week to think about it, but Nigel needed no time. He had accepted at once. That night he'd packed his bags, leaving Paris and poverty behind, and had presented himself at the mahogany reception counter of Danvers' House Auctioneers on the following Monday morning. And from that moment he had never looked back.

Until today. Until the appearance of James Dearing at the front door of San Felice.

The chime of the mantel clock returned him to reality and the present. He read through the letter on the monitor once more, just to be certain, then nodded with satisfaction and consulted the manual on his knee. He pressed, as instructed, a button on the menu bar and a dialogue box appeared, asking him to fill in the addressee's mailbox in the appropriate window. He typed *danvers@auction.lon.uk*, then pressed SEND. In nanoseconds, the missive was streaking through cyberspace toward its distant destination: the hard-drive of Sir Richard's private computer in a walnut-panelled office in London's Old Bond Street.

MESSAGE SENT, the screen announced. DO YOU WISH TO SEND ANOTHER MESSAGE? Nigel smiled and pressed NO.

'Marvellous,' he muttered aloud. 'Bloody marvellous business.'

No stamps, no waiting, no surly postal clerks. Yes, he thought with admiration, it makes one feel proud to be a part of the last decade of the twentieth century.

Cecilia Hathaway had come away from San Felice profoundly unsatisfied. More was going on, she knew, than met the eye, and having served for nearly twenty years as headmistress at a school of scheming adolescent girls, Cecilia wasn't one to miss the signs.

Nigel, of course, was deeply distressed by the events of the day. And, goodness gracious, who wouldn't be? A strange man killed in one's own garden – the police prowling about, showing by their looks that they suspected one of concealing something – an inquest shortly to be held in order to establish whether or not the death was accidental. Yes, Nigel had every reason to be concerned, the poor dear man. But the truth of the matter, although Nigel was of course innocent of any crime – of *that* she was perfectly certain – was that he *was* hiding something. She'd spent too many years prising the truth out of the secretive adolescents at Holford House not to recognize the tell-tale signs: the facile smile, the nervous, shifting eyes, the spidery tremor at the corner of the mouth. She could only assume that Inspector Bonelli had seen them too.

After the police had gone, she had tried in every way she knew to get Nigel to open up, to talk frankly, to put his trust in her. There was no reason for him to shoulder the burden alone when she was there, willing – more than willing – to help him. But he'd been unyielding: a block of granite. After an awkward cup of tea, offered merely to be civil, he'd muttered something about having 'things to do' and had driven her back down the hill in the grey Bentley to her cottage at the fork, dropping her at the garden gate. It was all very polite, very *comme il faut* – but also very distant, very cool and impersonal. There were things in his heart, troubles of some kind, that Nigel simply refused to share with her or anyone else. She thought of him sitting now, alone and comfortless, in the big empty villa at the top of the hill, and her heart went out to him. She knew only too well how devastating loneliness could be when one was troubled by something. She'd spent too many years living alone not to know its aching hollowness, its pangs and gnawing sorrows.

From his mat in the corner, Bunter, feigning rest, watched his mistress through narrowed eyes. He sensed the vibrations and felt her distress, but he knew, too, when to lie silent and wait.

For a time Cecilia sat at the kitchen table, distraught, feeling helpless, wondering what to do. For do something she must. It wasn't in her nature to sit passively by when a friend was in need. She drummed her fingers absently on the table and gazed around the room as if it were the landscape of a dream. *The lovely in life is the familiar*, her mind recited, apropos of nothing, *and only the lovelier for continuing strange*. Lines from a poem by Walter de la Mare. But they seemed a silly, mocking sentiment at the moment, and she brushed them impatiently aside.

I must *do* something, she thought, recalling herself to the present and its problems. Yes, but what?

Aye, there indeed was the rub.

She stood and, seeking inspiration, wandered around her little kitchen bright with pots of flowering plants. (Bunter followed with his eyes, moving no other muscle.) She threw the shutters open and stared hopefully out at the well-tended clumps of herbs – yarrow and meadowsweet, parsley and Ayurvedic coriander – growing in profusion in the garden. She was an expert herbalist and the garden was her pride and joy. Nature offered remedies for every ailment of the body but few for the bruised soul. If only there were *something* she could do for poor dear Nigel! If only there were some posset, some secret panacea, that she could supply to ease his pain. But inspiration failed her. She turned from the window and lit the gas-ring on the stove to brew herself a pot of rosemary tea. Rosemary was a circulatory stimulant and often helped, she'd found, to put a problem in perspective. When the tea was ready, she returned to her seat at the table and, like

Hercule Poirot, her favourite sleuth, began to review the evidence. There wasn't, frankly, much to review. The facts in the case were meagre and, it seemed now as she rehearsed them, quite remarkably uninformative . . .

A stranger, an American in a red sports car, had come out to San Felice, had talked briefly with Nigel, had met with an unfortunate accident. What precisely they had discussed, the substance of their conversation, Nigel had obstinately, in spite of all her well-intentioned prodding, refused to divulge. Why? she wondered; why had he been so secretive? Perhaps, she thought, it was because the man had brought him bad news. She turned the steaming cup in her hands, letting the aroma of the mixture float up and caress her senses. Yes, that was part of it, of course. There was bad news of some kind. But that didn't explain the hunted look she'd seen in his eyes or the two pink spots that stained the waxy pallor of his cheeks.

And then it hit her: *fear*.

Nigel was afraid. Yes, he was frightened of something. The hunted look, the blush on his cheek: they were signs of dread. She blamed herself for not having recognized them sooner. The American, then, had come to threaten him. Yes, that was it! Now at last she was getting somewhere.

But the American was dead.

Another thought struck her:

Yes, but he wouldn't be alone. *There must be others.*

And then she saw it all. Nigel was in danger – real danger – his life perhaps at risk. Merciful God! she thought, his life at risk! The imaginary fears that she'd felt for him on her walk up to San Felice earlier in the day returned, redoubled in strength now because they had a basis in fact.

Her heart beat faster. Her mind whirred. Her palms, she suddenly realized, were clammy with perspiration.

A plan began to form itself in her mind.

If Nigel wouldn't confide in her, if he was determined to resist her help, then she would act on her own. She'd protect him in secret, in her own way, without his knowledge. It was the least she could do for the man she loved.

She stood abruptly and, striding to the hall, plucked the telephone from its cradle. She would have the things she needed delivered from town. There was no dial tone. Blast! she'd forgotten the thing was out of order. Why did technology always seem to fail at those critical moments when one actually needed it?

Well, she'd have to do it herself. There was no time to lose. She'd already walked five kilometres today. Another three wouldn't hurt.

'Come, Bunter!' she said, snatching up a leash and her shoulder bag. 'There's work to be done.'

In an instant, he was at her side, his tail churning, his nails clicking in anticipation on the tile flooring. She latched the garden gate behind them and together they turned into the road, heading toward the hamlet of Valdottavo. There was a telephone there she could use to summon a taxi to take her into town. Bunter enjoyed a car ride with the wind from an open window blowing in his face and she took him along whenever she could, even though taxi drivers were occasionally less than enthusiastic about transporting an animal. None, however, had ever refused a lucrative fare on that account; and besides, Bunter was extremely well behaved.

They walked briskly, Cecilia's mind on the task ahead. The road was quiet and deserted, an unpaved country track. On a hillside ahead, an army of ant-like workers moved methodically through lines of laden vines, harvesting the vermilion fruit of the new vintage. Overhead, tufts of cloud scuttled across the sky. The air was humid, the sirocco that had come in overnight still dominating the weather.

The physics of the thing was simple enough and, in any case, she'd test the system thoroughly when it was in place in order to be quite certain it worked properly. This was no time to leave matters to chance. She made a mental list of the supplies she required: two photoelectric cells, a solenoid switch, power cells, clamps, a roll of coated copper wire, a halogen spotlamp, and one of those disposable Kodak cameras used by tourists. She smiled to herself. There weren't many women her age, she supposed, capable of devising so cunning a device. But then, there weren't many women her age, either, who'd studied two years of electrical engineering. The achievements of other women she knew were limited to needlework and birdwatching. But Cecilia had always been different. Back then, too, she'd been a pioneer – the only woman in her class. Although her love of literature had ultimately led her to abandon science for the arts and a career in teaching, she had always maintained a lively interest in electronics and mechanics; and more than once at the school in rural Somerset, when professional help was unavailable or too expensive to call, she had rewired a circuit or repaired an ailing electric motor. Behind her back her students, she remembered with a smile, had called her Miss Fix-It. Now she had an opportunity to put those skills to the test in a serious cause – and she found that she was quite looking forward to the challenge.

The campanile of the stone church at Valdottavo came into view over the brow of the hill and she quickened her pace. She was almost there. In half an hour she'd be in Lucca, purchasing supplies; in two hours, back home laying her trap.

There was a bounce in her step as she crested the hill and her heart was light. Bunter, too, had caught the mood and was frisking at her feet like a young pup.

'The game's afoot,' she said, grinning down at him.

'Aaarrgh,' he replied, concurring.

Yes, Cecilia thought with satisfaction, Nigel has a formidable ally in his corner – whether he wants me there or not.

The vaulted interior of the cathedral took Penny Morgan's breath away: hushed and solemn, it was a sumptuous expanse of gold, porphyry, and green-veined marble. The experience of stepping into its cool interior from the sunlit piazza was like that of being transported from ordinary time into some fabulous realm of the imagination – into Xanadu or Aladdin's cave. On every side, wherever she turned, frescos and sculpted stone met her gaze: Saint Martin on horseback dividing his cloak, canvases by Tintoretto and Passignano, altars adorned by Ghirlandaio and Filippino Lippi.

She started forward, dazzled, with Chad and Brooke trailing sourly in her wake. Her eyes, like finches, flitted from image to image, unable to settle, unwilling to rest.

'Oh! it's wonderful,' she breathed. 'Isn't it wonderful, kids?'

'Great,' Chad managed, unimpressed.

'Yeah, really cool, Mom,' Brooke agreed, adjusting the bra strap under her Nirvana T-shirt. 'Can we go now?'

'When you've learned something,' Penny said sharply. 'Now straighten up, young lady, and pay attention. I'm not going to have you ruining this for everyone else.'

They crossed the inlaid marble pavement to the octagonal *tempietto* of Matteo Civitali, executed in 1482, a screened structure of Carrara marble with fluted columns and a cupola surmounted by a delicate, Brunelleschesque lantern. Inside, hanging from the cross, was a carved figure of the crucified Christ depicted as the

Man of Sorrows, his large eyes looking out with patient forgiveness on an apostate world.

Opening her guidebook, Penny drew the children to her and read the relevant passage aloud in a soft, musical voice redolent of her Virginian ancestry:

'"The statue of the Volto Santo at Lucca is famous throughout Italy and much venerated by the faithful. According to legend, the crucifix was carved from a cedar of Lebanon by Nicodemus, the Pharisee who came to Jesus by night and, later, was present at the Crucifixion (John 3:1–21, 19:38–42). During the long period of persecution of the early Christian Church that followed under the emperors Nero and Diocletian, the holy image was carefully hidden until, eventually, it was put in an empty boat and entrusted to the sea. Guided by angels, the boat sailed across the Mediterranean and landed at Luni, where the holy image was discovered and loaded on to a cart drawn by wild oxen, who became miraculously meek, to Lucca. Since that time, the Volto Santo has been an object of veneration, responsible for many miracles over the centuries that mark the history of the town."'

'Do you believe all that stuff?' Chad asked, when she had finished.

'I don't know,' Penny said, looking into the careworn face of the hanging man. 'I suppose I want to. Some of it, anyway. Not the superstitious part about the boat being guided by angels or wild oxen becoming suddenly docile, I mean, but the older story about the love and forgiveness of the man who inspired such stories in the first place. That seems to me worth believing in. The world can be a pretty cold and unforgiving place, you'll find, Chad. You don't get far in it without needing your share of love and mercy. Anyway, I'd like to believe that the love we give to others will one day be rewarded; and it's comforting, too, to think that once, centuries ago, somebody loved us enough to die for all the terrible things we do to one another, even without meaning to.' She stopped, as if she'd said too much, and asked:

'But, tell me, what do you think?'

Chad shrugged. 'I don't know. I haven't really thought about it, I guess.' He added: 'A lot of it sounds pretty fishy, though, to me.'

'I suppose it does,' Penny said, putting her hand on his arm. 'But who knows,' she went on, and a kind of sadness seemed to creep into her voice, 'maybe life will some day make you want to believe in the reality of forgiveness and a transcending love. Then

73

the old stories will make more sense to you.' She pushed the mood aside and said, brightening: 'But, come on. There's something else I want you to see. I'm pretty sure you'll like it.'

She led the way down the nave to the north transept. There, behind a low iron railing, was the sarcophagus, in polished white marble, of a beautiful girl, her features serene and dignified in death. She was dressed in a long robe, belted, high at the neck, and her delicate hands were folded across her chest. Her head rested on two marble cushions, and at her feet, patient and watchful, as if his mistress were only sleeping, a small dog kept his eternal vigil. The gentle folds of the drapery and translucent quality of the girl's features, resigned, peaceful in death, gave the carving a reality of human pain and loss that spoke across the centuries, and, for the first time, Chad and Brooke were still and silent, as if standing over the body of someone they had known in life.

'Her name,' their mother said, 'was Ilaria del Carretto. She died in 1405, when she was only thirteen.'

'Wow, I mean she's really beautiful,' Brooke said, her voice full of wonder.

Chad's throat constricted and, for a moment, he could say nothing. Before they'd come into the church he had hoped, he remembered, to find a pretty girl inside, somebody who would make the visit memorable and take his mind off all the boring religious stuff. But he hadn't expected this. He hadn't expected a vision of love and death met together in the face of a girl whose life had ended, at the age of thirteen, six hundred years ago. He hadn't expected the centuries to melt away like seconds as he stood beside her marble tomb. He hadn't expected to find himself moved to the edge of tears.

'She died very young,' he managed to whisper.

But it was Penny who was crying. For the first time in all their many trips to monuments and churches, the three of them had shared a vision of the truth that lies in beauty, had shared the reality and power of an inspired intuition. It was the moment she had prayed for, fearing that it would never come. And now she stood, her arm around each of them, and the tears of shameless joy rolled down her cheeks.

Then, like mourners at a grave site, they pulled themselves away, retracing their steps over the marble pavement to the main portico, beyond which lay the ordinary world of sun and shade from which they had come and into which they would now return.

The door swung open and they stepped out into the glare. The precious moment they had shared, lingering until the light of common day flooded in to dissipate it, vanished like a ghost in moonlight as if it had never been.

'So, can I listen to my disc now?' Brooke demanded.

'May,' Penny corrected. '*May* I listen to my disc now – and of course you may, dear.'

They made their way across the piazza, heading for the car-park in Piazza Napoleone where they had left the car.

'Hey,' Chad said, 'there's Dad!'

Penny looked to where he was pointing, at a man sitting in the awning-covered patio-bar of the Hotel Universo.

'Oh,' she said, forcing a smile, 'his meeting must have ended early.'

But in her heart she knew it wasn't true.

6

Herr Doktor Professor Wilhelm Kleist – Willi Senior to his family – lifted his head from the binocular eyepiece of his Leitz micro-scope and, leaning forward, made a notation on the pad of yellow paper at his elbow. There was a ruminative, far-away expression in his ice blue eyes. He shook his head in incomprehension and rubbed his chin as if, somehow, that meditative act might help resolve the mystery. The experiment had not gone as anticipated. This time, after the changes he'd introduced in environment, he'd expected a series of subtle morphological variations in the organs of the upper thorax. But there was nothing he could see, nothing discernible at all. It was really, he judged, most curious – a most puzzling phenomenon indeed.

He lowered the silver-rimmed spectacles from his forehead, where he kept them out of the way when using the microscope, and looked absently around the greenhouse that he had converted into his laboratory. It was a spacious addition, attached to the rear of the villa, where the temperature and humidity were rigorously controlled with a view to replicating the conditions of the Vene-zuelan rain forest. At one end, the room was an office and laboratory, containing a sturdy desk, filing cases, a large metal work-table and an impressive array of scientific instruments. The other end, in striking contrast, was thickly planted with tropical trees and shrubs, and peeping between the fronds of ferns in hydroponic trays on the tiled floor, delicate orchids and other exotic flora flourished in the humid shade. Amidst the dense foliage one caught frequent glimpses of the glossy wings of large blue butterflies. There were forty or more of them in all, together with a large number of larvae of the same species in various stages of development – for the Blue Morpho, *Morpho menelaus* of the Linnaean family Nymphalidae, was the special subject of Professor Kleist's research. The insects were free to fly where they would, their domain bounded only by the glass walls of the greenhouse-laboratory, and the more venturesome among them would regularly leave their leafy sanctuary and land, sometimes on the desk or filing cabinet, sometimes on the professor's head or broad shoulders, fanning their iridescent wings in the various light. It was an odd fact that even the pungent smell of his eternally smouldering briar did nothing to deter them. But then, in some perverse way, perhaps they found the aromatic scent of his special-blend cavendish tobacco attractive. It was a topic on which he had more than once debated writing a scientific paper – for the phenomenon, as far as he could discover, had never been recorded in the literature.

The villa which the professor and his family had taken over for an eighteen-month sabbatical was owned by the University of Kiel and was offered, at a nominal rent, to senior professors on leave who, seeking uninterrupted peace and a warmer climate for their studies, wished to take advantage of the solitude of northern Tuscany. In fact, however, it had been Ilse Kleist's idea, not her husband's, to grasp the opportunity when it presented itself. Willi Senior could as easily have conducted his research in Minsk or Timbuctoo – or even, for that matter, in Kiel itself. Once buried in his work, he was oblivious to everything around him. All that mattered were his *Wanzen*, his bugs, and the rest of the world simply ceased to exist. But Ilse wanted to escape and had insisted they seize the chance to get away from the grime and pollution of northern Germany. They deserved a holiday in the south, she argued – and Lucca, of which in fact she had never previously heard, would be as good a place as any other located in the general vicinity of the Equator. She wasn't choosy providing it was a long, long way from the barren, wind-swept coast of the Baltic.

Willi Senior rose from his chair and arched his back, working out the kinks from sitting hunched so long over his microscope. The aching muscles in his neck and shoulders were an indication of encroaching age. Although only fifty-two, he was already monitoring with alarm the first signs of liver-spots on the back of his hands, and his mane of dark hair had grown silver at the temples and was salted with grey elsewhere. It was all very dismal, very depressing. *Der Film ist gelaufen*, he thought morosely, I'm washed up, finished. He was a big man, an athletic man, a rugby player in his youth – and the prospect of old age and a creeping senescence, of physical weakness and inability, was anathema to him. Willi Senior was one of those men who would, most assuredly, not go gently into that good night but would kick like the devil against the dying of the light.

Best not to dwell on the inevitable, he told himself.

Being fifty-two, after all, was a long way from being eighty-two – or, with any luck, even ninety-two. No sense worrying yet. He was in good health – robust, active, dynamic. And besides, he looked after himself: he exercised regularly, took a daily vitamin supplement, drank only in strict moderation, and ate his quota of broccoli (which he detested) and spinach. Yes, if there were any justice in the world, he'd live to be a ripe old age.

Certainly, it was his plan to do so.

He pressed his middle finger and forefinger against the carotid artery in his neck, just to be sure that everything was still on track, was as it should be. The pulse was strong and regular. *Mir fällt ein Stein vom Herzen*, he thought, expelling a long and thankful breath, well, that's a relief.

On the far side of the terrace, the twins, Dieter and Dietrich, aged fourteen, sons by his first wife, had cleared a large area and constructed a replica of the Russian steppes around Kursk and Kharkov. The ground was covered with battle formations of model tanks: German PzKw IVs and Panthers with swastikas on their turrets, and red-starred Soviet T-34 medium tanks whose V-12 engines had once, in the spring of 1943, carried them over the rolling, treeless steppes at speeds of more than thirty miles an hour. Inside a bulging salient around the town of Kursk, the Russian defenders had constructed eight concentric rings of anti-tank defences, but the Kleist twins were undeterred. With Dieter playing the role of General Kluge in command of Army Group North, and his brother taking the part of von Manstein in charge of the Fourth Panzer Army in the south, they had launched an all-out offensive on the Russian positions in a classic pincer *blitzkrieg*, throwing men and machines into the assault with enthusiasm and skill. There was nothing that the twins, voracious readers, didn't know about Operation Citadel. They had reconstructed the famous battle many times – and had so far discovered no fewer than fourteen ways in which the German forces, using *their* tactics, would without question have emerged victorious from the contest. If Dieter and Dietrich Kleist had had the power to turn back time and replay the battle at Kursk, the story of the war – and, who knew? perhaps of the world itself – would have had to be rewritten.

Willi Senior stood with his hands on his hips, watching his sons with a mixture of pride and anxiety etched on his features. They were an odd pair: stratospheric IQs coupled with depressingly narrow interests, socially backward and naïve, library cormorants when it came to German military history but not interested in much else. He watched as a puff of smoke rose from a column of Russian tanks temporarily blocking von Manstein's advance and shook his head. They were ascetic militarists, monkish tacticians who spent their days in a dream-world of imaginary blood-letting and a perversely patriotic reconstruction of the past. He wondered how he'd ever sired them and what role they were suited for in life, unless it was perhaps – *Gott behüte* – to start another war.

And then there was Willi Junior, his oldest son, now twenty-five. He was a strange and sullen boy, moody and bitter, unfocused and somehow afraid of life, a misfit like the twins but of another stamp, a darker and more enigmatic sort altogether. He'd never recovered from his mother's death and he resented his father's new-found happiness with another woman. For Willi Senior *was* happy with Ilse – wildly and deliriously happy. Their union had brought him more joy than he'd known for years, more than he'd ever thought possible after the loss of Mattie, his quiet and shy first wife. Oh, how different they were, those two wives who were a generation – and a universe – apart! How lucky he'd been to find Ilse, so young and beautiful, so vital and energetic! She had brought gaiety, renewed sensuality, and something remarkably akin to the kaleidoscope of a rediscovered youth back into the monotonous monochrome of his widowed existence. She was light and air, sunshine and shower – a shimmering vision of everything that made life wonderful and exciting and, in some mysterious way that he couldn't explain, eternally fresh and exhilarating day after passing day. He awoke each morning in an earthly paradise, with his own sweet Eve, newly created, lying at his side. He heard her voice in every bird that sang; he saw her face in every cloud and dancing bush, in every stream that burbled at his feet. He loved her to distraction with every ounce of his being, with his very soul – and he would, he knew in the darker places of his heart, have killed anyone who tried to take her from him.

In the distance a flash of light, the sun reflecting off a car's windscreen, caught his attention. The house overlooked a long valley and winding road that snaked its way up the mountainside to the villa at the top. The car was too far away for him to recognize, but he knew that it was Ilse coming back from town. The car was travelling too fast for it to be anyone else. He smiled a weary smile, hoping she wasn't about to present him with another speeding ticket. He'd pay it, of course, and gladly. It was his lot in life, like Leonidas at Thermopylae, to be there when she needed him, to protect her untamed spirit from the mercenary satraps of foreign laws and regulations. Love was not only blind, he had discovered, but also very expensive.

Suddenly he longed to see her, to hold her again in his arms and kiss her wine-sweet lips.

The experiment and his butterflies could wait. They'd still be there tomorrow. He closed the greenhouse door and turned the key in the lock, checking to be certain it was secure. He took no chances any more. Someone – he suspected the Italian maid who came in to do the cleaning – had carelessly left the door open and twelve of his Blue Morphos had escaped. Not enough to jeopardize his research, but too many to run further unnecessary risks. If it had been winter, he'd have lost the lot of them, delicate creatures that they were. As a result, he now kept them under lock and key.

He turned and looked down the valley. The car was closer now, only a kilometre or so away, and he recognized the glossy red paint of the leased Alfa Romeo. An eager thrill stirred in his chest and there was a vague lightness in his head, as if he were on his way to a first date. Her nearness often had that effect on him.

He pocketed the key and, walking quickly, crossed the terrace in order to meet her the instant she pulled into the drive.

Ilse geared down sharply and, leaning into the turn, shot like a bobsledder between the pillars of the wrought-iron gates. A polished plaque on the gatepost, mixing Italian and German, announced: TENUTA DEL COLOMBO. UNIVERSITÄT KIEL. She accelerated up an aisle of cypress and braked in front of the house, a two-storey structure of ivy-draped stucco with a hexagonal fish-pond in the centre of a circular drive. There, on the steps leading down from the villa, Willi Senior stood waiting for her. Was something wrong? Fear froze her heart like a block of ice and her head felt suddenly light. Why was he waiting for her? Did he suspect, did he *know*, what she'd been doing in town? *O großer Gott!* She looked around, her pulse racing, for Willi Junior's Volkswagen. It was nowhere in sight. He wasn't home yet, thank God.

Puh! She heaved a sigh of relief. She was safe then.

All the way back from Lucca she'd been unable to think of anything but her unexpected meeting in the car-park. The smutty little toad had wanted to sleep with her, had threatened to blackmail her if she didn't come across – and what had *she* done? Told him to get lost and pushed him out of the damned car in a fit of pique. Not an intelligent move. No, she hadn't been thinking properly there. She should, she realized now, have been more subtle – strung him along a little – teased and flirted with him to keep him off guard. But he'd taken her by surprise and she'd reacted out of instinct; and now he was angry and hurt – and consequently dangerous. Who could predict what he might do? He was capable of almost anything. Ilse shuddered, her mind full of vivid, unfocused imaginings. All she knew for certain was that she hadn't heard the last of the episode in the car-park. No, not by a long shot.

Stepping out of the car, she put on a brave, cheerful face. 'Hello, darling. What's up? *Stimmt etwas da nicht*, is something wrong?'

Willi looked perplexed. 'Wrong? No, there's nothing wrong. I saw the car coming and came out to meet you. Why should anything be wrong?'

'Oh, no reason,' she said airily, covering her tracks. 'I was surprised to find you waiting, that's all.' She ran her hand tenderly across his cheek and changed the direction of the conversation. 'Is your work not going well, my darling?'

'You're more important than work,' he said, taking her in his arms and kissing her lips. 'I miss you, *Schatz*. I miss you when you're away, even if it's only for a couple of hours.'

'I miss you too, *Liebling*,' she said, holding him out at arm's length and giving him a narrow, suspicious look. 'And I'm happy to learn that I'm more important to you than your old *Wanzen*. I should get a confession like that in writing, you know. It might come in handy some day.'

'I'll do it gladly,' he said, grinning, 'but I don't seem to have a pen on me.'

'Oh,' she said, stepping back with an innocent smile on her face, 'wasn't that a pen I felt in your trouser pocket just now?'

Willi Senior tipped back his head and roared with laughter. Mattie, his first wife, would have shrivelled with shame and died a thousand deaths before uttering such a salacious innuendo. Ilse, on the other hand, never hesitated to blurt out whatever came uppermost into her mind – and he loved it. It made him feel young again, carefree and spirited, like a roguish colt. It took away the sting, the bitter taste in his mouth of being fifty-two years old.

'You have a bad tongue,' he said, pecking her on the forehead.

'And you're a dirty old man,' she countered, brushing her hand across the front of his trousers. 'Now, help me in with these packages.'

He lifted a dressmaker's box and two smaller packages from the back seat. 'Vanity, vanity, saith the preacher,' he quoted, 'all is vanity.'

'If you want me to look nice, my love,' she said archly, 'you have to be prepared to make certain sacrifices. Anyway, it's just one or two little things for that poetry-award ceremony at Teatro del Giglio next week – and the soirée afterwards, of course. I thought you'd want me to look my best.'

'You look stunning in anything, *Schatz*,' he said, and then added without thinking, in a kind of Freudian slip, 'and even better in nothing at all.'

It had been his intention, when he'd left the greenhouse, to do no more than give her a kiss and a hug to welcome her home – but her sudden presence, the fetching sight of her in the lace-necked dress he'd given her for her birthday, the warm feel and honeyed smell of soft and yielding body when he'd taken her in his arms, had aroused other sensations. Suddenly, he wanted her, needed her right now. He could think of nothing else.

She recognized the signs. 'Oh, not now, Willi,' she groaned. 'It's been a long day. Won't it keep till tonight?'

'No. Let's get naked,' he whispered throatily. A libidinous leer, almost comical in its intensity, contorted his features into a mask of lust. 'Be daring, *Schatz*. Dare to be different.'

My God, she thought, I've unleashed a monster. It had been a mistake to let guilt and her fear of having been caught in the act with Peter trick her into playing the coquette so outrageously with her husband. Hindsight, of course, was always twenty-twenty. Without meaning to do so, she'd set Willi off – accidentally flipped his 'on' switch – when all she'd intended to do was let off a little grateful steam after a near miss.

'What about the twins?' she asked, clutching at straws.

He steered her up the steps and into the hall. 'They won't bother us,' he said. 'They're out on the terrace, blowing up Russians.'

She wondered why she'd even bothered to ask: the twins were always out on the terrace blowing up Russians. 'They might come in,' she warned, fighting a rearguard action.

He was not to be deterred. 'We'll take that chance,' he said.

He set the packages on the hall table and took her hands in his, drawing her toward the stairs. The vision of her naked body – her firm breasts, curving thighs, and golden, beckoning triangle of pubic hair – was almost more than he could bear. His throat was dry and tremors rippled through his groin, the precursors of a significant seismic event.

'And Willi Junior?' she tried.

'We'll take that chance, too.'

The look in his eyes told her all she needed to know. There was no point in trying to put him off. He was aroused and determined – a beast in heat. She'd seldom seen him like this, and it was always when he was feeling his years, when he was feeling maudlin and teary about how old he was getting and felt he had to snatch the opportunity to demonstrate his virility. God, the male ego was a silly, fragile thing – and women, damn it all, were always expected to be there, to pick up the pieces after a fall and put old Humpty Dumpty's libido back together again. Oh, what the hell, she thought, I'll humour him.

'All right,' she said, capitulating, 'let's go up and put some lead in that pencil of yours. But you'll have to give me a chance to shower first. I'm hot and sweaty from running around in town.'

Running around in town: an unintentional pun, and one that brought a smile to her lips when she realized what she'd said. Well, I guess it's just one of those days, she thought ruefully. It had started well, then gone rapidly downhill after that. An afternoon of satisfying sex with Peter Morgan – followed by sick, dirty hints from Willi Junior – and now here was Willi Senior waiting in line and wanting his turn in the saddle. All the attention was starting to make her feel a little like the town bike, ridden by everybody.

They mounted the stairs together and Willi locked the door behind them. Ilse took her time in the shower, letting the water steam and cleanse her, letting it drum against her skin like streams of aqueous bullets from the pulsing showerhead. When she was finished, she stepped out and wrapped herself in a thick, fleecy towel. She felt listless and worn out. Instead of filling her with a renewed energy, the larcenous water seemed to have drained away her little remaining strength, leaving her sapped and spent, like a used toothpaste tube. Oh God, she thought, of all days for Willi to want his damned ego bolstered . . .

Well, there was no help for it. Duty called.

The cheval mirror that stood beside the vanity was fogged and she wiped it clean with the towel, then turned herself carefully around in front of its silver reflection, scanning her neck and back for scars from her afternoon bout with Peter. He was an energetic lover and sometimes left scratches and bruises, even the odd love-bite. There was nothing this time, however, as far as she could see. And thank God for that! Willi had the eye of a hawk, and if he ever thought – ever even *suspected* that she was fooling around . . . Ilse gave an involuntary shudder. Well, suffice it to say that green was his colour and that he had a vile, feral temper when his jealousy was piqued. She'd seen it once before – and once was enough – when she'd flirted innocently with one of his junior colleagues at a party and Willi had knocked the poor devil senseless with an uppercut to the unsuspecting jaw. He'd apologized afterwards, of course – but, *Gott im Himmel*, what an embarrassment! And since then, Ilse had never dared to look sideways at another man, at least in public.

She finished drying off, then hung the towel on the rail and let out a long, weary breath that was almost a sigh. She crossed to the door and swung it open. The cool, dry air from the bedroom beyond hit her like an arctic blast, raising gooseflesh on her skin. Willi, naked and aroused, lay on the bed like a lateen-rigged dhow awaiting her arrival. She composed her face and tried to will herself into a suitably erotic mood.

All the world's a stage, she thought with a grimace – and, squaring her shoulders, she stepped out on to the boards.

Half an hour later, as they descended the stairs together, the front door opened and Willi Junior, wearing a furtive smirk on his pig-like face, shambled into the foyer. He was up to something. She could tell from his face. The bastard was plotting something.

She felt cold and suddenly frightened. She shouldn't have told him to go to hell. She shouldn't have mocked his passion and shoved him out of the car like that. She should have strung him along for a little and then let him down easily. But it was too late for that now.

'Where have you been?' Willi Senior asked, being pleasant.

Willi Junior shrugged. 'Out,' he said. 'Around. In town.' He gave Ilse a knowing, sidelong glance. 'Nothing special.'

He was lying. He was up to no good. It was written all over his fat face. The *Scheißwurm*, she thought venomously, the shitty little worm.

She wanted to scream, to rush at him and rip out his eyes with her nails. But her face, a stony mask, betrayed no emotion. She wouldn't give him the satisfaction of seeing her contempt, her terror. No, the next move in the nasty little game he'd started was his – but if he dared to cross her, by God, she'd strap him to a bed of white-hot coals and castrate him with a dull spoon. If the little weed thought he knew anything about being malicious, anything at all, he'd bloody soon discover that beside her he was a beardless stripling, a mere tiro in the arts of spite and revenge.

'I think,' she said in a toneless voice, turning to Willi Senior, 'that I rather fancy a beer, my love. There's a funny taste in my mouth. Shall I pour one for you too?'

7

The sommelier held the bottle cradled like a baby in a linen napkin for Bonelli to inspect. It was a Brunello di Montalcino, 1988 vintage, from the San Giorgio estate in Val d'Orcia. Bonelli nodded. Yes, it was the one he'd asked them to lay aside, their last bottle of what he'd been told was a pretty good vintage.

The steward drew the cork and laid it on the table.

'I think tonight,' Bonelli told him, 'the honour of the first sip belongs to my friend.'

The steward moved around the table and poured a small portion into Arbati's glass, catching the last drop on the bottle's lip with a deft twist of the wrist. The wine was deep in colour with a golden tinge at the edge where the light caught the meniscus. Arbati lifted the glass to his nose and inhaled. The bouquet was ambrosial, and the taste that followed, when he let the wine roll over his tongue, was rich and mellow, unlike anything he'd tasted in a long time.

'Very nice,' he said. 'In fact, it's quite wonderful.'

Bonelli grinned. 'I thought you'd like it,' he said, pleased. 'I remembered your passion for Brunello and, well – since this is a special occasion after all, I thought I'd splurge. I don't ordinarily drink this stuff, I want you to know. It's too expensive for my shallow pockets. Maybe I should become a writer like you.'

'Then become a novelist,' Arbati said, grinning. 'There hasn't been any money in poetry at least since Dante's time.'

The steward filled their glasses, then departed silently, leaving the bottle, still jacketed in its linen napkin, on the tablecloth between them.

When he had gone, Bonelli raised his glass and said:

'Well, my friend, I salute you – or, more precisely, I salute your achievement. How many policemen – and, more to the point, policemen whom *I* happen to know personally – are also poets who've won the gold medal of the Società delle Arti di Lucca? It's an impressive honour, Carlo, and it makes me very proud. The wine is my little tribute.' He shrugged and added: 'How can people say cops are philistines when you're out there writing prize-winning sonnets and odes? You've raised the profile of the whole profession, my friend.'

Arbati felt a flush of embarrassment rise in his cheeks. 'To hyperbole,' he proposed with a self-conscious grin. 'May it never lack friends or want followers. *Salute!*'

The Antica Locanda was full. Their table was in a corner and gave Arbati, whose back was to the wall, a clear view of the other tables. There was no one in the room he knew – he hadn't, of course, expected that there would be – but there was, as it happened, someone he recognized. Seated at a table with a pretty woman and two teenaged children on their best behaviour was the American who had left the Hotel Universo just as Arbati was checking in. He remembered him because the man had sensed that he was a detective and had done his best to steer clear – a phenomenon Arbati's trained eye had noted with interest, even though he was on vacation. The man was hiding something and had, ironically, unconsciously revealed in his body language his desire to conceal it. It was none of Arbati's business, of course. As far as he knew, the man had broken no laws and, even if he had, Lucca wasn't Arbati's jurisdiction. But he couldn't help at the time noticing the man's behaviour – just as he couldn't help noticing now that there was a subtle, unspoken tension, papered over with forced smiles, between the man and the attractive auburn-haired woman beside him who was presumably his wife. It was all just a part of being a cop. It went with the territory.

His meditation on the American was interrupted by the arrival of their meal, roast lamb for himself and braised rabbit for Giancarlo. The waiter set the steaming plates before them, replenished their wine, then disappeared as efficiently and silently as he had come.

For a time they ate in silence, savouring the food, then Arbati asked in a neutral voice:

'Anything interesting at the Questura?'

Bonelli raised an eyebrow. 'I thought you were on holiday.'

Arbati shrugged. 'Idle curiosity,' he said. 'You know what it's like.'

'Sadly, I do,' Bonelli agreed. 'You never really get away from it, do you? I went to the south of France last winter for a vacation and spent half my time wondering what was going on back here and the other half wondering what was happening on the local scene in Marseille. We should have been dentists or bank managers – something we could leave behind when we close the office door. Instead, we picked one of those jobs you carry around like a nose-ring twenty-four hours a day. It's like marriage in a way, isn't it? – which is,' he added, 'one of life's great traps that we've both so far managed to avoid.' He wiped his chin on his napkin and gave Arbati an elfish grin. 'At least I imagine you're still a free man. I don't recall a wedding, or even an invitation to one for that matter . . .'

Arbati gave a grunt. 'You nearly got one a couple of months ago,' he said, remembering Cordelia Sinclair, 'but I bailed out at the eleventh hour. At least I think I was the one who broke it off. I don't actually remember. I'll tell you about it some time. Maybe.' He turned the stem of his wineglass between thumb and forefinger, contemplating the mystery of decisions that seem to be made by circumstances rather than as acts of deliberate will. After a long moment, he said: 'But you haven't answered my question about what you've got cooking at the Questura.'

'Frankly,' Bonelli said, 'I'd rather hear about your love-life.'

'I'm sure you would,' Arbati said, 'but it will keep. Fill me in on what *you're* up to.'

Bonelli shrugged. 'There isn't much to tell, actually. Nothing much happens here. This isn't Florence, you know. I mean, we don't get big cases: Mafia bombs at the Uffizi, mass murders, high-profile corruption, kidnappings – that sort of thing. We have our share of robberies, of course, the odd extortion case, occasionally an isolated murder. But that's about it. Pretty tame fare for somebody from the big city. Certainly, we don't get headline-grabbers like that castrato business you had this past spring. What did the press call him? *Lo Squartatore*, "The Slasher" – yes, that's it, isn't it? Castration, revenge, death by straight razor: gripping stuff. The kind of thing pulp novelists sink their teeth into. No – no, nothing like that ever happens here in our little backwater, I'm afraid.'

'So, in other words,' Arbati offered, 'you hardly need a police force at all, is that what you're telling me? Come on, Giancarlo, you can do better than that.'

'Not much better, to tell you the truth.' Bonelli sipped at his wine. 'Well,' he said, 'there was something a little out of the ordinary that came up only this morning. It's probably nothing, a bizarre accident, but it may turn out to be something more. It's too early to tell.'

'Well . . .?' Arbati prodded.

'There was a call from one of the villas up in the hills. A man, the caller said, had been killed when the bronze statue of a Greek warrior toppled on him and the spear ran him through the chest. I investigated the thing myself. There are some questionable features that we're checking out – the dead man was carrying a concealed weapon, for example, and his hire-car was rented under a different name, maybe an alias. We'll know more in a day or two.'

'Death by art,' Arbati said, pursing his lips and leaning forward. 'I'm intrigued. Tell me more.'

Peter Morgan was having a terrible day. One of those black-cloud days when nothing goes right. It was bad enough that Jimmy hadn't shown up for their meeting, but then, to make matters worse, Penny and the kids had stumbled over him in a patio-bar in the middle of the afternoon when he was supposed to be in Florence. He'd told them his meeting ended early, that he'd just arrived back, but Penny hadn't bought it. She knew something was up: he'd seen it in her eyes. She'd wanted to send the kids off so that the two of them could thrash it out, right then and there – he'd seen *that* in her eyes, too – but he couldn't spare the time. Not just then. He had to find out about Jimmy first. Everything depended on it. Their whole damn future hung in the balance.

And so what had he done – ? Well, Christ, he'd quarrelled with her and stalked off in a huff, leaving her in tears. Damn, if life wasn't a bitch sometimes. The one person in the world who really cared and worried about him, and he couldn't bring himself to tell her anything, even with her eyes pleading with him not to shut her out. All he'd managed to do was shout at her and stomp off. Even the kids thought he was a real sonofabitch. Brooke had stood there crying with her mother and Chad had given him a cold stare, like he was a pile of doggie doo on the kitchen floor. Chad was protective of his mother: yes, Chad, he'd noticed in the past few weeks, was growing up. Peter shrugged. Well, soon everything would be back to normal. Once he got his hands on the money and paid off the gambling debts, he'd make it up to them. They'd go back to the States and pick up where they'd left off. There'd be no more dirty secrets: no more Ilse – no more mistresses, in fact, of any kind – and no more trips to the blackjack tables in Atlantic City. He'd get himself straightened out. Yes, everything would be all right. They'd pick up the pieces and start over.

But none of this could happen until the Ghirlandaio business was settled – which meant, first and foremost, finding out what had happened to Jimmy.

And it was at this point that a conventionally awful day had become a colossally horrific one. He'd gone to the hospital first, but no one named Dearing or answering to Jimmy's description had been admitted – so then he tried the Misericordia. That, he reflected sourly, had been his first mistake. The ambulance dispatcher, a hatchet-faced gorgon whose steel grey hair sat on her head like a metal helmet, had refused to be helpful, and no quantity of oil or charm had succeeded in extracting a jot of information from her. Her leaden lips were sealed; she would divulge nothing – all she did was refer him to the police: if his cousin was missing, she insisted waspishly, it was a job for the police, not the Misericordia. Roundly defeated, Peter had screwed up his courage and, despite his misgivings about the law, gone to the Questura with the same tale about his missing cousin. The police, as luck would have it, were intensely interested in his story – and just as interested, it seemed, in Peter himself. It had turned into a disastrous interview, a classic grilling. The only thing missing was a goose-necked lamp twisted into his eyes. Once they found out the missing cousin's name was Dearing, they had shown him into a room and started firing questions at him. Where had his cousin gone? Peter said he didn't know. Was he nervous, agitated in any way, when Peter had last seen him? No, not particularly – well, maybe a little: why? No answer, just more questions: had Peter and his cousin come abroad together? what were they doing in Italy? could they see his passport, please? how long was he staying? what was his address in Italy? his telephone number? On and on, interminably – then finally, perhaps an hour later, they told him he could go, that someone named Bonelli would be in touch in a day or two with more questions. Just what he needed: more fucking questions. Christ, it had been a nightmare.

And at the end of it all, he still knew bugger all about Jimmy. They'd told him nothing. They knew everything about him and he still knew nothing about Jimmy. The only thing he was sure of was that *something* – something that wasn't good – *had* happened to him. Otherwise, the police wouldn't have been so bloody interested. Shit! what a fucking awful day . . .

He dabbled with the spinach and ricotta pasta in his bowl, stirring it uninterestedly with his fork. Nothing appealed to him. He was sick of all this fancy foreign food. What he wanted was a plate of fries and catsup: something that would make the world seem normal again, even if it wasn't.

He didn't dare look at Penny. There was nothing he could say to make things better. She was angry, she was hurt – she knew he was hiding something from her. She'd probably guessed he had a mistress. (Had she also, somehow, found out about the gambling debts? About the Ghirlandaio business? *Oh, Christ . . .!*) He couldn't talk to her any more. He couldn't face her sad, frightened eyes. Chad and Brooke knew something was wrong, too. They'd sensed the vibrations and were sitting there at the table, not saying a word, picking at their meals with the funereal air of a pair of dyspeptic orphans. Brooke hadn't even grumbled about having to leave her eternal Sony Discman in the car while she ate. Damn it all! he thought with a sudden flash of fury, my family is going to hell in a hand-basket and I can't seem to do a damned thing about it. Shit!

He looked up from his plate and his eyes caught those of a man sitting at a table at the far end of the room. He recognized the face. Who was he? Then he remembered. It was that damned cop he'd seen at the Hotel Universo. Christ, there were cops everywhere he turned!

And why was the bastard watching him? He'd looked away when their eyes met, but there was no doubt at all that the man had been looking directly at him, staring at him . . .

In her cottage at the fork in the road, Cecilia Hathaway poured an ounce of Delamain cognac into a glass tumbler. It was a nightly ritual that she'd practised for many years. The brandy, she found, settled her stomach and helped her sleep. Every year at Christmas a delivery van rolled up to her garden gate and deposited a case of brandy and another of a sublime claret from Berry Bros & Rudd of St James's on her doorstep. The libations were the gift of Martin Witherspoon, Bart, of the hamlet of Bishop's Nympton in north Devon, the grateful father of one of Cecilia's youthful charges during her days as headmistress at Holford House whom she had acted decisively to preserve from a disastrous liaison with an itinerant farmhand. The girl had gone on to distinguish herself with a double first in history at Oxford and was now, after the last elections, the Conservative member for Taunton in Somerset. Her father, ever appreciative of Cecilia's timely intervention, annually expressed his gratitude with a boon of wine and spirits, and Cecilia could never pour her nightcap without a lively sense of his generosity and a fond memory of the action on her own part that had occasioned it.

She said goodnight to Bunter, already curled on his mat in the corner by the open hearth, then turned out the kitchen light and carried the glass, together with a single savoury biscuit (another part of the ritual), into her bedroom at the back of the cottage. She changed into a cotton nightdress, then slipped between the sheets, banked the pillows at her back, and settled in to read her Agatha Christie murder mystery. She'd read them all – many, many times – over the years; but she never tired either of Christie's skill or of Poirot's acumen, and so they were a perpetual pleasure to reread. Tonight, it was *The Murder of Roger Ackroyd*, one of her favourites. She preferred, at bedtime, to read only books she knew well: that way, she was never kept awake by the suspense of wondering what was going to happen next.

At ten thirty, when the chime of the pendulum clock sounded

in the hall outside her room, she closed her book and drained the last drop of her Delamain. She was precise about sleeping habits. For nearly fifty years she had turned out her light precisely at ten thirty, then said her prayers and fallen instantly into a deep and dreamless sleep, trusting to the watchful eye of the Almighty for protection. He had not failed her, nor did she expect him to. At six in the morning, like clockwork, she wakened with the earliest birds and shortly after the diurnal resurrection of the sun itself. She attributed her happiness and good health to the strictness of this inflexible regimen.

Tonight, as she lay in the velvet darkness awaiting the embalming fingers of sleep, her thoughts turned to Nigel and the dangers encompassing him. She wondered briefly and hopefully if he was still in the habit of saying his prayers at night – but, in case he wasn't, she had done it for him anyway. On the precipice of oblivion, some lines of Milton drifted through her mind like wisps of mist:

> On evil days though fall'n, and evil tongues;
> In darkness, and with dangers compast round,
> And solitude; yet not alone, while thou
> Visit'st my slumbers nightly . . .

Fleetingly, the thought crossed her mind of the ambush she'd prepared. Would anyone try to reach the villa tonight? Yes, perhaps . . . or then again, perhaps not . . . The morning light would reveal all . . .

And then, in the purity of innocence, she slept.

At Villa San Felice, Nigel Harmsworth turned out the lights and prepared for his vigil. There would be no sleep tonight. He was expecting something to happen; he was expecting trouble of some kind. And when it came, he intended to be ready for it.

An hour earlier, when he'd checked the computer, there had been (as he'd expected) an e-mail message from *danvers @auction.lon.uk*. It was, typical of his employer, phrased with a Spartan terseness:

Nigel,
Do nothing. Will arrive soonest. Hold the fort.

                              Dickie

And that was precisely what Nigel intended to do: *hold the fort.*

Donning a dark windbreaker to ward off the evening chill, he moved on to the terrace overlooking the single approach to the villa. It was from there that trouble would come. The other sides of the house opened on to steep and impassable hillsides.

His post was at the corner of the parapet in a sheltered nook in the shadow of a large terracotta amphora where he could see clearly without being seen. He sat in the chair he'd carried up from the garden earlier in the day and leaned the rifle, loaded and ready, against the stone jar. He hoped it wouldn't be necessary to use it, but he was prepared to take whatever steps were necessary in the event of unwanted intruders.

And then he settled back to wait.

The night was full of sounds. He'd forgotten how boisterous it could be. Crickets and other insects grated out tuneless nocturnes on serrated fiddles, a restless wind ruffled the leaves of trees and bushes, and somewhere in the chestnut woods a night-bird called to its mate: *Tu-whit! Tu-whoo!* Overhead, in pristine majesty, the moon sailed among scattered clouds attended in her stately passage by the winking rush-lights of a million stars.

For the first time in many years, he wished he had a cigarette.

Tu-whit! Tu-whoo! That eerie bird again, its mournful lament echoing through the forest like the cry of a soul in pain. *Tu-whit! Tu-whoooo . . .!*

When Peter Morgan left the restaurant, he didn't know what he was going to do. He needed time to think. Fortunately, since they had come to town in separate cars, he didn't have to put up with the long faces and freezing silences of Penny and the kids. They could drive home by themselves. He'd deal with them later. Right now, there were bigger things on his mind.

For a time, he wandered deserted back streets and took a stroll on the ramparts, weighing his choices, considering his options. In the end he decided there was really only one thing to do. He had to drive out to San Felice – now, tonight – and find out what had happened to Jimmy. There were two choices open when he got there: either he could snoop around quietly and see what he could turn up on his own, or he could pound on the door, shake the old bugger out of bed, and demand to know what the hell was going on. He decided to wait until he was actually on the spot before deciding which course to adopt. Best to spy out the lie of the land first, he told himself, and then react accordingly. Roll with the punches: that was his motto.

He took Via del Brennero, heading toward the mountains. On his left, the sinuous course of the Serchio unwound itself in a silver ribbon under a harvest moon, leading him with something like an insidious intent toward his destination. It was quiet, peaceful. He met no other traffic on the road. The night belonged to him. He picked a cassette from the dozen or so in the glove box – a selection of Julio Iglesias' greatest hits – and put it into the tape deck. Quiet music, lyrical music: music that offered the illusion of companionship. The soporific voice, rising and falling like the sea, seduced him out of reality and into a private world of subtle, intricate harmonies. His hands lay lightly on the wheel, his respiration deepened, his mind relaxed. He could easily have drifted off to sleep. Very easily. It had been a long and trying day.

He didn't see the rabbit until he was almost on top of the damned thing. It sat in the middle of the road, motionless and frozen, its round red eyes mesmerized by the circular glare of onrushing headlamps.

Peter wrenched the wheel hard, swerving out of the way at the last instant with a protesting squeal of rubber. It was a reflex act: he didn't remember until later that it was even a rabbit he'd turned to avoid. His heart was in his mouth. The tyres were off the tarmac and the car was slewing and skidding on loose gravel at the side of the road as if he'd hit a patch of ice. He struggled to regain control, to wrestle the machine back to safety, trying not to look at the high weeds slapping past under the bonnet or the anonymous black waters of the Serchio looming only a few yards away to his left. Although his knuckles were white on the wheel, he was surprisingly calm, his attention concentrated on the task in hand.

And then suddenly, miraculously, he was back on the road, hurtling through the night as if nothing had happened.

'Goddamn, that was close,' he heard his voice say in a remarkably steady tone. 'I nearly bought it there.'

He didn't feel very steady, however. His heart was racing and his forehead was bathed in a cold, clammy sweat. He slowed to a crawl and took a deep breath, then exhaled it slowly, thankfully. Yes, by God, it had been a near thing: one of those moments of blinding revelation that comes along to remind us – always when we least expect it – that life and death are only a heartbeat apart. He rolled down the window and let the night air flood in: a shower of reality, of returning sanity. He became suddenly aware that the Julio Iglesias tape was still playing – an incongruous, irritating, even mocking sound it seemed now – and he switched it off with annoyance. It was odd how the same music could have such different effects on the human nervous system, one minute caressing the senses, the next a tool in the hands of a sadist.

He brought the car back up to speed, putting the incident behind him. A sudden thought hit him. What exactly, he asked himself for the first time since setting out, do I think I'm doing? Jimmy was the one hired to look after the strong-arm tactics. What did he, Peter Morgan, a corporate lawyer, know about such things? He was the brains, Jimmy the brawn – the 'enforcer' as he preferred, somewhat theatrically, to style himself. Peter shook his head. Was he crazy? This wasn't a game they were playing: it was a big-money gamble with real, life-threatening danger. Nobody gave up two million dollars without a fight. So why in God's name, he asked himself, am I trekking out in the middle of the bloody night, alone and unarmed, to a lonely villa in the mountains?

The answer was simple: there *was* no one else. Until Jimmy put in an appearance, Peter was the only half-back in uniform. He was on his own.

That thought, he found, was far from being a consoling one. He didn't know what he might find when he got to the villa or how he'd handle things if the situation got rough. He wasn't experienced in this sort of work. He didn't even have a real plan, for God's sake – nothing concrete, no carefully thought-out strategy. If he were honest with himself in fact, he had to admit that he was just winging it – blundering along hoping that something would turn up, that a sudden inspiration would flash in his brain. All things considered, he thought glumly, it wasn't the best possible recipe for success.

And what if old Harmsworth was waiting for him? What if he were walking blindly into a trap?

He brushed the fear aside. Harmsworth was a grey-beard, a man over seventy years old. What threat could he be? He'd have drunk his hot milk and be fast asleep with his teddy bear by now. And besides, he didn't know Jimmy had friends lurking in the wings. Peter had insisted on the point when he'd briefed Jimmy on what he could and couldn't tell the old man. No, Harmsworth didn't even know that Peter Morgan existed.

He left the river valley and began to climb. He was close now and, in the bright moonlight, he began to recognize certain features along the way: the stone bridge with a humped back, the old church with its unfinished belfry, the scarred rockface where once, long ago, there had been a landslide. He slowed the car, keeping a sharp look-out for the junction where the fork led up a steep track to San Felice. There was no signpost to mark the turning, but there was, he remembered from the time he'd scouted the area with Jimmy, a cottage with a walled garden just where the road branched off to the villa . . .

Yes, there it was.

The cottage at the fork was in darkness, the occupant asleep. He'd expected that: it was past midnight. From here, it was another five kilometres up a winding track to San Felice. There were no other houses on the road which served as an extended private drive for the villa. He doused the headlamps, using only parking lights. The moon provided all the illumination he needed and he didn't want to announce his arrival with an unnecessary light-show – just in case there *was* someone keeping watch at the top. Better safe than sorry.

He swung right, up the gravelled track. The road was pitch black, the moon's light obscured by a thick cover of trees, and he found himself leaning forward, his nose practically on the windscreen, peering into the darkness trying to make out the grey ribbon of road in the dim glow of his parking lights. After fifty metres or so, the road, he knew, opened out and the driving got easier.

A shadow loomed on the road ahead. He stopped the car and got out. A heavy limb, too large to manoeuvre the car around, lay across the path, obstructing passage. Damn! he cursed under his breath. He'd have to drag the bloody thing out of the way. He grabbed one of the branches and gave a mighty tug.

Pfwaap!

A stab of light, like the sudden flashing on and off of a powerful search-lamp, split the night, blinding him.

'*Jesus Christ!*' he cried out, squeezing his eyes closed and twisting away. For several seconds, all he could see was a wavering blob, the residue of the original burst reverberating on his excited retinas.

What the hell was that?

His heart was pounding now, his mind racing.

Slowly, painfully, his sight returned. Now there were smaller spots, floating through his field of vision like stars on the surface of a midnight lake.

He listened, straining his ears to make out any strange or unusual sound, but there was only the monotonous, scratching cacophony of nocturnal insects. He looked around and then back down the road. There was nothing suspicious, nothing strange at all that he could see in the dim light cast by the parking lamps of his Alfa Romeo.

What the fuck was going on?

He moved cautiously to investigate, not knowing what to expect, like a man in a minefield, each step slow, each footfall calculated, deliberate. He could feel the blood pulsing in his neck.

He circled through the bushes at the edge of the road and came up on the spot from behind. It didn't take him long to discover the source of the sudden burst of light: a sealed-beam halogen spotlight on a metal stand. But what had set it off? He continued the search and turned up two photoelectric cells pointing at each other, one on either side of the limb lying across the road. When the limb was moved, the infra-red beam between the sensors was broken and the light was triggered. Peter furrowed his brow and scratched his head. But what the hell was it? Presumably a security device of some kind to alert the inhabitants of San Felice to the presence of trespassers. But why tell an interloper he'd been detected by flashing a bright light in his eyes? It made no sense. Old Harmsworth must be crazy as a coot. Loony tunes: a nut case.

Peter prowled the undergrowth at the edge of the road searching for a radio transmitter or some other clue as to how the signal was sent to the villa five kilometres away, but he found nothing. He never thought to look *up*, however, and so he didn't notice the disposable Kodak camera that Cecilia Hathaway had secured in a cleft of the holm-oak limb arching over the road, nor was he aware that the camera's 400-speed film had captured a perfect image of him tugging at the fallen branch, his face contorted into an agony of unaccustomed physical effort. In the background, as an added bonus, was the front of the Alfa Romeo with its number plate clearly visible. She had set her ambush with skill and care. She didn't mind if an intruder found the photoelectric cells or the halogen spotlight she'd used to floodlight the area and distract an intruder's attention away from the camera's automatic flash. The only thing that mattered was the camera itself and the photograph it contained. For that reason, she had buried the solenoid switch and the cable running from under the base of the spotlamp-stand to the gnarled tree where the camera was hidden, then carefully filled the trench and covered the ground above it with leaves and long grass. And now she had exactly what she wanted – a photograph identifying the person who was threatening Nigel – although, being fast asleep in her cottage a hundred yards away, she didn't yet know of her success.

Finding nothing more, Peter returned to the car, scratching his head, wondering what to do next. Should he press on to the villa or turn back? He decided to press on. He'd come this far and he might as well go the rest of the way. Nothing had really changed: he still had to know what had happened to Jimmy. But he had to be careful now. How many other boobytraps had that old coot Harmsworth set on the way up to the villa? Peter gave a grimace: God only knew.

Oh well, he thought, forewarned is forearmed – or so at least they say.

He drove at a crawl, his way lit by the moon riding at anchor directly overhead. He was as taut as a coiled spring, ready for anything – expecting at every moment to be blinded by another light, or have a telephone pole drop suddenly across the road in front of him, or feel the tyres blown out from under him by cat's-paws scattered on the road. Crazy old Harmsworth seemed capable of anything. A certifiable fruitcake.

He drove on – slowly, painfully, his heart in his throat. Half a mile . . . then a mile. Nothing happened: no lights flared, no poles fell across his path, no tyres blew.

He began to relax, to plot a strategy for what to do when he reached the top. He had to assume, having tripped the device on the road, that Harmsworth now knew that he was coming; and there was no telling how the old codger might react. He decided therefore to leave the car a piece down the road and to go in on foot. After he'd looked the place over, he'd make contact, find out what had happened to Jimmy, and play it by ear from there. It was still possible, of course, that Jimmy had never made it to San Felice, that he'd had an accident on the way. In that case, Peter would have to play the heavy himself. It was not a part he relished, but with Jimmy out of the picture, there was no alternative. He had to get his hands on that damned money. Everything depended on it.

The road wound up the mountain as if it had been designed by a serpent, writhing and turning back on itself in a series of switchbacks. At a point he judged to be about a quarter-mile below the villa, Peter turned the car around, facing downhill in case he needed a quick getaway, and set off on foot. The air was cool and he found himself shivering slightly, wishing he'd had the foresight to bring a sweater. Too late for that now, of course. He should have taken more time and planned the thing out better. At least, though, he was wearing a dark shirt and trousers: rudimentary but effective camouflage. Unless old Harmsworth had a pair of night-binoculars – which was unlikely – he'd never pick him out of the shadows. And that assumed, of course, that the old bugger was actually up there waiting for him. It could have been a stray dog or even one of those wild boars he kept seeing on Tuscan menus that had been rooting about and tripped the halogen device. Maybe the old boy had bolted out of bed, waited a few minutes to see if anything happened, then shrugged his shoulders, reset the alarm, and gone back to bed. With any luck, Peter prayed, that was exactly what had happened.

After a stiff climb, he reached the gates. A brass plaque glinting in the moonlight announced: SAN FELICE. The gates were closed. No doubt, Peter judged, they were connected to the alarm system. In any case, he wasn't about to tinker with them. There had to be another way. He moved along the stone wall, too high to climb, looking for a way in. Fifty feet further down he found what he wanted – a sturdy tree whose branches overhung the wall. He scrambled up the trunk, then eased his way out along a thick bough, using the branch above for balance. He hadn't done anything like it for years. Goddamn if it didn't make him feel like a kid again. Once beyond the wall, he squatted down gingerly on the branch and let himself down full length, dropping the last three feet to the ground with a gentle thud. Not a thing of beauty perhaps, but not bad at all, he thought, for an out-of-shape corporate lawyer.

Bent from the waist, he made his way carefully from bush to bush to the brow of a small rise where the house came suddenly into view below him. He was only fifty or sixty yards from the main entrance. He could see everything clearly: the shadowed grounds, the dark and empty windows, the sleeping house bathed in tremulous moonlight. Somewhere in the distance a lonely night-bird called to its mate: *Tu-whit! Tu-whoooo!* A long, drawn-out eerie sound.

Just as he hoped, the old boy had gone back to bed. No light showed in any of the windows. A good omen. He stood for a moment, a shadow in a world of shadows, surveying the layout before him. The floor at ground level was surmounted by a balustraded terrace, from the centre of which rose the two storeys of the main block. From his position behind the yew tree where he'd taken cover, the ground sloped gently down to the cobbled drive. There was no sign of Jimmy's Maserati. Did that mean he'd never made it to San Felice? – or did it merely mean that someone had moved the car? It was a question that needed an answer. Probably the garage was around the corner at the side of the villa. That, Peter decided, would be his first task: to try to locate the car.

He stepped from behind the tree.

There was a flat crack like a slap on bare skin and a bullet whined past his ear, severing a twig above his head. From the corner of his eye, as he threw himself down and rolled to safety, he'd seen the spurt of a muzzle flash off to the right, at the far end of the terrace.

He took several deep breaths, then eased his head up slowly, cautiously, until he could see the villa. There, right where he expected, silhouetted in the moonlight, was the hunched figure of the gunman. He was kneeling behind the stone balustrade, half hidden by a large ornamental pot of some kind.

There was obviously no point, now, in being coy. He took the bull by the horns.

'Nigel Harmsworth,' he called.

There was a long silence, then a wavering voice replied, 'What do you want?'

'I want to talk to you,' Peter called back, trying to sound reassuring. 'Put down your gun. I'm alone and unarmed.'

This time, the response was immediate: 'Don't come any closer. Stay where you are, I tell you, or I'll shoot!'

'I have no weapon. I just want to talk.'

'I don't believe you. Your friend had a gun. Now, clear off before I fill you full of lead.'

In other circumstances, Peter might have laughed. The old man had watched too many Westerns. Who did he think he was anyway – Jesse James?

'What friend?' Peter asked, keeping him talking.

'James Dearing. An American like you.'

Peter lay on his stomach, only the top two inches of his head showing above the rise. There was a pain in his shoulder where he'd landed when he'd thrown himself down on the ground, the front of his shirt was soiled and clammy, and he felt, lying with his face in the grass, as if he was shouting down a gopher hole. In the distance the eerie night-bird called again, and the sound hung in the air like an omen: *Tu-whit! Tu-whoooo!* It was as if he'd been warped by mysterious powers into a Keystone Cops movie scripted by Stephen King.

'Where is he now, this James Dearing?' he asked, his voice taking on a harder edge. He waited, but there was no reply. 'Are you still there, Harmsworth?' he called.

Finally, a hollow voice said:

'Dearing had an accident.'

'So, where is he? In hospital?'

'No, he's dead.'

Peter's chest froze. He couldn't believe his ears. This was a turn of events he hadn't expected in even his worst nightmares. 'Tell me what happened,' he said, his voice sounding dull and far away.

'A statue fell on him in the garden.'

'A statue . . .?'

'A second-century bronze warrior. The spear went through his chest. He died instantly.' He added as if it would somehow make things better, 'He didn't suffer. It was over in an instant.'

'Christ,' Peter breathed, closing his eyes. Jimmy dead! So, he was on his own now. He tried to pull his thoughts together, tried to find something – anything – to say to keep the old man talking.

'So, where's his car?' he asked.

'The police took it.'

'The police were here?'

'Naturally. I had to notify them. A man had been killed.'

Peter remembered the hour he'd spent at the Questura earlier that afternoon: the pursed lips, the suspicious looks, the endless questions. No wonder the cops had been so damned interested in what he knew about Jimmy Dearing. It all made sense now. But he could worry about that later. Right now, there was the matter of why Jimmy had come to San Felice in the first place and why Peter was there now, lying in the grass shouting up into the darkness at an addled lunatic with a hair-trigger finger.

'We still need to talk, Harmsworth,' he said evenly.

'About what?'

'About Ghirlandaio.'

A pause, then: 'Piss off.'

'Look, it's not that easy, Harmsworth. I'm not going to go away, you know; I'm not going to fold my tent and conveniently disappear into the sunset. Sooner or later, you're going to have to talk to me: we both know that. I know too much about you – about the Ghirlandaio and all those other paintings. So why not make it easy on yourself? Let me come up and talk to you – maybe we can work something out – or else you'll be spending the rest of your miserable life rotting in jail after I hand everything I've got on you over to the authorities. Don't be a fool, Harmsworth. You're going to have to make a deal with me, or I swear to God I'll sell you and that poncy boss of yours down the river.' He added, remembering an old film, 'And do you know something, old-timer? You won't last six months in the slammer – not alive – either one of you.'

The melodramatic threat was answered by two shots fired at random in Peter's general direction.

'Think about it,' Peter called, taking care to keep his head down.

'Bugger off,' came the terse reply.

Peter edged back down the hill, away from the villa and its crazed occupant. It was time for a tactical retreat. Harmsworth was going to be a tougher nut to crack than he'd anticipated. He needed a new strategy – and he needed it fast.

In the distant darkness the night-bird renewed its mocking call: *Tu-whit! Tu-whoooo! Tu-whit! Tu-whoooo!*

'Oh, fuck,' Peter muttered aloud, pausing to brush the dirt and grass from the front of his expensive Ralph Lauren shirt. 'What a goddamned fiasco this is turning out to be.'

PART TWO

A Case of Murder

1

The Lear jet touched down on the private runway outside the spa town of Montecatini and taxied to a position at the end of the strip. A light rain was falling and a lacy mist hugged the tarmac where the cold raindrops, forced high in their passage over the mountains, met the warm earth of the fertile, low-lying valley. A black limousine, its windows heavily tinted, waited for the plane to roll to a stop, then moved on to the tarmac and advanced warily toward it like a curious hyena approaching a resting cheetah. A panel in the side of the aircraft opened, unfolding an hydraulic ramp which descended with robotic precision to the ground and, a moment later, the figure of a man appeared in the opening. He paused, staring malevolently for an instant at the falling rain, then spat a command over his shoulder and an umbrella miraculously appeared above his head, held by a hand from behind.

Clutching the handrail, the man began to descend the steps slowly, cautiously, as if expecting to encounter a series of banana peels or fearing, perhaps, that one of the metal steps under his feet had been mined. Sir Richard Danvers, although only seventy-three, looked a good ten years older than his chronological age: he was stooped and fragile, thin to the point of anorexia, with the look of a revitalized skeleton over which a fresh suit of sallow skin had been recently stretched. Followed by his retinue – a pilot holding the umbrella and a portly woman in a nurse's uniform who had once, in better days, been his mistress – Sir Richard made his way without help step by agonizing step down to the waiting limousine, whose driver now stood rigidly in the drizzle holding open the car's rear door.

'*Buona sera, dottore,*' the man said.

'Bloody rain,' Sir Richard grunted by way of reply.

'*Sì, dottore,*' the chauffeur agreed.

Grasping the door frame for support, Sir Richard clambered painfully, like a rheumatic spider, into the plush leather interior.

No one moved to assist him: he had fired underlings for such gestures of concern and his employees knew better than to draw to his attention, even in minor ways, the obvious facts of his debility and infirmity. He was followed closely by the nurse, carrying a black bag like a doctor's case which contained a portable oxygen mask and the complex pharmacopoeia of drugs and elixirs required, he believed, to keep himself alive. The door closed behind them with a click. The pilot gave the chauffeur a malicious wink and, relieved of responsibility, turned on his heel and scuttled off under the umbrella to his waiting plane.

'*Madonna maiala*,' the chauffeur cursed under his breath, not certain whether the oath was aimed at the departing aviator or the surly old bastard he'd just delivered into his safekeeping. Well, he thought grimly, it will do nicely for them both.

He turned the car around and drove slowly – slowly enough, he hoped, to irritate the pilot of the Lear waiting to take off – up the middle of the runway. The cloud cover, he noticed, was thickening over the mountains: dark, heavy, pregnant with rain. They were in for a stormy night. At the end of the landing strip, he took the side road that led to the *autostrada*. In less than an hour he'd have delivered his two passengers to San Felice and be a free man again. Overhead, the Lear roared into the sky and climbed rapidly out of sight. He shot the unseen pilot a finger. '*Cornuto*,' he muttered and felt better for it.

In the sumptuous passenger compartment behind him, Sir Richard Danvers extracted a Ventolin inhaler from his pocket and took a puff, holding his breath to give the powerful expectorant a chance to clear his clogged bronchial tubes. At least he assumed they were clogged. Age had exacerbated his hypochondria, and any tightness in his chest was – if not the first symptom of a fatal heart attack – then at least an infallible indication of the onset of emphysema. Beside him, the nurse watched impassively. Medically speaking, his problems were severe arthritis and a punitive diet of wheat germ and low-fat milk recommended by an American dietary psychic. He ate nothing else and was slowly killing himself with his cure. She dared say nothing, of course. He retained her to confirm his own convictions, not to dabble in the black arts of diagnosis herself.

She waited until he had exhaled, then said: 'Shall I ring ahead and let Mr Harmsworth know that we've arrived?'

'No,' Sir Richard wheezed, waving her off, 'he'll know soon

enough. Get me Matajcek in New York.' The effort of getting out of the plane and into the car had exhausted him and he fell back into the leather upholstery gasping like a beached bream.

The nurse consulted a small book in her handbag, then, lifting the cellular telephone from its cradle, dialled the number. When the apparatus began ringing at the far end, she handed the receiver to her employer.

'Laszlo?' Sir Richard rasped. 'Danvers here. I'm ringing from Italy. What do you have for me on that Dearing chap?'

'Ah, Sir Richard!' the distant voice crooned. 'Yes, we've managed to track down your boy. He's a small-time con-man from the Lower East Side. Originally from Boston, but he's been living in the Big Apple for the past eight or nine years. Strictly little league: grifting, extortion, a bit of telephone fraud – that sort of thing. Nobody's seen hide nor hair of him for six or eight weeks. He seems to have gone to ground.'

'He's *in* the ground, actually,' Sir Richard said drily. 'He's dead. He came to Italy and had a statue fall on him.'

'Careless of him,' Matajcek observed.

'What *I* want to know,' Sir Richard said, 'is why he was here in the first place. And *that*, my friend, is what I'm paying you to find out. So, what do you have for me?'

There was a pause, then Matajcek's voice returned:

'The word on the street is that Dearing was working on a big job. It's all pretty sketchy, but he was bragging in the bars that he'd soon be on Easy Street for the rest of his days. He was a man, it seems, addicted to clichés.'

'And?' Sir Richard cut in impatiently.

'And,' Matajcek went on with a kind of verbal shrug, 'that's about it. No hard details – not yet, anyway. Except one: Dearing, it seems, was working for a big-time lawyer. Somebody from out of town. Philly most likely. They met two or three times in a tavern on West 57th.'

'What is this lawyer's name?'

'I'm working on it.'

'Then work harder,' Sir Richard growled.

'It takes time,' Matajcek countered.

'Time is something I don't have,' Sir Richard snarled. 'Find me the bastard, Matajcek, and find him quickly. I need to know what I'm facing here.' He added: 'Oh – and I'll want a full bio as well. Anything you can dig up: financial records, mistresses, underworld connections – that sort of thing. I need an Achilles' heel; something I can turn against him. Now, get on with it. You can reach me at San Felice. My nurse will give you the number.'

He passed the receiver to the nurse without waiting for a reply and collapsed against the leather seat, exhausted by the effort expended on the call. Matajcek was a good chap, a reliable man, but you had to sit on him. He'd come through in sticky situations in the past and he would, Sir Richard confidently believed, come through again. It was imperative that he should.

Cecilia Hathaway stepped from the taxi and unfurled her umbrella. Something had warned her, something in the barometric pressure or the cloud formations as she left the cottage, that she would need it before the day was done – and her instincts were infallible in these matters. It was spitting rather than actually raining as she emerged from the cab, but there was, she could tell, worse to come. The sky was dark and ominous over the mountains. She'd been wise to leave Bunter at home. He disliked rain and became profoundly agitated if there were thunder and lightning about. Yes, in spite of his disappointment at being left behind, he was best where he was – curled up securely on his mat in the corner of the kitchen. It was a long ride home and, though normally docile, there was no telling what mischief he might get up to in a strange vehicle in the event of a violent celestial disturbance. She'd try, however, to get back before the storm broke. It was the least she could do for him.

In her brisk way, she made her way from shop to shop making the purchases on her mental list – a spool of green thread, a new garden trowel, wooden clothes pegs, dental floss . . . Since she had never learned to drive a car and lived nearly twenty kilometres from town, she had learned to plan her visits into Lucca with care. One by one she added acquisitions to the accumulation of packages in her wicker basket. Her most interesting errand, however, was hardly routine and she had saved it on purpose until the last: a visit to the photographic supply shop in Via Fillungo where, the previous day, she had purchased an inexpensive disposable Kodak camera.

She had hardly been able to believe her eyes when, that morning, after her usual breakfast of muesli and fruit, she had walked up the road to inspect the trap she'd laid for nocturnal intruders attempting to make their way unseen up to San Felice. The heavy branch she had placed as an obstruction in the road had been pulled to one side and the halogen spotlamp lay on its side – which meant, since no one at the villa would yet have been up and about, that someone had travelled the road the previous night. Her first thought, of course, had been for Nigel: was everything all right? was he safe? She had retrieved the camera from the holm-oak limb stretching out over the road and returned at a trot to the cottage, then picked up the telephone – it had been repaired, thank heaven – and dialled the villa's number. It was answered by the cook, Signora Capponi, who lived in the servants' quarters at the rear. Yes, she said, Signor Harmsworth was at home, but he'd had a bad night and was in a foul temper. Did Signorina Hathaway wish to speak with him anyway? No, Cecilia had said, she'd ring later when he was in a more sociable mood. Then she had sat down to plan her next move. Over a cup of linden tea she decided that, for the moment, it was best to keep what she knew to herself. What was important was to discover what she *had*, in fact, discovered. And that meant having that film developed as quickly as possible.

The photography shop in Via Fillungo was a well-stocked emporium, selling not only film but a wide variety of cameras, lenses, tripods, and other accessories. A bell tinkled over the doorway as Cecilia entered, having first shaken the water from her umbrella and furled it carefully. That was one thing, she reflected with satisfaction, one could say about the English: they knew how to deal with inclement weather. Italians were always surprised and baffled by a sudden downpour, scurrying about with newspapers and makeshift bits of plastic held over their heads. *Semper paratus* was the British motto: always prepared.

The shopkeeper was busy at the counter with a customer – a German, it seemed, who spoke little Italian. They were huddled over a Minolta 700si camera and the shopkeeper was attempting, with florid gestures and exaggerated phrases, to explain its multifarious features. The customer was an unsavoury-looking character in his mid-twenties, pudgy and unkempt, with greasy hair and clad in a dirty pair of jeans. How he could afford so expensive a piece of technology was a mystery to Cecilia. A wealthy and extravagant father no doubt, she surmised. She watched them, locked together in conspiratorial absorption, with a sober expression on her face. Allies, she thought, remembering the war years and a father killed in Belgium. It was only to be expected of course that they should be examining a Japanese camera. Some things, it seemed, never changed.

'*Ich brauche Zeit zum Nachdenken,*' the customer said at last, straightening and stepping back from the counter.

The shopkeeper, mystified, screwed his face into a comic expression of incomprehension, not certain, it seemed, whether he was being complimented or insulted for his pains.

'*Zeit,*' the German reiterated, searching for words. '*Il tempo,*' he managed finally, tapping his temple with a fat forefinger. '*Il tempo per denken. Ritorno tardo. Capisci?*'

A light dawned. '*Sì,*' the shopkeeper replied, '*tornera più tardi. Sì – sì, capisco. Grazie, signore.*'

The German shambled off and the bell over the door tinkled his departure.

'*Ah! – Tedeschi,*' the shopkeeper muttered with an expansive shrug, turning, with evident relief, to serve Cecilia. 'And how may I help you, *signora*?'

She removed the disposable camera from her handbag.

'I'd like this film developed,' she said in Italian, setting it on the counter. 'As soon as possible, if you please.'

'But, *signora*,' he said, examining it, his eyebrows rising, 'only one picture has been taken. There are twenty-three exposures still left on the reel.'

'I'm perfectly aware of that,' she countered with a disarming smile. 'I only need the one, thank you. When will it be ready, please?'

'Tomorrow,' he said, shaking his head. 'In the afternoon.'

'I shall return for it then,' she replied, taking up her umbrella and wicker basket.

'That will be fine. Your name, *signora*?'

'Hathaway. Cecilia Hathaway,' she said, turning. 'Until tomorrow then. *Grazie, signore.*'

'*Prego, signora.*'

The look he gave her departing back suggested that, in his judgement, the English had just joined the Germans as one of the unexplained mysteries of the universe.

In the large room at the back of Villa San Felice that he had converted into a painting studio, Nigel Harmsworth threw down his brush in disgust. The colours, damn it, were wrong. He put his hands on his hips and tilted his head, glowering darkly at the large canvas, four feet square, that sat half-finished on the easel. The colours simply weren't *primitive* enough. The reds were too orangy, the greens needed more yellow, and the blues in the Virgin's dress were flat and lifeless. Nothing was right. The *idea* of the painting was brilliant, but the execution was execrable. It was meant to be a reworking of Botticelli's dramatic *Annunciation* in the Uffizi as Gauguin would have rendered it: the figures were Tahitian natives, the stalk of lilies carried by the kneeling angel of annunciation a bough of pale yellow hibiscus, the setting a tropical hut instead of a Renaissance palazzo, and the background a jungle clearing with thatched roofs peeking out of the lush foliage. There was no doubt that the conception was inspired, something that Gauguin himself might have approved. But the technique . . . the coloration . . .!

'Blast and damnation,' Nigel muttered, crossing to the french doors and staring out at the snow-capped tops of Apuane Alps in the distance. 'Perhaps the critics were right after all. Perhaps I can't paint worth a tinker's damn.' Or then again, he thought, perhaps it's just that I've been so upended by this Ghirlandaio business that I can't concentrate on anything at the moment.

He surveyed the garden below where James Dearing had been summarily dispatched only yesterday by a myrmidon's spear. The body, of course, was gone, but the fallen statue still lay on its side where the police had left it when they lifted it free of Dearing's corpse. It was the gardener's responsibility, of course, to see to its being returned to its pedestal; but, knowing Italians, that might take a week or more. The inquest into Dearing's death, on the other hand, was scheduled for tomorrow, on Friday morning at nine. In a bizarre twist of the usual pattern, Italian justice was moving more swiftly and efficiently than Italian restoration work. But what most surprised – and alarmed – Nigel Harmsworth was that the coroner should be holding an inquest at all. That Dearing's untimely demise was a tragic accident was obvious to everyone. Why should there even *be* an inquest?

It was not the result of the inquest, however, that Nigel feared. What frightened him was *who* would be there – for the man, Dearing's accomplice, who had come prowling around the villa at midnight and whom Nigel had run off with a few well-placed rounds from an old Lee Enfield rifle would doubtless be sitting quietly in the gallery, watching Nigel's every move, weighing his every word, silently plotting the revenge he intended to take for his friend's death.

Nigel shuddered.

He was doomed. The man – *men*, perhaps: for there might be others – knew where he lived, knew where to find him. They could pick him off at their leisure. And there was nothing he could do to protect himself, to strike back, because he had no idea who *they* were. He was a goldfish in a bowl – a sitting target. All he could do was wait.

He turned back from the window into the room. It struck him suddenly what a remarkably odd room it was, even for a painter. His large easel and a folding table spread with paints, thinners and a jar full of brushes stood in a lavish Polynesian setting that appeared to have been transported from the South Pacific, as if by magic, and dropped into the middle of an otherwise conventional Italian villa. The furniture was rattan with bright floral-print cushions, the matting on the marble floor was of woven reeds, and there were primitive artefacts – conch shells, a pile of coconuts, a three-pronged fish spear, several wooden masks and religious amulets – scattered about and leaning in corners. On the walls hung reproductions of Gauguin paintings: Tahitian women on a verandah, others with mango blossoms, a dark-skinned nude on a bed staring up fearfully as if at the apparition of Tupapau, the Tahitian Spirit of the Dead. Desiring to imitate Gauguin, Nigel had surrounded himself with the symbols – as many as he could conveniently obtain – of things like those that had once inspired Gauguin himself. As he grew older his imagination needed to be jump-started, and so he had decorated his studio in order to reproduce the atmosphere, the tropical ambience, of a Gauguin-esque paradise: it helped, he found, to concentrate his energies. There were, however, no naked native girls. He had considered hiring some locals with exceptional tans to play the role but decided against it since their presence might divert rather than focus his attention.

He had chosen to imitate Gauguin, not because he was a primitivist but because he was, in Nigel's view, the last great classicist – an artist who strove above all else for harmony and balance in his compositions and who struggled, against the post-Impressionist tide, to centre his vision on the expressive power of the human form. The old masters – Titian, Michelangelo, Leonardo – would, Nigel felt certain, have applauded the effort, would have praised Gauguin's desire to keep humanity and a human interest at the centre of his art. And that was the genius – for it *was* a kind of genius – in Nigel's own conception of an *Annunciation* in the manner of Gauguin. Like the Renaissance painters, Gauguin was the instrument of a revelation, religious in its own way, of a lost paradise recovered in the innocence and purity of a simple people, unspoiled by civilization and urban culture. There was a certain irony, therefore, in the choice of Botticelli's ornate humanist canvas as his model instead of a simpler, more transparently religious treatment of the same theme by Fra Angelico or Lorenzo di Credi – but then Nigel was partial to irony. It kept even the intelligent spectator on his toes and put those who missed the point, of course, quite firmly in their place. Yes, there was a good deal to be said for irony.

He stood back, arms folded on his chest, and considered the half-completed painting on the easel. He pursed his lips and tilted his head thoughtfully to one side. He stepped closer, then moved back again to consider it from a distance.

Yes, it had power. It had strength and grace. He'd overreacted a moment ago when he'd thrown his brush down and wondered why he'd ever been fool enough to become a painter. The colours were wrong in places of course – yes, he'd been perfectly right about *that* – but the conception itself was solid, and the execution of the two figures – the Virgin abashed yet regal and aloof, the angel submissive yet commanding – was subtly rendered and evocative. There was no doubt that it had real potential, that it was better, *much better* than anything he'd painted in a long time: that it was destined to become, indeed, with some reworking, his masterpiece.

He felt the winds of promise stirring in him and picked up his brush. He'd start with that background foliage behind the angel. The greens were too dusky, too *European*. They needed more vitality, more of that sun-tempered lemony gloss that one finds in tropical vegetation . . .

He took up his palette and, mixing yellow into the green, began to paint.

He didn't know how long he'd been working when he felt, rather than heard, the presence of another person in the room behind him. Remembering the incident of the midnight intruder, he wheeled around, his heart in his mouth, ready for anything.

In the doorway, grinning, stood Dickie Danvers.

'You old sod,' Nigel breathed, blowing out his cheeks, 'you

frightened the life out of me. How long have you been standing there?'

Sir Richard shrugged. 'Long enough,' he said with a wry smile, 'to warm myself in the flames of inspiration at work. Just like the old days, Nigel, eh? Ah, I remember them well! The creator's at his easel and all's right with the world.'

Nigel shook his head. 'Be serious, Dickie. You never painted a stroke more than you absolutely had to,' he observed, dropping his brush into a jar of turpentine and wiping his fingers on a paint-stained rag. 'You were always too busy making money.'

'True,' Sir Richard conceded. 'A hit, Nigel, a very palpable hit – as somebody in Shakespeare once remarked. Yes, I've always much preferred selling other people's inspiration to suffering its lamentable effects myself.' He looked around in mock horror, affecting to notice the room for the first time. 'But what in the name of all that's sacred have you *done* to the place? It looks like some rum dive in the tropics, old man. I leave you in charge of a perfectly respectable two-hundred-year old villa and you turn it into some sort of native shanty. Not what I'd call gratitude. Not at all.'

'Gauguin,' Nigel said, as if the name explained everything.

Sir Richard shuffled across the room and stood, hands on his hips, in front of the canvas on the easel. He looked, Nigel thought, frail and frightful, one foot already in the grave. Since they'd last seen each other – what was it? a year ago? a year and a half perhaps? – age had reduced his old friend to a walking skeleton. It was like being in the presence of the Grim Reaper himself. Lord, it was hard to believe, although he'd aged himself over the years of course, that they were separated by only nine months in age. His own descent to the inevitable grave, however, was being managed with considerably more grace and dignity.

Sir Richard considered the painting for a moment, then his lips cracked and he let out a wheezing cachinnation as if a salmon bone had lodged in his throat.

'Botticelli,' he said gleefully, recognition suddenly dawning. 'Why, you sly old dog, Nigel. A Tahitian *Annunciation*! Clever – very clever indeed.' He stroked his Vandyke beard in that meditative way he'd had as long as Nigel had known him and was silent for a long moment, bringing all his critical faculties to bear on the canvas. 'Capital,' he pronounced finally. 'One of your best, I think. Yes, splendid. You'll have no trouble selling it when the time comes.' He added: 'But the colours are wrong. There, for instance, in the Virgin's dress,' he said, pointing, 'that blue needs to be more blunt, more – what's the word I want? – more *primal*. You'll see to it, I expect.'

Nigel nodded. 'Of course,' he said, wishing he'd been working on the dress instead of the background foliage when Dickie had appeared. 'I felt the same thing myself.'

'Well now . . .' Sir Richard said, stepping back and looking his old friend up and down. They had known each other for over fifty years, had worked together as close associates for almost as long. 'You look tip-top, old fellow. Yes – yes, fit as a fiddle. Damn good to see.'

There was an awkward pause.

'And you?' Nigel ventured cautiously. 'How have you been?'

It was a perilous business to invite a hypochondriac to discuss his health – especially an ageing and obviously decrepit hypochondriac, where there was at least a fifty-fifty chance that the reality and imagination of serious illness had come to coincide.

Sir Richard shook his head. 'Not what I was,' he said lugubriously. 'Touch of emphysema, I'm afraid,' he said, tapping his chest. 'Ticker's not good either.'

'So, you've given up smoking then?'

'Crikey, no!' Sir Richard spat. 'That *would* kill me for sure. I'd sooner give up an eye.'

Nigel bit his tongue – then, hoping to divert the conversation into other channels, he asked:

'You came alone?'

Sir Richard was looking at the painting again. 'No – no, Molly's with me. She's in the kitchen mixing up one of my potions. She keeps me going, you know. Don't know what I'd do without the dear old girl.' He turned and took Nigel by the elbow. 'It's bloody good,' he said, nodding toward the canvas, 'bloody good indeed. It'll fetch a handsome bid, I'll wager. Well over a thousand quid, I should think. I'll handle the sale myself, naturally. *But change the blue in that dress first.* Now,' he said, his voice taking on a hard edge, 'tell me about this Dearing character. I want to know everything. We can talk in the library.'

Together, like an old man and his older father, they made their way along the echoing corridor. As they walked, Nigel detailed, as he had done once for Inspector Bonelli (only this time leaving nothing out), the fateful chronology of events on the morning of James Dearing's unexpected arrival at San Felice: his bluster and threats, his knowledge of the Ghirlandaio and a number of other forged paintings, his concealed Beretta pistol, his insufferable insolence, his sudden and deeply satisfying death.

Sir Richard sat rigidly in a wingback chair several sizes too large for him and listened, nodding occasionally, his face otherwise a stony mask.

'There can be no doubt then,' he said, when Nigel had finished, 'that he knew everything.' It was a statement, not a question. Sir Richard was a pragmatist where money was concerned.

Nigel could only concur. 'No doubt at all, I'm afraid,' he said.

Sir Richard pursed his lips. 'And this other chap,' he said, 'the one who came prowling around last night, was Dearing's accomplice you think?'

'No other reasonable alternative suggests itself.'

Sir Richard nodded. 'Quite,' he said. 'And he spoke, you say, with an American accent?'

'Yes.'

Sir Richard was lost in reflection for a moment, then, having reached a decision, he leaned back and steepled his fingers on his bird-like chest. 'So what are our options?' he asked rhetorically. 'First, of course, we must find out more about this second American. I've a shrewd idea already who he is – or at least who sent him. Matajcek is looking into that end of things in New York and he'll have something for us, I expect, by the end of the week. In the meantime, we'll dig up what we can here: check the hotels and villa rentals in the area – that sort of thing. Americans stick out and he has to be holed up some place. Once we have a clearer picture of what we're up against, we'll know how to deal with it. But as I see it, in the end we'll have only two options: a soft sell and a hard sell.' His voice took on a chairman-of-the-board tone. 'First, we try and buy him off. If he's working alone, we can be fairly sanguine, I think, about our prospects. I have money and a good deal of clout in the art world. He can't out-bluff me and he can't outflank me. If he tries, I'll use my influence and connections to expose *him* as a fraud attempting to destroy the reputation of a respected art dealer and connoisseur. The press will eat him alive. I'll explain this to him, naturally, and I expect he'll be reasonable in the end about a settlement.'

'And if he's *not* working alone?' Nigel hazarded. 'If the Mafia, for example, are involved?'

Sir Richard shook his head. 'They're not,' he said, smoothing down his beard. 'But even if they were, it wouldn't raise insurmountable barriers. The mob cares about three things: money, power, and image. For the right price and a little grovelling at the feet of the right people, even they can be bought. Honour among thieves, you know, and all that.' He gave a crooked grin. 'I know a few of them, as it happens. We belong to the same yacht club.'

'And if he – or they – *won't* be bought off, what then?' Nigel enquired. 'What's the hard-sell option?'

'We eliminate the problem at its source.'

'You mean *kill* him? Or them?' There was disbelief in Nigel's voice.

'Look,' Sir Richard said, leaning forward, 'death is never a pleasant alternative but it's sometimes the only solution. I have too much invested in keeping this Ghirlandaio thing quiet to fret about the odd corpse lying about. And so, my friend, do *you*. Think about it, Nigel; think about it carefully: prison – degradation – humiliation – never seeing the sun again. Think about it for ten minutes and you'll see that I'm right. We buy the enemy off or we take him out: those are our only choices. I won't hesitate for a moment to contract out for a murder or two if it means saving my own skin – and neither, if you think about it,' he added, indicating the luxury around them with a sweep of his emaciated, claw-like hand, 'will you.'

'Perhaps,' Nigel said, 'it won't come to that.'

'Perhaps not,' Sir Richard agreed; 'but, then again, it might. So my advice to you, old son, is to get used to the idea while the getting's good.'

Sir Richard had spent so many years abroad, in the United States especially, that he had acquired the irritating habit of interlarding his speech with Americanisms. The effect, on Nigel's sensitive and discriminating ear, was like hearing a Bantu tribesman, trained in an Oxford college, dropping into his English the odd click or grunt from his native language.

Molly DuBartas, Sir Richard's nurse, appeared in the doorway carrying a silver tray with cups, a teapot, a bowl of indigestible-looking white paste, a pitcher of low-fat milk, and a plate of buttered scones with honey.

'Ah!' Sir Richard groaned, collapsing into his chair with the air of a martyr. 'My farina.'

Nigel rose and took the tray. Molly, he couldn't help noticing, looked stunning. Nearly thirty years younger than her employer, she was in her early forties and had aged remarkably well. Oh, Nigel remembered how he had envied Sir Richard in the old days when he and Molly, then barely twenty and just out of nurses' training school, had started living together. He had lain awake at night imagining their love-making. He'd have sold his soul to have found her first and made her his – and even now, so powerful are the unfulfilled passions of youth, he still felt the same way.

'You look fetching,' he muttered in her ear, stooping to take the tray, 'as lovely as ever.'

'And you, Nigel,' she retorted, her words retaining the nasal inflection of her native tongue, 'have aged. How have you been?'

Molly was a Breton and a Huguenot and didn't mince her words.

'Well enough, I suppose,' he said, deflated. 'Fair to middling.'

He set the tray on the table and Molly handed Sir Richard his bowl of wheat germ and poured their tea.

'You should try one of these scones, Dickie,' she said. 'They're delicious. Freshly baked this morning.'

'What are you trying to do?' he snapped. 'Shorten my days?'

'On the contrary,' she said tartly, 'I'm trying to prolong them. If you'd eat some real food for a change instead of that muck you insist I make you, you'd live to be a hundred.'

'It's precisely because I *do* eat it,' he snarled, 'that I *will* make it to a hundred.'

'We'll see about that,' she said, biting into a honey-drenched scone.

They might as well, Nigel thought, have tied the knot formally. They bickered like husband and wife. But Dickie had never wanted marriage. He didn't want to be legally obliged to look after anyone. When he died, he said, he was taking everything with him. There had to be a way and he intended to find it.

They ate without speaking, only the monotonous ticking of the gilt bronze cartel clock above the mantel breaking in on the silence of their private thoughts.

Was Dickie *really*, Nigel wondered, prepared to kill if necessary in order to protect the secret of Ghirlandaio's daughter . . .?

2

The inquest into the death of James Douglas Dearing, late of New York City in the United States of America, took place in a bare courtroom at the Pretura, a heavily grilled palazzo in Piazza

Guidiccioni. A railing divided a small public gallery consisting of five rows of wooden chairs from the coroner's bench and the witness box at the front of the room. As a visiting official, Arbati took a seat beside Giancarlo Bonelli on the padded bench to the left of the coroner and directly opposite the witness box. It gave a superb view of the proceedings and allowed him to see, as well, both everyone who came in through the door at the back of the room and the faces of those seated in the chairs behind the wooden railing.

Arbati wasn't quite sure why he was there. Perhaps it was because he had nothing in particular planned for that morning and was at rather a loose end for something to do to fill the time. Perhaps it was simply out of curiosity, because of what Giancarlo had told him about the case over dinner in the Antica Locanda. Death by art was an intriguing notion, to say the least. Perhaps it was just because he was a detective and, try as he might, he could never seem to leave the Questura entirely behind him, even on vacation. And perhaps, he thought with a mental shrug, it was finally a subtle combination of all three motives. In the end it didn't really matter. He was an interested spectator, nothing more. It wasn't his jurisdiction – or, for that matter, his headache either.

One by one, the witnesses and other interested parties filed in and took their places: two elderly men, one apparently on his last legs, accompanied by an attractive middle-aged woman in a nurse's uniform; the American who had avoided Arbati in the lobby of the Universo and whom he'd seen again at dinner in the restaurant; an older woman, sharp-featured and hawk-eyed, carrying a furled umbrella (which meant she was English) and a wicker shopping basket; and, at the last moment, a gorgeous blonde wearing dark glasses who slipped unobtrusively into the back row of seats just as the coroner rapped sharply with his pen to bring the court into session.

Arbati nudged Bonelli. 'Who's the old gent with the Vandyke?' he whispered.

'Sir Richard Danvers,' Bonelli muttered back. 'He owns San Felice, where the death occurred. The man beside him is Nigel Harmsworth, the one who toppled the statue.'

'Danvers . . .' Arbati mused. 'Of Danvers' House Auctioneers?'

Bonelli nodded. 'The same.'

Interesting, Arbati thought. Death by art at the estate of a well-known dealer in art and antiquities. Yes, very interesting. Sir Richard was a wealthy and influential man and there were dark rumours about how he'd made some of his money, although nothing had ever been proved against him. Danvers' House had auction rooms in a luxurious palazzo in Viale Matteotti in Florence, not far from the Questura, which Arbati had visited occasionally. Only to look, unfortunately; never to buy. The prices were well beyond a humble policeman's salary.

'And the elderly woman?' he asked.

'Cecilia Hathaway,' Bonelli whispered back. 'Harmsworth's neighbour – and a bit of a busybody.'

'I've seen the American around. An odd fellow. What's his connection to all this?'

'The dead man's cousin,' Bonelli replied, 'or so he says. His name's Morgan, a lawyer from Philadelphia. He was expecting Dearing and, when he didn't show up, came along to the Questura to report him missing. I've interviewed him once. There's something dodgy there, but I can't put my finger on it. Wait until he takes the stand, you'll see what I mean.'

'And the girl at the back?'

Bonelli craned to get a better look. 'Don't know,' he said. 'Never seen her before.' He gave an elfish grin and wiggled his eyebrows. 'Wish I had though. She's a knockout.'

The coroner, Dottore Bindi-Santi, a large florid man with fleshy features who wore a monocle on a black ribbon which kept falling out and having to be replaced, rehearsed the formalities of the court and called the first witness.

Detective Giancarlo Bonelli took the stand and was sworn in. In economic language, devoid of sentiment or embellishment, he described the call that had taken him out to Villa San Felice on the date in question and what he had found there. When he had finished, he waited patiently until Bindi-Santi laid down the fountain pen with which he was making notes and looked up.

'And have the police,' the coroner enquired, 'been able to trace the ownership of the Beretta pistol in the possession of Mr Dearing at the time of his death?'

'The gun was not registered in Italy, *dottore*. Unfortunately, we have no way of tracing it.'

'It was manufactured in Italy,' the coroner said rather testily.

'Yes,' Bonelli explained, 'made here and exported, then brought back into the country by means and persons unknown.'

'Presumably by the deceased in an illegal manner, you mean.'

'*Possibly* by Mr Dearing, yes,' Bonelli corrected him patiently. 'But possibly also by someone else.'

'I see.' The coroner rubbed his heavy chin. 'And this hire-car – the, ah . . . Maserati – it was rented in Florence?'

'Yes. Three weeks ago. Under the name of Martin James Peterson.'

'And have you, inspector, managed to locate this Mr Peterson?'

'No, sir, and we are unlikely to be able to do so quickly. Both the passport and the credit card used for the rental transaction were forgeries. We thought at first that the name Martin Peterson might have been an alias employed by the deceased, but our enquiries in New York, via Interpol, indicate that to the best of their knowledge Mr Dearing did not use an alias. We're working on the assumption, therefore, that there is a second person involved – that Mr Dearing had a partner.'

'Whose identity is still unknown?'

'That is correct.'

'But you're working on it,' Bindi-Santi observed caustically, quite enjoying the spectacle of himself keeping Bonelli on the ropes.

'Yes, sir. We're still working on it.'

'I see – yes.' The coroner made an ostentatious jotting on the page in front of him.

Arbati watched this charade with a mixture of pity for Giancarlo and contempt for the pompous coroner who was taking such obvious delight in his own wit and acumen. No detective of his acquaintance would have handled an interview so crassly, but it was clear that the inquest was, in Bindi-Santi's view, largely an opportunity for him to parade himself to advantage in public. The elderly woman – Miss Hathaway – noticed it too, and disapproved. It was evident in the rigid line of her jaw and the little muscle trembling at the corner of her mouth. She might be a busybody, Arbati thought, but she's an intelligent judge of character. He found himself warming to her immediately.

'Now,' Bindi-Santi resumed, setting down his pen and squinting pontifically through his monocle, 'about this scrap of paper found in the pocket of the deceased. It contained, you say, only the single word *Ghirlandaio*. What do you make of that, inspector?'

'It may be relevant,' Bonelli said, 'or it may not. At this point it's impossible to say. It might be no more than a note to remind himself to see the frescos in the duomo. Anything I might say about it would, at this point, be purely conjectural.'

'But you're working on it,' Bindi-Santi said in a snide tone.

'We're in the process of following up all our leads,' Bonelli replied evenly, 'and that is one of them. I have the feeling it may prove to be an important one.'

'But you can't say why.' A sarcastic statement, not a question.

'Not at the moment, no.'

'Well, it seems to me, Inspector Bonelli,' the coroner said, heaving himself back in his chair with a theatrical sigh of exasperation, 'that the police have rather a lot of work still to do on this case.'

'It seems indeed,' Bonelli agreed, 'that we do.'

'Very well then, inspector,' Bindi-Santi said with an airy wave of his hand, 'you are dismissed. I have no more questions.'

Bonelli left the stand and took his place on the bench beside Arbati. 'Christ!' he muttered under his breath. That expletive seemed to Arbati, too, to say it all.

The next witness called was Nigel Harmsworth, who gave his evidence in clipped, precise phrases in a rather bookish Italian. What struck Arbati about the scene, however, was not the spoken language but the unspoken body language that went on in the courtroom during his testimony. Sir Richard Danvers sat smiling darkly to himself, drinking in every word and taking, apparently, a bleak and sadistic satisfaction in the details of Dearing's death. Peter Morgan's face, on the other hand, was expressionless and revealed nothing of his thoughts – but his dark eyes never once, Arbati noted, left Harmsworth's face: the American was intent and totally focused, oblivious to all around him, like a cat stalking a canary. Harmsworth himself, despite an unruffled exterior, was sweating bullets: his eyes flickered back and forth between the coroner and the American as if he were following the ball in an imaginary tennis match. He was the helpless canary, limed on a limb, who *knew* he was being stalked. And then there was Miss Hathaway: she too had picked up the signals between Harmsworth and Morgan and she had fixed the American with a cold, narrow, Medusa-like stare that would have unmanned a fighter pilot. There was real hate in that gaze, and it was prompted, Arbati suspected, by something more than a passing or merely neighbourly affection for Nigel Harmsworth. Only mothers and those in love are capable of generating such passion.

Arbati, quietly vigilant, was the watcher of these watchers. It was a position in which, over the years, he had often found himself. Watching came naturally to him and he'd become something of an expert in reading the moods and thoughts of people too preoccupied with themselves to be aware of the existence of others. It was an ability that had served him well in more than one investigation. Heard melodies are sweet, ran a line in a poem he'd once read, but those unheard are sweeter. As with melodies, so it was too, he'd often discovered, with thoughts: not always sweeter perhaps, they were certainly more revealing than the imprecise and often deceptive words employed to cloak them. During Harmsworth's testimony, there was more meaning in the silent messages passing between the participants than there was in anything spoken aloud in the court – and Arbati, unobtrusively observant, heard it all.

'You say, Signor Harmsworth,' the coroner said, furrowing his heavy brow, 'that Mr Dearing was unknown to you and that you have no idea why he drove all the way out to San Felice to see you? I find that very strange.'

'I can only repeat, m'lord,' Nigel said, 'what I have already said. The man was, and still remains, a stranger to me. I had never seen him before. He had no time to unfold his business before the unfortunate accident occurred.'

'Whether or not Signor Dearing's death was accidental,' Bindi-Santi unctuously reminded the witness, 'is the purpose and prerogative of this court to determine.'

'Yes, m'lord.'

'And do you not find it odd, Signor Harmsworth,' the coroner said, picking up the thread of his argument, 'that the deceased should have been armed with a pistol when he came to visit you?'

'I do indeed, m'lord. I find it quite remarkably odd and utterly inexplicable. It is not, you understand, something I would do myself. I have always been rather fearful of firearms and prefer not to have them about.'

Several other equally inane questions followed from Bindi-Santi, succeeded by equally urbane and polished answers from the witness, and then Nigel was excused and Peter Morgan took the stand and was sworn in. In the case of the American, who spoke little Italian, the services of a translator were required, and a heavily built woman who could have been a lorry driver was summoned from the corridor outside where she had apparently been waiting.

'I see from your deposition,' Bindi-Santi said, addressing Morgan, 'that you are the deceased's cousin.'

'Yes, your honour.'

'And by profession, you are a lawyer?'

'Yes. From Philadelphia.'

At the word *Philadelphia* Sir Richard Danvers, who had seemed to be dozing, gave a sudden start and his eyes flew open as though he'd received an electrical shock. Arbati noted the reaction with interest. What was so special about being a lawyer from Philadelphia? Curious – very curious indeed. And another curious thing: ever since the American had taken the stand, the mysterious blonde at the back, who had so far taken no interest in the proceedings and might have been in the wrong room but too embarrassed to make a scene by leaving, was suddenly alert and attentive. Since she was wearing dark glasses, Arbati couldn't see her eyes, but there was something in her manner, something in the way she sat forward perched on the edge of her chair . . . They're lovers, he thought suddenly – and no doubt *she's* the cause of the tension I noticed the other night at dinner between Morgan and his wife. Additional food for thought. Yes, there was more to this case, more by a long shot, than met the eye at first glance.

Bindi-Santi went instantly and ineptly for the jugular. 'What,' he demanded portentously, 'did your cousin, the deceased, drive out to San Felice to discuss with Signor Harmsworth?'

'I haven't the faintest idea,' Morgan said calmly.

'You – well, I . . . er . . . Explain yourself, sir!' the coroner blustered, stymied.

'Certainly,' Morgan replied suavely. It was apparent that he was more at home in a courtroom than the flustered coroner. 'Jimmy Dearing,' he began, 'was a cousin – a second cousin, in fact. On my mother's side. Not a close relation, you know, but you do what you can when it's family. Anyway, my aunt telephoned me from the States to say that Jimmy was coming over and asked me to keep an eye on him. If you know anything about him, you'll know that he's had a rather chequered career, as one might say, and hence the call from my aunt. She was worried about him. I agreed to see him, to do what I could, and arranged to have him meet me at the Hotel Universo two days ago. I waited in the room all afternoon and, when he didn't show up, I went to the Questura and reported him missing. It was the responsible and logical thing to do.'

Arbati listened to the story carefully – and his antennae were on full alert. There was something wrong, something slightly off-centre. Maybe it was the *too* polished delivery, maybe something in the man's self-confidence, verging on arrogance, that warned him to be suspicious. Morgan was a crafty customer, and his story, Arbati sensed, was a tissue of ingenious fabrications. He didn't know *how* he knew this: it was only a hunch, nothing more – an intuition. But he *knew* he was right. He'd interrogated too many criminals over too many years not to know the difference between innocent truth and clever prevarication. Yes, Giancarlo was right about the American: there was something dodgy – and something, too, downright *dangerous* – about the man.

Bindi-Santi, sensing nothing except his own discomfiture, blundered mercilessly on. 'And he didn't tell you, when you were talking to him, why he was coming to Italy? I find that hard to believe, Signor Morgan.'

'The arrangements were made through my aunt,' Morgan replied. 'I never actually spoke with Jimmy himself – so, no, I don't, as it happens, have any idea why he was coming.'

'None at all?'

'None whatsoever,' Morgan replied definitively.

'Was your cousin in the habit of carrying an unregistered firearm?' the coroner asked hopefully.

'Your honour, I was as shocked and dismayed by the discovery as Mr Harmsworth here. If I had known, I'd have made him get rid of it, naturally.'

Relentless in self-destruction, Bindi-Santi insisted on posing several more questions, depressing further still the value of his already-deflated inquisitorial stock, before he could finally bring himself to dismiss the witness and call a half-hour recess to consider his decision. He needed no time to render a judgement: the only possible verdict, given the evidence, was death by accidental means. He needed the time to salvage what he could of his bruised vanity.

Outside, while they waited for the court to reconvene, Bonelli leaned against one of the black Carabinieri Fiats parked in the piazza and lit a cigarette, offering the pack to Arbati.

'Well,' he said, 'what do you think?'

'I think,' Arbati said, tapping out a cigarette, 'that you're looking at the tip of a very large iceberg.'

As the inquest was dragging its weary length along at the Pretura, Willi Kleist Junior was nervously pacing his room at Tenuta del Colombo in the hills beyond Bagni di Lucca, psyching himself up for the encounter with his father. He hated his father. Willi Senior was everything Willi Junior wasn't but wanted to be: big, strong, athletic, handsome, rich, and sleeping with Ilse – the last item being a private fantasy that Willi Junior had masturbated himself raw trying to imagine for himself. One afternoon when he'd heard them rutting behind the closed doors of their bedroom, he'd run downstairs and, in a fit of pique and despair, thrown open the door to his father's laboratory, leaving the butterflies inside free to escape. It had made him feel better for a while, but only marginally so. There was no lasting pleasure in striking out anonymously at his father; what he really wanted was to *be* the man he had learned, dreaming of Ilse, to envy and loathe.

Now, however, he had an idea. Something more subtle and satisfying than the blind rages and impotent furies that were his usual response to his own inadequacy. But in order to pull it off, he needed his father's help. Not that the old man would actually *know*, of course, that he was helping his son into bed with his own wife. But that was the genius of it, the thing that brought a grim smile of satisfaction to Willi Junior's pouty lips whenever he thought of it: his father was to supply the means of cuckolding himself. Nemesis was what the ancient Greeks called it – at least, if his memory of the course he'd once taken in Sophoclean tragedy was accurate, that was what they called it. Yes, he thought darkly, *ich werde die Nemesis des Altes sein*, I'll be the old boy's nemesis.

That thought was the spur he needed to prompt him to action. He ran a brush through his lank, stringy hair that never quite did what he wanted it to and made sure his shirt was tucked in all the way around – Willi Senior was a Tartar for neatness – then locked his door and pocketed the key. He'd locked his bedroom door since he was twelve years old: the secrets inside were *his* secrets and he intended to keep them that way. There was a hamper for dirty clothes in the hall outside and every Monday he stripped and made his own bed, leaving the soiled linen outside his door. Nobody but Willi Junior himself ever entered the room. It was an asylum from pain and humiliation, a refuge from the realities of life. It was the amniotic sac he wished he'd never left.

He descended the stairs and shambled, his hands in his pockets, across the terrace toward his father's greenhouse-laboratory. Dieter and Dietrich – *die schwachköpfigen Zwillingsbrüder*, as he called them, the nerd twins – were refighting the battle of the Kursk salient and were so engrossed in the task of blowing up Russians that they didn't notice him pass. No one, in fact, ever seemed to notice him unless for some reason he was brought to their attention. It was one of the many gripes he had against the world.

He opened the greenhouse door and stepped inside. His father was at the desk bent over the binocular eyepiece of his Leitz microscope, his spectacles stuck on top of his head where they were out of the way. Around his immobile form, blue butterflies fluttered in the foliage like scraps of wind-tossed silk, pausing to rest, then rising again to the secret rhythm of some atavistic impulse stored in the blueprint of their genes. The place had the hushed, somnolent air of a library reading room, the only audible sound the low distant hum of the generator that kept the temperature and humidity inside the greenhouse at a constant level.

He closed the door softly and advanced across the tiled floor, standing for a time unnoticed and unheard beside the hunched figure of his father. Finally, as if reluctant to intrude, he asked:

'What are you working on?'

'Ah, Willi!' his father said, looking up. 'I didn't know you were there.'

'I just came in. I wondered how your work was going.'

Willi Senior gave his son a quizzical look. It was unusual for Willi Junior to show any interest in entomological research. The subjects of Willi Senior's study were typically dismissed by the members of his family as *die Wanzen Vaters*, Dad's bugs.

'Fine,' he said, a little sceptically. 'Very well, actually.'

'What are you doing, exactly?' Willi Junior asked. 'I mean, what's the project you're working on at the moment?'

'Well,' his father replied, trying to keep the explanation simple, 'I'm examining the internal structures of larvae that were isolated and fed on a high-nitrate diet. I want to see if there's any mutation or visible deterioration of organ function.'

'Sounds interesting,' Willi Junior said, leaning over the microscope. 'Can I have a look?'

'Yes, of course,' his father said, surprised, pleased. 'Certainly. By all means.' He rose and let his son take his place. 'What do you see?'

'A long white squiggly thing.'

'The intestine,' Willi Senior said. 'What you're looking at is a longitudinal section of larval abdomen.'

'Great.'

'Let me show you something else,' Willi Senior said, removing the glass slide and placing another under the lens. 'We'll need to

127

jump the magnification for this one,' he added, adjusting the instrument. 'Now, have a look at that.'

An oval image of browns and reds, like the pattern in a kaleidoscope, filled the eyepiece.

'Wow!' Willi Junior breathed. 'That's really something. What is it?'

'A transverse section of larval thorax. Sort of a *CAT* scan for caterpillars. The colours are metachromatic dyes injected before dissection to highlight the organs.'

'Neat. What's the red blob in the middle?'

'A cross-section of the heart.'

'*Klasse!* This is great stuff, Dad.'

Before he knew it, Willi Senior had shown his son a dozen or more slides, flattered and delighted by his interest. Perhaps, he thought guiltily, he'd been too hard on the boy, too rash and harsh in his judgement of him. Maybe there *was* something there after all – some potential, some spark of hope that he'd find a vocation and start a life of his own.

'You know, Dad,' Willi Junior said as his father removed the slide of an adult male Blue Morpho's brain, 'I was wondering if photographs of these slides – you know, blow-ups made right through the microscope – would help you with your work? Then you wouldn't have to keep changing slides and resetting the magnification levels all the time. You could line the pictures up on a table all at once and compare them.'

Willi Senior walked blindly into the trap.

'I suppose so,' he said, rubbing his chin. 'Yes, it might be quite useful. Why do you ask?'

'I was thinking,' Willi Junior said, 'of taking up photography. I'd need your help, of course. Not much at first. Just a camera and some developing chemicals. I've been reading up on it and it sounds like it might be just the line of work for me. I could start with portraits and that sort of thing, and maybe start a little business when we get home: weddings, graduation photos, stuff like that. It would get me out on my own, earning my own keep.' He knew all the right buttons to push. 'Gradually,' he enthused, 'I could work my way up to the fancier stuff: close-ups, filters, special lighting. There are a lot of good jobs in medical pho- tography and I'd be able to help you with your research. I'd really like that.' He paused fractionally, then said earnestly, 'What do you think?'

'It sounds expensive,' Willi Senior said sceptically.

'Not really, Dad. Not at the start. I know exactly what I'd need. I've researched the whole thing very carefully.'

And he had, too. He knew precisely the equipment required for the job. The Maxxum 700si camera he had his eye on was fully automatic, functioned in low light without a flash, and was virtually silent in advancing the film from frame to frame. It was pricey, but it was also the perfect tool for his purpose. Moreover, his bedroom was set up for immediate conversion into a dark-room: he'd cleared the desk in readiness for the trays of developing fluids and put an infra-red bulb in the overhead fixture. All that was left – the only remaining obstacle – was the money needed to purchase the camera and supplies.

That hurdle did not remain an impediment for long.

After twenty minutes of pleading, promises, and intense cajoling, he left the greenhouse with a smile on his face and a cheque for a thousand Deutschmarks burning a hole in his trouser pocket.

When she'd left the cottage at eight that morning, she had been quite certain that there would be rain. There was a certain heaviness in the atmosphere that infallibly in her experience – well, *almost* infallibly – foretold the coming-on of rainy weather. But when Cecilia Hathaway emerged from the Pretura after the inquest, the sun was shining and there wasn't a solitary cloud in the sky.

She shrugged and put the furled umbrella under her arm. Better safe than sorry. *Semper paratus*, she reminded herself, always be prepared – and, adjusting her sun-hat on her head, she set off at a brisk, businesslike pace across Piazza Guidiccioni in the direction of Via Fillungo.

Nigel, of course, had been completely vindicated. The coroner – pompous fool though he was – had returned the only verdict possible in the circumstances: death by accidental causes. Yes, it was a relief that Nigel no longer had the threat of criminal prosecution hanging over him. He could put the unfortunate incident behind him now and get on with his life. At least, she *hoped* he could – but she was worried. That American, the dead man's cousin, was up to no good. He was a smarmy weasel if ever she'd seen one – and he was, too, she'd sensed, a desperate and dangerous man. There was a dark fury, a *thwarted greed*, somehow – though she didn't know what it meant – bubbling under the smooth surface of his spurious calm. And Nigel, she knew, was terrified of him: she had seen it in his eyes, in his nervous, skittish movements. Yes, Peter Morgan was someone to be watched, and watched very closely indeed.

The shops along Via Fillungo were doing a thriving business and the pavement was crowded with eager shoppers, anxious to disburden themselves of travellers' cheques in exchange for shoes, jewellery, and crafted leather handbags. The photographic supplies shop, however, was empty when she entered its dark interior. The proprietor was behind the counter polishing a large and doubtlessly criminally expensive telephoto lens with a lint-free cloth. He looked up hopefully when the bell over the door tinkled.

'Ah, *signora!*' he said, laying aside the lens.

Cecilia opened her bag and took out her purse. 'Is my photograph ready?' she asked.

'*Ma, certo, signora,*' the man replied. 'Your name again is . . .'

'Hathaway. Cecilia Hathaway.'

'*Ma sì,*' he said, tapping his forehead. 'I should have remembered.'

He hunted through a cardboard box of labelled folders, removed a thin envelope and passed it across the counter to her. 'That will be four thousand lire, please,' he said.

She counted out two two-thousand lire notes.

He said: 'It is a strange picture, *signora.* I couldn't help but notice.'

'I'm rather a strange woman,' she replied with an enigmatic smile, replacing her purse and turning away toward the door. '*Grazie, signore.*'

'*Prego, signora,*' he said, a look of baffled wonder spreading over his face.

At the door, she nearly bumped into a large, shambling youth, his eyes bright with purpose, who brushed past without seeing her in his haste to get inside. He would surely have run her down had she not, in a quick-footed manœuvre, nimbly evaded his headlong progress. He was, she noticed then, the same boorish individual who'd been pricing cameras the last time she was in the shop, and this time he was clutching a large wad of bills ostentatiously in one pudgy paw.

'More money than good sense!' she muttered, stepping out into the street and closing the door firmly behind her.

Once outside, she tore open the envelope and removed the single photograph it contained: a picture of a man straining at a large fallen limb and, behind him, a white Alfa Romeo saloon with the licence plate clearly visible: LU 889456.

'Heavens above!' she breathed, hardly able to believe her eyes.

The man in the photograph was Peter Morgan, the American lawyer, Dearing's cousin.

It took a moment for her brain to assimilate the information, then she stuffed the photo into her handbag and started off, her mind reeling, down Via Fillungo toward Piazza Napoleone. She shouldn't have been surprised, of course – not after the hostility toward Nigel she'd seen radiating from Morgan during the inquest. No, she should have been prepared. Still, at first, it had been a shock.

But what did it mean?

It meant in the first place, she reflected, gathering her thoughts, that everything she'd sensed about Peter Morgan was perfectly accurate. He was a thoroughly nasty piece of goods – an evil and unscrupulous character. In the second place, it meant that Nigel, who was afraid of him, was in serious trouble of some sort and, quite possibly, in serious danger as well. Peter Morgan, she judged, was the cold, calculating type of desperado capable of almost any monstrous act, even murder. Like Poirot, Cecilia had an instinct for these things.

The question was: What should she do with the information she possessed? How could she best use it to help Nigel? For she *was* determined to help him . . .

She decided to mull it over, since it was nearly one o'clock, while she ate lunch. She was beginning to feel peckish and they did a nice Milanese cutlet, she remembered, at that little outdoor café in the corner of the piazza. What was it called? Stella Polare: that was it. Yes, she'd go there.

It was barely a two-minute walk and the place, when she reached it, wasn't crowded. She ordered inside, then took a seat outside under the awning where there was less commotion and where she could watch people passing in the piazza. She enjoyed people-watching: seeing how they dressed, what shopping bags they carried, guessing where they were from and how they earned their living. They never seemed to notice people sitting in res-taurants looking out at them and, as a result, acted in perfectly ordinary, unselfconscious ways. It was rather like looking in from outside on a human aquarium.

As she settled into her seat and looked around, she noticed, at another table further down, Inspector Bonelli and the other detective who had been at the inquest. It was not, however, as a policeman that she knew Inspector Bonelli's companion. To her, he was Carlo Arbati, the poet, and she had recognized him from the photograph on the jacket of his book the first moment she'd set eyes on him that morning at the Pretura. He was a policeman too, of course; she knew that much about him. No one, unfortunately, could make a decent living nowadays simply being a poet. But she preferred to think of him as a weaver of words rather than an unraveller of crimes. It gave him more dignity; it placed him in a cultured, more refined perspective.

What were they talking about, she wondered? Were they discussing the inquest they'd just left? – or a new volume of poems that Arbati was working on? – or perhaps what he was proposing to say in his acceptance speech at the awards ceremony next Friday? It was interesting to speculate, to imagine. As she watched them, it struck her again, as it had in the courtroom, what a pleasant and genial man Arbati looked to be. Such a sensitive, intelligent face, and so warm and open a smile!

He happened at that moment to turn his head and their eyes met. Although he didn't know her, he smiled and gave a brief nod, and she turned away in embarrassment and confusion. It was one thing to spend an idle moment watching people; it was quite another, thank you very much, to be caught in the act of actually doing so.

Her discomfiture was relieved in the same instant, mercifully, by the arrival of her food. The white-jacketed waiter placed before her a plate containing a breaded cutlet and small green salad, a glass and a half-bottle of sparkling water. She never took wine with lunch; invariably, though she was fond of it, it upset her digestion in the middle of the day.

'*Altro, signora?*' the waiter enquired.

'*No, va benissimo,*' she said, opening the napkin on her lap. '*Prendero un caffè dopo.*'

'*Sì, signora.*'

As she ate, she debated what to do about Nigel. It was an awkward situation. She should, she knew, show him the photograph and tell him how she had come by it. Then, at least, he'd know what he was up against. But she had a feeling that he already knew more than enough about Peter Morgan: how else could she explain the cat-and-canary looks they had given each other during the inquest? Besides, Nigel had been acting quite remarkably oddly since the accident. He'd grown moody and

132

withdrawn, and she was uncertain how he might respond to her 'meddling' (as he would doubtless construe it). And then there was the problem of Sir Richard Danvers. She had been disturbed to find, when she'd arrived at the court that morning, that he was now on the scene. Nigel, presumably, had called him down from London, since Sir Richard owned the property on which the accident had occurred. But no good could come of it. She had met Sir Richard once, years ago, at a party in London and had disliked him intensely – an emotion which she had every reason to suppose had been fully reciprocated on his part. He was a mean-spirited and self-centred cad with – she was certain – a black streak of flat-out dishonesty running right down the middle of his blighted personality. Oh yes, it had been a mistake to summon Sir Richard. It was like inviting Attila the Hun to a *fête champêtre*. He was bound, sooner or later, to start butchering the men and abusing the women.

She decided, finally, that she had no option but to withhold the photograph from Nigel. It pained her, but there was really, in the circumstances, no alternative. Which left her still with the problem of what, precisely, to do about it herself . . .

And then she knew: quite suddenly and decisively, she *knew*.

Her coffee arrived and she bolted it down with an unseemly haste. There were things to find out, arrangements to be made. Yes, there wasn't a moment to be lost!

She rose to depart.

'*Buon giorno*, Signorina Hathaway,' said a voice at her shoulder.

It was Inspector Bonelli and Carlo Arbati, just leaving themselves. In her excitement, she hadn't noticed them approaching.

'*Buon giorno*, inspector,' she replied.

'Permit me,' Bonelli said, 'to introduce an old friend. Detective Inspector Arbati, from Florence.'

'A pleasure, inspector,' she said, extending her hand. 'Indeed, a very *distinct* pleasure since you are also Carlo Arbati, the poet.'

'Oh,' Arbati said, slightly abashed, 'do you know my poems?'

'Quite intimately, inspector. I own copies of both *Fòglia di luce* and *Tommaso incredulo*. I am also, as it happens, a member of the committee that recommended you receive this year's gold medal – an award which, if I may say so, you most richly deserve. I was perfectly delighted when I learned that you had agreed to come and accept it in person. We are greatly honoured.'

'The honour, Signorina Hathaway,' Arbati said, reddening, 'is entirely mine.'

133

'How very kind of you to say so,' she replied, flattered. 'Well, I expect we'll be seeing rather a lot of you, inspector, over the next few days. I must say I'm looking forward to the awards night and your talk. We feel it was rather a coup getting you to come, you know. I trust you won't disappoint us.'

'I trust not,' he rejoined with a grin.

They walked in together to the cashier to pay their bills.

'You will, I imagine,' Bonelli said, turning to Cecilia, 'be relieved by the coroner's verdict. I know that Signor Harmsworth is a close friend.'

'Very relieved indeed, inspector,' Cecilia replied, 'but I think the matter is far from being closed – and so, I believe, do you. Now, if you will excuse me, gentlemen,' she said, retrieving her change and returning it to her purse, 'I have rather a pressing engagement. Good day to you both.'

'A strange lady,' Bonelli observed as they crossed Via Veneto to the Questura.

'A clever and determined lady,' Arbati suggested, 'and a lady, I'd say, on a mission. I'd keep an eye on her, my friend, if I were you.'

3

The camera was a great success. In the three days he'd owned it, Willi Kleist Junior had shot off seven rolls of film, mostly inside buildings in poor lighting conditions. He wanted to test its capabilities and be absolutely certain that, when the time came, there'd be no surprises for him of a technical nature. He would, he knew, only get one chance and he couldn't afford to mess up. There was no margin for error, no second kick at the cat if he blew the first one.

And the camera had performed magnificently. Exactly as the man who'd sold it to him had promised, the Maxxum 700si was fully automatic and completely idiot-proof. It metered the light and set the lens aperture automatically, adjusting both to the speed of the film loaded in the camera. All the operator had to do was point and shoot. A complete klutz could get perfect pictures every time – an important consideration given that Willi Junior was, as klutzes go, pretty well as close to being complete as human nature allowed. Mechanical contrivances were enigmas to him – Rosetta Stones with moving parts – and he normally did his best to avoid them. But the Maxxum 700si was different. It made him feel, for the first time in his life, that he had real power in his hands, that he had control of his fate and the future. It was better than owning a gun. And, he thought with a grim smile, it was just as lethal too, in its own way.

Having nothing better to do with his time, and wanting, as well, to test his new toy under the most gruelling conditions he could imagine, he had spent the morning photographing the inside of a cave in the Garfagnana, using *ISO* 1000-speed film and only the light from a sealed-beam torch for illumination. The results were beyond his wildest expectations. The prints that emerged when he swished the exposed paper around in the developer were detailed and crystal-clear, as if they had been taken in broad daylight. He didn't care about the pictures themselves – boring shots of jagged rocks – but only about their *quality*. And the quality was superb: every bump and crevice looked as if you could reach out and touch it.

I'm ready, he thought proudly. I'm ready whenever I get the green light.

He stood in the middle of his bedroom at Tenuta del Colombo like a paratrooper awaiting the jump-signal, his face bathed in the eerie shadows cast by the red dark-room light above his head. Around him were the weapons of his trade: on the desk, trays of developer, bleach, fixer, and stabilizer; on a table, the old enlarger he'd picked up at an auction sale he'd seen advertised in the paper; on his bedside night-stand, a half-dozen books on the art of photography and film development; on cords strung around the walls, damp prints of the interiors of dark churches and gloomy public buildings hung up with plastic clothes pegs to dry. The photographs of the cave by torchlight had been the final test. He didn't know what conditions he might meet when the time came, but they couldn't possibly be worse than that. He had put the camera through its paces and come through with flying colours. And now, he knew, he was ready.

The telephone rang.

He did not rush to answer it. His father was in his laboratory; the nerd twins were on the terrace blowing up Russians. Ilse was alone in the house. He waited until the instrument stopped ringing, then, when he was sure she'd answered it, he picked up the receiver and, holding the plunger down with his finger, let it up slowly so that it made no noise, no crackle or click on the line that would attract her attention and warn her off. Then, holding his breath, he pressed the earpiece to his ear and listened.

'. . . *free this afternoon?*'

A man's voice, speaking in English.

Willi Junior smiled a crooked smile. It was the call he had been waiting for. Thankfully, every German schoolboy learned enough English to get by in the language. If the call had been in Italian, he'd have been in trouble; but the caller spoke English – and the voice, he was certain, was the same one he'd heard the last time.

'*What time?*' Ilse's voice.

'*Say, about three? The usual place.*'

A pause, then Ilse's voice again: '*Okay, fine. I'll be there.*'

There was a click and the line went dead.

Willi Junior replaced the receiver and his smile broadened.

'Showtime!' he grinned.

He dressed in dark clothes and a pair of rubber-soled shoes, then put a new roll of film in the camera and slung it around his neck. There was no hurry. It was just past noon. He had almost a three-hour head start. He didn't know how he was going to do it; all he knew was that, come hell or high water, he was determined to find a way. He just had to get there and then play it by ear.

He skipped down the stairs into the front hall. He could hear Ilse singing to herself in the kitchen, sounding happier than a married woman meditating adultery had any right to be.

'I'm off into town for the afternoon,' he called.

'Be back for dinner at eight,' she called. 'It's the twins' birthday, remember, and your father expects you here.'

'I'll be back,' he said, his hand on the knob, 'and I'll be hungry.'

The knock on the door was unexpected and Bunter, asleep by the hearth dreaming his doggy dreams, scrambled to his feet as if he'd been prodded by a hot iron.

At the sink in the back kitchen, Cecilia was potting out fennel seedlings she intended to grow indoors over the winter and heard nothing. Fennel was her preferred treatment for indigestion and, while most of her herbs were dried and stored in labelled jars in a large cupboard outside the sitting-room, she liked her fennel fresh. It was, she had discovered, more effective that way. She was humming to herself and looked up with a smile when Bunter appeared in the doorway.

'What is it, boy?' she asked, wiping a stray wisp of hair from her eyes with the back of her arm. 'Do you need to go out?'

'Aaarrgh!' Bunter replied, dancing, his nails clicking on the tiles.

'All right then,' she said. 'I'm just coming. Be patient.'

'Aaarrgh! Aaarrgh!'

The knock sounded again, more loudly, and this time Cecilia heard it too.

'Well now,' she said, wrinkling her brow, 'I wonder who that could be?'

She pulled off her rubber gloves and slipped the heavy canvas apron over her head. She was expecting no one. Had she ordered something from town and then forgotten about it? No, not that she could recall.

She paused in the hall and straightened her skirt in the mirror, taking the time to run a quick hand through her hair. Goodness, she thought, I look a frightful sight!

'Well,' she told Bunter, 'whoever it is will just have to take me as I am.'

She opened the door and looked out.

'Nigel,' she said, her face lighting up, 'what a pleasant surprise!'

Bunter saw matters differently. His ears had fallen and he was emitting a low, ominous rumble from deep in his throat. Left to his own devices, he'd have made short work of the old man. There was bad chemistry between them and there had been right from their first meeting.

'Do come in,' Cecilia smiled. 'I've been wondering how you were getting on since the inquest. Oh, Bunter, *do* behave yourself. Nigel is a friend.' She turned back to Nigel. 'Everything *is* all right, I trust?'

'Yes, fine – fine,' he said with forced jocularity, keeping a wary eye on the brindled Cerberus blocking his path. He disliked dogs on principle. This one he detested with passion. 'Actually,' he said, 'I've been feeling rather guilty, I must confess, about the way I've treated you since this dreadful Dearing business began. It's rather put me off my stroke, I'm afraid. In short, Cecilia, I've come to apologize.'

'You poor, dear man,' she said, her heart melting. 'There's no need for that, I assure you. Now, do come in. I'll fix us a nice pot of tea.'

She led the way to the sitting-room, a cosy enclave of chintz upholstery, matching curtains, and framed prints of pastoral landscapes. A glass-fronted bookshelf contained a cosmopolitan mixture of titles in English, Italian and French, in addition to bound translations of Dostoevsky, Cervantes, and the inevitable Ibsen. On the mantel over the fireplace stood an elegant pair of Staffordshire figurines and a fine reproduction of an eighteenth-century bracket clock. The window was open and a soft breeze from the garden stirred in the petals of a vase of freshly cut roses, filling the room with their sweet fragrance.

'Just make yourself comfortable,' she said. 'I won't be a moment. There are copies of *Punch* and the *Times Literary Supplement* there on the table.'

'I'll be fine,' Nigel said, sitting. 'You run along. I'll find something here to occupy me.'

Bunter stood at the end of the sofa glaring at him with distrust and transparent loathing. He had stopped his guttural rumble in obedience to his mistress's command but reserved the right to maintain the intimidation factor with narrowed eyes and raised hackles.

'Goodness!' Cecilia said beaming, still unable to quite believe her eyes, 'but this *is* a pleasant surprise.' It was the first time in the nine years she'd known him that he had ever dropped in on her unannounced. How very sweet and thoughtful of him! 'Well,' she said, collecting herself, 'I'll be right back then. Bunter, you come with me.'

'And I'll still be here,' Nigel said with a smile. 'Don't worry.'

In the bright, yellow-trimmed kitchen, she put the kettle on and took down the teapot, then set out a silver tray with a lace mat and her best cups and saucers. As an afterthought, she arranged a small plate of Peek Frean assorted biscuits, which she kept in a sealed tin for special occasions. Her heart was light and she felt almost like singing. I'm acting like a lovesick schoolgirl, she thought with a silly grin. But she didn't care: she was content with the moment – even though it wouldn't, alas, last forever. She'd overcome her disappointment on that score years ago. At least, she was quite certain that she had. Nigel was a friend and there was nothing more in it.

The kettle began to whistle and she let it come fully to the boil, enduring its shrill screech, before taking it off and heating the pot, then pouring the remainder of the liquid over the tablespoon of leaves that she placed in the bottom. Good tea required the water at precisely 212 degrees Fahrenheit and not a fraction of a degree lower.

When she returned to the sitting-room, Bunter did not accompany her. He had been sent to his mat for the duration of the visit. Nigel was leafing through a picture magazine and he rose gallantly, offering his assistance, when she appeared in the doorway.

'Thank you,' she said, allowing him to take the tray. 'Just there on the table will do nicely.'

He deposited it on the table she'd indicated in the middle of a group of comfortable wingback chairs, then took the seat opposite her.

'Milk?' she asked, pouring.

'Please,' he said. 'A little.' He leaned forward and took the offered cup. 'I was just reading,' he said, 'while you were making the tea, about Africa. An article on the nomadic pygmy hippo of the Serengeti. Fascinating business.'

'Central Africa,' Cecilia said firmly, 'is a part of the world I should never care to visit. As far as I can ascertain, it's all tall grass, swamps, and tsetse flies. Not my sort of place at all.'

'I rather fancy you're right,' Nigel said, adding in self-defence, 'though it's tolerable enough in magazines and on the telly. But one needn't trouble going oneself, of course, if David Attenborough is prepared to do so for one and report back.'

'An altogether superior arrangement,' Cecilia agreed, setting down her cup. 'I was surprised,' she said, changing the topic and attempting to keep her voice as neutral as possible, 'to see Sir Richard at the inquest. Is he stopping long at San Felice?'

'It's hard to know,' Nigel said with a shrug. 'He thought he should put in an appearance since the accident had occurred, after all, on his estate. Apparently there was some question, too, of an insurance claim. The Americans, it seems, are particularly swift to launch liability suits. How long he'll stay, of course, is anyone's guess.' He added, 'I wasn't aware, actually, that you knew Dickie. I take it then that you've met?'

'Yes, at a party once,' she remarked rather coldly, 'many years ago. It was not, I must confess, a particularly pleasant experience.' She reached forward and took a cream biscuit with a raspberry jam centre. 'For either of us,' she said.

'I'm sorry you didn't get on,' Nigel said – adding reflectively, 'Dickie can at times, I know, be a quite difficult personality.'

Which, Cecilia thought, was putting it very mildly, all things considered.

'Indeed,' she agreed.

They sat in silence for a time, each thinking his own thoughts.

'I was wondering – ' Cecilia began, reviving the conversation.

But just then the telephone sounded in the front hall. 'Well, the thought will keep,' she said, rising. 'Excuse me, Nigel. I won't be a moment.'

She did not receive many calls and she was quite certain she knew in advance who would be on the other end of the line this time. It would be her friend Adriana from the Motor Licence Bureau in Palazzo Ducale. She had expected her to call before now, but the information Adriana was hunting out, quietly and as a personal favour, must have been more difficult to obtain than anticipated.

When she reached the telephone, she lifted the receiver and, putting a hand over the mouthpiece, said aloud: 'Hello? Yes, but I can't talk now, I'm afraid. I have someone with me.' She uncovered the mouthpiece and said softly, *'Pronto.'*

'Sì,' she said, listening. *'Ottimo!* Just let me jot that down.'

What she wrote on the pad at her elbow was: *Peter Morgan. Via Giuliano, 17. San Leonardo.*

'Mille grazie, Adriana. Ciao.'

At last, she had what she needed. San Leonardo was a village at the foot of Monte Pisano on the far side of Lucca. The house would not be hard to find. Now she was ready; now she could act.

She depressed the plunger with her thumb, breaking the connection, then said aloud: 'That will be fine, *signora.* Ring me next week and we can arrange a time. Yes, thank you. Goodbye.' Then she replaced the receiver and, slipping the paper securely down the front of her dress, walked back to the sitting-room. She had already decided at lunch in town the day of the inquest to act without telling Nigel what she was doing, and she still thought it by far the best course. She would work better alone – without distractions, without objections.

'Sorry for the interruption,' she said, taking her seat. 'It was a lady who's making me a set of bedroom curtains. She wondered when it would be convenient to bring them round.'

'Ah!' Nigel intoned melodramatically, 'the multitudinous minutiae of our daily lives!'

'More tea?' she asked.

'Yes, please,' he said, passing the cup across. 'You said as the telephone rang that you were wondering about something. You've rather piqued my curiosity. Do you remember what it was that you were about to ask?'

'Certainly,' she replied, 'I was wondering how you were getting on with that painting you showed me the cartoon for. An *Annunciation*, as I recall, in the manner of Gauguin. I thought it a splendid and most original notion . . .'

Over a second cup of tea, they talked about Nigel's painting and discussed her plans for the reception following the literary awards at Teatro del Giglio – for Cecilia was chair of the committee in charge of the event – and then Nigel, looking in mock horror at his watch, rose to take his leave.

'It has been a most exquisite pleasure seeing you again,' he said, touching her hand to his lips in that old-fashioned way he had. 'I trust that all is forgiven, and I promise faithfully that I shall not be so uncivil to you ever again in the future.'

'You old tease,' she said, reddening, 'there never was anything to forgive. As you well know.'

She walked him to the front door.

'I hope, by the by,' she said, holding it open, 'that you *are* planning to attend this year's awards ceremony. The committee has worked hard to put on a first-class show, and it just wouldn't be the same without you.'

'My dear lady,' he replied with a flourish, 'I never miss a gathering of artists. Wild horses would not keep me away.'

'Until Friday night, then,' she said.

'Until Friday night,' he replied.

When he had gone, she closed the door and leaned back against it dreamily. We could, she thought, have been very happy together if fate had only sorted the cards differently. But that was not to be, she knew, and there was no point in bemoaning the ifs and might-have-beens that life had never offered except in imagination. She gave a shrug, then gathered up the tea things, returning with them to the kitchen where Bunter waited, his tail churning, glad that they were alone together, just the two of them once more.

There were a dozen or so passengers on the platform waiting to board the train for Viareggio when Arbati arrived at the station at twenty minutes to ten. He intended to spend a quiet day alone on the *lungomare*, away from distractions, reading his Umberto Eco novel and making notes for his talk to the Società delle Arti on Friday. He would build the talk, he had decided, around the challenges facing the poet in an age when prose fiction is the vogue and poetry has largely fallen into disfavour. What was it that motivated a poet to spend hours on end in his room polishing verses when there was no prospect of financial reward – or even, in most cases, a measure of recognition – for his labours? The answer, of course, was a sensuous love of language and an irrepressible drive to discover and express the *essence* of experience, to capture the evanescent moment and distil its meaning into memorable and evocative images. He knew pretty well what he wanted to say but he still needed two or three quiet hours to lick it into final shape. It wouldn't, he thought, be a difficult task, and he was rather looking forward to it.

Among his fellow passengers on the platform, he noticed, was the family of the American lawyer from Philadelphia. What was the man's name? – Morgan, that was it: yes, Peter Morgan. The woman was attractive, in her late thirties perhaps, fair-skinned in the way that Americans are or, at least, appear to southern Europeans to be. She was carrying a beach bag with the tip of a yellow towel peeking out of the top. The boy – about sixteen, Arbati judged – was a handsome lad with long blond hair and the body of an athlete. He was spinning a volleyball on the tip of his index finger in the way Arbati had once seen a visiting troupe of black basketball players do. His dark-haired sister, slightly younger, was lost in the world of her Sony Discman. Her eyes were closed and she was swaying rhythmically to the beat of an unheard band mixing their magic through her stereo headphones for her alone. They were, he thought with a twinge of envy, an idyll of the best that twentieth-century civilization had to offer: an ordinary family off on its way to an ordinary day at the beach. Morgan himself, their father, was nowhere in sight. And there was nothing ordinary, Arbati reflected, recalling the inquest, about Peter Morgan: on the contrary, there was something sinister about him, some dark and nefarious purpose that oozed through cracks in the polished veneer of his personality and spread down out of sight to corrupt the hidden depths of his soul. Had the other members of his family, Arbati wondered, seen it too? – or were they, like other families he'd encountered in his work, innocently blind to the demon lurking on their doorstep?

Morgan's wife interrupted the thought by looking up at that moment and catching Arbati's eye, then looking quickly away as if she'd been caught with her hand in the cookie jar. How strange, Arbati thought: there was recognition in that glance. He furrowed his brow. I know who she is, of course, because I saw her with her husband at the Antica Locanda, *but how does she know who I am*?

She wasn't at the inquest, after all. It was strange – yes, very strange indeed.

He shrugged and let it go. It didn't really matter and, in any case, he had other things to occupy his mind.

The tannoy speaker overhead crackled, and a muffled, tinny voice sounding as if it emanated from the bottom of a petrol tank announced: 'Treno per Viareggio, La Spezia, Genova, e Torino in arrivo sul binario cinque.' The train pulled in, powered by overhead wires, and eased to a stop. The automatic doors hissed open. Five or six disembarking passengers descended and then those waiting on the platform began to board. Once aboard, Arbati walked the length of two carriages looking hopefully for an empty compartment but found none and settled finally for one containing a soldier in shirt-sleeves and an old gentleman impeccably attired, as if on his way to a wedding or a funeral, in an immaculate three-piece suit. Neither paid Arbati the slightest attention as he slid the door open and joined them.

After only a minute or two, the train eased forward, gathering speed, and soon they were flashing through the countryside, the imposing bulk of Monte Pisano rising on their left. Arbati crossed his legs and watched the passing scenery. The trip to Viareggio was under half an hour. There was no point in trying to get into his novel: Umberto Eco's dense prose required more than a twenty-minute train-ride to begin to unravel into sense.

The trip went quickly and the train, like a winded sprinter, coasted into the station at Viareggio and rolled to a stop. Taking down the overnight bag containing his book, sunscreen and bathing towel, Arbati descended to the platform and made his way out into the street. Viareggio was a holiday town – a place of sun and sand, of gaudy libertà villas, of beach umbrellas and fluttering flags. Running north from the town for perhaps thirty kilometres was the Tuscan Riviera, a narrow strip of coastal plain lined with bathing establishments sandwiched between the blue Mediterranean and the snow-streaked marble flanks of the Apuane Alps.

In no hurry, he wandered up the esplanade past art nouveau villas and the garish fronts of competing gelaterie, taking in the sights, soaking up the atmosphere of the place. There were people and cars everywhere and the sun beat down from a cloudless, copper sky. Roller bladers in spandex shorts wove in and out of pedestrians strolling along the esplanade and a pair of girls on bicycles sailed sedately past, a small dog yapping their approach from a wicker basket on the handlebars. It was noisy, it was gaudy, it was (he had to admit) even rather tacky in a way; and yet he'd always had a special place in his heart for Viareggio: it was too full of life and splendid, innocent fun to dismiss it, as some were quick to do, as just another lamentable modern instance of *haute vulgarisation*.

At a seaside resort called Guido he turned in and rented an umbrella and beach chair, then changed into his bathing trunks. Once on the beach, he rubbed his skin until it glistened with a UV sun-tanning lotion, then opened his Umberto Eco novel and settled back to read. Now *this*, he couldn't help thinking, is living: the sea at my feet, the mountains at my back, the sun on my chest, a book in my hand, and not a blessed care in the whole wide world.

He didn't know how long he'd been lost in his reading when a shadow fell across the pages of his book. He looked up.

'Hello,' said the woman standing above him. 'You don't know me but I'm Penny Morgan. If I'm not mistaken, you're Carlo Arbati, the poet, aren't you?' She spoke in a lilting Italian tinged with the soft drawl of her Virginian background.

'I am,' he said, lowering his book.

'I recognized you from your picture,' she said – then added in explanation, 'the one here on the jacket.' She held out at arm's length a copy of *Tommaso incredulo* and went on, sounding slightly flustered: 'I noticed you, actually, at the train station in Lucca. I have to confess that I've been following you ever since, hoping to work up enough nerve to ask you to sign it for me. You must think me very forward.'

'Not at all,' Arbati said, sitting up. 'I'd be delighted.' He had only his towel and tanning lotion with him and he gave a comically forlorn look around at the empty sand and said, 'I hope you had the foresight to bring a pen for me to do it with.'

'Yes, there's one in here somewhere, I'm sure,' she said, fumbling in her bag as if afraid that he would disappear before she could find it.

Arbati smiled to himself. It never ceased to surprise and embarrass him the way people became tongue-tied and agitated in the presence of a writer, although he'd certainly never thought his talents entitled him to any special consideration. 'You should have asked me to sign it at the station,' he said. 'It would have saved a lot of trouble. I don't bite, you know.'

'Of course not,' she said, reddening. 'It's just that – well, to tell you the truth, you're the first real live author I've ever met. I thought you might be tired of having silly sallys chasing you down for your autograph.' She fished the pen up from the depths of her leather shoulder bag. 'There!' she said triumphantly, holding it out. 'I knew it was in there some place.'

Arbati took the offered pen and opened the copy of *Tommaso incredulo* to the title page. 'It's *Penny* Morgan, is it?' he asked, to be certain. 'As in "A *penny* for your thoughts"?'

'Yes, that's it,' she said. 'You know, I really do appreciate this, Signor Arbati – ' She stopped suddenly, fearful of having made a gaffe, and said in a worried voice: 'It is proper to call a poet *signore*, isn't it?'

'Well, yes,' he said, handing the book back with a smile, 'but there's no need to be so formal. Especially out here. The beach is a place for casual wear, not for tuxedos. You can call me Carlo and I won't be offended. In fact, I'd prefer it.'

'That's very gracious,' she mumbled, looking down at the sand with a pleased smile.

'And you won't mind then if I call you Penny?'

'Yes – no – of course you may – I mean, I'd be flattered.'

There was a sweetness in her confusion that reminded him of Cordelia Sinclair, the American girl that he'd come within an ace of asking to marry him. Penny Morgan had the same reticence and vulnerability, the same grace and fragile beauty that had drawn him to Cordelia. Was there some fatal attraction about Americans, he wondered? – or was it just that he needed a break from Umberto Eco's labyrinthine prose and, as a result, welcomed her timely interruption? Whatever the cause, he realized suddenly that he wanted her to stay.

'I was just about to order myself a drink,' he found himself saying. 'Perhaps I can offer you something?'

'Oh, no,' she said quickly, 'no, thank you very much. I'd be imposing. It's very kind of you to offer but I've taken too much of your time already.'

'On the contrary,' he said, 'it would give me great pleasure if you stayed. And besides,' he added with a sly grin, 'I'm intrigued to know what possessed you to bring along one of my books for a day at the beach. It seems a remarkably odd choice of leisure reading, at least to me.'

He stood and offered her a chair.

'You're quite sure . . . ?' she said hesitantly.

'Perfectly,' he replied, nodding. 'To tell the truth, I'd far sooner talk to you than be forced back to my novel. It's rather boring and

I was getting tired of it. Poet's honour.' He crossed his heart with a melodramatic flourish.

'Oh, all right,' she said, laughing. 'A Campari on the rocks, if I'm not in the way.'

The silver tinkle of her laughter reminded him again of Cordelia.

He summoned a waiter and ordered their drinks. 'Now,' he said, when the waiter had gone, 'you were about to tell me how you happened to be carrying one of my books around in your beach bag.'

'Well,' she replied, 'as it happens, it's hardly accidental. I brought it along with me to *study*. I'm planning to attend the literary awards night at Teatro del Giglio – I've been planning to go, in fact, since the day the posters went up – and I'm reading your poems in preparation.' She gave him a disarming smile. 'I'm getting to know them pretty well too, you know,' she said. 'You can even ask me questions if you want.'

'I don't think that will be necessary,' he countered with a laugh. 'And if you've been, as you say, *studying* them, it might well prove an embarrassment for *me*, because I'm not sure I remember some of them all that well.' He added, wrinkling his brow: 'What strikes me as odd, though, is that you're an American – '

She nodded. 'From Virginia, although I live in Philadelphia now.'

'So how is it,' he went on, 'that you come to be interested in Italian poetry?'

'Oh, there's nothing very mysterious about it,' she said, feeling more and more at ease with this charming man whom only moments ago she had considered distant and olympian and had had to screw up her courage even to approach for an autograph. 'I majored in modern languages when I was at college and Italian was my special study.' She gave a self-deprecating grin. 'That was quite a few years ago now, of course, and I'm afraid my skill with the language isn't what it used to be – as you've undoubtedly noticed.'

He had, a little, but he let it pass.

'And poetry?' he asked. 'What attracts you to poetry in the age of the mystery novel and spy thriller? It's not something most people have any interest in reading nowadays.'

'Well, I'm not most people, I guess,' she replied with a grin. Then she went on, her eyes lighting up suddenly: 'Poetry has been a passion with me for as long as I can remember. I even thought

146

at one time that I wanted to become a poet myself. I dabbled at it for years, but then one day, perhaps foolishly, I sat down and read over everything I'd ever written and – well, let's just say that it was a pretty devastating experience. I haven't written a line since. But at least,' she added in a deft and gentle compliment to Arbati's achievement, 'my failures taught me to appreciate other people's successes. I know good poetry now when I see it; and I know, too, what goes into making it.'

The waiter arrived with their drinks and they sat for a time in companionable silence, sipping and watching the sun glinting like a tray of diamonds on the wave-tops rolling in toward the shore.

'And what is it,' Arbati asked eventually, reviving the conversation, 'that brings you to Italy now? Not poetry, surely.'

She shrugged. 'No. A vacation – at least that's what it's supposed to be. I'm here with my husband and two children. Those are the kids over there,' she said, pointing, 'Chad and Brooke.'

Arbati followed her finger to a blue-and-orange beach umbrella on the far side of the café. Brooke was slumped in a chair, her feet propped up on the table bobbing and tapping to the beat of her Sony Discman. Chad stood to one side watching a group of teenagers, two or three years older than himself, who had set up a net on the sand and were playing a heated game of volleyball. The girls were bare-breasted and Chad's eyes were popping out of his head. His father's genes, Arbati thought laconically, remembering the ravishing blonde who had turned up at the inquest to keep an eye on Peter Morgan.

'Chad is sixteen,' Penny said, 'and Brooke a year younger. We've been pretty much on our own, the three of us, since we arrived. Peter – that's my husband – was supposed to be sharing the time with us, but he's always away at meetings . . . or doing other things. So we've had to make our own fun without him.'

The fractional hesitation in her voice told Arbati everything. She knew, or at least she suspected, that her husband was having an affair and was confused and deeply hurt by his betrayal. If she had been a European, instead of an American, she'd probably have taken the matter more in her stride. But he understood the cultural environment she'd grown up in and his heart went out to her.

'So it hasn't,' she concluded glumly, 'been much of a family vacation after all. Not really.'

The shouts and youthful enthusiasm of the volleyball game reached them across the sand like sounds from another world.

'Tell me about your husband,' Arbati said. 'What does he do?'

The question was out almost before he realized it. What was he doing, he wondered? But he knew the answer to that question: like a good detective, he was prying loose information. Once a cop, always a cop. The Dearing case, of course, was Giancarlo's, not his – and really, he had no business getting involved, even on the periphery: it wasn't his jurisdiction or his problem. But he couldn't help himself. And there was something more, too, something beyond mere professional interest that lay behind his probing issues that were none of his concern. Instinctively, he liked and admired this woman – her frankness, her sweetness, her vulnerability: so different in every way from her husband's dark and secretive guile – and he wanted, in some deep and hopelessly chivalric way, to help her if he could, to protect her somehow from the fate he feared lay waiting in store for her when the truth about her husband finally came out.

'Oh, Peter?' Penny said. 'He's a lawyer.'

'Interesting,' Arbati said casually. 'Criminal law?'

Penny shook her head. 'No, corporate,' she said. 'Take-overs, taxation appeals – that sort of thing.'

'And he's working on something or other while he's over here, I gather,' Arbati prodded. 'You said he was away a lot of the time.'

'He wasn't supposed to be,' she said. 'This was just a holiday – or so the kids and I thought. But almost as soon as we arrived, Peter started making excuses and going off to meetings. I don't know what it's all about and he won't talk to me about it. It's something important, though, and it's eating at him. He's been a bear to live with, especially in the past week. I think the deal or whatever he's working on must have gone sour. Anyway, he bites our heads off if we dare mention his being away so much; so we just grin and bear it. There really isn't much else we can do.'

She had revealed more than Arbati had expected, and her openness had the effect of making him feel ashamed and guilty about the way in which he was abusing her confidence in order to find out about her husband's business dealings. He hadn't intended to distress her when he'd asked that first innocent question about what Peter Morgan did for a living, but now he was afraid he'd opened a Pandora's box of private recollections that could do no more than cause her pain, and he wished he could turn back the clock and unask the question. He should, he told himself, have had the good sense to leave well enough alone in the beginning.

'Well,' he said, steering for calmer waters, 'I'm sure it will all work out in the end.'

'I hope so,' she said, forcing a smile. 'I truly hope so.'

She was silent for a moment as if struggling with a difficult decision, then went on in a far-away voice as though communing with her own deepest fears: 'He's gotten himself involved in something he can't handle. I can feel it every time we're together. I don't know what it is, but I know there's something terribly, terribly wrong. He's afraid of something and he won't tell me what it is. Oh God, I want to help him, but I can't talk to him any more – ' She stopped abruptly and dug in her bag for a tissue. 'I'm sorry,' she said, wiping her eyes. 'I have no right to push any of this off on to your plate. You'll be sorry I ever came over and introduced myself.'

'Not at all,' he said with a fresh stab of guilt.

It was Arbati's turn to make a decision. He stared at the horizon where the sea and the sky came together in a narrow blue line, and revolved the choices in his mind. Finally he said:

'There's something I should tell you, Penny, although perhaps you know it already. I'm a policeman as well as a poet, and if you think there's anything I can do to help – anything at all – all you have to do is pick up the telephone and call me. I'm at the Hotel Universo, Room 209.' He put his hand on her arm and squeezed gently. 'I want you to promise me you'll call if you need me.'

When she looked up, her eyes were full of tears but they were tears of gratitude, not sorrow. She wasn't alone any more in a strange and foreign land. She had found a friend – or rather, a friend had found her.

'I promise,' she said, wiping her tears. 'Yes, I promise, Carlo.'

Willi Junior parked his battered Volkswagen in a cul-de-sac beside the Hotel Celide. The place was just beyond the city walls and it was inconspicuous. Since his car was easily recognizable – *ein verdammter Schandfleck*, his father called it, a damned eyesore – he'd put it safely out of the way where no one would notice it or, for that matter, ever think to look for it. Securing the Maxxum 700si around his neck, he locked the car and set off at a shambling gait for the centre of town. It wasn't far, a ten-minute stroll through Porta Elisa and along Via Santa Croce, then left down Via Beccheria for a couple of blocks.

Piazza Napoleone, when he reached it, was remarkably quiet: a few tourists strolling the cobbles with guidebooks and cameras, an orange *CLAP* bus that rumbled, spewing fumes, past the front of the Palazzo Ducale, a dozen pigeons strutting in circles under a row of huge plane trees in the misguided expectation of manna dropping from heaven to sustain them.

It was just past one o'clock when he turned under the awning-covered entrance and pushed open the glass doors of the Hotel Universo. He knew this was the place: it had to be. *The usual place,* the man on the telephone had said. It had to be the Hotel Universo because that was where he'd seen Ilse come out the day he'd waited for her in her car and she'd pushed him out when he'd accused her of having an affair. Yes, this was it all right. 'The usual place,' he muttered to himself, running the bitter euphemism over his tongue.

The lobby was empty. There was only the concierge, a middle-aged man with thinning hair, who stood behind the reception desk shuffling papers and generally making himself look busy. Willi Junior took a seat in one of the faded leather armchairs that dotted the lobby and settled in to wait.

What would happen, he wondered suddenly, if Ilse were the first to arrive and spotted him sitting there?

But *that* wouldn't happen, he reflected – no, not in a million years. Ilse never arrived early and never simply 'arrived' anywhere; Ilse *made entrances*. There was always a well-calculated sense of the dramatic about her timing: she made certain she was the last to enter and the first to leave a room so that everyone would turn and notice her. While Willi Junior tried to slink into rooms unnoticed, Ilse, afflicted with the vanity of the beautiful, made grand entrances and exits. Yes, she would arrive, as she always did, at the last minute.

After ten minutes, the concierge looked up and asked if he could be of service.

Willi Junior shook his head. 'No,' he mumbled sullenly in his fractured Italian, 'I'm waiting for somebody.'

The man shrugged and went back to his work, looking up every now and then with a raised eyebrow as if surprised and slightly annoyed to find him still there. Willi Junior ignored him. He fiddled with the knobs on his camera, played with his fingers, stared out of the window, put his head back and squinted at the fat cherubs on the ornamented ceiling. Time dragged by. No one came in and no one went out. There was only the eternal concierge, unobtrusively vigilant, hunched over his paperwork. Willi Junior shifted his position a dozen times, trying to get more comfortable, trying to make the time go faster with an illusion of activity; but nothing helped. The ticking of the grandfather clock set in a niche in the wall grew louder in his ear, until each mechanical *tick* and *tock* reverberated like a cannon shot in his brain.

He waited, fidgeting, for over an hour.

Finally, at twenty past two, the door opened. A man, tall and good-looking, wearing a red Lacoste shirt and dark glasses, entered the lobby and crossed to the reception desk. He walked straight past Willi Junior without even turning his head.

'Good day, Franco,' the man said to the concierge.

English.

Willi Junior's ears pricked up like antennae.

'Ah, Signor Morgan . . .' the concierge replied, looking up with a smile.

'A room for the afternoon, if you please,' the man said.

It was the same voice he'd heard on the telephone. Willi Junior's heart skipped a beat, then hammered in his chest like an Indian tom-tom. This was his man.

While the concierge turned away to fetch a key from the bank of pigeon-holes behind him, Willi Junior, moving at the speed of light, made a bolt for the stairs and scampered up, taking them two at a time and clutching the camera to his chest to prevent it from banging against something. At the top he ducked into a linen locker, leaving the door ajar so that he could see if the man went on up the stairs to the top floor. From his vantage point he had a clear view of the corridor stretching away to the rooms on the second floor.

He was still catching his breath when the man appeared at the head of the stairs and walked swiftly to the second door down from his hiding place. He didn't look around or even check the room number; he knew exactly where to go: the place was obviously familiar to him. He unlocked the door – and then he did something odd. Instead of simply going in and closing the door behind him, as Willi Junior expected, he stopped and took a match-folder out of his pocket, then bent it in half and stuck it across the latch cover to prevent the tongue from engaging.

Willi Junior grinned darkly from his retreat. *Ein Sonntagskind bin ich*, he thought, it's my lucky day! It would save him the

151

trouble of picking the lock – assuming, of course, that he was actually capable of doing so. He had the tools for the job in his pocket and he'd practised on the locks at Tenuta del Colombo; but given his lack of mechanical ability, there was still no certainty of success. Well, he reflected with satisfaction, none of that mattered now. The gods, it was clear, were smiling on him. And Willi Junior believed in the gods: powerful unseen forces had so often thwarted his desires when it was obvious no human agency could possibly be involved that he had come to accept their existence as axiomatic. It was pleasant, for a change, to have them on his side.

He waited five minutes, then crept along the hall and pressed his ear carefully against the door, making certain not to dislodge the match-folder. He could hear, muffled and in the distance, a high wailing sound as if someone were being crucified. What on earth was the man doing? Willi Junior wrinkled his brow. Was he *singing* . . .?

He pushed the door open an inch . . . then another . . . slowly, carefully, holding his breath, the blood pounding in his temples, expecting every instant to hear a shout and find himself running for dear life back along the hall. But there was no shout. There was only the dreadful caterwauling and, when he listened carefully, the far-off sound of running water. The man was in the shower. Willi Junior let out his breath with an audible sigh. Truly, the gods *were* smiling on him today.

'I can hear the drums, Fernando-ooo . . .' the man wailed.

There was no time to lose. Willi Junior slipped inside the room and replaced, as expertly as his trembling fingers allowed, the match-folder which had fallen to the floor. He needed a hiding place. He looked around. There was only one possible place: a huge wooden armoire with a full-length mirror on one of its double doors. It was massive and appeared to be solidly constructed: a perfect retreat. He pressed himself against the wall – he didn't know why; it just seemed the proper thing for an intruder to do – and eased his way, step by step, toward the concealing safety of the distant sanctuary. The wardrobe, thank God, was empty: just a few heavy-gauge metal hangers suspended at one end. He shouldn't have been surprised that it was empty, of course. The man had been carrying no luggage; there was nothing for him to hang up.

' . . . and see the firelight shining in your eyyyesss . . .'

Willi Junior stepped inside the cavernous shell and pulled the door closed tightly after him. There was no light and it was close and warm and woody, like being trapped inside a coffin. He almost panicked at the thought – but it was, after all, *only* a thought, only a silly and imaginary fear. He made himself be calm, made himself think of other things. Where was Ilse now? he wondered. He checked the luminous dial of his Tag Heuer watch – an expensive gift from his father on his eighteenth birthday. Two thirty: yes, she'd be on her way by now. Somewhere around Borgo probably, driving like hell as usual – and driving straight into the trap he had set for her. He smiled to himself in the Stygian blackness. Once he had pictures of them in bed together, once he had the *proof* he needed of her infidelity, he'd have her eating out of the palm of his hand. Then she could refuse him nothing – *nothing* – or else he'd take the pictures straight to Father and she'd be out on her pretty little butt, everything she'd worked and schemed so hard for up in smoke. Yes, soon – very, *very* soon – he'd have her right where he wanted her.

The pipes banged, the water stopped, and soon he could hear the man moving about in the room beyond his hiding place. Willi Junior held his breath. What was the man doing? A clink of ice on glass. He was fixing a drink at the minibar. Now the man was humming to himself – the singing, if that's what it was, was reserved apparently for the shower – and Willi Junior could hear his damp naked feet padding around outside on the tile floor. He moved away from the armoire, then moved back toward it: closer . . . closer . . . Willi Junior bit his lip and felt the blood pulsing in his neck. What could he do if the man opened the wardrobe door and found him? Burst out and make a run for it, he decided. He had the element of surprise on his side and the man was probably only wearing underwear, or maybe nothing at all. Why get dressed when you're only going to take it all off again? Yes, Willi Junior told himself, if he made a bolt for the door and ran like hell, he'd get away easily. But the man wouldn't open the wardrobe. What was the point? If he'd been planning to hang up his trousers and shirt, he'd have done it when he first took them off before his shower . . .

The man moved away again. Willi Junior's shoulders relaxed and he let his breath out in a long, slow exhalation as if he were surfacing after a deep dive.

Scheiße, he thought, that was a close one –

'Well, aren't you a sight for sore eyes.' A woman's voice: Ilse's voice. 'Oh – and what big hairy gonads you have, Grandpa!' She must have arrived just as the man was standing in front of the wardrobe door, perhaps admiring his naked body in the mirror.

'Can I get you a drink?' the man's voice asked.

'Sure,' Ilse said. 'A gin and tonic, thanks. You've had your shower, I gather.'

'Just finished. You?'

'At home. Before I came.'

The sound of ice clinking on glass.

What was she doing, Willi Junior wondered? Was she undressing? The thought of her naked body made him feel light-headed and he could feel the gentle pressure of a nascent erection pressing against the tight denim of his crotch. Oddly, he had never given a moment's thought to the physical effects of what he'd be witnessing. He'd thought of the pictures only as pictures – and not even dirty pictures at that.

There was a long silence, and then Ilse's voice:

'Oh, Peter – you beast.'

What were they doing, Willi Junior wondered? It was all he could do to stop himself from opening the door a crack and peeking out. Too soon, he told himself, it's still too soon.

'Ohh,' Ilse moaned. 'Ohhhh . . .'

The talking had stopped. They must be into it now, he thought. He strained his ears to pick up every sound. There were little grunts of pleasure now and the breathing was deeper, heavier. Willi Junior eased the door open and looked out. They were on the bed and Ilse was on top of him, straddling him, moving up and down rhythmically, and her breasts were jumping with little rubbery shudders at the bottom of every downstroke. *The pictures*, his mind shouted, *the pictures*! He raised the camera and exposed three quick frames. The camera made no noise – not that any of the participants, including Willi Junior, would have noticed if a gun had been fired.

The man reached up and fondled Ilse's breasts, then flipped her over on to her back and took the upper position.

'Ohhh . . .!' Ilse cried, moving toward climax.

'Ahhh . . .' the man groaned, increasing the tempo.

'Shit!' Willi Junior muttered, hearing the old wardrobe creak under his weight as he shifted position to get a better view.

In pulling the door closed and stepping back into the blackness, his head hit the line of heavy metal clothes hangers on the rail above him and set them ringing and clanging in the enclosed space like the carillon in Tchaikovsky's *1812 Overture*.

Peter Morgan came off the bed like Priapus unbound and headed for the wardrobe.

'*What the hell* – !' he roared.

Ilse, in a coital daze, rolled her unfocused eyes like a Cumaean sibyl, still uncertain of what was happening.

Peter threw open the wardrobe door, exposing Willi Junior's trembling form crouched in the corner. He took the meaning of it in at a glance: the camera, the terrified eyes, the hysterical burbling noises issuing from Willi Junior's constricted throat. Without a word he reached in, grabbed the cowering figure by the shirt-front and heaved him bodily out of the armoire, opening a long and nasty gash on the side of Willi Junior's head where the flesh made contact with the sharp protruding lip of the window sill.

'Willi!' Ilse wailed from the bed. '*Oh, my God! what are you doing here?*'

Now in possession of her faculties, she sat with the sheets pulled demurely up to her neck, staring open-mouthed with round, stupid, disbelieving eyes at the crumpled figure of her stepson on the tiles below her.

Peter Morgan, who had started forward with clenched fists to finish the intruder off, froze in his tracks.

'Wait a minute,' he hissed. 'What the hell's going on here? Do you *know* this creep?'

Ilse stared at him dumbly, then nodded almost imperceptibly.

'So who the fuck is he?' Morgan demanded.

'Willi Junior.'

'Christ,' Morgan spat. 'So, what's he doing here? Spying for your old man?'

Willi Junior, blood flowing down his face from the deep slash on his temple, followed this exchange in mute terror, his head bobbing back and forth between the speakers like an umpire at a tennis match.

'More likely spying for himself,' Ilse replied coldly, once more fully in control of herself. 'I imagine he was planning to use the pictures to blackmail me into bed with him.'

'Why, you greasy little shit!' Morgan spat, scarcely able to credit what he was seeing and hearing.

Collecting himself, he bent down and ripped the camera from around Willi Junior's neck.

'I should kill you, you miserable sonofabitch,' he breathed in a low, menacing voice, speaking directly into Willi Junior's panic-stricken face, 'but I won't do that because I'm a decent kind of guy. Now, get your sorry ass out of here before I change my mind and rip your miserable balls off.'

And then he straightened up, opened the back of the camera to expose the film, and then, very calmly and deliberately, wound up like a major-league pitcher and hurled the Maxxum 700si against the wall with all the brute force he could muster.

Half crawling and half running, Willi Junior scuttled for the door. He'd lost everything, even his camera. His eyes burning with tears of terror, humiliation, and impotent rage, he blundered down the narrow stairs and out into the brilliant afternoon sunshine. If he hadn't run quickly out of breath, having to throw himself, wheezing and spluttering, over the bonnet of a car parked on the far side of the piazza, he might have kept running forever.

4

Dickie Danvers appeared in the doorway of Nigel's painting room with a wide grin splitting his withered face from ear to ear.

'We've found the swine,' he announced. 'I just now got off the telephone with Matajcek in New York. That lawyer from Philadelphia – you remember, the one Matajcek told us had met two or three times with Dearing in a bar on West 57th – well, it turns out it's the same Peter Morgan who testified here at the inquest. There's no doubt about it.'

Nigel laid his brush aside and said,

'That's hardly a news flash. We had already reached that conclusion ourselves, as I recall.' He added, 'Without Matajcek's help.'

'Yes,' Sir Richard beamed, 'but now it's confirmed. *Confirmed.*'

'I suppose that makes a difference,' Nigel said sceptically.

'He isn't Dearing's cousin either,' Sir Richard cackled gleefully, ignoring Nigel's irony. 'He lied to the police, old chap. Dearing has no cousins.' He rubbed his hands together. 'We've got the blighter now. We've got him right where we want him.'

Nigel turned his attention back to the painting on the easel. It was coming along very nicely. The greens in the background vegetation were finally the right shade and the blues in the Virgin's dress were almost there. There was still a problem with the angel's left wing, but that would sort itself out when he extended the fronds of that palm tree to balance it. Yes, all in all, it was coming along very nicely indeed.

'And now that we've "got" him, as you so elegantly phrase it,' he said, forcing his mind back to the problem in hand, 'what exactly are we proposing to do with him?'

'I should have thought that was obvious, old chap,' Sir Richard said, fondling the hair on a coconut that lay on the table beside him. He'd never understood why Nigel couldn't paint like other painters, why he always had to tart up his studio with fish spears and voodoo masks to get himself into the mood. When he'd done those Fra Angelicos some years back, he'd turned the whole place into a damned monastery, chucking out the comfortable chairs and hanging pictures of Savonarola's execution all over the place. Now he'd turned the place topsy-turvy again and converted it into a bloody sambo shanty. Coconuts indeed! 'We're going to go out and talk to him, of course,' he said. 'We're going to lay out the facts and present him with certain alternatives.'

'And if he doesn't like our alternatives?' Nigel ventured.

'Humph!' Sir Richard snorted. 'He has no choice.'

'He will, however,' Nigel replied reasonably, 'if we present him with alternatives.'

'Don't bandy words with me, old fellow,' Sir Richard said, bridling. 'You'll only piss me off.'

'All right,' Nigel said, mollifying him, 'what alternatives then?' It was clear that Dickie had no intention of clearing off and leaving him in peace to get on with his painting. Peter Morgan might be given alternatives, but Nigel, at the moment, had none. He swirled his brush in a jar of turps and then sat himself down, like an obedient charge, on the rattan sofa opposite Dickie's chair. 'I'm listening,' he said. 'Now, what exactly do you have in mind?'

'Well,' Sir Richard said in a conspiratorial voice, leaning forward, 'the way I see it, our friend Morgan is up to his neck in caca. He's a gambler back home and not, I gather, a very proficient one, because he owes his shirt – something in the order of half a million dollars – to a mob of sleazy loan-sharks in Atlantic City. Anyway, somehow – I don't yet know how – he stumbled over the fact that the Ghirlandaio in Chicago is a forgery, and suddenly he thought he'd found a way out of his dilemma. He did some digging and traced the painting back to Danvers' House, then did a little more digging, put two and two together, and settled on you as the forger. A nice piece of deduction actually, if you think about it.'

Nigel listened with an impassive face. It was all perfectly possible, of course.

'Now,' Sir Richard went on, 'Morgan is a lawyer with a reputation to maintain, so he wanted to keep his own hands clean. Hence, enter James Dearing – a minor thug from the Lower East Side, possibly supplied by the loan-sharks in Atlantic City. Dearing's on board to handle the dirty work, while Morgan looks after the research, the planning and the head work. They plan to scam us out of a couple of million quid, split the profits, and retire to the Bahamas – something like that, anyway. Except that Dearing gets himself knocked off. So now Morgan is on his own, but he doesn't know a bloody thing about playing the heavy. When Dearing goes missing, he goes to the police and lies about being Dearing's cousin – which gets him dragged into the inquest – which put us on to him in the first place – et cetera, et cetera, et cetera. In short, Morgan is an incompetent crook. He's out of his depth and definitely out of his league when he decides to tangle with somebody like me.' He twisted vigorously at the point of his beard, as if it were Morgan's neck he held between his gnarled fingers. 'As I fully intend, incidentally, to show him.'

Nigel had no idea where all this was leading, and the appalling *mélange* of American slang and the Queen's English in Sir Richard's schizoid vocabulary was giving him a brutal headache.

'Look, Dickie,' he said, rubbing his temple, 'this is all very interesting, old man, but what precisely *is it* that you intend to do about Morgan?'

'All right,' Sir Richard said, 'I'll cut right to the chase. I intend to meet with him, tell him what we know and at the same time try to find out exactly how much he actually knows about us, then give him the following choice: (a) I'll cover half his gambling debts in exchange for any hard evidence he has on the Ghirlandaio and any other paintings he alleges we forged; then he goes back to the States and forgets he ever met us, or (b) I'll use all my influence – starting with the Italian authorities – to have him discredited and, with any luck at all, tossed into jail. He's already perjured himself in open court by claiming to be Dearing's cousin. What other laws has he broken? I know people down here who can find that sort of thing out.'

'And when,' Nigel asked, his headache intensifying, 'do you intend to present him with this ultimatum?'

'We, Nigel – *we*,' Sir Richard replied, leaning back with a smile. 'We're confronting him together, old fellow.' He consulted his watch. 'In about an hour, as a matter of fact. Bruno is bringing the car around now.' He added, in answer to Nigel's unspoken question: 'Morgan was required to state his address in his deposition to the court. I had a friend wheedle the address out of somebody in the coroner's office – for a small fee, of course. The Italians are always so terribly accommodating, I find, when there's a small fee involved.'

'And what happens,' Nigel ventured, 'if Morgan rejects both of your options?'

Sir Richard waved the objection aside with an airy hand. 'He won't. He can't afford to.'

'He may not see it that way,' Nigel persisted. 'And what then?'

'Then,' Sir Richard said flatly, 'we shall have to think of a more dramatic solution, shan't we?'

'Where's your sister?'

'In a record store up the street,' Chad said, stepping over the low planter dividing the outdoor café from the piazza beyond. 'She's hunting for a Janet Jackson tape.'

He turned a chair backwards and straddled it, leaning his arms on its back.

'What did you buy?' Penny asked, indicating the bag he'd set at his feet.

'Nothing much,' he shrugged. 'It's just a shirt.'

She gave him a funny maternal look. 'Well, let's see it, silly,' she said.

He opened the bag and held up a T-shirt with the Italian flag and the words *Ciao! Italia* stamped on it.

'Sharp!' she said, admiring it. 'It'll look good on you.'

'Yeah, I kind of liked it too.'

The day was humid, a sirocco coming in, and the sun lay hot on their shoulders. They watched as a group of children holding ice-cream cones and all licking furiously were herded across the piazza by their handlers in the direction of the ramparts. A school day-trip of some kind: a history lesson made palatable by a *gelato* bribe.

'Would you like a drink?' Penny asked.

'Sure,' Chad said. 'A Coke, I guess.'

She called the waiter over. '*Una Coca Cola, per favore.*'

'*Nient'altro?*'

'*No, grazie.*'

When he had gone, she turned back to Chad and said:

'Is there anything you'd like to do in town before we head back? Your father has a meeting of some kind going on at the house. When I rang to ask him about our tickets to Rome next week, he said he couldn't talk. I think he'd prefer if we didn't rush back.'

Chad shook his head. 'No, I don't think so. Nothing in particular.' Then a thought struck him. 'Well, actually,' he said, 'I'd kind of like to have another look at the tomb of the girl we saw in the cathedral. You know, the white marble one. If you don't mind, I mean.'

Penny nodded. 'Ilaria del Carretto, in the duomo. No, I don't mind at all.'

'It's weird, you know,' he said, opening up in a way that was becoming more frequent with him, 'but I keep thinking about her. How she died so young, I mean, and so long ago. I keep seeing her lying there with her little dog. I can't seem to get her off my mind.'

'Yes,' Penny agreed, nodding, 'she's hard to forget.'

He's growing up, she thought. He's not a little boy any more; he really is growing up. And she felt a lump – whether of pride or sorrow she didn't quite know – forming in her throat.

'It's almost like I actually *knew* her or something,' he said.

'Well,' Penny said, 'in a way maybe you do know her now, Chad – and so the centuries don't seem to matter as much any more. I mean, knowing somebody is really nothing more than having strong feelings about another human being. It's easier, I suppose if the person's still alive, but the feelings carry on after they're gone. I feel that way about my mother, for example, and she died before you were even born. Most of the time I can't convince myself that she's gone because she was always there for me when I was growing up.'

'Yeah,' he said, nodding, 'maybe that's right. I just thought it was kind of spooky, you know, her being a stranger and having been dead so long. But maybe it doesn't really matter after all. The feelings that join us are more important than the centuries that keep us apart. I know I'll never forget her anyway – which means, I suppose, that in a way she *is* still alive. In my mind, I mean – like Grandma.'

His drink arrived and he sipped it thoughtfully. A bus rumbled past, changing gear noisily as it rounded the corner, and a pair of old gentlemen engrossed in animated conversation rolled by, gesticulating, on their bicycles. In the sky, high above, puffs of cloud floated like cotton balls and a group of four or five pigeons, on their way some place or other in a hurry, swept over the piazza like a formation of miniature fighter jets.

Penny took off her sun-glasses, then took her compact out of her purse and checked her face in the mirror. There were smudges of mascara under her eyes and she wiped them away with a tissue.

Chad waited until she had finished before he said:

'You were crying again, Mom, weren't you?'

She gave him a pained smile but said nothing.

'You can talk to me,' he said. 'I know what's going on, you know. I'm not a kid any more.'

'I know that, Chad,' she said, looking away. 'Of course, I do.'

'It's Dad, isn't it?' he persisted.

'Oh, it's a lot of things, sweetheart,' she said evasively, 'and some of them are my fault too.'

He ran his finger around the top of his glass.

'He's having an affair, isn't he?' he said finally.

'What makes you say that?' Penny asked with a shock of surprise.

Chad shrugged. 'The two of you fight all the time,' he said, 'and you're always crying. I mean, am I not supposed to notice that something's wrong?'

She didn't know how to answer him. He was at that awkward age between boy and man when sometimes one and sometimes the other held the ascendancy. She didn't want to alienate his trust and insult him by fobbing him off, but she couldn't bring herself either – no, not yet . . . not so soon – to treat him as an adult. It was a painful learning experience for them both.

'Of course not, darling,' she said, trying to say something while saying as little as possible. 'It's just that – well, your father and I are going through some hard times right now, but everything will be just fine. You wait and see.'

'There's another woman, isn't there?' he said, refusing to be put off.

There was, she noticed with a start, a steely coldness in his eyes that she'd never seen before. No, he wasn't a little boy any more.

'I don't know,' she said, trying to be honest. 'Maybe. I don't know what to think any more. I don't know what's happening to us. I can't talk to him any more. He's like a stranger.'

Chad reached across the table and, taking his mother's fragile hand in his own, looked her unblinkingly in the eye.

'You'll always have me, Mom,' he said. 'I'll always be there for you. You know that.'

'Yes, sweetheart,' she said, smiling bravely, fighting back her tears, 'I know that.'

'And I won't let him hurt you, Mom,' Chad said earnestly. 'I'll kill him first.'

The word had travelled quickly through the family by a kind of unspoken telepathic osmosis: *er hat schlechte Laune*, Willi Senior was in one of his 'moods'. Nothing was said: everyone simply *knew* – and steered a wide, careful course around him. The cook had set his breakfast eggs and ham before him without her customary cheerful salutation and disappeared back into her kitchen as if the devil were on her tail. The twins had masticated their wholegrain cereal in sullen silence and then fled to the terrace, where confronting hostile Russian divisions was a prospect considerably less daunting than facing the basilisk mask of their father's malignant stare. Ilse and Willi Junior had not even put in an appearance at the familial board. Ilse declined to leave her room and Willi Junior, whose battered Volkswagen was not in its accustomed spot over the oil stain in the drive, was apparently not even at home.

Willi Senior spent the morning in his greenhouse-laboratory. He didn't take his usual coffee in the garden, and his morning newspaper lay, untouched, on the table in the hall. The hour for lunch came and went, and finally the cook, taking fate by the nose, dared to penetrate his sanctuary and deposit on the desk at his elbow a tray containing a salami sandwich, two dill pickles (imported from Germany because he couldn't survive abroad without them), and a glass of beer. He didn't look up from his microscope long enough to acknowledge either her presence or her solicitude.

He spent the afternoon chloroforming specimens. Capturing the unsuspecting butterflies – who had, no doubt, come to consider him a harmless fixture of their environment – in a large diaphanous net, he placed them individually in sealed jars into which he had previously inserted gauze pads saturated with $CHCl_3$. They fluttered briefly, but death quickly supervened and their large blue wings grew still.

He was in the midst of this procedure when he noticed through the laboratory window the tell-tale plume of dust rising on the dirt track that led up the hillside to Tenuta del Colombo. It meant that a car was approaching. He released the hapless victim that he was carrying, ignorant of its fate, toward the bottles of death and then he laid aside his net. He left the greenhouse and walked, without haste, through the villa to the front door, where he stepped out under the portico and waited, his arms folded across his chest.

The old green Volkswagen Fox wheezed up the last hundred metres of road and passed through the entrance gates, then rolled up the lane and sought out its normal resting place in an inconspicuous corner of the drive under the shadow of a large cypress. Willi Senior, his face blank and inscrutable, watched his son approach and said nothing.

'He! hallo, Vati. Ich – ' Willi Junior began.

'Come with me,' his father said icily, twisting on his heel and disappearing into the house.

As he turned, the curtain in an upstairs window fell back into place where Ilse had let it go and stepped back out of sight.

Obediently, his head bowed, Willi Junior followed his father down the echoing corridor and into the high-ceilinged, book-lined sanctum of the library.

'Sit,' Willi Senior commanded, pointing at a chair.

Willi Junior sat, his heart pounding, and his father stood above him, glaring down. When he spoke, his voice was velvet over steel:

'What happened to your head?' he demanded.

'I had an accident,' Willi Junior stammered. 'I – I fell.'

'You're lying.'

'I was on the ramparts. It was dark. I tripped over a stump and there was an iron railing . . .'

'You're lying.' Willi Senior's lips were a white line stretched thin across his face and his voice was low, menacing, scarcely audible. 'You weren't here last night. It was the twins' birthday and you were expected. Where were you?'

'I – I forgot. Look, Vati, I – '

'You're lying,' Willi Senior spat between clenched teeth. 'Now, where were you, *verdammt noch mal*?'

Willi Junior said nothing. He sat with his hands in his lap, twisting his pudgy fingers as though attempting to wrench them free of their moorings. His face was drained of colour and his bad eye, which blinked involuntarily, was flashing frantically like a distress signal on an Aldis lamp.

Willi Senior walked to the window and stood, hands locked behind his back, staring out at the drive and the olive-coloured hills falling away to the boulder-strewn course of the Serchio three kilometres away. He was silent for several minutes, as still as stone. Finally, he turned and, in a voice that seemed to have run off a glacier, said:

'I'm not a fool, boy, so don't take me for one. Something happened in town yesterday, something involving you and Ilse. I don't know what it was – not yet – but I promise you, *mein Junge*, that neither of us is leaving this room until you tell me exactly what went on.' He turned back and stared out of the window again. 'If you refuse,' he said without turning, 'you can go upstairs, pack your bags, and get out of my house. Now. Today. You decide: you have two minutes to make your choice.'

Willi Junior looked as if he'd been stunned by a mallet-blow. His mouth fell open, his eyes bulged and the bad one stopped fluttering, and his breathing seemed to have stopped. He had always in the past been able to manipulate his father and was totally unprepared for a decision so abrupt, so dramatic, so draconian. He was speechless. His mouth opened and snapped closed several times like that of a beached porpoise, but no words came out.

And then his mind took over: *Wait a minute! what have I done? why should I suffer for Ilse's transgressions? It is she, not I, who is at fault, who is the deceiver and the fornicator. Let her, then, pay the price for her sins.* The idea made him almost smile. For perhaps the first time in his whole life, he suddenly realized, all he had to do was tell the truth. Yes, by God, the truth would set him free.

'All right, *Vati*,' he said softly, 'I'll tell you what happened.'

Willi Senior turned and faced him. 'Go on,' he said.

'It's not something you're going to like hearing,' Willi Junior began, 'but you have a right to know it anyway – '

'Get on with it,' his father said, a note of asperity creeping into his voice.

'Ilse is having an affair.'

164

A deep crimson, beginning at the neck, crept up Willi Senior's face like an incoming tide. He struggled for a moment to regain his composure, then said in a strangled voice:

'How do you know this?'

'I caught them in bed together. The man saw me and threw me against the wall. That's how I cut my head.' He almost added, 'He also broke my camera,' but stopped himself in time. He could hardly find a reasonable explanation to account for his being there to take pictures. It was the truth certainly, but not the whole truth, that would set him free.

'Where was this?' Willi Senior asked in a far-away, disembodied voice, as if his mind were incapable of processing the data reported by his ears.

'At the Hotel Universo.'

'And who was the man?'

'I don't know, *Vati*. He was an American.'

Willi Senior's voice, when he finally regained the power of speech, was the voice of another creature, the low guttural moan of a wounded animal:

'*Ich werde den Hurensohn erschlagen,*' he snarled, 'I'll kill the sonofabitch.'

The inhuman accent sent a chill up Willi Junior's spine and his father's eyes, like flaming carbuncles, made him want to melt out of sight – and out of range – through the marble floor.

Willi Senior threw open the door and stamped to the bottom of the stairs.

'Ilse!' he howled up the echoing staircase. 'Ilse you *liederliche Schlampe*, you lickerish slut, get down here! Now! This instant!'

Cecilia had the taxi drop her at the bottom of the road.

She had debated coming by bus but had decided, given the importance of the mission, that the substantially higher cost of a taxi was not, in the circumstances, unwarranted. The future for Nigel, and indeed – who knew? – perhaps for herself as well, hung in the balance. She had seen this Peter Morgan in action at the inquest, had there had the opportunity to assess his character, and had judged him a thoroughly nasty piece of goods – a man capable of almost any imaginable villainy. Yes, she would certainly need her wits about her when she confronted him.

On the way to San Leonardo she had plotted her strategy for the encounter. Her opening salvo – since the best defence was an aggressive offence – would be to place before him, without comment, the photograph of him taken at midnight on the road to San Felice. Let him explain to her what he'd been doing there when other people were in bed. He would make up some story, of course, but she'd have him back on his heels. Then, before he could recover, she'd inform him that she had deposited a copy of the photograph with the police – which was, in a sense, true, since she'd dropped one off in a post box, sealed in a manilla envelope addressed to Inspector Bonelli, on her way through town. She expected that the inspector, when it arrived, would simply throw it out since it had arrived without explanation or meaning; but she couldn't tell an outright lie, not even to a dishonest character like Morgan – lying simply wasn't in her nature – and so she'd disarmed conscience in advance by mailing the photo. Then finally, while Morgan was reeling from this second blow, she'd demand to know why he was threatening Nigel and warn him that, whatever his game, she intended to see that it failed. She shrugged. It wasn't a great plan perhaps, but it was certainly a serviceable one. If it did nothing more, she thought cheerfully, it would put the wind up him and let him know that she meant business.

She got her bearings and marched up the hill, the leather soles of her walking shoes crunching purposefully on the gravel under her feet. The house was at the end of the road on an elevation giving a panoramic view over the valley and set apart from the neighbouring houses in a private grove of ilex and conifers. It was a large house – obviously expensive and well appointed – but she had expected that: Peter Morgan was a man of means. What she hadn't expected was to find Sir Richard Danvers' long black limousine parked in the drive. The chauffeur, smoking a cigarette, was leaning against the side of the car with his cap tipped back and a bored expression overspreading the features of his listless face. There was no one else in sight.

She slipped into the cover of a patch of shrubbery and, moving stealthily, made her way around the house so that she could approach it from the rear. There were pine cones underfoot and she did her best to avoid them, not wishing to alert any listening ears there might be to her presence. In the branches overhead, a daw croaked and flapped ponderously away, and she cast a poisonous look after its departing form. What on earth, she wondered, was Sir Richard doing there? – and of all the exquisitely inopportune moments for him to have chosen to show his miserable face. It threw her plans into a tizzy, into complete disarray. Damn and blast him anyway! she thought irritably.

But curiosity was more powerful than irritation. She pressed forward, descending into a small ravine at the bottom of which burbled a brook, over which she leapt with agility. Was it possible, she thought, landing expertly on the balls of her feet, that Sir Richard and Peter Morgan were in something together? that Nigel had accidentally stumbled over the scheme and that they were threatening him? Why, after all, had Sir Richard turned up when he had? The accident at San Felice did not require his presence; he could easily have handled any insurance claim through his lawyers, from London. Yes, the more she thought about it, the more suspicious his presence on the scene seemed to become. Well, she thought, clambering up the far bank and twisting aside the sprigs of bramble that stretched out to catch at her skirt, he has *me* to contend with now. Let's see how the old buzzard handles that!

She peered over the lip of the ridge and found herself looking down on the back of the Morgan villa. There was a terraced patio and a swimming pool, some clothes hanging to dry on a line, but no one in sight. Did Morgan have a family or did he live alone? She had never thought until now, she realized, to ask herself that question. Not that it mattered. She was interested only in Morgan himself – and of course, now, in the mysterious presence of Sir Richard Danvers as well.

Moving from tree to tree and bush to bush, she made her way carefully, quietly down the slope to the house. Bent from the waist, she crept along the outside of the low hedge surrounding the patio and reached the corner of the building. She pressed herself against the wall and caught her breath Whew! this sleuthing was an arduous business. She could recall no instance where Poirot had been required to dirty his spats in rough terrain; he enjoyed the luxury of drawing-room detection. If Agatha Christie were still alive, Cecilia thought, I'd send her a note suggesting that verisimilitude demands a more active physical role for her little Belgian detective.

The day was warm and the windows were open. There's no help for it, she thought, I'm simply going to have to snoop. She paused at the first window and listened, but heard nothing. The second produced the same result ... and so also the third. She had now reached the front corner of the house. Pressing herself flat against the wall, she peered cautiously out. The chauffeur was thirty yards away, stirring the gravel in the drive with the polished toe of his shoe. There were ornamental shrubs across the front of the house. She waited until the man looked away, attracted by some sound in the distance, then took a deep breath and slipped noiselessly around the corner and into the bushes. At the second window she struck 'pay dirt', an apposite phrase she remembered from an American movie. There were voices – loud voices – coming from inside the room. She stationed herself behind a clipped yew and raised herself slowly, inch by inch, until she could see over the sill and into the room. It was a study or library of some kind, filled with expensive-looking computer equipment and, in the centre, a grouping of high-backed chairs on a Turkish carpet arranged around an oval table. In one of the chairs, glowering and silent, sat Sir Richard Danvers like a disgruntled spider in the centre of its web. In another, smiling expansively and waving a huge cigar, was Peter Morgan. The other two chairs had their backs to her and she couldn't see whether or not anyone was sitting in them.

'You can puff and blow all you want, *old chap*,' Peter Morgan said derisively. 'It's no skin off my ass. I've got the goods on you, plain and simple. You've seen the photocopies – you know what I know – and we both know you're up shit creek without a paddle.'

'I have friends in the Carabinieri,' Sir Richard said darkly.

'And I,' Morgan countered, 'have friends in the American Consulate. So tell me, *old fellow*, is this a game of my brother is bigger than your brother, or what? Come on, man, face the facts. I've got you by the balls, so why not just pay the piper and be done with it?' He added ominously, 'Because if you don't, Sir Richard, I swear to God I'll turn this stuff over to the press and you'll go up in smoke, you and your whole fucking empire. Think about it.'

He rose and poured himself a drink from a cut-glass decanter on the sideboard, raising the decanter in Sir Richard's direction. Sir Richard waved him off with a brusque, imperious hand.

'Suit yourself,' Morgan said, returning to his chair and settling back with an indifferent puff on his cigar.

'Your price has gone up,' Sir Richard said in an accusing tone.

'Of course it has,' Morgan replied with a shrug. 'You killed my friend, Jimmy Dearing.'

'That was an accident,' said a third voice. 'Even the coroner has officially pronounced it death by misadventure.'

Cecilia's heart froze in her chest. *That was Nigel's voice.* Oh, dear God! she thought, what's *he* doing in the middle of this mess? Her mind was spinning. Suddenly, she couldn't make sense of any-thing any more. What *was* going on? Had Sir Richard tricked Nigel into participating in some nefarious scheme that Morgan had discovered and was now blackmailing them over? Nigel would never do anything dishonest. No, she couldn't – *she wouldn't* – believe it. Oh, nothing made sense any more . . .

'The coroner was a jackass,' Morgan said. 'I think you murdered Jimmy when you found out what he wanted.'

'That is a preposterous suggestion, sir!' Nigel blurted. 'It's a – *a damned lie!*'

'It's what I think,' Morgan replied evenly, 'and it's why the price has gone up.'

Cecilia could hardly restrain herself. She wanted to leap through the window and throttle the miserable Yank with her bare hands – and for tuppence and a dare she'd have done so, too.

'You're asking too much,' Sir Richard said. 'If I pay you, it will ruin me.'

Morgan tipped back his head and laughed.

Recovering himself, he said: 'Let's be serious, Sir Richard, shall we? You're worth ten times what I'm asking. Look, old buddy, I've managed in one way or another to get my hands on some pretty detailed records of your financial affairs.' He gave a sweep of the hand indicating the sophisticated computer equipment around them in the room. 'It's the magic of the electronic age, old man.' He sipped at his bourbon, then leaned back in the chair, his cigar locked in his teeth in a most offensive way, and said without bothering to remove it: 'You have until Friday night to make up your mind. That's almost three days.' He stood up, indicating that the meeting was at an end. 'I imagine,' he said, 'that you'll both be attending that arts-do at the Giglio Theatre on Friday night. Everyone else will be there – including me, as it happens, since I promised my wife in the interest of family harmony that I'd trail along behind her. You can let me know your decision then. But just remember, gentlemen, if I don't hear from you, I'm going to start mailing off anonymous brown-paper packages to every major newspaper in North America and Europe. They'll eat you alive, old buddy.'

Sir Richard struggled to his feet. 'We'll consider your offer,' he said stiffly.

'It's not an offer,' Morgan said, removing his cigar. 'It's an ultimatum.' He added: 'Pay up and we all win, Sir Richard; try something cute and nobody wins. And like the man said: Winning isn't everything, it's the *only* thing. I'm sure you'll see things my way when you're feeling calmer and have had a chance to think things over. I find, incidentally, that I do some of my best thinking in the shower. You boys should try it.'

They were moving toward the door, Morgan with his arm around Sir Richard's resisting shoulder and Nigel trailing behind. By the time they reached the portico, Cecilia was already scuttling down the ravine behind the villa with lightning in her eye and fire in her heart.

Something, it was quite clear, had to be done about that horrible American. She could deal later with Sir Richard and whatever mess he'd managed to drag Nigel into. For the moment, it was Peter Morgan who was the single and immediate object of her attention and her ire.

5

The literary awards ceremony, held annually on the last Friday of September, was the highlight of the Lucchesan social calendar. It was held in the auditorium of the Teatro del Giglio, a building unprepossessing enough from the outside, but inside an elegant neo-classical opera house – indeed, a miniature La Scala – with three tiers of semicircular boxes adorned with gold and outfitted with plush red velvet seats. Limousines began arriving at six thirty bearing local dignitaries, the wealthy and influential, foreign visitors of stature, and what was left of the old hereditary nobility languishing in apartments in town or amassing new fortunes in the hills on estates producing wine and olive oil. By seven o'clock the seats were full, the audience a shimmering sea of emeralds, diamonds, and pearls. A hush fell over the hall as the prize-recipients, preceded by the executive committee of the Società delle Arti, filed on to the stage and took their places in the two rows of padded antique chairs flanking the podium.

There was a brief welcoming address from the Marchesa di Lena, a frail old dowager of over eighty who was the honorary president of the Società, and then the active president, Signor Paolo Borghese, rose and introduced the prize-winners, each of whom was presented with an embossed *medaglione d'oro* in a polished rosewood box lined with blue satin and a cheque for five hundred thousand lire. There were recipients for poetry, the novel, the novella, and drama. Following the awards, each of the recipients was invited, in turn, to address the gathering and to read a brief selection from his work. Arbati, the first to be called, tackled the issue of the role of the poet in the modern world and then read from his new volume entitled *Tommaso incredulo* – the 'Tommaso' of the title being, not Arbati himself, but a fictional *alter ego*: an empiricist, a neo-Aristotelian realist – the antithesis, in fact, of everything Arbati himself cherished and held dear. The poem he chose was addressed to the ideal woman whom he'd never met and was entitled '*Museé des Beaux Arts*':

If I were a painter, I would paint
Effulgent landscapes, deep in summer heat;
Resplendent grass and forests, and the faint
Lines of distant hills. Trim slopes of wheat
Reclining in the sun, and kindly herds
Of cattle, browsing gentle fields.
Waterways, beneath high clouds, and soaring birds;
Chalk hillsides, limestone wealds;
A million rain-soaked leaves: benignity
Suffusing wood and stream and pond. And dignity.

If I were an artist, I would etch
Huge trees with complex fronds, and uncouth roots;
Archaic bark, and antique moss. And I would sketch
The skeletons of their branches, their autumnal fruits.
The way the wind tousles their drooping manes,
Foliage-slanting shafts of sunlight, ancient scars,
The timorous plants beneath, in shaded lanes;
Snowfall at night, and half-glimpsed stars.
The strength of massive boles in copse and chase;
The wonder of vast realms of time. And grace.

But most of all, I would draw you. Beneath my dark
And lyric lead your beauty should unfold.
The planes and volumes of your face would arc
Above your glowing shoulders; I would mould
The wonder of your back and hips, the swell
Of breasts and buttocks, and the burnished shell
That is the helmet of your hair; your tender glance;

The garment of your nakedness, worn with nonchalance.
All these would be my subject, be a toy
Caressed with brush and hand in reverence. And joy.

Tommaso is a painter. He creates
Bleak shores, and rubbish dumps, and rusted wire,
The loneliness of life on dank estates,
Absurd iconic jokes, the rotting mire
Of wreckers' yards, and garbage underfoot;
Hand-tinted photocopied trash, and junk
Assembled from industrial grime and soot.
Pinball arcades, the haunt of tough and punk,
The photorealist gloss on car and van.
But then, of course, he is a happy man.

Embarrassed to see himself in printed copy in booksellers' windows, his uneasiness disappeared when he read his verse aloud. It was as if, somehow, the words were no longer *his* words but had, by some mysterious alchemy of art, become the words of all men who had ever loved and sought the grace of beauty in their lives. He read in a deep sonorous voice, utterly unaware of an audience listening beyond the footlights, and when he had finished, took his place among the chairs behind the podium, yielding the platform to the next speaker.

The rest of the ceremony passed in a blur, the narcotic effect of the poem draining away slowly from his system like the vestiges of a dose of laudanum. And then, quite unexpectedly, he found himself outside, his hand being grasped by bejewelled matrons and portly gentlemen in dinner jackets: '*Oh, Signor Arbati, that was wonderful – simply divine*'; '*Well done, old man. Nice bit of poetry there. Yes, yes – very good indeed*'; '*There were tears in my eyes, Signor Arbati – real tears – oh, thank you so much for coming.*' The words washed over him like grains of sand piling up over a wreck, drawn by the resistless power of the tide.

He lit a cigarette and eased his way to the edge of the crowd. There was still the reception to get through and then a formal dinner (by invitation only) at the Marchesa di Lena's palazzo. God, he thought, how will I survive it all?

'Hello there,' a voice said at his elbow.

It was Penny Morgan, the American he'd met on the beach at Viareggio. 'Oh – hello,' he said.

'I was impressed,' she said, smiling. 'You read beautifully. I'm glad you chose "*Musée des Beaux Arts*". It's my favourite, I think, of all your poems.'

He looked away, embarrassed now that it was over, now that he spoke with only his own everyday voice. 'Thank you,' he said. 'I'm pleased you enjoyed it.'

'I'd like you to meet some of my family,' she said, covering his unease. 'This is my husband Peter and my son Chad. Brooke, our daughter, didn't come; she wasn't feeling well.'

'Nice evening,' Peter Morgan said, extending a hand. But his mind – and his eyes – were elsewhere, searching the crowd for someone. Arbati thought he knew who that someone would be: the mysterious blonde from the inquest.

After a banal exchange about the ceremony and the weather, husband and son both drifted away, leaving Arbati alone with Penny. He was not sorry to see them go. The night was warm and they stood together, watching the flow of life around them, under a sky now speckled with winking stars. The scent of her perfume curled up to his nostrils like a memory of flowers and he noticed, not for the first time, how elegant and strikingly beautiful she was in the lace-trimmed dress of black satin that flattered her contours with an understated grace. Around them, in twos and threes, people were setting off across the piazza toward the illuminated façade of Palazzo Ducale. He looked around, but there was no sign of Peter Morgan or the boy, Chad.

'May I walk you to the reception?' he asked, offering his arm.

'It would be an honour,' she replied, taking it.

Like an old married couple, they walked along beside the Hotel Universo under a line of venerable plane trees arching over them in a leafy canopy.

'How are things at home?' he ventured, trying to sound casual.

She was silent a moment, then said:

'Oh, not very good, really. He's tense and irritable all the time. This afternoon he shouted at Brooke and called her some pretty nasty things. It's the reason, actually, she didn't come tonight. I think she wanted to.' And then she added in a less guarded voice, 'Chad thinks he's having an affair.'

'And you?' Arbati asked.

She looked away. 'Yes, he probably is,' she said. 'But there's something else too, something that's upsetting him terribly and keeping him on edge all the time as if – oh, I don't know – as if he'd done something dreadful and feared that the police were after him. It's not me, I know that. It's something bigger.'

173

'Have you tried, since we talked at the beach, to get him to talk about it?'

'Many times. He just turns cold and tells me to mind my own business. I'm about at my wits' end, I'm afraid.'

'My offer of help still stands, you know,' he said gently, reminding her.

She nodded in the darkness beside him. 'I know, Carlo,' she said. 'I know it does.'

The night surrounded them like an old familiar blanket and they walked on, arm in arm, not speaking, taking the long way around. They could see the lights glowing in the windows of Palazzo Ducale, and just as they reached the portico, the door opened and Giancarlo Bonelli emerged.

'Ah – Carlo! there you are,' he said. 'I looked for you at the theatre but missed you in the crowd. You did a marvellous job, my friend. Marvellous.' He sounded out of breath. 'Look, I'm going to have to give the reception a pass, I'm afraid. Something's come up at the Questura; but I wanted to catch you first and congratulate you. Damn good job, old buddy.'

Arbati gave an embarrassed smile.

'Marvellous,' Bonelli said, moving away. 'I'll catch you later, okay? We'll have a drink.'

Arbati nodded. 'Later will be fine,' he said, 'and so will a drink, if you're buying.'

'A promise,' Bonelli said, waving.

'A man in a hurry,' Penny observed, watching his departing back.

'An old friend,' Arbati said, shaking his head. 'Giancarlo Bonelli – Inspector Bonelli, actually. We were at the Carabinieri academy in Florence together.' He added with a grin, 'He told me when I arrived here, you know, that crime in Lucca had been cancelled in honour of my visit. It seems he had a looser grip on the situation than he imagined.'

She gave a silvery laugh – the kind of laugh that made him wonder how her husband could bear to treat her so abominably. He'd often wondered that about married people. Familiarity, it seemed, too often bred, if not contempt, then certainly indifference and a callous insensitivity to the feelings of others. If Penny Morgan had been his wife, he knew, he'd have treated her with the dignity and respect she deserved. She was, with her quiet beauty and sweet diffidence of manner, an attractive and loving woman, and she deserved a much better bargain in a husband than she had received. As he held the door open for her to pass through, his heart hardened another notch against Peter Morgan.

The reception was in the Statue Gallery on the second floor, a domed arcade lined on either side with Roman replicas of Athenian statuary. They climbed the Royal staircase together and joined the throng. Tables groaning under the weight of hors d'oeuvres were placed along the walls and white-jacketed waiters circulated carrying trays loaded with fluted glasses of champagne.

'I'd better mix,' Arbati said.

'Of course,' she said. 'Thank you for squiring me so gallantly to a party being held in your honour. It was more than duty required.'

'And more,' Arbati replied, 'than pleasure anticipated.'

'Oh, you poets,' she said, reddening, 'you have such a way with words.'

Arbati took a glass of champagne from a passing waiter and moved among the guests, shaking hands, chatting, being gracious. It was interesting to discover in a strange city how many people he knew – many of them, oddly enough, visitors like himself. Many of them, too, from foreign lands. And the other odd – and quite remarkable – thing, now that he came to think of it, was how many of them had something to do in one way or another with the strange death of James Dearing. There were the Americans, of course: the Morgans. Peter Morgan over there, standing by that statue of Aphrodite with his superior smile and bored eyes. He was here because his wife had dragged him, not because his Mammonish spirit had any affinity with literature or art. At the inquest he'd claimed to be Dearing's cousin, but Arbati had his doubts. Penny had mentioned nothing about a visiting cousin and she seemed, although Arbati hadn't cared to pry, to know nothing about the inquest into Dearing's death: surely an odd fact. It was, apparently, one of the many secrets about himself that her husband had kept from her. And then there were the English: Cecilia Hathaway, Nigel Harmsworth, and Sir Richard Danvers. An odd assortment of personalities if ever there was one. Sir Richard Danvers, cold and calculating, eyeing the paintings and running a surreptitious palm over the rump of the marble goddess at his side as if assessing its potential for profit in his auction rooms. And who was the woman hovering officiously there beside him? She'd been at the inquest too. A private nurse: someone apparently to carry his pills and cater to his whims. And then there was Nigel Harmsworth, over there standing by himself rolling the stem of his wineglass between thumb and forefinger, aloof and rather stuffy, but at the same time foppishly cultivated with the floppy handkerchief in his breast pocket, his paisley cravat and his stylish silver-headed walking-stick – apparently an artist himself, a painter. And finally there was Cecilia Hathaway, brisk and efficient, chairwoman of the reception committee, moving among the guests making introductions and keeping the conversational ball in play – the expatriate who had thrown herself into the life of her adopted country with verve and passion, although reserving (as Arbati had intuited at the inquest) her greatest and most private passion for a fellow countryman: for it was clear that she was deeply in love with Nigel Harmsworth, although the feeling was not, Arbati guessed, reciprocated on his part. Yes, they were an interesting group – a distinct and distinctly memorable trio.

At that moment he happened, in turning to take a second glass of champagne, to look over at the head of the staircase. There, on the arm of a large and distinguished gentleman with ice blue eyes, was the mysterious blonde from the inquest. She was, in her white evening gown and without her sun-glasses, a most extraordinary and radiant creature – or such, at least, was her external form, for below the surface Arbati sensed a coiled tension and something like fear, as if she were afraid of encountering someone she'd rather not meet.

'The Kleists,' said the pinched and bespectacled woman beside him, following his gaze. For the past ten minutes he'd been half listening while she'd fulminated against the iniquity of gratuitous sex in the cinema, apparently under the misapprehension that he was a screenwriter of some sort.

'Excuse me?' Arbati replied, forcing his attention back to her.

'Their name is Kleist,' the woman repeated. 'He's a science professor from Germany. An entomologist, I believe. All the visiting notables staying in the area get an invitation to the reception and it's rather a point of honour with them, as I understand, to attend.' She added, to illustrate her own pedigree: 'I met the Kleists, as it happens, at a private dinner party last month at Villa Mansi. An interesting and rather pleasant couple – in a very *German* way, of course.' She gave Arbati a knowing and stony stare. 'It's a second marriage for the professor, you know,' she muttered *sotto voce*, leaning forward into his shoulder, '*un matrimonio de ghiandole*, a marriage of glands.'

'Yes, I dare say,' Arbati replied distractedly – for at that moment

176

he had witnessed the most extraordinary series of eye and body signals passing between the Americans and the arriving Germans. As the Kleists entered the gallery, Peter Morgan had given Frau Kleist an indiscreet wink; she, noticing him, had flinched as if she'd received a physical blow; her sudden movement had, in turn, alerted her husband to the exchange and the professor, his face going instantly crimson and his eyes bulging, now looked as if he were attempting to suppress, for civility's sake, the unexpected detonation of several sticks of dynamite in his intestines. Meanwhile, the remaining Morgans – mother and son – had also seen the exchange: Penny had turned and fled from the room, and Chad, casting his father a look normally reserved for convicted felons, had hurried after her. It was, in a nutshell, a tragi-comedy of star-crossed recognitions. If Chad and his mother had merely suspected Peter Morgan was having an affair, they were in no doubt about it now. If Professor Kleist had entertained the innocent belief that the young wife on his arm was pure and chaste, he had just been rudely and peremptorily disabused of his delusion.

Engrossed in her own judgements, the poisonous harpy who had trapped Arbati and was loath to release him while any juice remained had noticed nothing of this. 'The ungainly whelp with them,' she confided with a sniff, referring to Willi Junior who was slouching along behind his father, 'is a son by the first marriage. An incorrigible layabout and wastrel, from what I gather.'

'He seems to have injured his head,' Arbati observed, merely to say something. And indeed, Willi Junior wore a large bandage covering nearly half of his left temple.

'The result, I shouldn't wonder,' the lady at his elbow pronounced with enthusiasm, 'of being apprehended *in flagrante delicto* by an irate husband. Really, *signore*, the morality of young people today is positively the most dismal and shocking comment upon the so-called progress of our modern civilization. Why,' she said, wagging a skinny finger under his nose and off again on her hobby-horse, 'when *I* was a girl . . .'

After ten minutes of nods and pained smiles, Arbati finally broke free, feeling considerable affinity with a man released into the sunshine after many years in a subterranean dungeon. Heaven preserve us, he muttered under his breath, from Jansenist harridans!

Having replenished his drink, he noticed Peter Morgan standing by himself, as he had been for much of the evening, beside a statue of Philopoemen, the Arcadian general forced to drink poison by the hostile Messenians who captured him in 182 BC. Penny and Chad had returned and were putting up a brave front in another part of the room, while Morgan himself, sublimely indifferent, seemed neither to have noticed nor to care about the turmoil he had caused by his earlier indiscretion. He sipped his drink and watched Arbati approach with a look of supercilious bemusement spread on the features of his face.

'You're from the United States, I gather,' Arbati said, breaking the ice. He didn't know why he'd come over to talk to a man he had considerable motive to dislike, but something had prompted him. Curiosity, perhaps – or the impromptu hope that he'd learn something that would help Penny. Or perhaps it was just old-fashioned courtesy. He didn't know – but there he was anyway, the ice (for better or worse) truly rent and shattered.

'From Philadelphia, yes,' Morgan replied without interest.

'A lawyer, I understand,' Arbati persisted, smiling. 'An interesting line of work.'

'You seem to know a lot about me,' Morgan replied coldly. The dark eyes were appraising and predatory, weighing Arbati up as if he were a potential client – or a prospective meal.

'I met your wife on the beach,' Arbati explained. 'At Viareggio. She asked me to autograph her book for her. She happened to mention in passing that you were a lawyer.'

Morgan looked away, bored. 'Yes,' he said, 'I believe she may have told me something of the sort.'

The man was insufferable, but Arbati, never one to admit defeat easily, tried again. 'If you don't mind my asking,' he enquired pleasantly, 'what is it that brings you to Italy, Signor Morgan? Business or pleasure?'

'Both, as it happens,' Morgan grunted. 'Not that it's any particular concern of yours.'

The man was gratuitously offensive, an unsociable boor, and Arbati began to appreciate what his family was going through living with him. Had he always been like this? No, surely not, or someone as refined and sensitive as Penny would never have married him – although what she might ever have found attractive in the arrogant brute, he had to confess, eluded him completely at the moment. Well, he decided finally, enough was enough – and he'd definitely had enough.

'It is evident,' he said with cool civility, 'that we have nothing of mutual interest to discuss, *signore*. So I will bid you good evening.'

He turned away, seeking more companionable society, and had taken only a step or two when Morgan swirled suddenly, spilling his drink, and slapped at his back.

'Damn!' he cursed. 'What the hell . . .!'

Arbati turned back to see what had happened.

Morgan was twisting left and right, staring wildly about him and grabbing at the small of his back with his free hand. Anger and bafflement mingled on his face in equal proportions. He had expected when he'd wheeled around to find someone to shout at. But there was no one. The party ebbed and flowed around him in the way that parties do, with no hint that anything untoward had taken place.

But Arbati's sharp eye had caught sight of a tiny stain, no more than a drop or two, on the back of Morgan's grey silk suit jacket, just where he had slapped and held the fabric against his body. The stain was blood and Arbati knew instantly that, whatever had happened, it was more than a prank. He scanned the room with narrowed eyes in the direction from which the projectile – for instinct told him it had to have been a projectile of some kind – had come. There was nothing unusual, nothing suspicious that he could see. The perpetrator who had fired the weapon – a small bore revolver with a silencer, perhaps? – had melted innocuously into the surrounding activity. The other guests were talking, laughing, chewing, sipping their drinks. No one was moving away; no one was staring; one or two people cast cold glances at Morgan, sniffing at his bizarre behaviour; but no one except Arbati had noticed, it seemed, that anything was seriously amiss.

He caught a passing waiter by the sleeve. 'Call for an ambulance,' he said. '*Subito!*'

The man took one look at Arbati's face and scuttled off.

Arbati turned back to Morgan who was still staring around in angry bafflement and rubbing his back.

'You'd better sit down,' he said, taking the glass from Morgan's hand and easing him down on to the floor with his back against the wall. 'It's possible you've been shot. You mustn't move around. Help will be here in a minute. I've summoned an ambulance.'

Swiftly and efficiently, he posted waiters at the exits with instructions that no one was to enter or leave the building.

'You,' he said, taking one of them aside, 'get down to the Questura. Ask for Inspector Bonelli. Tell him he's needed here on the double. Now, move!' The Questura was in the south-west corner of Palazzo Ducale, only two minutes away. Hopefully, Giancarlo would still be in his office.

A circle had formed around the stricken man and Arbati had to push his way through. Where was Penny, he wondered? Did she know what was happening?

'Stand back,' he snapped. 'An ambulance is coming. Leave room for them to get through.'

It took Peter Morgan just under ten minutes to die.

He complained of blurred vision and dizziness, of a parched throat and mouth. His pulse, when Arbati felt the carotid artery in his neck, was rapid and erratic. With symptoms like these, it was clear Morgan had not been shot with a conventional revolver. Something more sinister – but what? he wondered – was going on. Then suddenly Morgan opened his mouth in a wordless scream, his eyes bulged in pain, and he slumped sideways, as if his heart had exploded in his chest. When Arbati felt again for a pulse, there was nothing. He closed the staring eyes and, out of decency, unfolded his handkerchief over the lifeless face.

'All right, keep back now, everyone,' he ordered, standing. 'There's nothing more we can do. Touch nothing. The police will be here soon, and they'll be wanting a statement from each of you. Try to remember now, while it's fresh, whether you saw or heard anything strange – anything at all – no matter how insignificant it may have seemed at the time.' As he spoke, his eyes scanned the room, searching for Penny.

She was against the opposite wall with Chad, looking over at the commotion on the far side with the disinterested fascination that people display at the scene of accidents and disasters. It was strange they never connected tragedy with themselves, never had a presentiment that the event might touch their own lives: he'd known relatives to stand outside a shooting scene with the same dispassionate absorption as the spectators around them, even though they might have known from the address that the victim was quite possibly their own flesh and blood.

He crossed the room and took her by the arm, guiding her to a nearby chair.

'It's your husband,' he said softly. 'He's dead, I'm afraid. He's been murdered.' He turned to Chad. 'Look after your mother, my boy. I'll be back as soon as I can.'

180

There was a commotion on the stairs and Giancarlo Bonelli, flanked by two uniformed officers, appeared through the hushed crowd that parted to let them pass.

'What's up?' he asked, spotting Arbati.

'Murder,' Arbati replied. 'Over here.' He added: 'Poison of some kind, I suspect.'

Bonelli knelt and lifted the handkerchief covering the dead man's face.

'*Porca miseria!*' he whistled. 'Dearing's cousin.'

PART THREE

Denouement

1

'The question is,' Arbati said, holding a piece of the glass tubing that had arrived with the autopsy report up to the light and turning it speculatively in his fingers, 'what precisely was the thing fired from? What was the murder weapon?'

The projectile, just over five centimetres in length and now in two pieces because Morgan had broken it when he'd twisted his body after it went in, was a slender pipette, hollow and now empty, that had been sharpened at one end on the bias like a syringe. The solution it held had been released into Morgan's system through the open tip and at the break where the tube had snapped inside his body.

Giancarlo Bonelli, standing at the window, shifted his weight from one leg to the other and shook his head.

'That,' he said, without turning, 'is a major mystery. My men searched every guest leaving the reception thoroughly and found nothing – nothing at all.' He took out a cigarette and lit it, tossing the spent match out into the cobbled courtyard below the window. 'And the other strange thing,' he went on, 'is that the weapon, whatever it was, apparently made no noise. Not one of the statements we took from the guests at the reception mentions anything about anyone hearing anything unusual. No bang, no pop, no report of any kind. It's as if the damned thing had been thrown like a dart – but someone would have noticed that. You don't wind up at a crowded party and chuck a glass javelin into someone's back without *somebody* thinking that what you're doing is distinctly odd and remembering it.' He shook his head. 'And, as it happens, it couldn't have been thrown or even rammed home by hand,' he added. 'The tube was buried in the intestines, just missing the liver, more than three centimetres below the skin, and there was no indication that the end had been broken off, as there would have been if the weapon had been something like a glass dagger. No, the thing was actually *fired* from something at close range – a mechanical weapon of some sort.'

Arbati frowned. 'Very odd,' he said. 'And there was nothing left behind in the room? Nothing that might have served as a weapon? A hollow tube of some kind, a piece of heavy elastic, a rubber sling – anything?'

Bonelli shook his head. 'We turned the place upside-down,' he said. 'There wasn't so much as a hairpin we overlooked.' He pressed his lips into a thin white line and flicked the ash irritably from the end of his cigarette. 'No, whatever the weapon was, it must have gone back out the door with whoever brought it in with them in the first place. We had it right in our hands, damn it, and we let it get away – which means, of course,' he added, 'that it didn't *look* like a weapon. It must have been disguised in some fashion.'

They were in Bonelli's office on the second floor of the Questura in Palazzo Ducale. The forensics report on Peter Morgan's cadaver and a letter seconding Arbati, *pro tempore*, to the Lucca constabulary had come through from Florence that morning. Bonelli had requested that Arbati be formally involved in the investigation since he'd been present when the murder occurred and since, as well, he knew something about the victim and had met a number of the prime suspects. The fact that Sir Richard Danvers, a powerful man with influential connections, was among those suspects made Arbati's tact and his experience with important cases an asset that Bonelli wanted on his side. He could sense in his bones that the case was a delicate and intricate affair, fraught with pitfalls and hidden dangers, and having his old friend right there on the spot, willing to be co-opted, was an opportunity not to be missed. The Carabinieri commander in Florence had fortunately seen matters the same way, and Arbati, as a result, was now on the team. When the time came, Bonelli of course would make the actual arrest or arrests since Lucca was his jurisdiction, but Arbati had been given full investigative powers and a free hand to play his cards pretty well as he saw fit.

'We can assume, I think,' Arbati said, running his eye over the forensics report, 'that our killer knows a thing or two about drugs. I can't imagine that atropine is a terribly common medication.' He looked down at the document that lay before him on the desk and furrowed his brow. 'What exactly,' he said, looking up again, '*is* the therapeutic use for the stuff anyway?'

'According to Doc Bindi-Santi,' Bonelli replied, 'it's used mainly in eye drops. Normally a 1% solution of atropine sulphate in sterile water. It dilates the pupils, apparently.'

Arbati raised an eyebrow. 'Our victim, however,' he said drily, 'didn't die from enlarged pupils. I was there; I know.' He ran his finger in a zigzag down the closely typed autopsy report from the forensic sciences laboratory in Florence. 'And how in God's name are we supposed to make any sense out of all this other gobble-degook?' He found the place he was looking for and tapped the page with his finger. 'Here, just listen to this bit, for instance,' he said, reading aloud: '"atropine inhibits the muscarinic actions of acetylcholine on structures innervated by postganglionic cholinergic nerves and on smooth muscle tissue, not so innervated, which responds to endogenous acetylcholine..."' He let his mouth fall open and crossed his eyes in mock idiocy. 'We're simple working cops, for heaven's sake, not research scientists. Do you have any idea what any of this actually *means*?'

'The bottom line,' Bonelli said with a straight face, 'is that one possible effect of a toxic dose of atropine is to induce uncontrollable ventricular tachycardia. And that, if you read on in the report, is precisely what happened to our victim.'

Arbati threw up his hands. 'Oh, don't *you* start with me!' he moaned.

Bonelli gave a simpering grin. 'I couldn't resist,' he said. 'You asked for it.'

'Well, now that you've had your fun,' Arbati said patiently, 'what exactly *did* happen to Signor Morgan?'

'In simple words,' Bonelli resumed, 'his heart tore itself apart. The atropine caused it to beat wildly out of control until *poof!* it just sort of blew up. Like a cart bumping down a rocky hillside until it shatters itself to pieces with the violence of its own momentum.'

Arbati nodded, remembering the erratic pulse he'd felt in Morgan's neck.

'But the interesting thing,' Bonelli continued, 'is that our murderer took something of a risk by using atropine at all. It seems that, while it may be fatal, it isn't always so. According to Doc Bindi-Santi, doses up to 1000mg have been given without the patient dying, although in other people much smaller doses have been lethal. It's unpredictable stuff: deadly for some, not so deadly for others. So, our killer was taking a chance – which might suggest,' he added, 'that, contrary to what you were saying a minute ago, he *doesn't* in fact know very much about drugs and was simply lucky. Maybe he – or she, for that matter – is just an amateur with a Deïaneira touch.'

'An interesting thought,' Arbati conceded.

'The fly in the ointment there, however,' Bonelli went on, 'is that the liver biopsy and urine sample taken from Morgan both suggest that the atropine was highly concentrated, in fact, virtually pure – perhaps 80% or 90%. In that strength, a little bit goes a long way.'

'Which means, I assume,' Arbati said, filling in the gaps, 'that it wasn't a commercially prepared solution.'

'Exactly,' Bonelli nodded. 'A normal adult dose by intravenous or intramuscular injection is 0.5mg, with a range of 0.4 to 0.6mg. It's used in surgery when the pulse rate and blood pressure drop abnormally. Since it speeds up heart action, it's used to restore the cardiac rate and arterial pressure. But Morgan had enough of the stuff floating around in him, or so it seems, to stop a bull elephant in its tracks.'

'Which surely,' Arbati said, furrowing his brow, 'brings us full circle, doesn't it, to the original argument? The murderer must have known exactly what he was doing. He gave a dose large enough to be absolutely certain of its effect.'

'Almost certain,' Bonelli corrected. 'As I said, atropine is unpredictable stuff: some it kills, some it doesn't.' He flicked the butt of his cigarette out on to the cobbles and turned back into the room. 'What it does mean, however,' he said, 'is that our killer didn't pick up his supply of the stuff at his corner pharmacy. In that concentration, you either steal it or you refine it yourself. You can't buy it in a pure form on the open market.'

'Well, that narrows the chase enormously then,' Arbati said with an ironic moue. 'We're after somebody who's either a chemist or a thief. There can't, I suppose, be many of either of those around.'

'Something like that,' Bonelli agreed. 'Or an avid gardener, of course. Atropine is an alkaloid derived from deadly nightshade – the Latin name for which, by the way, is *Atropa belladonna*. According to the dictionary I consulted, Atropos was one of the classical Parcae, the Fates. The other two were Clotho and Lachesis, but they don't seem to have had any deadly plants named after them.'

'Fascinating,' Arbati said dully. 'And no doubt it's information that will prove vital in our investigation.'

'I just thought you'd be interested,' Bonelli replied with a grin.

'The problem, however, is that you can grow the stuff – night-shade, I meant – almost anywhere. Out behind the house, in a greenhouse or a herb garden, even in a window box. A fact which,' he added, 'I'm afraid rather broadens the chase for us again, doesn't it?'

Working with Giancarlo, Arbati reflected, was going to be a real pleasure.

'You're a gold mine of arcane trivia,' he said. 'Is this how you spent your time before I joined the team?'

'I'm an avid reader,' Bonelli said with an unrepentant shrug.

'As a writer myself, that pleases me no end,' Arbati said, standing and working a kink out of the muscle in the calf of his leg, 'but right now we've got a murder to solve – so,' he went on, sitting down again and seeking to open a more productive investigative furrow, 'what do we know about the guests at the reception? All of them had the opportunity, of course, but how many of them had a motive to want Peter Morgan out of the way?'

'Very few, in fact, it seems,' Bonelli said, taking a sheaf of papers from the top of the filing cabinet and depositing it on the desk in front of Arbati. 'We can rule most of them out right at the start. Including waiters and serving staff, there were seventy-seven people in the Statue Gallery at the time of the murder. We've interviewed all of them. Most had no idea who the victim was or why anyone might want to kill him, and background checks have confirmed that there was, in virtually every case, no connection with the victim.' He crossed the room and sat down, tipping the chair back on its hind legs and sticking his feet up on the corner of the desk. 'There are eleven exceptions,' he went on, taking out a pack of Nazionales, removing one, and tossing the pack on to the desk where Arbati could help himself. 'Three people remember seeing Morgan around town: in a shop, at a restaurant, coming out of a hotel – that sort of thing. But they knew nothing about the man, not even that he was an American.'

'And the other eight?' Arbati asked, lighting a cigarette and dropping the burned-out match into the already half-filled ashtray on Giancarlo's cluttered desk.

'Interestingly enough, they're all connected, in one way or another,' Bonelli said, 'with the inquest into the death of James Dearing.'

Arbati pursed his lips and nodded. The information didn't really come as a surprise.

'First,' Bonelli went on, 'there's the grieving widow and Morgan's son. Neither was at the inquest, as you'll remember, and neither, when we questioned them, had ever heard of James Dearing – or so they claimed – or had any knowledge that he was Morgan's cousin. Morgan, they say, never mentioned either Dearing or the inquest to them. It's possible they're telling the truth, but why would Morgan have been so secretive about his own cousin? It doesn't add up.'

'If he *was* a cousin,' Arbati said softly.

Bonelli raised an eyebrow. 'Do you have any reason to think he wasn't?'

'No, not a reason exactly. Call it more a lurking suspicion – a hunch.'

'Oh dear,' Bonelli said, shaking his head. 'Another of those famous Arbati hunches, is it? I thought they'd pounded those out of you years ago, *amico mio*, at the academy where all Carabinieri life begins and takes on its inflexible shape.'

'On the contrary,' Arbati said, 'as soon as I got out from under their thumbs, I started giving my hunches free rein. Criminals, I've found, unlike Carabinieri cadets, don't spend a lot of their time boning up on standard psychological profiles. They tend to go off on their own. We'd be well advised to do the same, if we want to catch up with them.'

'Well, be that as it may,' Bonelli said, 'the surviving Morgans had an adequate motive for homicide, with or without cousin – or non-cousin – Dearing. Morgan, it seems, was having an affair, and both the wife and the son knew about it. The boy, in fact, told me he was glad his father was dead. Not a great deal of filial love there, I found.'

'Morgan had put them through a lot,' Arbati said neutrally, 'but not, I think, enough to call for such desperate measures. I've talked to Penny – Signora Morgan – a couple of times and she's told me a little of what was going on. Frankly, I don't think either Penny or Chad is the murdering type.'

'Perhaps not,' Bonelli said, raising an eyebrow, 'but we can hardly rule them out at this stage of the game either.' He gave Arbati a hard look, wondering how deep his interest in the widow Morgan ran. He'd seen them, he remembered, going into the reception at Palazzo Ducale together. Was there more to it than that . . .?

'No,' Arbati said, 'we can hardly rule them out at this point, I agree.' He drew on his cigarette, then tipped back his head and blew a long, thoughtful stream of smoke at the ceiling. 'Which brings us next, I suppose,' he said, looking down again at Bonelli, 'to the Kleists.'

'It does indeed,' Bonelli replied, surprised. Arbati had officially been on the case for only a little over an hour. Already, it seemed, he knew as much as Giancarlo did about it himself and he'd been working at nothing else for the past three days. 'But just how the hell,' he asked, shaking his head in wonder, 'do *you* know about the Kleists? And what, for that matter, leads you to think of them as possible suspects?'

'Would you believe – a hunch?'

'No.'

'Well then,' Arbati grinned, 'it must have been a deduction.' He ground out the butt of his half-smoked cigarette in the ashtray and went on, 'Signora Kleist, as I realized when I saw her again at the reception, was the mysterious blonde at the Dearing inquest. The one, you remember, in the dark glasses who came in late and sat at the back of the room. She'd come to keep an eye on Peter Morgan, her lover. Maybe they had plans for lunch or something of the sort after the inquest was over. Anyway, when I saw her again at the reception, she was with her husband – and it was clear from the thunder-and-lightning look on Professor Kleist's face when he saw Morgan that he'd somehow twigged to the dark deeds going on between Morgan and his wife. If looks could kill, Giancarlo, I can tell you Morgan would have been struck dead on the spot, and I had the distinct impression that if it hadn't been a public gathering the good professor would have bounced his wife's lover off the wall a few times to soften him up and then gutted him with his pocket knife. He was mad as hell. Mad enough, I'd say, to kill.' He added, perhaps a little smugly: 'And therefore the professor is a prime suspect in the murder, QED.'

'It goes even further,' Bonelli said with a grin of his own. Maybe there *was* after all, he thought, something he could tell Arbati about the case that he didn't already know or hadn't already worked out for himself. 'You remember the young Neanderthal who was with the Kleists at the reception?'

'Yes, vividly.'

'Well, as I discovered when I talked to them, he's the professor's eldest son by a first marriage They call him Willi Junior and the father Willi Senior – although it's hard to imagine there's any biological connection between the two of them, isn't it? I mean, it's like trying to get your mind around the idea that somebody

191

like Zero Mostel is Charles de Gaulle's son. Well, in any case, it seems that young Willi caught Peter Morgan and Ilse Kleist in bed together at the Hotel Universo. I got this from Professor Kleist himself, after a little prodding – and his wife and the boy both confirmed it. Anyway, young Willi was hiding in the wardrobe trying to get dirty pictures – I ask you, Carlo, what *is* the world coming to? – but Morgan caught him at it, smashed his camera, roughed him up a bit, and tossed him out on his slimy ear.'

'Which accounts for the bandage he was wearing at the reception.'

'Exactly.'

'As well, of course,' Arbati added, 'as giving him a pretty good motive for wanting to see rough justice served on Morgan.'

Bonelli nodded. 'Yes, I'd say so,' he said. 'A definite possibility.'

'An interesting scenario,' Arbati mused, staring out at the empty windows on the far side of the courtyard which Bonelli's office overlooked. 'And when exactly did this little bedroom farce take place?'

'Last Monday afternoon. Four days before the reception at Palazzo Ducale.'

'Leaving plenty of time,' Arbati said, pursing his lips, 'for either Kleist *papà* or Kleist *figlio* to plot his revenge and then carry it out.'

'Precisely.'

'And Frau Kleist?' Arbati enquired.

Bonelli shook his head. 'At this point,' he said, 'there's no obvious motive. Morgan was her lover and she's one of the few people I talked to who actually seems to have liked him.' He shrugged. 'But stranger things have happened. Think of Lucrezia Borgia. Maybe Ilse Kleist just has a motive we know nothing about.'

'Which brings us finally then,' Arbati said, 'to the three *Inglesi* who were present at the Dearing inquest: Nigel Harmsworth, Cecilia Hathaway, and Sir Richard Danvers.'

'Last but not least,' Bonelli said, nodding. 'I interviewed all three of them myself. There's something strange going on there, but I can't put my finger on it. Harmsworth and Sir Richard are – or rather *were*, I suppose, since Dearing and Morgan are both dead – involved in something fishy with the Americans, and my guess is that they didn't like each other very much.'

'I'd say that's putting it mildly,' Arbati said. 'I was watching them at the inquest. Harmsworth was terrified of Morgan, and Morgan, it was clear, had no love for either Harmsworth or Sir

Richard. But the most revealing moment, I thought, was when Morgan mentioned during his testimony that he was a lawyer from Philadelphia. It was an offhand remark as I remember it, but Sir Richard nearly swallowed his tongue. The word Philadelphia rang some kind of bell in his brain and, from that point on, he was perched on the edge of his seat, soaking up everything the American had to say. But the interesting part is this: I had the feeling – though it's nothing more than a feeling – that Sir Richard had just then discovered something about Morgan that Harmsworth had known or suspected all along but hadn't for some reason bothered, or perhaps trusted Sir Richard enough, to tell him. If I'm right, it's a curious fact, given that Harmsworth and Sir Richard are such old friends.' He rose and walked slowly to the window, turning and leaning back against the sill. 'I agree with you, by the way,' he went on, his mind reviewing clips of the inquest, 'about there being something – and as you say, probably something fishy – going on between the English and the Americans. They were covering something up, and the coroner was too slow-witted to pick up the signals and pry loose whatever they were hiding. The problem is that *we* still don't have any idea what it was either, and hence we have no way of knowing whether or not it might be a motive for murder. Who knows? Maybe they were negotiating time-shares in a Mediterranean condo, or acting as intermediaries in a peace initiative for Bosnia, or forming a committee to save the Brazilian rain forest? You don't have to actually *like* the people you're sometimes forced to work with. It could be any of a thousand things – and not all of them lead to an atropine dart in Morgan's back.'

Bonelli was unconvinced. 'No,' he said firmly, shaking his head, 'there's something sinister there. I can feel it. And whatever it is, it has something to do with Ghirlandaio. I'd be willing to stake a year's salary on it.'

'Ghirlandaio?' Arbati said, puzzled. 'The Renaissance painter, you mean?'

'The same,' Bonelli nodded. 'I forgot to mention it – it's somewhere in that stack of reports you're taking away to read – but our friend Dearing had a slip of paper in his pocket with the word *Ghirlandaio* on it. Nothing else: just that single name. I'm convinced it's an important clue but I can't find anything else in the case to link it with. At least, not so far. Harmsworth denies having any idea why Dearing might have had the name in his pocket. He's lying, but I can't prove it.'

193

'It's just a *hunch* then,' Arbati said with a wry grin.

'*Touché*,' Bonelli said, grimacing. 'It is, I suppose, though I hate like hell to admit it.' He dropped his feet to the floor and leaned a shirt-sleeved elbow on the desk. 'And that leaves us still with Signorina Hathaway,' he said, 'and I must confess I have no idea how she fits into the equation, unless somehow, in ways I don't understand, she was involved with Harmsworth and Sir Richard in whatever enigmatic little game they were playing with the Americans. I can't see, otherwise, why she'd want Morgan out of the way.'

'Oh,' Arbati smiled, 'there's a simple enough reason for that, I think. Signorina Hathaway is hopelessly – and *hopelessly* is the right word – in love with Signor Harmsworth. My guess, in fact, is that she's been suffering, with no hope of a cure, from that particular malady for some considerable time, probably for several years. She'd do, I think, almost anything to protect him. Now, since she was well aware that Harmsworth was terrified of Morgan – she saw what we saw at the inquest, after all – there was nothing to prevent her from deciding to remove a threat to the man she loved by removing the evil agent of that threat. Love, my friend, is a powerful motive and murder is a definitive solution.'

'Ah, love . . .' Bonelli reflected, shaking his head. 'The things, alas, we do for love.'

Arbati nodded. 'Signorina Hathaway is a tough and resourceful lady. I don't think she'd let much get in her way if she wanted something badly enough. And besides,' he added, 'poison is a woman's weapon. Yes, I think there's no doubt that we can include Signorina Hathaway in our list of candidates for this particular crime.'

The bells of San Michele pealed in the distance and Bonelli looked at his watch.

'Well,' he said, standing and stretching, 'a good morning's work, I'd say.' He added with a grin, 'We've assembled our cast of villains and there's not, you'll notice, an Italian among them. Americans, Germans, and English: a cast of exiles, *amico mio*. Who says the Italians are a violent people? We just clean up after the other nations.' He crossed to a wash-basin that stood in the corner and ran some water over his hands, then squinting into a grimy mirror suspended from a nail in the wall, smoothed down what remained of his thinning hair. Finished, he turned on his heel and, plucking a pair of dark glasses from his breast pocket, said: 'I'm

194

beginning to feel distinctly peckish. Lunch is in order, I think –
and besides, if I remember correctly, I owe you a drink.'

'You do,' Arbati said, levering himself on to his feet, 'and lunch
is an excellent suggestion.'

Bonelli paused with his hand on the doorknob and turned.

'I'm glad you're here, my friend,' he said. 'There's something
unsavoury about this case and I have the sinking feeling that
we're not going to like what we find when we come to the end of
it.'

2

The house was a large modern villa perched on a shoulder of
Monte Pisano overlooking a valley of neat rectangular fields with
the *autostrada* laid out across the landscape like a black ribbon in
the distance. For privacy's sake, the house was set back from the
road on a small eminence and girdled by a grove of lacy conifers.

Bonelli parked the Carabinieri Fiat in the cobbled drive and
together he and Arbati climbed a flight of terracotta steps, which
looked freshly swept, to the front portico. The day was warm and
sunny and, high overhead, unseen wires pulled patches of cloud
across the sky. It was the kind of day, Arbati couldn't help
reflecting, more suited for stretching out under a beach umbrella
and contemplating nothing in particular than it was for chasing
down leads in a murder investigation.

Bonelli pressed the button on the brass plaque beside the door
and inside, like a far-off angelus, the muted tintinnabulation of a
chime echoed in the silence. After a few moments the door swung
open and Chad Morgan appeared with a book in his hand, his
place held open with a crooked index finger. The book, Arbati
noticed, was Dickens' *Great Expectations* – not the sort of thing he
would have expected to find in the hands of a sixteen-year-old,
unless, of course, it was a school text and therefore mandatory
reading.

'Mom's in the kitchen,' he said in halting Italian, letting the two
policemen in and showing them down a hall into a spacious, well-
appointed room with large windows opening out, through a frame
of trees, on to a panoramic prospect of the valley. 'You can wait in
here, if you want. I'll tell her you're here.'

Arbati looked around the room. The Morgans, it was evident, lived very well. There was a suite of chairs and a matching sofa upholstered in olive green leather, expensive chrome-and-glass tables, a large television set nestled in the middle of a built-in entertainment centre containing the latest electronic gadgetry, a desk with a state-of-the-art computer and laser printer, and on the walls what seemed to be original canvases by Kandinsky and Paul Klee. The owner of the villa, an auto parts magnate in Torino, no doubt extracted a handsome monthly rent-cheque to protect his investment.

A moment later Penny Morgan appeared in the doorway, wiping her fingers on a gingham apron. 'I'm sorry,' she said, looking up, 'I was baking. I wasn't expecting – ' She stopped, catching sight of Arbati, and straightened her dress as a reflex. 'Oh, Carlo!' she said, smiling. 'What a pleasant surprise.' Patches of pink confusion bloomed suddenly on her cheeks.

She looked, Arbati thought, in spite of her surprise at seeing him, relaxed and oddly – indeed almost disconcertingly – normal, given all that had recently happened in her life. She appeared happy and domestic; her hair was tied back with a negligent ribbon, she wore no make-up, and there were traces of flour on her forehead where she had flicked a tuft of hair out of the way with powdered fingers. She didn't strike him as looking like a recent widow at all.

'I thought, inspector,' she said, turning back to Bonelli, 'that I'd already answered all your questions – or perhaps there's something new?'

Bonelli shook his head. 'No, nothing new, *signora*,' he said a little stiffly. 'Police work, I'm afraid, is the rather tiresome business of tramping over the same ground again and again until you eventually notice something in the bushes that, for some reason, never caught your eye before.'

She gave him a disarming smile. 'So, we're about to beat the bushes again then, are we?'

Bonelli nodded. 'Yes, I'm afraid so, *signora – col vostro permesso.*'

That smile again: she had taken Bonelli's measure and could, if she had chosen, have wrapped him around her little finger. For all his bravado in private, Giancarlo had always been intimidated by a pretty woman. They left him tongue-tied and feeling exposed, like a small boy in a round hat and short trousers. She said:

'You make it sound, inspector, as though I have a choice. But I don't for a moment suppose that I really do.' Without awaiting a reply, she turned to Arbati, although her words were still addressed to Bonelli. 'And is Carlo – or perhaps I should say, Detective Arbati – investigating the case now too?'

'I am, yes,' Arbati intervened. He added, 'And it's still Carlo, I hope.'

'Yes, of course,' she said, looking away a little flustered. 'Well,' she went on, regaining her composure, 'if we're going to be here for a while, I suggest you both sit down. I'll fix us some coffee. I was just about to make some for myself anyway.' She turned in the doorway. 'Is there anything else I can offer you? I've just finished a batch of rather splendid-looking pecan tarts.'

'No, thank you,' Arbati said, patting his waistline. 'Coffee will be fine for me.' He added: 'Perhaps, however, you could ask Chad to join us. I'd like to hear what he remembers of events the other evening.'

'Certainly,' she said. 'And you, inspector?' she asked, turning to Bonelli. 'Can you be tempted?'

'Too easily, alas,' Bonelli confessed. 'Yes, I'd love a tart. I have a bit of a sweet tooth.'

She disappeared and returned shortly, preceded by Chad carrying cups of coffee on a tray and a plate of crusty tarts. She had, Arbati noticed, taken the time to remove her apron, run a comb through her hair, and put on some lipstick. She was, in fact, a remarkably attractive woman: tall and slender with a face at once strong and sensitive dominated by a pair of hazel eyes that looked out on the world with understanding and sympathy, and a hint, too, of surprised irony, as if anticipating the fact that life never serves up quite what one expects it to. If he were ever to fall in love again, Arbati knew, it would be with someone like Penny Morgan. You'd never have to wonder what she was thinking, never have to guess at her moods, her joys and secret sorrows: you could read everything she was feeling in her eyes, those frank and faithful mirrors of her soul. He'd noticed that about her, he remembered, that first day on the beach at Viareggio – and it struck him again now.

Chad set the tray down without a word and slipped into a corner of the sofa, making himself as inconspicuous as possible. Arbati gave him an encouraging smile. It was only natural that the boy should be apprehensive about being questioned by the police, especially in a strange country. He was still a teenager and, no matter how grown-up he thought he was, it was bound to be a daunting experience for him.

197

Penny distributed the mugs, offering milk and sugar, then took a seat beside her son and said in her frank way: 'Well, where do we begin?'

'At the beginning, I think,' Arbati said. 'We need to know everything you remember about the night of the reception and the days leading up to it, whether the details seem significant to you or not. Solving a crime is a little like putting a skeleton together from a pile of bones belonging to different species: not everything is relevant and some parts that are important don't look at first as if they possibly could be; but eventually, if you work at it long enough, a pattern begins to emerge, the right pieces seem to jump out at you, and the puzzle falls into place. I don't want you to tell us simply what you *think* might be important. Give us all the bones, however unimportant they seem, and then let us go away and work out what belongs and what doesn't.' He gave this little speech in some form or other whenever he interviewed witnesses: it reduced his headaches later on from their tendency to omit crucial data while editorializing and unconsciously overstating their memories of what they'd seen and heard. 'All right, then,' he concluded, 'so I want to know what you *actually* remember, not what has seemed, since then, to become meaningful or memorable about those memories. Okay?'

Penny and Chad both nodded dutifully.

He began with easy questions, speaking slowly for Chad's benefit, switching occasionally to English, making certain that the boy understood. He took them back through events on the evening of the reception, step by step, prodding them to reconstruct the occasion as if they were reliving it for a second time: where were they standing? what were they looking at? who were they talking to? what did they see and hear? He was interested not so much in *what* they said, as in *how* they said it. The intonation and body language were as important as the verbal responses themselves. Gradually, the questions became more pointed, the answers more revealing.

'And when you left the room after you'd realized that Frau Kleist was your husband's mistress,' he asked softly, 'where did you go?'

It wasn't easy asking such questions, reviving such memories, pressing her to relive the pain of her betrayal, but there was a job that had to be done. It was possible, though not probable, that she was implicated: she might have known for certain about her husband's infidelity beforehand, then run out of the room as if she'd only just discovered it and retrieved the weapon loaded with an atropine pipette that she'd hidden outside or in another part of the building. She might be a consummate actress, her apparent shock and grief parts of an elaborate alibi to throw the police off the scent. Not that he believed any of it for a minute, of course; but he had to clear her of guilt before he could, in conscience, trust in her honesty: he had to eliminate her from suspicion in order to validate her innocence. Sometimes, he reflected, being an investigator could seem a remarkable perversion of the very values it was instituted to defend and preserve.

'Oh, I don't know,' Penny said a little hoarsely, remembering. 'I just ran. I was pretty sure he was seeing someone else, of course, but I wasn't prepared to be confronted with it in public. It was the humiliation, I suppose, that made me run. I just wanted to escape, to get away as far and as fast as I could. I might never have stopped running if Chad hadn't caught up with me and made me sit down on a bench. Once I'd had a good cry, I knew I'd survive – and then we went back into the reception. I thought I'd have it out with Peter at home later, once we were alone. I didn't know if he was planning to leave me or just having a casual fling. I guess I never will, now.' Tears brimmed in her eyes but she kept control of herself. 'And, who knows,' she added with a martyred smile, 'maybe that's for the best. Perhaps I wouldn't have been strong enough to handle the truth.'

'And how long,' Arbati asked, hating himself for having to continue, 'were you outside before you returned to the reception? Do you have any idea?'

'Not long,' she said, 'but I don't really know. Time seemed to have stopped. I was outside, then back inside – and then you came over and told me that Peter had been killed. It was all so fast and yet at the same time seemed somehow to be happening in slow motion, like a movie with half the frames cut out, that I don't really have any sense of how long anything took. I'm sorry I can't be more helpful, but it's all just a kind of blur in my mind.'

'And you Chad?' Arbati said, switching to English. 'Is that what you remember?'

Chad nodded. 'Pretty much, yes. We weren't outside for very long, and we hadn't been back inside very long when Dad got killed.'

'And while you were outside,' Arbati pressed gently, 'you sat on a bench for a few minutes and then came straight back into the reception, is that right? You didn't go any place else or do anything in particular.'

'Yes, that's right.'

'And you didn't, either of you, bring anything back into the reception with you?'

'No.'

Arbati paused, then said: 'I have to ask you a difficult question now, Chad, and I want you to think carefully and be very truthful when you answer it, okay?'

The boy nodded, his face long and grave.

'I have to know,' Arbati said softly, 'what you thought of your father. Did you love him?'

Chad gave a quick glance at his mother, then looked back at Arbati. 'No,' he said, 'not very much. He was a bad father.'

'In what way was he a bad father? Did he beat you?'

'No, nothing like that,' Chad said, shaking his head. 'He shouted at us a lot – all of us, even Mom – but he never beat us. The yelling got worse when we came over here. Back in the States, he spent a lot of time away from home and we didn't see much of him. He was never there for us when we needed him.' He stopped for a moment, then went on, his dark eyes flashing: 'But mainly it was because he was hurting Mom. He was seeing that other woman and didn't seem to care what it did to Mom. I hated him for that.'

'How long had you known he was having an affair?'

'For about a week,' Chad said. 'I guessed it the day we visited the cathedral. When we came out, we saw him in a café when he was supposed to be at a meeting in Florence. He said he'd gotten away early and had just arrived back, and then he blew his cork when Mom didn't believe him – well, none of us did, really – and he called her a dirty, prying slut and a bunch of other things. That's when I knew. I'd suspected something before, but that's when I knew for sure.'

The boy's honesty was transparent and Arbati heaved a silent sigh of relief. He couldn't rule them out completely as suspects yet, but the omens were all good. He knew now what he needed to know about their movements and attitude to events on the night of the reception. There had been no surprises in what they said: their stories were consistent and believable. It was time to find out if they knew anything – whether they *knew* they knew it or not – that could lead him to the murderer. He accepted Penny's offer of a second cup of coffee, looked longingly at the plate of scrumptious pecan tarts (of which Bonelli had demolished three), then took the questions off in a different direction. What did they know about James Dearing? Nothing, they said; they'd never heard of him until Inspector Bonelli had asked them the same question when he'd first questioned them. Did Morgan have enemies in Italy that they were aware of? Did he receive threatening calls or letters? Whom did he meet in Florence and what was the nature of their business? Were they certain, in fact, that he ever actually went to Florence on business...? Every question met a brick wall. Peter Morgan had kept his family in the dark about his affairs. His life was a closed book, a stony enigma, a sealed tomb. Finally, Arbati said, without much hope of being rewarded for his pains:

'Does the name Ghirlandaio mean anything to you? There's a chance it may be significant in connection with whatever business your husband was conducting while he was here.'

A look of recognition dawned in Penny Morgan's eyes. 'It's odd you should ask,' she said. 'Only yesterday, when I was looking in Peter's credenza for some scrap paper, I stumbled over one of those portable strongboxes people keep their valuables in. It was locked of course, but the police had given me Peter's effects, including a little key on a brass medallion that I'd never seen before. He must have always carried it with him. Well, anyway, curiosity got the better of me – so I fetched the key and opened the box. I thought, I suppose, that I might learn something about a man that I didn't, it seems, know very much about, in spite of the fact that I'd been married to him for eighteen years. Inside the box were our traveller's cheques, Peter's ruby ring, and a brown envelope marked "Ghirlandaio" which contained five or six letters and some legal documents, all having to do with some forged paintings. I must confess I was a little disappointed.' She shrugged. 'I leafed through the material but none of it made any sense, so I closed the box up and put it back where I'd found it. I would probably never have thought of it again if you hadn't mentioned the name Ghirlandaio. It's such an odd name, isn't it?'

'Do you suppose, Signora Morgan,' Bonelli interjected with a little more enthusiasm than strict professional disinterest would have dictated, 'that we could possibly have a look at what's inside that envelope?' From the beginning, he'd been convinced there was a Ghirlandaio connection and now, at last, something concrete had dropped out of heaven to corroborate his instinct.

'Of course,' she replied. 'Shall I get it for you now?'

'Yes, please,' he said, leaning forward, 'if it's no trouble.'

'It's no trouble at all, inspector,' she replied, rising. 'It's less than ten feet away.'

She crossed to a desk that held a computer, a laser printer, and a plastic floppy-disc caddy. Opening the top drawer, she removed a key and then, turning, stooped down out of sight, resurfacing momentarily with a white, asbestos-lined security box which she placed on the desk and unlocked.

'I hope it's something useful,' she said, returning and handing a manilla folder to Bonelli who was grinning in anticipation like a Cheshire cat.

He removed the contents and scanned them quickly, his eyebrows working vigorously, then passed the sheaf without comment across to Arbati.

'I think, in fact,' he said, turning to Penny and doing his best to suppress his delight, 'they're likely to prove extremely useful.' He went on in a more neutral voice: 'If you have no objection, Signora Morgan, I'd like your permission to keep them for a few days. They're something we should study carefully, and I'd like to have some of the information they contain confirmed by experts. We'll return the documents, of course, as soon as we have finished with them.'

'Yes, I suppose so,' Penny said, nodding. 'I don't see why not. They're really of no use to me.'

Arbati scanned down a page typed on embossed letterhead from the Rijksmuseum in Amsterdam. Addressed to a Mr Jonathan Barnes of Chicago, Illinois and dated 10 March 1991, it read:

Dear Mr Barnes,

I have now concluded my examination of the portrait entitled *Young Girl with Lilies*.

It is perfectly true, as you point out in your letter of 22 October last, that Vasari, in his *Vite de' più eccellenti Architetti, Pittori, e Scultori Italiani* (second edition, 1568), describes a painting by Ghirlandaio depicting his own daughter, Regina, in a prospect of lilies. This picture was lost in the eighteenth century, its last recorded owner being Pierre d'Armanteuil, comte de Beauséant, who was guillotined in 1789 and whose estates were subsequently sold off. At that point, the Ghirlandaio (along with many other priceless artefacts) disappeared and has not, according to my enquiries, been seen since. You

202

will understand, then, my anticipation in undertaking to clean the work for you and to assess its value for public sale.

I must report however that, after the most scrupulous examination, I have concluded that the painting is a forgery. The pigments are chemically inconsistent with those employed by artists of the late Quattrocento and the canvas – a fragment of which I took the liberty of submitting to spectroscopic and carbon analysis – has been artificially aged. I am afraid there can be no doubt about these conclusions, which might perhaps have eluded a less meticulous eye. The forgery is a clever piece of work but a forgery nonetheless, and I must conclude, with considerable regret, that the lost portrait of Ghirlandaio's daughter is still lost.

I deeply regret, sir, being the bearer of such tidings, and remain, yours truly,

Frans van den Eshof, D.Litt. (Oxon.)
Curator-in-Chief

It was instantly clear why Giancarlo was anxious to take the documents in Peter Morgan's Ghirlandaio file away to be studied and analysed. If they confirmed what Arbati suspected, then the results of their investigation might well lead, not simply to the apprehension of a murderer, but to the collapse of Danvers' House, one of the largest and most prestigious auction houses in the world – not to mention the indictment for art fraud of Sir Richard himself and God only knew how many others who were involved with him: Nigel Harmsworth almost certainly, and perhaps Cecilia Hathaway as well. Having effectively ruled out Penny and Chad as potential murderers, they had narrowed the field to the English and the Germans. Peter Morgan had, almost certainly, been killed in retribution either for his promiscuity or for his greed – and the interviews to follow, Arbati reflected, were likely to bring a lot of hoary old skeletons clinking and clanking out of the closet.

He slipped the documents back into their manilla folder and, when he looked up, Penny was staring at him with frank, questioning eyes:

'Do you have any idea what they mean?' she asked in English. 'I couldn't make head nor tail of them.'

'They mean, I'm afraid,' Arbati replied, 'that your husband was quite possibly blackmailing someone and was murdered when the scheme went sour.'

She was incredulous. Her eyes opened wide and for a moment

203

she could say nothing. When words did come finally, they tumbled out incoherently in a turbulent stream of denial. 'Peter? Blackmail? It's – it's – well, it's *preposterous*! I can't believe it.'

'And why is that?' Arbati asked evenly.

It was Chad who answered. 'I can believe it,' he said in a quiet voice. 'One day – I guess it was about two weeks ago – when I was reading in my room, I heard Dad shouting over the telephone to somebody. He was talking about this guy Ghirlandaio and he said something about making a killing on the deal if whoever he was talking to would get the lead out and put the squeeze on the old bastard. I didn't think much of it at the time – Dad was always yelling at somebody about something – but it sounds to me like we knew a lot less about him than we thought we did. If he could cheat on you, Mom, he could cheat on anybody. That's what I think anyway.'

Penny Morgan turned and looked at her son with tear-filled eyes. 'I suppose you're right,' she said, yielding. 'We really didn't know him very well, I guess, did we? It's just that I'm having a little trouble at the moment accepting that I could have been so blind – and so gullible. I don't know whether to sit down and have a good cry or go out to the kitchen and start breaking dishes.'

There was nothing more to be learned from the Morgans and Arbati and Bonelli, anxious to be away, rose to take their leave. At the front door, Arbati turned back. It was an awkward moment. He wished there was something he could say, something he could do to make it easier for her. But there was, he knew, nothing he could offer.

'How long will you be staying on here?' he asked.

Penny shrugged. 'Until the police have finished with us, I suppose. Then we'll go back to the States and start over. Life goes on.'

He shifted awkwardly. 'If there's anything you need . . .'

'Of course,' she said, giving him a wan smile. 'Your offer still stands, I know. Thank you, Carlo.'

Chad stepped forward and put his arm around his mother's shoulder.

'We'll be fine,' he said.

Arbati studied the boy's resolute face for a moment and then nodded. 'I believe you will,' he said, smiling. 'Yes, son, I truly believe you will.'

*

Bonelli pulled the car smoothly off on to the narrow verge in front of the cottage and shut off the engine.

It was a distinct pleasure, Arbati reflected, to be driven around for a change by someone who considered a car a convenient and necessary method of transportation instead of, in some perverse way, a mechanical extension of the libido. Giorgio Bruni, his partner in Florence, fell into the latter category – and Arbati never entered a car with him without a small prayer and the helpless sensation that his number in the cosmic lottery was about to be drawn. With Bonelli at the wheel, on the other hand, there was time to enjoy the scenery and he arrived at his destination rested and not rattled into gibbering incoherence as if he'd just stepped off a carnival ride. Yes, he'd miss Giancarlo when it was all over, in more ways than one.

After leaving the Morgans' villa in San Leonardo, they had driven back to the Questura, gone carefully over the contents of the Ghirlandaio file and sent off a half-dozen faxes to corroborate its details, then walked up the street to Trattoria da Leo for a lunch of fresh rolls, a creamy wedge of pecorino cheese, and a substantial bowl of red bean and shallot soup. The investigation was falling nicely into place and they could afford, they felt, to linger over the carafe of house *rosso* they'd ordered with their meal. The afternoon was already mapped out: a visit to the *Inglesi* at Villa San Felice with a stop at Cecilia Hathaway's cottage on the way up. It would be instructive, given what they now suspected about a Ghirlandaio connection, to hear what all three of them had to say. The documents in Morgan's folder didn't convict anyone of murder, although they made it probable that, in due course, a number of other serious charges would eventually be laid. For the moment, their visit was a scouting expedition – an effort to assess how best to proceed when the faxes they'd sent had provided them with more information – and it was with that limited expectation that they had stopped at the fork in the road and were now approaching, up a flagstone path flanked by well-tended rosebeds, the front door of Cecilia Hathaway's cottage.

There was no bell and Bonelli knocked. From inside came the bark of a dog – a single, sharp yap. The windows were open and the breeze was billowing the chintz curtains in what was probably the sitting-room.

They waited.

Arbati looked around at the freshly painted windows, the prickly rose stems heavy with scented blooms, the lichen-spotted stone of the waist-high wall encircling the property. Nothing was untended, nothing allowed to go to seed. Signorina Hathaway, it was obvious, was a proud and fastidious occupant.

Bonelli knocked a second time. Again, the reply came in the form of a single, sharp *rruuff!*

He waited briefly, then squinted in through a lace curtain to the narrow hallway beyond. In the middle of the floor, four-square and immovable, stood a brindled bull terrier looking up at the door like Leonidas defending the pass at Thermopylae.

'Maybe she's at the back and can't hear,' Bonelli said. 'Let's have a look.'

They made their way around to the small enclosed yard at the back: a concrete fishpond in the centre, a potting-shed to one side, along the other side an impressive herb garden, sectioned and set out in neat, rectangular beds divided by rows of wood chips. A place for everything and everything in its place. The only signs that labour ever took place were a wheelbarrow tipped on end beside the staved rain barrel under the downspout and a pair of rubber boots, venerable with age and use, that stood in untenanted repose on a mat outside the back door. There was no sign that anyone was about.

Bonelli rapped on the door; then, making a visor of his hands, he put his face against the sidelight and peered in. There, confronting him, holding the middle of the floor in what looked to be a summer kitchen, was the brindled bull terrier.

'*Rruuff!*' the dog said.

'*Rruuff!*' Bonelli replied, and the animal tipped its head on one side and gave a puzzled look. 'Let that be a lesson to you,' Bonelli said, turning away with a smug grin. 'Teach you not to trifle with the police.'

Arbati was in among the herbs, down on his haunches examining something.

'No one at home,' Bonelli announced. 'We can try later, if you'd like.'

Arbati plucked a sprig from the plant he was bent over and popped one of the ruffled leaves into his mouth. 'Peppermint,' he said. 'Want some?'

Bonelli wrinkled his nose. 'No, thanks,' he said, 'I like my foliage cooked.'

The road to San Felice was up a narrow unpaved track with a series of dramatic switchbacks. Bonelli negotiated the curves with skill. About two-thirds of the way along, at a point where the road passed through an umbrageous grove of towering chestnuts, they saw Cecilia Hathaway coming toward them, moving briskly downhill in the direction of her cottage.

'A tough old bird,' Bonelli observed with something akin to wonder. 'It must be four or five kilometres to the top. Not a thing I'd care to try on a hot day, even at my age.'

'A pity we weren't a little sooner,' Arbati mused. 'It might have been useful to have seen the three of them together.'

'Shall I stop? We could pick her up, then give her a lift home later.'

'No,' Arbati said, reconsidering. 'No point in muddying the waters at this stage. Keep going. Harmsworth and old Sir Richard, if he's in one of his truculent moods, will be quite enough for one visit, I should imagine.'

Bonelli slowed to a crawl and eased the little Fiat almost into the bushes to give her passage.

'Good afternoon, gentlemen,' she fluted as she sailed past, raising the gnarled wand of her stout ashplant in salutation. 'A beautiful day for a walk, don't you think? So wonderfully warm and invigorating.' And then suddenly she was behind them, striding away, so swiftly that their muttered greetings fell upon the empty air.

And just what, Arbati wondered, was she doing up at San Felice . . .?

Bonelli increased their speed and soon a pair of tall, wrought-iron gates hove into view. They passed through and up a broad cobbled drive to the imposing façade of the villa itself, the Guinigi escutcheon embossed ostentatiously over the central door on the terraced second floor. It was an imposing sight with the mountains in the background and Arbati was duly impressed.

'Wait until you see inside,' Bonelli grunted. 'It's enough to convince you that crime in fact does pay, and very handsomely too.'

The door was opened by Molly DuBartas, Sir Richard's nurse. The look on her face, when she saw who had rung the bell, was one of bored resignation – the sort of glazed stare she reserved for door-to-door encyclopaedia salesmen and the representatives of religious societies hawking *Watchtowers* and other certificates of salvation.

'Ah, inspector,' she said in a flat, nasal inflection. 'To what do we owe the pleasure? Another round of questions, I suppose?'

'I'm afraid so,' Bonelli replied. 'This, by the way,' he went on, 'is Detective Inspector Arbati from Florence. He's been assigned to assist our local force with the investigation.'

'Ah, yes, the poet,' she said without interest, turning away. 'Well, if you'll just follow me then, gentlemen.'

She led them through the marble foyer where classical statues stared sightlessly from scalloped niches, then down a series of echoing corridors to a sequestered room somewhere at the back of the villa. Pausing at the door, she said officiously, her hand on the handle:

'Sir Richard is having his thermal treatment. Be as brief as you can. He tires easily.'

She opened the door and they found themselves in a large windowless room dominated by a commercial tanning device reminiscent in size and shape of a cut-away of an iron-lung machine. Sir Richard, naked and emaciated, lay stretched on his back under a mirrored hood like a kipper on a griddle, his eyes protected by circles of black felt, his genitals obscured by a strategically draped towel. Light streamed down and around his supine form, giving him the uncanny appearance in the otherwise darkened room of a high-tech Messiah awaiting the divine touch of resurrection.

'It's the police again, Sir Richard,' the nurse said.

'Christ,' Sir Richard muttered, moving only his lips, as if he were glued to the pallet under him, 'can't a man even brown in peace? Are you there, inspector?'

'I'm here,' Bonelli replied.

The English, Arbati reflected, were an unaccountably eccentric race. Why a man should choose to lie inside under artificial lights on a day when it was 30 degrees Celsius outside and not a cloud in the sky was an inexplicable mystery. If he wanted a tan, he'd have been better in his bathing-trunks on a recliner out on the terrace, with a scotch and soda in his hand.

'Well, what do you want?' Sir Richard rasped. 'Spit it out, man.'

Bonelli flinched, unaccustomed to being addressed so brusquely. 'There are one or two questions I'd like to ask you and Signor Harmsworth,' he said with studied civility. 'And we'd like to have another look around the property, if you don't mind.'

'Would it matter if I did?' Sir Richard grunted, still moving only his lips. 'Molly, what time is it?'

'Just coming up to three twenty, Sir Richard.'

'All right,' Sir Richard said. 'I have another ten minutes to bake before I'm done. Nigel will be in his studio, no doubt, painting.

You can pester him until I'm ready – or you can troll around the grounds, if you like, sniffing for clues. Suit yourself. I'll see you when I'm finished here. And close the door behind you when you leave.'

Gritting his teeth, Bonelli retreated, leaving Sir Richard to his rays.

'Shall I show you the way to Mr Harmsworth's studio?' the nurse enquired.

'Thank you, no,' Bonelli said, needing air and open space, 'we'll start outside, I think.'

With Arbati, he crossed the terrace and descended the travertine steps to the garden below. As they started down, Arbati noticed out of the corner of his eye that the nurse stood in a window, watching them from behind a set of half-closed curtains.

'Damned old tyrant,' Bonelli grumbled under his breath. 'No respect for the bloody law, that's his problem.' At the bottom, he stopped in his tracks. 'Hello,' he said, 'what's this?' The statue of the Greek warrior lay on the ground beside its broken pedestal, exactly where, two weeks earlier, he and his men had lifted it free of Dearing's pinioned body. The grass around the recumbent figure had been meticulously trimmed, but the statue itself had not been moved. 'How curious,' he said, scratching his head. 'I'd have thought Sir Richard would have had it repaired by now. He's not the sort, I shouldn't have thought, to leave such an eyesore lying about. Everything else about the place is so neat and tidy.' He added, for Arbati's benefit: 'This is the spot, incidentally, where James Dearing met his untimely end.'

'So I gathered,' Arbati replied, stooping to examine the base of the statue and the concrete pedestal from which it had fallen. 'Rather a heavy object,' he observed. 'It must have taken a good deal of force to dislodge it. I'm surprised old Harmsworth had enough weight to do it.'

Bonelli nodded. '*Tottered* was his word. He said he *tottered* into it after a glass of sherry.'

'He must totter like a sumo wrestler then,' Arbati said, rising and dusting off his hands.

Bonelli sat down on one of the wrought-iron chairs grouped around a matching pedestal table and took out a package of cigarettes. 'There's time for a smoke, I think,' he said in a long-suffering tone, 'before we have to go in and face the old lizard again. You want one?'

'Yes, why not,' Arbati said, sitting.

When, feeling stronger and more civilized, they finally remounted the steps and crossed the terrace to the back of the villa, they met the nurse coming out of the door.

'Oh,' she said, surprised – or feigning it handsomely, 'I was just on my way to fetch you. Sir Richard is ready now. They're waiting for you in the studio.'

She led the way through a maze of corridors and up a flight of stairs, coming eventually to an airy room overlooking the mountains through tall french doors. It was, however, one of the oddest rooms Arbati had ever seen. On one side, a grouping of rattan chairs and a sofa in bright floral upholstery set around a wicker table, in the centre of which stood a pyramid of coconuts stacked like hairy cannon-balls. On the walls, under a gilt rococo ceiling, primitive artefacts (spears, carved masks, and the like) hung from hooks, together with unframed and curling prints of Gauguin paintings – Tahitian women on beaches and mats and beds with mangoes and flowers, an aureoled madonna holding a dark-skinned child, also with a halo, on her shoulder – affixed to the plaster with pieces of Sellotape. In the centre, an old wooden table loaded with jars, tins, soiled rags and twisted tubes of paint set beside an easel on which was propped what appeared at first glance to be an original Gauguin painting of the Annunciation. The *mélange* of European and Tropical, the civilized and the savage, took Arbati's breath away. It was like being cast, without warning, into one of Hieronymus Bosch's bizarre nightmares.

'Ah, the constabulary!' announced Sir Richard. He was dressed in casual slacks and an open-necked white shirt which hung loosely on his skeletal frame, and he sat, legs crossed, not rising as they entered, twisting in his fingers a medallion suspended from the gold chain around his neck: an image of opulence at ease. 'Come in, gentlemen. I suggested we meet here so that Nigel could show you what he's been up to. You're a poet, inspector,' he said, giving Arbati a sardonic grin. 'Have a look at that painting' – he gestured at the Gauguin on the easel – 'and tell us what you think.'

Nigel Harmsworth, who had risen the moment the two policemen came in, and who now stood by awkwardly in embarrassed silence until Sir Richard gave him the fillip, stepped forward with Arbati to the easel.

Arbati studied the painting for a long minute – and then it hit him. Although painting wasn't his specialty, he'd visited the Uffizi too often not to recognize a Botticelli composition when he saw one, even if the features and garb of the figures depicted in it had been transported to Polynesia. The texture and coloration were remarkably – indeed, almost miraculously – Gauguinesque; but the picture was in the final analysis, like all imitations of the masters, somehow unsatisfactory: an unsettling mixture, like the room in which he now stood, of the real and the bogus. There was no doubt that Nigel Harmsworth could paint, that he understood technique. What he lacked was an *inspiring vision* – and in trying to appropriate Gauguin's vision and make it his own, without sharing Gauguin's commitment and genius, he had produced something clever but not powerful, something remarkable but not memorable. Like all good imitators, Nigel Harmsworth was a clever copyist, an astute mimic – in short, an artist *manqué*. But Arbati had no desire to insult the man who stood beside him awaiting his verdict. Sir Richard Danvers, on the other hand, whose brinkmanship had prompted the unfortunate interlude, was another matter entirely.

Stepping back from the canvas and folding his arms across his chest, Arbati said reflectively:

'It's a very interesting piece indeed and extremely well executed, to my untrained eye, from a technical point of view. The use of Botticelli's *Annunciation* as the compositional model implies, perhaps, a certain unintentional irony in the conception – a confusion of the superstitious with the supernatural – but on the whole the work strikes me as something of which Gauguin himself might well have approved. I think Mr Harmsworth is to be complimented on his accomplishment.'

Sir Richard's jaw dropped as if he'd taken an unexpected blow to the solar plexus, then shut with an audible snap. He was accustomed to holding the upper hand in an encounter, especially when the topic was art, and was not easily persuaded to accept a setback gracefully.

'I'm glad you like it,' he managed finally in a strangled voice. 'Now, what are these questions you want answered?'

After that, the interview went smoothly. Bonelli picked tactfully around the edges of the Ghirlandaio business, careful not to reveal too much of what they knew and suspected. Nigel Harmsworth, still flattered by Arbati's praise, was urbane and voluble, though cautiously reserved in his responses. Sir Richard, smarting and affecting an infinite boredom, restricted himself to terse phrases and monosyllabic grunts.

'Well then,' Bonelli said, standing, 'that about wraps it up. I thank you both for your time.'

The others, save Sir Richard, stood too.

'I'm intrigued, Signor Harmsworth,' Arbati said as they moved toward the door, 'to know why, inspired by Gauguin, you've filled your studio with objects, not only from the South Pacific, but from Africa and South America as well. That fertility mask I recognize as Zulu, and that blow gun, surely, must come originally from the Amazon basin.'

Nigel smiled. *'Ambience,'* he said, 'is a general rather than a specific thing. I find that all I need is a tropical atmosphere *grosso modo* to get the creative juices running.'

'Interesting,' Arbati said. 'And where in Italy did you manage to lay your hands on some of these things – that Amazonian blow gun, for example? It must be rather a rarity over here.'

'Ah, yes – well, that *was* a piece of luck, as it happens. I tripped over it quite by accident,' Nigel said with considerable pride, 'in a little antique shop in Perugia. Apparently they'd bought up the effects of a South American traveller. There were a number of other items in the same vein, but it was the blow gun that took my eye. Would you like to see it?'

'Very much,' Arbati said, 'if it's no trouble.'

'None at all,' Nigel said, standing on a chair and reaching it down. 'Lamentably, no curare came with it,' he added with a grin, 'so I've been reduced to keeping it as an ornament.'

Arbati turned the hollow wooden tube over admiringly in his hands, then held it up endwise to the light and squinted down its interior length.

'Fascinating,' he said, handing it back.

As they left the room, Nigel was standing on the chair returning the weapon to the security of its hooks and Sir Richard, scowling, was still ensconced immovably in his chair, licking his wound. It was Molly DuBartas, Sir Richard's nurse, who guided them back to the foyer and closed the large oak door firmly behind them.

Back in the car, Bonelli inserted the key and switched on the ignition, then turned to Arbati.

'A neat trick with the blow gun,' he said. 'Any chance it's our murder weapon?'

Arbati shook his head. 'I wondered that myself, of course,' he said, 'but it was covered with dust and the bore inside was dirty.'

'Maybe he has another one besides his display model,' Bonelli offered.

Arbati considered the suggestion for a moment, then said: 'It would take more puff to operate, I imagine, than either Sir Richard or old Harmsworth could generate. And besides,' he added, 'a blow gun isn't exactly the sort of thing you can wander around with in your hand and not get noticed. Somebody at the reception would have seen something.'

'Damn,' Bonelli grunted, wheeling around the fountain in the middle of the drive, 'I'd hoped we might have tumbled on to something there.'

3

The next afternoon Arbati and Bonelli drove out to Tenuta del Colombo in the hills beyond Bagni di Lucca to interview the Kleists. The Germans were, even to Bonelli who had questioned them earlier in the week before Arbati joined the team, something of an enigma. They were a taciturn family, reluctant to divulge their secrets and air the family's laundry in public – which was hardly surprising since they all had things to keep quiet and feel penitent about: Ilse for being apprehended *in flagrante* with the deceased, Willi Junior for being a prurient misfit and an incompetent peeping Tom, and Willi Senior for knowing so little about his family that he let it all happen in the first place. The unanswered question, of course, was whether these private guilts were in any way connected with a larger guilt over the demise of Peter Morgan – and *that* it was the purpose of Arbati's and Bonelli's present excursion to attempt to determine. There were also, apparently, two other Kleists: Dieter and Dietrich, twins in their early teens who, according to Bonelli, were a precocious and stuffy pair of hot-house brats obsessed with eking a *Wehrmacht* victory out of the Kursk salient with toy soldiers and model tanks. They, of course, having stayed at home the night of the reception, were not – whatever their other problems might be – directly implicated in the police investigation into Morgan's death.

On the whole, Arbati reflected as they drew up beside a battered Volkswagen Fox parked in the drive, the visit to the Kleists didn't promise to be a particularly diverting or jovial affair.

They mounted the steps to the portico and Bonelli rang the bell. After a moment the door was opened by Ilse Kleist, dressed in a demure broomstick skirt and high-necked blouse that did little, however, to obscure her evident charms. Still, Arbati noticed, she was hardly the radiant creature he'd last seen at the reception in Palazzo Ducale in a stunning white evening gown that had drawn every eye, including his own, in her direction. There was something in her look – an anxiety, a wariness, an uncertainty trembling below the surface calm – that took the edge off her magnetism and made her seem, if not exactly ordinary, then certainly less vivacious and vibrant than before.

'Oh, inspector,' she said, seeing Bonelli. 'I was just going out to do a little shopping. I suppose I need to stay now. Will it take long?'

'I shouldn't think so,' Bonelli replied. 'A few questions. Nothing much. Half an hour perhaps.' He spoke slowly, enunciating the words clearly, since her Italian was not strong. 'This is Detective Inspector Arbati, from Florence. Perhaps you will remember him from the awards ceremony at Teatro del Giglio.'

'*Ja*,' she nodded, recognition dawning. '*Der Dichter*.'

'Yes, the poet,' Bonelli agreed. He went on: 'Is your husband at home? Also your stepson? We would like to talk to them as well.'

'*Ja*,' she said. 'Willi Senior is in his *Treibhaus* and Willi Junior is upstairs.'

'Fine,' Bonelli nodded. 'Good. Would you take us to your husband, please?'

She nodded. '*Bitte, kommen Sie mit.*'

'*Il professore*,' Bonelli said to Arbati as they started off, 'speaks a passable Italian. Something he learned at school, I gather. He'll be our translator.'

She led them back through the house to a terraced patio at the rear. On a patch of open ground off to one side, Dieter and Dietrich Kleist were on their hands and knees hurling Panzerdivisions against the hapless Russians. They looked up briefly, without interest, as their stepmother passed with the two policemen.

'The Hun twins,' Bonelli muttered to Arbati with a jerk of his head.

At the greenhouse, Ilse checked the screen for butterflies, then opened the door and slipped inside. '*Mach schnell!*' she said, hurrying them in. '*Die Schmetterlinge müssen nicht entfliegen.*'

Dressed in rubber boots and what looked like an old trout-fishing hat, Professor Kleist was back in the bushes bent over some orchids in a hydroponic tray. When the door opened, he looked up from his place in the foliage. A blue butterfly, disturbed by the motion, lifted from his hat where it had been resting and flapped away into the shady security of the dense undergrowth.

'Ah, inspector,' he said, emerging – 'and, if I'm not mistaken, it's Signor Arbati, isn't it, the poet?'

'Detective, actually,' Arbati said. 'I've been seconded and assigned to the Morgan case.'

'I didn't realize,' the professor said, wiping his hands on a dry cloth, 'that you had a second string to your bow. Rather an odd combination, isn't it, poems and policing?' He grinned, catching himself. 'You don't need to answer that. I cut up bugs and play the cello: rather an odd combination itself, I'd say.' He tossed the cloth on to a corner of the desk, then said: 'You have more questions for us, I assume. Shall we go up to the house?'

'Here will be fine,' Bonelli said. 'We won't be disturbing you for long. I wonder, though, whether your son could join us as well.'

The professor turned to Ilse. 'Fetch Willi Junior and bring him here,' he said in German. 'Now,' he said, turning back to his visitors, 'let's see if we can find some chairs in all this clutter for us to sit on.' He liberated an old rocking-chair loaded with books and rounded up three slatted folding-chairs from the patio, drawing them into a semicircle round his desk. 'There,' he said, taking the swivel chair behind the desk himself, 'that should serve the purpose. Please, gentlemen, make yourselves comfortable.'

Shortly, Ilse returned, Willi Junior trailing reluctantly in her wake with a sour expression on his face as if he were about to be forced to eat raw worms. He was an ungainly young man: overweight and slovenly in appearance, shambling in gait, with a hint of sly maliciousness in his pig-like eyes. He was still wearing a large bandage over the cut on his temple that Peter Morgan had inflicted when he'd tossed him out of the armoire in the hotel room.

They were an interesting trio, Arbati noticed, a study in contrasts, as they took their places around the desk like a seminar class coming into session: Ilse subdued and slightly anxious, Willi Junior moodily withdrawn and belligerent, Willi Senior frank and hearty, playing the genial host. Arbati distrusted on principle the phenomenon of the relaxed and too-helpful witness because too often they had something to hide, but the professor's affability wasn't overdone and seemed authentic and unforced. It wasn't, however, something that Bonelli had encountered, Arbati knew, on his earlier visit to Tenuta del Colombo: then, the professor, embittered by the all-too-recent discovery of his wife's infidelity, had been taciturn and glacially remote. So why the sea-change? What had prompted it? Was it an act? – or was the professor, perhaps, simply a man who had come to terms with a painful reality and made his peace with the world? In the end, the second alternative – assuming Willi Senior's equanimity *was* in fact genuine – was perhaps the only sensible attitude to take in the face of what had happened. But that was a question that Arbati, who'd never himself been married, found himself ill equipped to answer.

'Well now,' Willi Senior said when they were all seated, 'what are these questions, inspector, you'd like to put to us?'

'To begin with,' Bonelli replied, 'there's no need for us to cover in detail the ground that we covered the last time. Inspector Arbati has read my notes from that session and is up to speed on what was said.' He opened his pad on the desk and moistened the lead of his pencil on his tongue. 'There are, however,' he went on, 'one or two little points that still need to be clarified . . .'

The purpose of the visit was not so much to elicit new information as it was to verify the information they already had and to give Arbati, who'd never met the Kleists, an opportunity to study their reactions and assess their stories at first hand. Gently, discreetly, Bonelli took them over the events at the Hotel Universo and then on to the evening of the reception, Professor Kleist repeating the questions in German and translating the responses. Arbati listened, watching their eyes and noting their body language, weighing the content of their replies. Around them, tropical butterflies fluttered in the leafy silence and the only sounds were the hum of a generator and, occasionally, the shrill cry of a distant bird. There was a vague unreality about the proceedings, like conducting an investigation in a jungle clearing with an interpreter fashioning laborious sense out of the incomprehensible babblings of the local tribe.

When Bonelli was done, Arbati said casually:

'Tell me, professor, do you ever have occasion to use atropine in your work?'

'No, never,' the professor replied, wrinkling his brow. 'Why do you ask?' Then he caught Arbati's drift. 'Ah, I see – so atropine was the drug employed, was it? A heart drug. A bit chancy as a murder weapon, I should have thought. Terribly unpredictable stuff. In my line, though, there's never any call for it.' He fished a key out of his pocket and pushed it across the desk. 'That's my drug cabinet over there,' he said, pointing to a high cupboard secured with a padlock. 'Have a look if you want.'

Arbati left the key where it was. 'I don't think that will be necessary,' he said. 'I'm perfectly willing to accept your word for it.'

Professor Kleist nodded, one professional to another. 'I appreciate that, sir.'

When they were finished, it was Professor Kleist, still attired in rubber boots and his old fishing hat, who showed the two policemen back through the house to the front door, leaving Ilse and Willi Junior alone in the greenhouse-laboratory staring distrustfully at one another in the eerie silence of the butterflies.

At the front door, Professor Kleist held out his hand. 'Good luck with your investigation,' he said. Then he went on: 'I had a motive, and so did Willi Junior, to kill Herr Morgan – but we didn't, even though we were present at the scene, have the opportunity to commit the crime. I think you know that. The three of us were together the whole time, never out of one another's sight, not even to go to the toilet. If Willi Junior had killed Herr Morgan, you can be certain that Ilse would gladly have told you. If I had done it, Willi Junior would, I know, have found a way of telling you or, at least, a way of trying to blackmail me into buying his silence.' He drew himself up in a dignified way to his full height. 'As you've seen, gentlemen, there are problems in my family that require attention. They are largely, I regret to say, the result of my own neglect. I need to take them in hand – and I assure you that I intend to.'

Bonelli backed the car around and started down the drive.

'Well,' he said, when they were under way, 'do you believe him?'

Arbati was silent a moment, then nodded. 'I do,' he said. 'None of the Kleists murdered Peter Morgan. Ilse had no motive, and the son is too maladroit to open a can of tomato paste without making a botch of it and cutting his finger in the process. He's certainly not capable of carrying out a sophisticated murder in a public place without being noticed by someone.'

'And the professor?'

Arbati smiled to himself. 'Oh, Professor Kleist,' he said, looking out at the purple outline of the distant mountains, 'would never shoot you in the back or stoop to using poison. No, he'd kill you with his hands, face to face. I saw that the night of the reception when he realized who Morgan was. If it hadn't been a public

217

gathering, he'd have torn him limb from limb in a fit of rage right on the spot. He's a man of reflex and passion – hot-tempered, but the kind who cools off quickly. When it comes to murder, there isn't a shred of premeditation in him.' He added: 'And our crime was certainly the product of careful planning and premeditation.'

'All of which leaves us,' Bonelli said, 'with the finger pointing at one of the three *Inglesi:* Signor Harmsworth, Sir Richard Danvers, and Signorina Hathaway.'

'Four,' Arbati corrected. 'Let's not forget Signorina DuBartas, Sir Richard's nurse. No doubt she knows her poisons and she probably has an array of blood-tubes in her little black bag.'

To relieve the tension Ilse took a lingering bath, then dressed solemnly for dinner. Something, she knew, was about to happen. They all knew it. For a week, since he'd learned about her adultery, Willi Senior had been moody and uncommunicative. He hadn't shouted or hurled recriminations at her; he'd hardly, in fact, spoken to her at all – and then suddenly that morning, as if a momentous decision had been reached, the clouds had risen from his face and he'd returned to being his normal self. But something had changed: there was a certain reserve now in his affection, a kind of caution in his warmth. At lunch, shortly before the police had arrived, he'd announced that he wanted everyone present that night at dinner, that some changes were going to be made around the house.

Ilse didn't know what it meant. All she knew was that, as the hour approached, the butterflies in her stomach fluttered more violently and a nameless dread around her heart tightened its insidious and encircling coils. At first, she hadn't loved her husband: no, not really. He was old and tired, a man with half his life already behind him. She'd been using him, she knew – his wealth, his status, the security he offered – for her own ends. But over the seven years of their marriage, without her even noticing it herself, she had been slowly, secretly falling in love with him. It was the little things: the way he laughed and yawned and held his head, the way he twisted his lip up when he shaved, the whistling grunt he gave when something in the newspaper amused or irritated him, the funny way he talked out loud to himself when he thought he was alone. Without her realizing it, familiarity had bred content. She had thought, at first, that Peter Morgan was an escape from a humdrum reality that was closing in around her, suffocating her; but Peter was a trap, a delusion of her own restlessness. He gave her satisfying sex, but he was too shallow and self-involved to give her anything meaningful or more. In the days following the end of their affair and Peter's sudden death, Ilse had come to see that love was the tremulous expectation of the little things in life that bring peace and happiness and the security of belonging. She had discovered that, for her, love was Willi Senior with all his quirks and foibles – and yet now, at the very moment of finding it, she felt certain that she was about to lose it all.

She finished her hair in the bathroom mirror – how drawn she looked and pale! – and then descended the curving staircase to the main floor. In the dining-room, where the ticking of the long-case clock was clearly audible in the strained silence, the others were assembled at the table awaiting her. Willi Senior, as always, rose and held out her chair. The cook brought their meal on a wheeled trolley and, when she had disappeared back into her kitchen, Willi Senior offered up to the Almighty a perfunctory blessing for the food – and then they ate in a funereal silence punctuated by gestures and whispered requests for grated Parmesan or the salt. Willi Senior watched them with assessing eyes: Ilse, picking nervously at her plate with averted eyes; Willi Junior, louring and sour, satisfying his appetite, shovelling sustenance with a liberal hand; Dieter and Dietrich, on their best behaviour, sensing trouble, managing their utensils with a laboured intensity.

The first course came and went, then the dessert. The cook appeared and cleared away the dishes, bringing coffee and schnapps. They heard her in the kitchen, loading the dishwasher, tidying up, and then the back door closed with a gentle bump, the creak of her bicycle echoed past the window and she was gone, finished for the day.

'This family,' Willi Senior said, pouring schnapps and plunging *in medias res*, 'is in need of repair. We are no longer, in fact, a family: we are a collection of selfish egos masquerading as a family, and the situation in which we have landed ourselves has become intolerable.'

The others watched him in silent apprehension, not knowing what to expect.

'Partly,' he went on, 'I blame myself for what has happened. I have been preoccupied with my work and neglected my duties as husband and father. I have taken my hand off the tiller and, as a result, the vessel is in danger of tearing herself apart on the shoals.

That is about to change; I am, as of today, reclaiming the tiller.' He gave a stern look around the table as if daring their dissent. 'But I am not alone in my guilt: each of you has a share in the blame; each of you has contributed to bringing us into the sorry state in which we find ourselves. That, too, is about to change. For the past week, I have given this whole business my most serious attention – in fact, I have been able to think of nothing else – and I have reached several decisions. The judgements you are about to hear are not negotiable and they take place with immediate effect.' Again, he raked them with his eye. 'I hope I make my meaning perfectly clear,' he said unnecessarily.

His stony look met with a chorus of silent nods.

'Very well, then,' he said, turning first to Dieter and Dietrich. 'Your war-games are over. Tomorrow you will pack up your tanks and soldiers and send them back to Germany. I want them out of this house. They can be stored in the attic when we return until you understand that your infatuation with the Third Reich is a dangerous flirtation with an evil that true Germans want put behind them forever. I am old enough to remember what Hitler did, not for us, but to us; and I have no desire to see you glorify, even in play, what history has taught us to abhor. I only hope for your sakes that I have acted in time.' He lifted two books from the floor beside him – one of Schiller, the other of Goethe – and passed them down the table. 'Since you want to discover the past, you can start with a past worth discovering. When you've finished reading them, we'll sit down together and discuss what they contain. For the moment, I have nothing more to say to you. *Gute Nacht.*'

Silently, the two boys rose and, taking the books under their arms, departed, closing the door behind them softly.

When they had gone, he turned to Willi Junior. For a moment he was silent, then words began to come slowly, wearily, as if they had travelled a long distance:

'I have been patient with you for too long. I have waited, hoping against hope, that you would pull your life together and find an honourable profession. I have given you money and a home; I have sent you to expensive schools – but you are lazy and rudderless. Worse, you are dishonest and a schemer. You have abused my hospitality, manipulated my love, and dishonoured my name.'

'Oh, come on, *Vater*,' Willi Junior interjected, trying to lighten the tone, 'let's not overstate – '

'BE QUIET BOY!' Willi Senior thundered, cutting him off.

The violence and suddenness of the outburst drew a sharp intake of breath from Ilse seated at the far end of the oval table, tears brimming in her eyes.

Struggling to regain his composure, Willi Senior ground his fist in his palm and fought to bring his breathing under control. Finally he said to his son in a distant and glacial voice:

'Nothing you can say now will help. It would only make matters worse.' He removed an envelope from his pocket and passed it across. 'In there you will find a cheque for five thousand Deutschmarks, the last money you will see from me. You are to pack your things and, as soon as the police permit it, leave this house and go back to Germany. You must find yourself a job and a place of your own to live. I have done all I can – all I am willing to do – for you. You must work out for yourself how and where you can fit into the new Germany. I hope, in due course, that we shall hear from you, and that what we hear will be good. Now, go. There is nothing more that we have to say to one another.'

Speechless, deflated, Willi Junior took the envelope and, like a man in a dream, made his way painfully toward the door. With his hand on the handle, he turned back into the room as if to speak.

'No,' Willi Senior said, forestalling him. 'No words. Just go.'

The door clicked behind him.

When he had gone, Willi Senior rose from the table and crossed to the fireplace, resting his head against the cold marble of the protruding mantel and staring down into the dead ashes on the grate. In her chair at the end of the table Ilse sat with silent tears streaming down her face. For a long time neither spoke. Then, finally, Willi Senior, mastering emotion, began to speak in a low, unsteady voice:

'Ilse, I hardly know what to say to you or what to expect you to say to me. From the first moment I saw you, I loved you and could think of no one else. I tried in every way I knew to please you, to make us happy together. I thought we *were* happy; but I was wrong. Perhaps you have never loved me, I don't know; perhaps you have thought me a love-sick old dolt and laughed at me behind my back, longing to be with someone else. It doesn't matter. I have always been devoted to you and, fool that I am, I always will be, as long as I can draw breath. You are the heart of my heart.' He turned slowly from the fireplace and faced her. 'But you have betrayed me. You have made a mockery of my love, and

221

the pain of your treachery is something that I cannot describe to you. You have made me an old man overnight, a man with nothing left to hope or dream, and I face the future with uncaring indifference.'

'Oh, Willi, I'm so . . .' she said, sobbing, but then her voice faltered.

He put his finger to his lips. 'No,' he said softly, 'no, don't say it. The past is past. I have no hatred in me any more for what is done. I did at first, but that anger has passed, leaving me empty and afraid. What can you tell me, Ilse, to ease my pain? When you look in your heart, is there anything at all that you can find to say?'

She sat for a moment in the embalmed silence, where only the clock spoke, trying to bring herself under control.

'I can tell you,' she said at last in a strangled voice, 'that I know now, after all that has happened, that I love you with my very heart and soul. But can you believe me?'

He stepped behind her chair and laid his hands gently on her shoulders. 'You can tell me so, *Schatz*,' he whispered, bending to kiss her tear-stained cheek, 'and I will believe you.'

4

Having spent two days mulling the case over, one of them on the beach at Viareggio ostensibly catching up on some of his lost vacation, Arbati was convinced he now knew how the murder had been carried out and who the murderer was. To an outsider, his conclusions might well have seemed no more than an inspired hunch; but they were, in fact, the result of a rigidly logical process of deduction. It was, as usual, the little things – the inconsistencies and overlooked details – that had led him, step by irrefragable step, to the truth. The answers to the faxes Bonelli had sent out in order to verify statements in the Ghirlandaio file they'd obtained from Penny Morgan had confirmed his suspicions. And now, beyond the shadow of all reasonable doubt, he *knew* . . .

The problem that remained, of course, was to *prove* what he knew, to produce evidence that would stand up in a court of law. Deductions, however tightly argued, didn't impress judges or prosecutors. They wanted hard facts, solid evidence like fingerprints or a signed confession, and in this case there was only one possible piece of physical evidence – the murder weapon itself, with or without fingerprints – if, that is, the murderer hadn't had the foresight to dispose of it. But Arbati didn't think this murderer would be inclined to destroy so clever a toy. He didn't know why he thought so; he just had a hunch about it.

Given the complex psychological relations existing among the suspects in the case, it was best, he'd decided, to see the four *Inglesi* together. Proving his suspicions would depend, in the final analysis, on the murderer being manoeuvred into a confession of guilt – and for *that* to happen, he knew, he needed not only Bonelli's help but the unwitting assistance of the remaining suspects in the case. It would be a tricky business but, handled dextrously, it would work – or so, at least, he had managed to convince himself. The crucial first step was to bring the four suspects together, and this had been accomplished by the simple expedient of having two uniformed Carabinieri pick up Cecilia Hathaway and deposit her at San Felice with word there had been an important break in the case and that Inspectors Arbati and Bonelli would be along shortly to discuss its implications with the four of them. That would stir the pot. Thrown together, they would start talking, start *speculating* about what the police had discovered. Imagination, once unleashed, is infinitely more potent than reality. They would debate among themselves, they would spin theories, they would secretly suspect one another – and one of them would begin to sweat. And then, when the pot was simmering nicely, Inspectors Arbati and Bonelli would arrive and bring it up to a full and rolling boil. *That* at least, Arbati thought with crossed fingers, was the theory.

'How long has she been there now?' he asked.

'Almost an hour,' Bonelli replied. 'Nervous?'

'Like it was my first date,' Arbati said with a pained grin.

Bonelli turned in through the gates and steered up the curving drive lined with clipped yew that led to Villa San Felice. The two Carabinieri who had delivered Signorina Hathaway sat in their car in front of the main entrance, puffing cigarettes. They might be needed later, but it didn't seem probable: two frail septuagenarians, a fit but elderly woman and a middle-aged nurse were unlikely, even in the event of a full-scale revolt, to require the services of a burly back-up. But prudence, as those who enforce the law know all too well, is never misplaced.

The two detectives parked behind the escort Fiat and advanced on the heavy oak door of the villa. Bonelli rang the bell and stepped back. It opened after a moment to reveal the gaunt, unsmiling face of Molly DuBartas.

'They're waiting in the library,' she said without preamble. 'Follow me.'

She led them down a corridor hung with portraits from the noble past to a set of double doors at the end. Swinging them open with a dramatic flourish, she announced in a gravelly voice: 'The police.'

Three grey heads swivelled in unison. Sir Richard, shrivelled but tanned, squatted rheumatically on an antique *fauteuil* like a toad on a rock. Nigel Harmsworth and Cecilia Hathaway, together yet apart, were disposed like bookends at the extremities of a long sofa, he twisting the stem of a sherry glass in delicate fingers, she perched precisely on the front half of her cushion like the vicar's maiden aunt. Around them, on silent shelves, the leather-bound wisdom of Western civilization, unopened for decades, dozed in dignified obsolescence.

'Damned well about time, too!' Sir Richard snorted, seeing the two detectives. 'You've kept us waiting long enough. This better be bloody good.'

With his customary civility, Nigel rose from his seat, and the detectives crossed the hand-woven Indian carpet to the chairs he indicated. Molly DuBartas moved silently into place on a hard-backed chair beside Sir Richard's armchair, completing the circle.

'I don't think,' Bonelli said, opening his notebook on his knee, 'that you'll be disappointed on that score, Sir Richard.'

'I should bloody well hope not,' Sir Richard grunted waspishly

'Before we begin,' Nigel proposed, 'may I offer anyone a drink? I was just about to replenish my own.'

Sir Richard waved the suggestion aside with a claw-like hand. 'Oh, do sit down, Nigel, and stop being so damned accommodating. They're on duty. They probably can't take a drink, even in Italy.' He turned back to the detectives. 'Now, what's this all about? You've given us the heebie-jeebies with all this mystery.'

It was Arbati who spoke.

'We have nearly completed our investigation into the death of Peter Morgan,' he said with slow deliberation, 'and we have reached the point where it has become apparent to us' – he paused, giving a hard glance across at the quartet of attentive faces opposite, then went on – 'that one of you sitting here in this room is a murderer.'

'Rubbish!' Sir Richard snorted. 'You can prove nothing of the sort.'

'Yes, quite. Perfectly absurd,' Nigel chimed in.

The two women said nothing. Molly DuBartas' eyes opened a fraction wider – whether in fear or surprise it was impossible to say – and Cecilia Hathaway, unflappable and inscrutable, sat with her lips pressed in a thin rigid line.

Arbati continued:

'We have been aware for some time that the late James Dearing and the late Peter Morgan were involved in a scheme of some kind – we guessed that it was blackmail: correctly, as it turns out – to put pressure on Signor Harmsworth and, through him, on you, Sir Richard. We strongly suspected, too, that in some important way the painter Ghirlandaio featured in this scheme. You will recall from the Dearing inquest, which all of you attended, that the name Ghirlandaio was found on a scrap of paper in Signor Dearing's pocket. But what did a forgotten Quattrocento painter have to do with whatever Dearing and Morgan were plotting against Signor Harmsworth and Sir Richard? That was a question which, for a long time, we could not answer – until, that is, certain documents fell almost by accident into our hands. From these documents we have been able, following the same trail used by Peter Morgan, to uncover the existence of a series of forged paintings – all of which, as it happens, originated at Danvers' House Auctioneers and were sold privately over a period of some thirty years to wealthy collectors: always to individuals, never to museums or galleries, where their authenticity would be carefully scrutinized. These collectors, satisfied with the reputation and expertise of Danvers' House, did not feel it necessary to seek a second opinion and so the paintings were never vetted by outside experts.'

'This is malicious slander,' Sir Richard blustered. 'You can't prove any of it.'

'In fact, we can – all of it,' Arbati said evenly, 'or at least enough of it so that legal proceedings against you will shortly be placed before courts in the United States, France, Italy, Canada, and the United Kingdom. There is, for example, an investment banker in the United States – a certain Mr Jonathan Barnes of Chicago – who has registered sworn affidavits that a painting in his possession entitled *Young Girl with Lilies*, purportedly by Domenico Ghirlandaio, is a forgery purchased from and authenticated by Danvers' House in the year 1947.'

'I know no one by the name of Barnes,' Sir Richard said sulkily.

'Perhaps not,' Arbati said, 'but you certainly knew his maternal grandfather, Harry Simon Hillier II, to whom you sold the painting in question. Your signature is on the bill of sale, and Signor Harmsworth's signature appears on the certificate of authentication accompanying it. Mr Hillier, it seems, was a fastidious bookkeeper whose papers passed to his grandson following the probate of the will in 1990. Mr Barnes has known since shortly thereafter, when he had the painting cleaned and assessed by a Ghirlandaio specialist at the Rijksmuseum in Amsterdam, that the work was a forgery. What he didn't know – and what we ourselves have only recently discovered, thanks to Peter Morgan's detective work – was that Danvers' House had sold upwards of thirty other forgeries to private collectors around the world. Mr Barnes had thought he was alone; he had assumed that, although Danvers' House had made a grievous mistake, it had, like his own grandfather, simply been taken in by a clever forgery. He took no legal action against you because, not being a litigious man, he believed you had made an honest mistake. What he has learned from us, Sir Richard, has led him to revise that opinion and to look for a legal remedy. Others, I assure you, will follow.'

Sir Richard looked as though a thunderhead had stalled directly above him and was about to pour its contents down on him alone.

'Even if what you say is true,' he growled, 'it doesn't convict me of murder. Or Nigel either. So tell me, inspector, just what precisely *is* the point you're dancing around in telling us all of this?'

'My point, Sir Richard,' Arbati said patiently, 'is that Peter Morgan knew about your activities and was blackmailing you to keep this knowledge quiet.'

'You *know* this?' Sir Richard sneered. 'Or is it merely a hypothetical construction of your own invention?'

'We know,' Bonelli interjected, 'that three days before Signor Morgan died your chauffeur drove you to the Morgan villa in San Leonardo and waited outside for over an hour at a time when we also know, from Morgan's widow who telephoned while you were there, that her husband was having an important meeting in the house and was angry at being disturbed. She and the children remained in town, killing time, until they could be quite certain that the meeting was over.' He added almost nonchalantly: 'We also know, of course, what you and Signor Harmsworth talked about in the car on the way back home. The discussion, Sir Richard, was, I gather, quite animated and even vitriolic on your part. I questioned your chauffeur myself. He has been a most co-operative witness.'

Sir Richard's mouth fell open and then snapped shut. Betrayal by an inferior was a concept he had neither experienced nor even allowed himself to entertain as a possibility. It was his custom to speak freely, abusing whomever he wished, and to be rewarded by a loyal silence from underlings. The prospect that others might have the temerity to treat him as he routinely treated them was a bitter and overwhelming revelation. It was a bad moment for him: a moment of painfully anguished reckoning.

'Blackmail, of course,' Arbati said, bridging the gap smoothly, 'is a powerful motive for murder. On the basis of the violent threats against Signor Morgan made by you to Signor Harmsworth on the way back to San Felice, we can, Sir Richard, put together a very convincing circumstantial case against you for homicide.' He paused, then went on in a more meditative strain: 'But blackmail is not, in this particular affair, the only possible motive to account for Signor Morgan's untimely demise. Love, and a desire to protect a loved one from harm, is also a possible motive. I think you know, Signorina Hathaway, that I am referring now to you.'

Cecilia Hathaway sat like the Sphinx, staring straight ahead. No feature twitched, her eyes did not blink, not a muscle in her body moved.

Arbati continued:

'On the same afternoon that Sir Richard and Signor Harmsworth met with Peter Morgan at his villa, you took a taxi to San Leonardo and were let off, at your own request, at the bottom of the road on which the Morgan villa is located. Lucca is a small town, Signorina Hathaway, and there are few cabs. The driver who took you to San Leonardo recognized your description immediately when we questioned him; he remembered you vividly and thought it strange that you should have asked to be let out in the middle of the road instead of at one of the houses.'

He paused, giving her an opportunity to speak – to deny, to object, to qualify what he had said. She sat rigidly, looking straight ahead. She had nothing to say.

He shrugged and went on:

'I ask myself, what possible reason can you have for visiting Signor Morgan? – for I can imagine no other cause that would take you to San Leonardo, a small community with no shops or attractions, no interesting churches or historic buildings. You did not visit any of the other houses in the area: we know this, *signorina*, because we have questioned everyone in the neighbourhood. Therefore, you must have gone up to the Morgan villa. But why? Only one possible reason presents itself: you had determined to visit Signor Morgan because, since the Dearing inquest, you had known he was threatening the man you loved – perhaps you even knew *why* he was threatening Signor Harmsworth, I don't know – but you intended, being a woman of decision and action, to do something about it. And what exactly, I ask myself, *did* you intend to do? Here I am presented with two alternatives: either you planned to confront Signor Morgan and warn him off, perhaps even threaten him in return, or else, Signorina Hathaway, you planned to kill him. In either case, you were prevented from accomplishing your purpose because, when you arrived at the villa, Signor Morgan had visitors – in fact, Sir Richard and Signor Harmsworth. It must have come as a surprise to you to find them there; but their presence would only have deepened your concern for the power Morgan must hold over Signor Harmsworth and thus have heightened your determination to resolve the issue, at a later time, in some definitive way. You would not have had long to wait. As chairwoman of the organizing committee for the reception at Palazzo Ducale, where guests had been required to sign up in advance, you would have known that Signor Morgan and his family were planning to attend, and it would have been an easy matter for you to defer your plan for three days until that event took place.' He stopped and gave her a quizzical look. 'I am surprised, *signorina*, that you remain silent in the face of such grave allegations.'

She returned him a stony stare. 'I am silent, inspector,' she said finally, 'because I have nothing to say. The case you make against me is entirely circumstantial. You may speculate as much as you please. Your vivid imagination – to be expected, one supposes, in a poet – and airy guesses about why I went to see Signor Morgan and what I might have intended to do prove nothing.'

Arbati took a deep breath and continued: 'Very well then, Signorina Hathaway, I must tell you that my concerns are not prompted by speculation alone. Signor Morgan was killed by a massive overdose of atropine. As an expert herbalist, you are, I assume, aware that atropine is a poisonous alkaloid of deadly nightshade?'

'I am, naturally.'

'And you are no doubt also aware that in the garden at the back of your cottage there are several nightshade plants. I saw them there myself.'

'I am perfectly aware that they are there, of course. I planted them myself.'

'For what purpose?'

'I suffer from angina, as it happens, and small doses of atropine relieve the pain. I also keep it on hand because atropine is a reliable treatment for mushroom poisoning – especially as an antidote to the toxic alkaloids in such species as *Amanita muscaria*. I am fond of mushrooms and, while one is careful, inspector, mistakes are always possible. I prefer to be prepared.'

'And you possess, I assume, given the size of your herb garden, an extensive herbarium?'

'I do. A large cupboard outside my sitting-room holds all my preparations in carefully labelled glass-stoppered bottles.'

Arbati nodded. 'Including the atropine?'

'Yes.'

'And it is there now, this bottle of atropine, if I wanted to see it?'

For the first time, Cecilia Hathaway betrayed a hint of emotion: a tic rippled at the corner of her lip and an anxious look flickered for an instant in her eyes. But she said nothing.

Arbati repeated his question.

'No,' she said finally, rather waspishly, 'as a matter of fact, you couldn't see it. It's missing. When I was looking in the cabinet the other day for something else, I noticed that it was gone.'

Arbati gave a surprised look. 'Gone?' he said. 'And can you explain what might have happened to it?'

'No, I cannot.'

The others in the room all stared at her intently. Even Sir Richard stopped fidgeting with the wispy end of his Vandyke beard and fixed her with a steely glare.

Arbati said slowly:

'Either you are protecting someone with your silence, Signorina Hathaway, or we must assume that you disposed of the atropine yourself. But why, I wonder, if you had disposed of it, would you confess to having possessed it in the first place? Frankly, I am baffled. Perhaps there is something more you wish to tell us?'

'I have nothing more to say, inspector. Nothing at all.'

'You are quite certain?'

She nodded peremptorily. 'Perfectly certain,' she said.

Arbati rubbed his chin thoughtfully. 'If you persist in taking this line, *signorina*,' he said, 'it is my duty to warn you that I will be left, I fear, with no alternative but to take you into custody. Think carefully, therefore. Are you absolutely certain that there is nothing more you'd like to say?'

'This has gone far enough,' Nigel Harmsworth interjected before she could respond. 'It was I, inspector, who removed the atropine from the herbarium. I took it one day when I visited Signorina Hathaway. While she was busy in the kitchen preparing us tea, I snooped around and found her herb cabinet.'

Arbati's shoulders seemed to relax fractionally. 'I see,' he said in a neutral voice. 'And *when* was this, Signor Harmsworth? Do you happen to recall?'

Nigel shrugged. 'A week ago, perhaps more. I don't remember exactly.'

'Do you remember, perhaps, which day of the week it was?'

'A Monday, I think,' Nigel said, furrowing his brow. 'Yes, it was the day I'd been into town about having my electric razor repaired. I dropped in on Cecilia on the way home.'

'In other words,' Arbati pressed, 'the day *before* your visit with Sir Richard to Morgan's villa, which took place on the Tuesday?'

'I suppose it must have been.' Nigel shrugged. 'Is that important?'

'Time is always important,' Arbati replied, then asked: 'And for what purpose did you remove the atropine, Signor Harmsworth?'

'I'd rather not say,' Nigel replied unhelpfully.

'I see,' Arbati said, giving a thin smile. 'Then I shall tell *you*, Signor Harmsworth. You took it in order to murder Peter Morgan at the reception in Palazzo Ducale that coming Friday evening. On Monday, you already knew what you were going to do and had taken the steps necessary to procure the poison. On Tuesday afternoon, a day later, when you left the Morgan villa with Sir Richard, it was, as we know, Sir Richard who made violent threats against Morgan and whose threats were overheard by the chauffeur. But angry people often say things – unfortunate things that later appear incriminating – merely as a way of releasing frustration, of letting off steam, without ever intending to carry their words through into action. It is the silent ones, Signor Harmsworth, who are more subtle and more dangerous. You said nothing on the way back to San Felice in the car because actions are more fulfilling than words: you had made your decision to kill Signor Morgan, you had removed the atropine from Signorina

230

Hathaway's herbarium in preparation – and you were awaiting only the arrival of the proper moment to strike.'

'Rubbish!' Sir Richard snorted. 'A load of utter rubbish! What are you blathering about, man? Nigel isn't a murderer. He's protecting Miss Hathaway out of a misguided sense of chivalry and honour. We can all see that.'

'No, Sir Richard,' Arbati replied, 'I'm afraid I don't see that at all. I see, in fact, exactly the reverse. The chivalry belongs to Signorina Hathaway: it is *she* who is attempting with her silence to protect *him*.'

'Prove it,' Sir Richard grunted, 'if you can.'

Arbati turned back to Nigel. 'You will recall, Signor Harmsworth, that when Inspector Bonelli and I visited you in your painting studio several days ago, you pulled a chair over and fetched down an Amazonian blow gun from the wall for me to look at. Now, the most perplexing aspect of this case for us, right from the beginning, has been the problem of the weapon that was used to deliver the poison that killed Signor Morgan. I wondered whether the blow gun might have been the weapon. It wasn't, of course. I knew that the minute I had it in my hand: it was covered with a film of dust and the bore inside was clogged and dirty. There was the problem, too, of how you would have been able to get such an object into the reception and then out again without being noticed. Inspector Bonelli's men searched every guest leaving the reception and found nothing; they would not, we can be quite certain, have permitted a blow gun to slip through their inspection. At first then, I must confess, I was disappointed – but then, as I thought about the problem further, Signor Harmsworth, I was struck by something odd. That day in your studio, you had climbed on to a chair without difficulty – even, I may say, with remarkable agility for a man of your years; similarly, at the inquest into Signor Dearing's death, you had walked to and from the witness box with ease, you had stood under oath for a considerable time with no sign of discomfort or arthritis. And yet at the reception in Palazzo Ducale, I remembered, you were carrying a cane – a rather distinctive silver-scrolled walking-stick with a T-bar instead of a crook at the top – precisely the sort of innocuous, everyday object that the police would not think to confiscate or examine too closely. The more I thought about it, the more I became convinced that I had discovered the weapon that had delivered the fatal dart.' He paused and gave Nigel a penetrating look. 'I would like to see that walking-stick, Signor

Harmsworth. I would like to learn how you used it to murder Signor Morgan.'

Nigel's shoulders slumped and the fight went suddenly out of him. 'Yes, all right,' he said in a strangled voice, 'I did it, just as you say I did.' He paused for a moment, gathering his strength, swallowing several times, and then went on: 'The walking-stick is hidden in the wardrobe in my room upstairs. No doubt you will find it eventually. Shall I save you the trouble of tearing the place apart and get it for you now?'

'That won't be necessary, sir,' Bonelli interjected. 'My men will fetch it down later when you tell them where it is. Perhaps you'd just be good enough to tell us now, for the record, how the device works.' He sat with the pencil poised expectantly over his notepad.

'Very well,' Nigel nodded. He turned back to Arbati. 'It's odd, inspector, that you should have noticed the blow gun, for it was what gave me the idea in the first place. That,' he added, 'and the Bulgarians.'

Arbati pursed his lips, remembering. 'Yes, the Bulgarian Secret Service agent,' he said, 'who killed a defector on a crowded London street corner in broad daylight with a poison-tipped umbrella. That crossed my mind too.'

Nigel went on:

'I needed a weapon that was silent, inconspicuous, and easily transported. The blow gun, as you pointed out, is too obvious – and I wasn't certain, either, that I could either muster the breath or attain the accuracy necessary to employ it successfully. I remembered the Bulgarians then – but an umbrella is conspicuous if it isn't raining or at least likely to rain, and I didn't fancy, in any case, that I'd get away with walking around indoors with an umbrella for very long anyway. Somebody would have noticed and remembered seeing me. Then I had an idea. I had an old cane with a bar across the top like a shooting-stick that I hadn't used for years, not since I attended county cricket matches back home in England and used it to sit on as I watched. The handle, padded on the outside with rubber, was made of sturdy metal and already hollow and it had rather attractively ornate silver rosettes at either end for decoration. I bought a powerful spring that fitted inside and connected it to a simple triggering device operated by pressing a button that I could feel through the rubber around the handle. I remembered the glass tubes that Molly uses to take samples of Dickie's blood to test his fasting blood-sugar. They were too large for what I had in mind, so I bought a piece of glass tubing the right size, cut it to the required length, melted one end closed and sharpened the other with a file, used a syringe to load it with the atropine I'd prepared, and then put a thin wax seal over the end to prevent the drug from leaking out. I knew the wax would break away on impact and the atropine ooze out because I'd conducted several experiments with melons. Then, once I'd bored a small hole in the centre of the rosette, I loaded the tube and glued the rosette back in place, trusting that even if the cane were examined no one would notice anything odd about it.' He gave a thin, painful smile. 'Well, I was right about that. Nobody did notice anything, at the time. Anyway,' he went on, 'I had no difficulty the night of the reception in Palazzo Ducale crossing behind Signor Morgan in the flow of guests, firing the dart into his back as I went by, then stepping quickly out of sight behind one of the statues lining the gallery – a rather fine reproduction of Praxiteles' Hermes with the infant Dionysus on his arm, as I recall.' He gave Arbati a quizzical look. 'If I remember correctly you were the person talking to Signor Morgan at the time.'

'I was,' Arbati nodded. He crossed his legs, straightening the trouser crease over his knee, then said: 'And that brings us, Signor Harmsworth, to the death of Signor James Dearing.'

'Ah,' Nigel said with a tired smile, 'you know about that too, do you?'

'Dearing's death was not, I think,' Arbati said, 'precisely an accident in the sense that the coroner concluded. I have examined the statue in the garden and the pedestal from which it fell. It strikes me as highly probable, from the cracks on the base, that the statue had fallen before and been badly repaired. I suppose you knew that the pedestal was weak and that the statue could be easily toppled?'

Nigel nodded, looking down at his feet.

'Why don't you tell us what happened,' Arbati said softly.

For a long moment, Nigel contemplated the polished tip of his hand-tooled shoes, then he looked up and said: 'I have never liked Americans. They are brash and uncultivated. Signor Dearing was a particularly appalling specimen. When I discovered what he wanted, I led him down to the garden and let him talk. I didn't intend to kill him – I only wished to silence him, to get him out of my life. He was younger and stronger than I. I thought the statue would incapacitate him, perhaps knock him out, and then I could ring for assistance, since I was alone in the house. Then later, since

Dearing had made plain both how much he knew about Dickie and me and what he wanted to extort from us in return for his silence, I could call Dickie in London and we could decide how best to proceed in the matter. I had no way of knowing that the warrior's spear would pin the poor devil to the turf. I cannot say, however, that I was entirely sorry when it did.'

'And what exactly,' Arbati pressed, '*did* Signor Dearing know about you and Sir Richard?'

Sir Richard sprang forward in his seat. 'Say nothing, Nigel,' he growled. 'Tell him nothing he doesn't already know. I have friends in high places. We can still contain the damage. I'll look after your legal expenses, of course.'

Nigel threw his former employer a withering look. 'Don't be pathetic, Dickie. It's too late for shabby deceptions and high-priced lawyers. The game's up, old man.'

'Nigel, I warn you – ' Sir Richard spluttered, stirring rheumatically in his chair as if he were attempting to rise.

'Keep your seat, Sir Richard, and be quiet,' Bonelli said bluntly, 'or I shall have you forcibly restrained.'

'It all started just after the war,' Nigel said. 'I was starving in Paris, painting historical and mythological subjects that no one wanted to buy. They were good – no, better than good – but they were out of fashion. Well, one day out of the blue, Dickie – we'd been at the Slade together in London, several years before – turned up at my garret-studio, took me for a magnificent lunch at the bistro Benoît in Rue Saint-Martin and, over dessert, made me the most interesting proposal. I should, he said, come to work for him at Danvers' House. Doing what? I enquired. Painting old masters, he replied. I hated the direction modern painting was taking; I was also starving – in short, I was intrigued. Which old masters? I asked. The lost paintings, he replied, mentioned by Vasari in his *Vite de' più eccellenti Pittori Italiani*. The plan was a simple one: I would recreate the lost paintings from Vasari's descriptions, imitating the pigments and ageing the canvases, reproducing the works in the manner and style of the artist concerned, then Dickie would use the resources of Danvers' House to sell them to private collectors as recent discoveries. The war had played rather nicely into our hands. The Germans removed half the paintings in Italy and France and took them away to private collections in Germany; the Russians in their turn, when they overran the Reich, took much of what the Germans had pilfered and spirited it away behind the Iron Curtain. The art world after the war was in turmoil. No one knew where anything was; known paintings had disappeared and unknown paintings began to surface almost every day. In the confusion, it was easy for us to pass off our counterfeits, especially in America where there was more money and greed for culture than there was caution or knowledge. We began with Ghirlandaio's portrait of his daughter, and after that I painted, I believe, twenty-four others: a Cimabue, two Uccellos, a Verrocchio, several Mantegnas – even a Michelangelo. I could supply you with a complete list, of course, if you should require it. Well, there isn't much more to tell. The paintings sold like hot cakes, Sir Richard became extremely wealthy, and then when I retired finally from the fray a decade ago, he gave me this villa rent-free and expenses paid for services rendered. And so it would have remained if Signor Dearing hadn't come sticking his nose in where it didn't belong.'

Through all of these revelations, Cecilia Hathaway had sat with a succession of emotions – anger, shock, horror, pity, sorrow – flitting successively across the hawk-like features of her face. She felt used and betrayed; she felt sadness and shame for what he had done – but under it all, the power of her love refused to accept that he could possibly be, in spite of everything else, a cold-blooded murderer.

'But why, Nigel,' she said in a quavering voice, entering the conversation for the first time since her own interrogation, 'why did you kill Signor Morgan? Dearing's death was an accident but Morgan's was an act of premeditated murder, a horrible crime. I don't understand what on earth could ever have possessed you to do that.'

He could not face her eyes. He looked away.

'For a reason,' he said, 'that I am ashamed to confess to you, Cecilia, or to anyone else.' He took a deep breath and went on in a faltering voice. 'I did it because, if Morgan had been permitted to ruin Sir Richard, I knew that I would lose San Felice and be thrown into poverty. I am too old to start again. I couldn't face the prospect of losing everything – the peace, the security, the beauty of this place. They were all I had to make my life worth living. I am a tired and selfish old man. I killed to protect my way of life, to cling to the material comforts that made the prospect of old age tolerable.'

There was no possible response to this admission of weakness and wickedness, and Cecilia sat in silence looking at his averted face with unbelieving eyes.

The surrealistic calm was broken by Inspector Bonelli:

'Nigel Harmsworth,' he said, rising, 'I place you under arrest for the wrongful deaths of Peter Morgan and James Dearing. Be advised that all that you have said can and will be used against you in a court of law.'

'What about me,' croaked Sir Richard. 'Are you proposing to frog-march me off in chains too?'

'No, Sir Richard,' Bonelli said in a coldly official tone, 'not for the moment. But I must ask both you and Signorina DuBartas to remain in Italy and to keep me informed of your whereabouts until this matter has been fully resolved.' He added: 'And to ensure that you do, I must ask you to surrender your passports.'

Outside, the two detectives and Cecilia Hathaway, whom they were presently to drive home, watched as the Carabinieri Fiat containing Nigel Harmsworth, head bowed and face averted, turned in the drive and sped off down the winding track that led toward Lucca.

Cecilia watched it disappear with tear-filled eyes.

'May I visit him sometimes?' she asked.

Arbati held the rear door of the car open for her. 'Of course, *signorina*,' he said gently. 'Now more than ever he will need your comfort and support.'

5

It was one of those crisp early autumn mornings when the sun shines brightly and the air, clear and bracing, rides down into town from the mountains with a hint of snow on its breath. Feeling the chill, Giancarlo Bonelli buttoned the front of his suit jacket and hurried across the piazza to the Hotel Universo. Arbati was in the lobby, waiting in one of the faded leather armchairs, his single suitcase packed and ready to go beside him.

'What time's your train?' Bonelli asked.

Arbati checked his watch. 'Just over an hour.'

'Then there's time for a coffee,' Bonelli said. 'I'll pay,' he added with a grin, snatching up Arbati's case. 'I owe you that much at least.'

They crossed the piazza back toward the Questura, stopping at their usual café on the corner of Via Vittorio Veneto. Bonelli ordered two *caffè latte* and they stood at the counter, sipping the rich brew while Bonelli filled Arbati in on the latest developments in the case. Sir Richard, fulminating and protesting his rights, was now in custody on the strength of warrants sworn out by the Italian owners of three forged paintings sold by Danvers' House in the mid-fifties. There were outstanding warrants in half a dozen other countries as well. By the time it was all over, Sir Richard would need several lifetimes to serve out the prison time he was going to accumulate as the cases came to trial. Danvers' House itself was in a shambles and would be driven into receivership. Molly DuBartas, Sir Richard's nurse, innocent of any implication in the art fraud or the murder of Peter Morgan, had fled the country as soon as her passport had been returned to her – doubtless, Bonelli surmised, on the hunt for another frail and wealthy septuagenarian whom she could nurse to the grave in the hope of being handsomely rewarded in the will for her ministrations.

'And Signorina Hathaway?' Arbati enquired.

'A tough and capable lady,' Bonelli observed. 'A thoroughly admirable woman. She has, I understand, cashed in her insurance policies and is making all the necessary arrangements for Signor Harmsworth's defence. She visits him daily and is managing, in spite of everything, to keep his spirits up.' He sipped his coffee thoughtfully, then added: 'If he'd married her years ago, as he should have done, he wouldn't be in the mess he's in today.'

Arbati grinned. 'What's this I hear?' he said, feigning shock. 'Are you, my old bachelor friend, making an argument in favour of marriage?'

'Ah – no,' Bonelli replied, retreating awkwardly, 'I'm making an argument restricted to Signor Harmsworth's particular case. He's old enough to need a woman's guiding hand. You and I, my friend, are still young enough to know better.'

Arbati's grin widened. 'Stick to police work,' he said, shaking his head. 'With arguments like that you'd make a lousy prosecutor. Now, drink up. I have a train to catch.'

Bonelli's car was in the courtyard outside the Questura. He stuck Arbati's case in the rear seat, then drove them out through Porta San Pietro, hooking around on to Viale Cavour and drawing up in front of the station. It was only a two-minute drive. Bonelli hated goodbyes: there was an implicit finality about them that distressed his spirit and made him feel ineffably sad. Like funerals, he wanted them over as quickly as possible.

He lifted out Arbati's case, setting it on the pavement, then held

237

out his hand. 'If you don't mind, I won't wait around for the train,' he said. 'I should be getting back to the Questura.'

Arbati nodded. 'There's no point in staying,' he agreed, understanding.

Bonelli shuffled awkwardly, delaying the moment. Then he said: 'I'm glad you happened to be here, Carlo. I couldn't have done it without you.' He gave a lopsided, pixie-ish grin. 'It takes an artist, I guess, to catch an artist.'

'Maybe it does,' Arbati said, returning the grin. 'Yes, maybe it does.'

He watched as Bonelli pulled away, waving, then turned and walked through the nearly empty terminal building to the platform beyond. He was sorry to be leaving Lucca, even if his stay hadn't ended up being the well-deserved rest he'd been looking forward to for months. Lucca was always a joy to revisit: one of the unspoiled treasures of an older, quainter, quieter Italy that had somehow survived the onslaught of culture-seeking packaged tours. Florence would be a madhouse by comparison. But Florence, too, was home – and he wasn't sorry to be going back.

There were a few scattered passengers idling on the platform in the morning sun, perhaps a dozen, and among them – to Arbati's surprise – were Penny Morgan and her children. They stood in a silent group apart, looking lost and vaguely out of place, like strangers at a country fête. It was the first time he'd seen the girl – what was her name? Brock, was it? Breck? No, it was Brooke, he remembered – without her eternal Discman and earphones.

He walked over and joined them.

'*Buon giorno*,' he said, tapping Penny on the shoulder. 'You folks are off on your way home from the look of it.'

'Oh, Carlo!' she said, turning. 'Yes, we fly out of Fiumicino tomorrow. It's been a difficult time. There's nothing to keep us here, now.'

He nodded. 'I'm sorry things had to work out as they did . . .'

They stood in awkward silence for a moment, then Arbati said: 'I hope you've had help with the arrangements.'

Penny nodded. 'Yes, the authorities have taken care of everything. They've sent Peter back to the States and our bags will follow in a day or two. Everyone has been very kind.'

'I'm glad,' Arbati said.

'You're going back to Florence?' she asked.

'Yes,' he nodded, 'there's nothing to keep me here now either.'

The tannoy crackled overhead and a tinny voice announced:

'Treno per Pisa, Livorno, Grosseto, Civitavécchia e Roma in arrivo sul binario quattro. Treno per Montecatini, Pistoia, Prato e Firenze in arrivo sul binario tre.'

They passed through the *sottopassaggio* together and mounted the steep flight of concrete steps to the strip of platform running between the two sets of tracks. There was a heavy rumbling and their trains arrived from opposite directions almost simultaneously, pulling into the station with a hiss of releasing airbrakes.

'Goodbye then, young lady,' Arbati said in English to Brooke as she clambered aboard.

'Goodbye,' she said, giving him the best smile she could manage.

Chad followed his sister aboard, and Arbati hoisted the heavy bag the boy had been carrying on to the carriage step where he could grasp it.

'Goodbye, Chad, and take care of your mother.'

'I will,' the boy replied. 'Don't worry.'

Arbati turned back to Penny who still stood on the platform. It was she who spoke first.

'Well, goodbye, Carlo,' she said in Italian. 'I'll think of you often. Whenever I open the book of poems you signed for me.' Her eyes were moist and full. 'I have it here in my purse, as it happens – just like the last time we were in this station together, remember? One of life's little ironies, I guess.'

'I'll think of you too,' he said, meaning it.

'If we'd met under different circumstances,' she said, giving him a brave smile, 'the story might have had a different ending.'

He nodded. 'It might have,' he said, bending to kiss her cheek. 'Yes, I think it might well have been different.' He added: 'Another of life's little ironies.'

He handed her aboard, then, turning quickly away, mounted the steel steps of the carriage opposite. The train was not crowded and he found an empty compartment easily. He retrieved his Umberto Eco novel and put his case in the overhead rack, then settled into the window seat, looking out at the train across the platform. He could not see her. She had gone.

A shrill whistle sounded. Then another.

The two trains lurched, pulling apart, going their separate ways in opposite directions.

Arbati opened the novel on his knee. He'd need another vacation, he knew – next time a real one – if he were ever going to finish the damned thing.